艺海观澜
——新语境下的文艺论丛

楚惬 著

吉林大学出版社

长 春

图书在版编目（CIP）数据

艺海观澜：新语境下的文艺论丛 / 楚惬著 . -- 长春：
吉林大学出版社，2019.10
　　ISBN　978-7-5692-5805-9

　　I.①艺… II.①楚… III.①文艺评论－中国－当代－
文集 IV.① I206.7-53

中国版本图书馆 CIP 数据核字（2019）第 251116 号

书　　　名：艺海观澜——新语境下的文艺论丛
YIHAI GUANLAN——XIN YUJING XIA DE WENYI LUNCONG

作　者：楚　惬　著
策划编辑：朱　进
责任编辑：矫　正
责任校对：崔吉华
装帧设计：童慧燕
出版发行：吉林大学出版社
社　　址：长春市人民大街 4059 号
邮政编码：130021
发行电话：0431-89580028/29/21
网　　址：http://www.jlup.com.cn
电子邮箱：jdcbs@jlu.edu.cn
印　　刷：三河市嵩川印刷有限公司
开　　本：787mm×1092mm　　1/16
印　　张：23
字　　数：370 千字
版　　次：2019 年 10 月第 1 版
印　　次：2023 年 4 月第 3 次
书　　号：ISBN　978-7-5692-5805-9
定　　价：72.00 元

序

　　楚惬是我指导的 2016 级艺术硕士戏剧专业的研究生。他在河南师范大学学习的三年时间里,取得了惊人的成果:发表了十几篇论文,创作了十几部戏剧等艺术作品。在我从教这三十多年里,还没见过这么努力、这么优秀的学生!我赞赏楚惬的不只是他的学习精神和学习成就,而且还包括他极高的情商。他有发自内心的对老师的尊敬。对老师的指导,他总能谦虚地接受。老师交给他的任务,他总是二话不说迅速、漂亮地完成。同学之间,也总能做到友好相处。经常听我指导的其他研究生说,楚惬又送给了他们什么什么书了。楚惬在校期间两次获得国家奖学金,其创作的作品也多次获得全国法治动漫微电影作品奖、黄河戏剧奖·理论评论奖、"创意河南"艺术设计大赛奖等。可以说,楚惬的三年研究生,进步很快,收获满满!

　　楚惬取得的成就源于他刻苦努力的学习。俗话说,功夫不负有心人。楚惬在学习上是位有心人。他有理想、有抱负,对自己的学习和未来有明确的规划。他读书常常会熬到夜里三四点。我曾非常担心他的身体,建议他注意作息时间。但他说习惯了,晚上读书效率高。在写论文方面他也是个拼命三郎。记得他最早交给我的论文,问题很多,我在他论文上的批注已经满了。他虚心接受,认真修改,进步很快。我曾建议他多学习别人的论文。他就将有关论文打印出来带在身边,抽出时间就认真揣摩。正是这样认真的学习精神和刻苦的学习态度使他在三年内迅速成熟,逐步走进了学术殿堂。

　　《艺海观澜——新语境下的文艺论丛》收录了楚惬在研究生学习期间的一些研究成果。其中个别篇目是我与楚惬合作完成的,多数是他自己的创造。难以忘记,他刚入学,我们就一起去荥阳调查狮子鼓、笑伞。后来他曾多次感慨说,在调研中收获很大,学到了很多东西。这种务实的科研态度确实是应该坚持的。楚愒对当代艺术发展也很关注。集子中的不少篇目是对当代戏剧等艺术的评论。楚愒在校期间看了不少戏。他对新上演剧目最为关注,并且养成了看过戏后写评论的习惯,不管能不能发表,都要写。他的不少论文就是这样产生的。这种对当代艺术的关切使他的研究很接地气。更值得一提的是,楚愒不仅努力于理论学习和研究,还积极进行创作实践。作为河南省作家协会、戏剧家协会的会员,近年来他还写了不少剧本,其中一些已经发表,并被搬上了舞台,受到了观众的欢迎。

学海无涯。对于一个初入学术门径的年轻人来说,还有很远的路要走。楚愒的研究还有很多不成熟的地方,需要学习的东西还很多。但我相信,只要有一颗热爱学术的心,坚持不懈,就一定会有所成就。希望楚愒在未来的发展中,能够继续脚踏实地,不断进取,在学术上取得更大的成就!

丁永祥

2019 年 10 月 13 日

目　录

含烟带月碧于蓝

——豫剧《秦豫情》的艺术创获

摘要：西安市豫剧团剧作《秦豫情》打破了地方戏原有的地域性及程式化，在演出时融合了舞蹈、话剧、秦腔元素等舞台呈现方式，在继承河南豫剧传统的基础上大胆创新，用独特的艺术手段展示了豫剧的魅力和强大的生命力。剧作着笔于小人物的悲欢离合，讴歌了河南人在灾难困苦面前的坚毅豁达精神，赞扬了陕西人民宽厚包容的优秀品格，对秦豫两省人民之间的相互宽容、风雨同担的友谊作了形象生动的诠释，具有较高的艺术成就和较强的时代意义。

关键词：《秦豫情》；豫剧；继承；创获

由陕西和河南两地青年剧作家杨林、雷琳静、甄业共同编创，李利宏编排，徐俊霞领衔主演的豫剧《秦豫情》（剧作原名《河南担》，刊载于《剧本》杂志 2016 年第 8 期），带着三秦大地的质朴乡风和豫中人民的历史记忆于近期成功在郑州上演。《秦豫情》融合了舞蹈、话剧等艺术元素，以新的艺术手法展示了河南豫剧的独特魅力，显示了豫剧这一地方剧种强劲的艺术生命力。

历史记忆：悲伤情节中的温馨感动

西安市豫剧团所编创的豫剧《秦豫情》给梨园吹来一股清新的春风。它讲述的是 1942 年那段关于一个时代、两个地域的集体记忆，是历史和人民的双重记忆，也是历史和人民的双重伤痛。战祸频仍的中原地区因为遭受旱灾蝗灾，庄稼颗粒无收，饿殍四陈。无奈之下，居住在豫中平原上的河南人只得拖家带口地朝着他们心中的"长安城"一路讨要寻求生路。生存的不易和世俗的欺凌不断摔打、折磨着这些逃荒者仅存的自尊。

该剧总导演李利宏说："历史习惯于大而化之，而人性的光辉往往体现在微小处的大抉择。生动地表现出那个极端岁月中小人物的喜怒哀乐，能够令观众体会到'爱'的伟大，'希望'的力量，'生命'的潜能，'人'的高贵。"[1]《秦豫情》既是审美的赋格，又是象征的隐喻。剧作者以社会底层小人物的视角来进行同样命运人物的审视和叙述，将宏大历史叙事中经常被忽略和遗忘的社会底层人民，经过戏剧艺术的打磨和对人物形象的塑造，使之真实而又艺术地呈现在了舞台之上。剧场大幕缓缓拉开，"呼啦啦的河南担，铺天盖地，一眼望不到边……"[2] 一群河南逃荒者以舞蹈和戏剧动作相杂糅的舞台表演，整齐划一且极具震撼力的场景，一下就吸引了观众的注意。当衣衫褴褛、饥寒交迫的逃荒者用尽浑身最后一丝气力喊出"可算是……有活路了"[3] 的时候，凄婉悲恸的呐喊，借由河南方言的迸发，直抵人心。带着浓厚时代气息的舞美布景，一下就把观众带到了那段遥远而让人痛心悲怆的岁月。

剧作从一个全新的角度来观照和讲述 1942 年发生在河南人身上的那段多灾多难的悲惨命运，着笔于小人物在那样一个"人吃人"的时代洪流中的生存与发展；讴歌了河南人在大灾大难面前表现出来的坚毅、顽强、豁达、豪迈的"河南担"的可贵气节，突出了陕西人的包容、质朴、勤劳、善良的高尚品格。

小勤和他爹随逃荒人群历经磨难与坎坷，一路讨要着来到了他们心目中那个"遍地是馒头"[4] 的长安城，但四野茫茫，举目无亲，人无立锥之地。尽管在初入长安时，和"老陕"曾发生过一些细微的冲突，但经过戏剧矛盾的冲突与化解，父女俩很快便取得了大家的谅解和宽容，终于有了安身立命的一席之地；然而，那稍事缓和的氛围并没有维持多久，一位双目"失明"的算卦先生"鸠占鹊巢"，这又使得小勤父女二人再次为落脚之地犯了难。小勤开始是别扭的、不情愿的，但在明白这个艺人的"特殊"身份后，果断地把方便让给比自己更苦难的人。刚刚还在和小勤吵嘴的"砖头"吆喝着"叫我说，咱各家各户，相互挪挪，挤出个三尺五尺的地方，就能让她爷儿俩住下——"[5]众河南逃荒者们齐声道"中！中！中！"[6]簇拥着整部戏剧情节朝着和美完满发展。从此，小勤不辞辛苦、披星戴月，给大华纱厂洗油纱。流畅欢快的板式配乐，行云流水般的戏剧舞台表演动作，小勤及一众浣纱女人们娴熟的"举石凿冰""冰水浣纱"，编剧、导演与作曲者匠心凝萃出了这么一段天成之作，更是呈现出了戏剧与话剧、舞蹈艺术交融的审美新范式。在坎坷艰苦的生活里小勤乐在其中，至少在那样一个温饱都难以维系的时代里又重新燃起了希望的灯火。福无双至，祸不单行。正当生活一点点好转的时候，小勤回家途中在下坡时和一架拉满瓷器的架子车相遇，慌忙地左躲右闪中导致车辆倾翻，让张大遭受了极大的经济损失。怒冲冲、气鼓鼓讨要赔偿的他，不曾想，在追讨赔偿瓷器的矛盾"拉锯战"中，诚恳、诚信、宽容、包容、礼让的雨露，竟滋润出了一朵美好的爱情并蒂莲花，也唱响了一曲"真情、亲情、爱情"情愫浓重的歌！

审美化的人性主题：中和、宽容、诚信

古人认为情绪的过度，不利于人七情的调节、社会的安定和天地的秩序，"在人与自我的关系上，表现为节制；在人与人的关系上，表现为和谐；在人与天命的关系上，表现为认同"。[7]应该说豫剧《秦豫情》体现了古时候"中和"的审美理念。这是一部打破了地域局限，有筋骨、有道德、有温度的好戏，不仅是演唱陕西、河南两地的风俗和生活，更展现了在饿殍千里的历史时代背景下，伟大的中原儿女与命运抗争的精神。这部戏的色调整体是悲凉的。虽然，悲惨凄苦的社会环境让主人公小勤等人的人生坎坷多舛，但是，全剧在不少地方仍坚定地洋溢着融融的暖色调，如同春雨绵绵，点点滴滴，滋润了观众心田。譬如，小勤父女二人穷途末路之际又添新债，小勤毅然站了出来承下了这份亏欠，给张大写欠条、拿出了仅有的钱，彰显了"河南人"人穷志坚的品格。"尽管已是灾民，已经一无所有，但河南人

要脸！"[8]张大损失惨重，当看到小勤父女俩极端贫苦而无力还债的处境时，顿生怜悯之心，表现出了三秦子弟坦荡宽广的胸怀。还有小勤难产的危难之际，乡亲们表现出极大的热情，千方百计出手相帮，其情可嘉，其情可赞！换言之，《秦豫情》不仅让观众看到了我们民族曾经有过的苦难，还让人们看到了苦难中人民的奋起，以及善良、忠厚、坚韧、乐于互助等传统美德伴随着人性之美的传播、扩散。全剧的戏剧处理，足可见编创这部戏曲的剧作家、导演，乃至每一位参与演员的功力与付出！

一部好的文学艺术作品必然是贴近人民的，反映时代的，直抵人心的。豫剧《秦豫情》中的戏剧冲突看似一直在表层激荡，实则在激流之下更蕴藏着诚信和虚伪、友谊和私欲、宽容和狭隘相互博弈的汹涌暗流。剧中女主角小勤的人物形象设计，为了生存，随家人流落异乡，饥寒中仍不失子女孝义；落户长安（西安）后她自强不息、乐观向上，用柔嫩的肩膀扛起父女二人生活的重担。"瓷器"矛盾中，男主角张大这一人物形象呈现在了舞台上，土生土长的陕西娃，满车瓷器破碎，追讨"肇事者"之时，虽言语过激却也不失为一种率真自然的情感流露；明白小勤一家人遭受的苦难时又热情慷慨地伸出援手，用陕西人的那份质朴沁润着小勤受伤的心灵；筹谋生路，制作工具，日久生情，就连表白也是那般的憨厚淳朴而又逗趣观众，张大的人物形象情感饱满、敢恨敢爱。小勤这一人物的设定显然是寄托了剧作者的极大偏爱，在戏剧文本中，剧作者不吝笔墨地刻画、塑造她的血肉和灵魂。同时，剧作者对每一位戏剧人物形象的刻画又都是保持着清醒和理智的，用深刻的笔调使每一位剧中人物的思想情感变得丰满而立体，由这样的角色所演绎的故事必然是感人至深的。情节缓缓铺展开来，人物性格随着一件件故事的发生而层次性地铺展开来。小勤大大咧咧的性格最终发展成了莽撞和疏忽，直接导致张大的一车瓷器毁于一旦，恐惧和贫困让她惶恐万分，匆忙逃回家中躲藏；当张大找到贫户区并给予"河南人"整个群体猛烈鞭挞和谴责的时候，她羞愧万分，毅然站出来承担责任，包赔损失，态度诚恳而感人；当张大风风火火赶到贫户区来找那对落难父女索赔时，靠出卖自己来维持生计的吕嫂先是用颇为戏谑意味的搔首弄姿来糊弄张大，后又发自肺腑地将自己心中的和整个"河南担"群体心中的那份苦完完整整地掏出；张母迟迟不肯接受这样的儿媳妇，其泼辣偏执的手段超出常人所能够接受的程度；当小勤挺着肚子、顶着瑟瑟寒风伫立街头叫卖胡辣汤却始终难以卖出一碗时，张母悄然托别人买下小勤的胡辣汤，为的就是让自己表面不愿接受的"儿媳妇"能够安心在家养胎，那一刻的张母不再似之前那般偏执泼辣，而是慈爱得如世间任何一位母亲一般；当小勤难产命在旦夕时，为"巧"占小勤父女二人栖身之地而冒充盲人的马虎，猛然良心发现，毅然蜕下了"谎言"的躯壳为小勤祈愿，也为寻求自己心中那份关于原罪的解脱。在长安的一隅，"河南担"们互相帮扶、抱团取暖的精神，如一簇红艳艳的牡丹，暖了观众的心，也赢来了一阵阵发自内心的掌声。不同于以往该主题剧作选题定位的"高"，剧中的角色与情节都不是"高大全"，而是一个个生活在社会最底层、在大灾大难之下苟延残喘着的中原大地上最具代表性的河南形象。正是这样真实的人物刻画和舞台呈现，方寸间的演绎才能够在短暂的时间里让观众感受到对人性质朴美的观照与再审视。

艺术融合：秦腔和豫剧的兼收并蓄

《秦豫情》蕴含着浓厚而强烈的创新精神。它摆脱了一味注重事件交代、情节堆凑，而忽视戏剧人物性格塑造与内心情感揭示的窠臼，真正专注于人物主体，回归对人性的关注，把陕西秦腔元素和豫剧唱腔有机结合到了整部戏剧作品之中，珠联璧合、水乳交融。应该说，这是一次带有西安地域风味的豫剧成功演出，更是一次有益探索。为了强化戏剧的艺术效果，作曲兼收并蓄，对秦腔与豫剧两种不同地域文化下孕育的声腔和旋律进行了有机地融合，是创新性的舞台形式对现代豫剧融合豫陕地域特色的大胆尝试。陕西与河南两地社会底层小人物之间所发生的故事，秦腔音乐与豫剧行腔的碰撞与搭配，让《秦豫情》呈现出不同于传统豫剧的审美新感受。

摒弃旧模式，敢于创新路。《秦豫情》的舞美设计虽不同于传统戏曲舞台"一桌两椅"的布景，却力求舞台的干净和无杂物，采用组合式、多景深的舞台布景。其舞美设计极力打破地方戏曲程式化的传统审美思维局限性，将巨大的舞台布景——"城门"悬在舞台空中。深灰色的城门布景弥散着古朴厚重的地域氛围；斑驳的枯树，历经沧桑；破败的旧楼，满目忧伤，它不仅吸收九朝古都长安的深邃底蕴，也融入了中原古都的地域特色，这种对地域文化的形象的诠释,这种带有明显秦豫两处地域色彩的舞美设计,不仅形成一种独有的地域风韵,还带给观众(受众)一种全新的审美感受。同时,《秦豫情》充分运用现代戏剧舞台美术的经验与创新实践,既呈现出电影般的视觉张力与审美细腻,又极具现场演出的震撼效果。从而使剧中塑造的人物形象所传递出的人生况味亲切温馨,在观众的心底久久激荡。

李渔在《闲情偶寄》中说:"古人呼剧本为'传奇'者,因其事甚奇特,未经人见而传之,是以得名,可见非奇不传。'新'即'奇'之别命也……是以填词之家,务解'传奇'二字。"[9]戏曲不仅是中华优秀传统文化的瑰宝,还是民间智慧的集大成者;而市井阶层最强烈的审美要求就是"故事",即叙事的传奇性。它提醒我们,倘若叙事性的剧作在情节铺陈和故事叙事上不能讲述一个"情理之中,意料之外"的故事,接受者(观众)就会觉得索然无味。《秦豫情》的编创者显然是深谙此理的,因此才会极大限度地给观众留下回顾自身生活经历的想象空间,让他们自己在陕西、河南两地戏剧艺术建构的场域内体悟剧情故事,领略秦腔、豫剧的艺术魅力,感悟陕西与河南两地深厚的情谊。它没有刻意将剧作者自身的立意、倾向、评价灌输给观众,而是采用白描的叙述手法,平静地诉说,在融合两地之间的方言俚语、民情风俗的基础上,将人物的命运、心态情感,以及故事脉络展现给观众,让审美和社会教化的功能完美结合,体现出剧作家高超的艺术匠心。它所塑造的舞台形象在价值取向上,虽然讲述的是特定年代和特定区域的故事,但故事中主人公身上的那种执着精神,对人生的美好期许和那善良淳朴的品性,都是能超越时间和永恒的东西,即使在当代也能触动人们的灵魂质素,代之而起的便是强烈的演出效果。在这里,如果没有博采众长,凝聚两种戏剧艺术精华,是不可能的。究其内在的艺术内蕴来讲,它是具有审美现代性的,并没有落入单纯表现灾难年景下劳动人民深重灾难的俗套,而是挖掘了人性深处更根本的东西,讴歌河南、陕西两地人民之间自古就有的纯洁高尚的优良传统;尤其是宽容、诚信、包容的情怀,蕴藏着典型的正能量和高昂的主旋律。换言之,《秦豫情》所要张扬的正是今人所失去的东西,以这样的视角重新审视那段满目疮痍的苦难历史,剧作者、导演拨开历史的重重烟云,凭借着一腔艺术热情和审美追求,以兼具了感性与理性的观照视域,用洞悉一切的戏剧视野带领着观众走进新的审美维度。之所以如此,应该说是与剧作者能融合秦腔、豫剧两个剧种的艺术优势,使其珠联璧合而不失豫剧的艺术主体性。

精准的舞台表演:角色的生活化和个性化

《秦豫情》从文学剧本到舞台演出实践,其唱腔设计和舞美呈现上也有着巨大的突破。于热闹中求宁静,于曲折中求单纯,于浅显中求深远。据悉,在排演过程中,导演李利宏在传统戏曲程式化动作的基础上进行了大胆的创新与尝试,而剧作者在情节紧张的"节骨眼儿"处独运匠心地写下了大段唱词,通过导演、作曲的二度艺术加工,流畅自然地展现在舞台之上。大段唱词行腔给观剧者以酣畅淋漓的感觉,行云流水般的唱腔让舞台活色生香。那段历史年代中真实的元素充满着浓厚的地域色彩,令观剧者产生了极大的时代共鸣感。国家一级演员、第二十四届中国戏剧梅花奖获得者徐俊霞是位有着丰富舞台演出经验的豫剧旦行表演艺术家。在豫剧舞台演唱方面,徐俊霞精准地拿捏到了与角色形象之间的融合与疏离。这份超越于角色本身的艺术体悟,流淌出强烈的思辨气质,完美地契合了《秦豫情》中主角小勤在人物塑造上的寄托。她的精湛演技做功与凌驾角色自身的体悟力,赋予了主人公鲜活的生命。她的成功,体现在对主人公的感情、心态、性格的体验与把握,其次是自出机杼地将传统戏曲动作有机化合进了当代戏曲舞台艺术表演当中,恰如其分、自然流畅。既是生活化、性格化的,又是规范化、戏剧化的。一场剧演下来,细细品味和揣摩,一颦一笑、一招一式、一举一动都有章法可循,都是精心设计过的,继承了传统戏剧美学意蕴,同时又兼具了现代豫剧的创新,绝无随意和故弄玄虚的痕迹。

上海戏剧学院的陈多先生在《戏剧美学》一书中有着这样的表述:"舞容歌声,动人以情,意主形从,美形取胜。"[10] 简明扼要地将戏剧审美特征做了这样的总结。徐俊霞唱腔应当是遵循了如此原则,把真情熔铸进角色里,当快则快,宜慢则慢;该细腻时,则婉转;应抒情时,就舒展。如小勤和张大的"刮目相看生敬慕——"那段,由怨恨到谅解,由朦胧到清晰,由相识到相爱,层次清晰,合乎情理且感人至深。三秦韵味的豫剧唱腔嘹亮悠扬,似奔涌不息的黄河水倾泻而出,大段唱词发自肺腑,经由声腔和思维的双重加工,令听者大快朵颐,直呼过瘾。将真挚的情感化劲于声腔,三秦儿郎的朗利和豫中逃荒者的质朴都借由唱段和念白原原本本地再现于舞台之上。于是,这种似山涧清泉、林中幽兰的艺术特色,让观众在欣赏之时绝不仅是简单地跟着戏曲的发展情节走,而是伴随着戏剧人物的喜怒哀乐同频共振。

以故事酝酿音乐,以音乐演绎人生。倘若按照电影类型商业片和艺术片进行区分,《秦豫情》无疑是"艺术"的。它没有政治功利,没有主题先行,没有为了某种理念而喋喋不休地说教,而是单纯地"用一种十分真诚的、充满激情的心态",生动而真实地将河南逃荒者的历史进行了艺术的崇高再现。这是一部没有严格意义上"坏人"存在的现代悲剧。开场,舞台上的长安城门布景所呈现给观众的满目苍灰色格调,把观众带进了特定的时代文化氛围之中,创造了一种静谧、古朴、灰暗、苍凉又有点心酸的逼真意象,寓意着主人公面临着的不幸遭遇。在宏大历史背景下讲述最底层人民生动、真实而痛击人心的故事,传递着跨越了时代和地域的人情与人性体悟,将残酷美与崇高美并举,更拉近了观众与剧中人物的心理距离。两者互为表里,既互相激发,又水乳交融。在这里,豫剧《秦豫情》理所当然地传播着社会所亟须的正能量,决然不是那种居高临下的说教,而是要通过人物身上所折射出的人性至美的光芒,"润物细无声"地感染观众,用艺术的形象来洗涤人们的心灵。

结　语

总之,无论是在剧本,还是在音乐、布景、表演等方面,豫剧《秦豫情》都做出了成功的探索。而引领这种艺术创新精神的动力,既有常香玉时代赋予豫剧成为全国著名地方剧种的盛名,更是杨林、雷琳静和甄业等青年剧作家,李利宏导演以及徐俊霞等演员对当下豫剧的热爱与创新。它的成功告诉我们:豫剧艺术的出发点永远植根于生活的沃土,而这片沃土,不仅在河南,也在外埠。豫剧的生命之花能够开遍四野,它的艺术生命力在于每一个喜爱它的人。

参考文献：

[1] 张丛博. 戏里戏外都是浓浓"秦豫情"[N]. 大河报，2017-08-30（A1·16）.

[2] 杨林，雷琳静，甄业. 河南担[J]. 剧本，2016（8）：32.

[3] 杨林，雷琳静，甄业. 河南担[J]. 剧本，2016（8）：33.

[4] 杨林，雷琳静，甄业. 河南担[J]. 剧本，2016（8）：33.

[5] 杨林，雷琳静，甄业. 河南担[J]. 剧本，2016（8）：36.

[6] 杨林，雷琳静，甄业. 河南担[J]. 剧本，2016（8）：36.

[7] 翟文铖. 论汪曾祺创作的儒学美学精神[J]. 理论学刊，2010（8）：124.

[8] 杨林. 关于《河南担》[J]. 剧本，2016（8）：59.

[9] 李渔. 闲情偶寄[M]. 上海：上海古籍出版社，2000：25.

[10] 戴平. 生活永远在逻辑之外[J]. 上海戏剧，2014（12）：25.

[11] 杨林，雷琳静，甄业. 河南担[J]. 剧本，2016（8）：42.

The Color of the Water of Jialing River Seems Dark Blue Rather than Dark Green at Dusk —The Artistic Creation and Reflection of The Henan Opera *The Friendship between the People of Shaanxi and Henan Provinces*

Abstract: The modern Henan Opera *The Friendship between the People of Shaanxi and Henan Provinces* created by the Henan Opera Troupe of Xi'an(capital city of Shaanxi Province) cast off the regionalism and stylization of local opera, incorporated dance, modern drama, Shaanxi Opera (popular in the northwestern China) and other performing forms into the opera, brought forth new ideas on the basis of inheriting the traditions of Henan Opera, and demonstrated the charm and vitality of Henan Opera with unique artistic means. The opera depicted the joys and sorrows of the small folk, eulogized the indomitable spirit of Henan people in face of disasters and hardships, praised the generous and kind characters of Shaanxi people, interpreted the profound friendship between the people of Shaanxi and Henan Provinces, and had artistic quality and epoch-making meaning.

Key Words: *The Friendship between the People of Shaanxi and Henan Provinces*, The Henan Opera, Inheritance, the Artistic Creation and Reflection

The Henan Opera *The Friendship between the People of Shaanxi and Henan Provinces* (the original name of the opera is *The Shoulder Pole that Henan People Carried to Flee from Famine*, was published in the 8th issue of the magazine *Script* in 2016) created by three young scriptwriters of Shaanxi and Henan Provinces including Yang Lin, Lei Linjing and Zhen Ye, directed by Li lihong (the national first-level scriptwriter and director) and played by Xu Junxia (a national class-A actor) was successfully performed in Zhengzhou recently with the simple character of Shaanxi people and the historical memory of Henan people. The opera combined dance, modern drama and other artistic elements, demonstrated the unique charm of Henan Opera with new artistic methods and showed the strong artistic vitality of Henan Opera.

The Historical Memory : Warm Moments in the Woeful Plots

The Henan Opera *The Friendship between the People of Shaanxi and Henan Provinces* created by the Henan Opera Troupe of Xi'an brought innovative elements to the performance of the opera. The work told the story of 1942, which was a collective memory of one era and the two regions, and the bitter years of history and people. In the war-ridden years, the Central Plains region suffered from severe drought and plague of locusts, and the farmer reaped nothing at harvest time and starved to death. In desperation, the Henan people living in the Central Plains were forced to leave their home and begged all the way to ideal Chang'an (the former name of Xi'an) to earn a living. The difficulty of survival and snobbish ways of the world kept torturing the remaining self-esteem of these people fleeing from famine.

The director Li lihong said : " The history is grand, while the charm of humanity is often reflected in choices on small things. The expression of the joys and sorrows of small folk in that hard time showed the audience the greatness of love, the power of hope, the potential of life and the nobility of human beings. " The scriptwriter depicted the characters from the perspective of the ordinary people with same fate. These people, who were at the bottom of the society and often neglected in the grand historical narration, were presented to the audience through the processing of the opera and shaping of the image. The stage curtain was raised slowly; the actors sang behind the curtain : "There are so many people carrying the shoulder poles, but we carry the shoulder poles just to earn a living", while a group of actors who played Henan people that fled from famine carried the shoulder poles in the forms of dance and movements of opera, and their uniform and shocking movements attracted the audience's attention immediately. When ragged, hungry and cold refugees used all their last strength to shout : "We finally find a way to live!", the audience were deeply moved by such mournful cry in the form of the Henan dialect. And then the beautiful stage scenery with a strong flavor of the times brought the audience to that distant and sad time.

The opera told the tragic story of Henan people in 1942 from a brand-new perspective, focused on the survival of the people with low social status in the hard times, eulogized Henan people's perseverance and heroic spirit in the face of great disasters, and highlighted Shaanxi people's noble character of simplicity, diligence and kindness.

The protagonist, 14-year-old Xiao Qin and her father went through hardships and difficulties with the other Henan people fleeing from the famine, begged all the way to Chang'an, where they thought it was so prosperous a place that people could eat steamed bread at random. But the fact was they had neither friends nor relations to turn to, let alone finding a shelter to live. Although they had an argument with other famine refugees who came to Chang'an early, Xiao Qin and her father quickly won everyone's understanding and finally had a place to settle down and live after the resolution of the conflicts. However, the slightly warm atmosphere did not last long. A fortune-teller shamelessly occupied the place of Xiao Qin and her father, which put the latter in an awkward situation. Xiao Qin was reluctant to leave at first, but she gave the place to the fortune-teller without hesitation after knowing that the fortune-teller was blind. Seeing Xiao Qin's behavior, the character called Zhuan Tou who had quarreled with Xiao Qin just now shouted : "Let's move room for Xiao Qin and her father to live!" "Yes!"the other famine refugees said in chorus, which pushed the whole story into pleasant atmosphere. From then on, Xiao Qin washed gauze for Dahua Cotton Mill tirelessly from before dawn till after dark. The scriptwriter, director and composer depicted the scene that Xiao Qin and other women washed gauze with icy water through the cheerful incidental music and the actors' skillful performances, which was the crystallization of wisdom and presented a new aesthetic paradigm by integrating the opera with modern drama and dance. Xiao Qin still had a hope for tomorrow although the life was hard. However, misfortunes never come singly. On the way home, Xiao Qin met a man called Zhang Da who carried a handcart loaded with porcelain on the downhill, she hurriedly gave way to Zhang Da but caused the handcart overturn, which made Zhang Da suffer great economic losses. In great anger, Zhang Da asked Xiao Qin for compensation, and he never thought that he would fall in love with Xiao Qin for her sincerity and honesty in the process of getting alone with Xiao Qin.

The Theme of Humanity : Moderation, Toleration and Honesty

The ancients believed that stable mood is beneficial to the adjustment of human emotions, social stability and the order of heaven and earth, "which manifested the moderation in the relationship between people and ego, the harmony in the relationship between people, the self-identity in the relationship between people and destiny"[7]. The Henan Opera *The Friendship between the People of Shaanxi and Henan Provinces* embodied the ancient aesthetic concept of moderation. It was a great opera that broke down the regional limitation, showed the customs and life of Shaanxi and Henan provinces, and eulogized the spirit of the people in Central Plains fighting against disaster under the historical background of great famine.

On the whole, the tone of the opera was sad. Although the protagonist Xiao Qin and others suffered many hardships and difficulties under the miserable social environment, the whole play was still brimmed with warm atmosphere in many parts and touched the hearts of the audience. For example, Xiao Qin and her father lived a poor life, but Xiao Qin took the only money she had and resolutely signed an IOU (I owe you) to compensate Zhang Da for his loss, and she said: "We're forced to leave our home and have nothing, but we have self-respect!"[8], which demonstrated the determined character of the Henan people who were in poverty. Though Zhang Da suffered great losses, he felt sympathetic when he saw the poor life of Xiao Qin and her father, which showed the generosity of Shaanxi people. Besides, the villagers did everything possible to help Xiao Qin when she had a difficult childbirth, and their kindness was commendable. In other words, the Henan Opera *The Friendship between the People of Shaanxi and Henan Provinces* showed the audience the hardships our nation once suffered, the unremitting struggle of the people in the sufferings, and the traditional virtues of kindness, simplicity, tenacity and helpfulness as were as the beauty of humanity. The opera was a crystallization of labour of the scriptwriter, director and every actor.

A good literary and artistic work must be close to the people, reflect the times and touch the hearts of the people. The conflicts in the Henan Opera *The Friendship between the People of Shaanxi and Henan Provinces* seemed to insignificant, but in fact it was a struggle between honesty and hypocrisy, friendship and selfishness, tolerance and narrow-mindedness. In terms of the image of the leading lady Xiao Qin, she was compelled to leave the native place with her family to earn a living, and attended to her elderly father in hardships. After settling in Chang'an, she kept optimistic and took the responsibility to take care of her father. As far as the image of the leading man Zhang Da as concerned, he was a native Shaanxi young man and spoke harshly when he faced the broken porcelain and asked for Xiao Qin for compensation, which also was a natural expression of emotion; he offered assistance generously and warmed Xiao Qin's fragile heart with the kindness of Shaanxi people after knowing the hardships that Xiao Qin's family had suffered; he helped Xiao Qin to look for a new means of livelihood and made tools for her, and showed his love to Xiao Qin in a simple and rustic way, which made the audience cannot help laughing. The scriptwriter had a preference for the image of Xiao Qin, and depicted her story and personalities with long length. At the same time, the scriptwriter remained rational on the portrayal of each character, and depicted the thoughts and emotions of each character vividly with an exquisite style of writing. Based on this, the story must be touching. And the plots and personalities of the characters were presented to the audience with the development of the story. Xiao Qin's rashness caused the handcart loaded with porcelain overturn and made Zhang Da suffer great economic losses, and she fled back to home in terror, then she resolutely promised to compensate for Zhang Da's losses when Zhang Da came to the poverty-stricken area and condemned the whole group of Henan people. Mrs Lǚ, a prostitute of the poverty-stricken area, first fooled Zhang Da with sexy gestures, and then said the pains of her and that of the whole group of Henan people in a sincere way after knowing that Zhang Da intended to seek compensation from Xiao Qin and her father. Zhang Da's mother, a shrewish and stubborn woman, was reluctant to accept Xiao Qin as the daughter-in-law, but she quietly asked others to buy Xiao Qin's spicy soup so that Xiao Qin could feel at ease at home before delivery after seeing that Xiao Qin stand on the street to sell spicy soup in cold day. At this moment, Zhang Da's mother was no longer as shrewish and stubborn as before, but a loving-mother as any mother in the world. Ma Hu, the fortune-teller who had pretended to be blind to occupy the shelter of Xiao Qin and her father, returned to his good conscience after knowing that Xiao Qin had a difficult delivery, thus he exposed his lie to pray for Xiao Qin and felt relieved of the burden on his conscience. The spirit of Henan people who lived in a corner of Chang'an helping each other touched the audience deeply and evoked prolonged applause. Unlike the previous plays of the same topic, the characters in the opera were not of high ranking, but a group of ordinary Henan people in the Central Plains who lived at the bottom of society and suffered form great disasters. It was the real characterization and vivid performance that enabled the audience to contemplate the pristine beauty of human nature.

The Artistic Integration : The Integration of Shaanxi Opera and Henan Opera

The Henan Opera *The Friendship between the People of Shaanxi and Henan Provinces* brought forth new ideas for it got rid of the old pattern of focusing on the explanation of story and the accumulation of plots rather than the characterization of characters and the revelation of inner feelings. The opera focused on the characters and the humanity, incorporated the elements of Shaanxi Opera and Henan Opera into the whole work. Thus, it was a successful performance of Henan Opera with Xi'an regional features. In order to strengthen the artistic effect of the opera, the composer combined the singing and rhyme of Shaanxi Opera and Henan Opera bred under the two different regional cultures, which was a bold attempt to incorporate the regional characteristics of Henan and Shaanxi provinces into the modern Henan Opera. The story of the figures with low social status of Shaanxi and Henan provinces, and the combination of Shaanxi Opera and Henan Opera, made the work present a new aesthetic feeling differing from the traditional Henan Opera.

We should constantly bring forth new ideas in the creation of opera. Unlike the traditional opera stage scenery with one table and two chairs, the stage art design of the Henan Opera *The Friendship between the People of Shaanxi and Henan Provinces* strove for the clean stage without much decoration, adopted the stage scenery with miserable scenes, threw off the traditional aesthetic conception of local operas, and suspended the stage prop — the gray city gate — in the air, which heightened a primitive and profound regional atmosphere. There were other stage props, including the withered trees that witnessed the vicissitude of the life, and the dilapidated old buildings that embodied the profound history of Chang' an — the ancient capital of nine dynasties — and the regional characteristics of the ancient capital of the Central Plains, which was a vivid interpretation of the regional cultural and characteristics of Shaanxi and Henan provinces, and brought a brand-new aesthetic conception to the audience. At the same time, the opera drew inspiration from the experience and innovative practice of modern opera stagecraft, and presented the audience a film-like visual effect and aesthetic notion.

In *Casual Expressions of Idle Feeling*, Li Yu (1611 — 1680, an outstanding playwright and litterateur in the transition period between Ming and Qing dynasties) once said : "The ancients called the script legend for its strange affair that passed on without anyone seeing it, which differs from the new story. Thus, the scriptwriter must write a story full of strange tale and ideas." [9] The opera is not only the treasure of Chinese excellent traditional culture, but also the crystallization of wisdom of the folk. The strongest aesthetic demand of the ordinary people is the story, that is, the legendary nature of narration, which reminds us that the audience would feel dull if a narrative play cannot tell a story of strange tales and ideas. Obviously, the scriptwriters of the Henan Opera *The Friendship between the People of Shaanxi and Henan Provinces* knew this kind of situation and left enough imagination room for audience to review their own life experience, so that the audience could understand the story under the regional cultures of Shaanxi and Henan provinces, appreciate the artistic charm of Shaanxi Opera and Henan Opera, and feel the profound friendship between Shaanxi and Henan people. The opera did not deliberately imbue the audience with the scriptwriters' conception, inclination and judgement. Instead, it told the story through the straightforward style of writing, showed the audience the fate and emotion of the characters as well as the thread of the story on the basis of integrating the dialect and folk customs of Shaanxi and Henan provinces, and realized a perfect combination of aesthetic education and social enlightenment, which showed the great originality of the scriptwriters. In terms of value orientation, the opera told a story of a specific era and a specific region, while the protagonists' perseverance, hope and kindness could transcend time and touched the heart of the audience, and realized a successful performance. Thus, it was impossible to combine the essence of the two local operas without making extensive use of the expertise from all quarters. In terms of the inner artistic connotation, the opera had modern aesthetic notion rather than adopting the traditional pattern of expressing the hardships that the labouring people suffered in hard time, and eulogized the fine traditions that had existed between the people of Henan and Shaanxi provinces since ancient times, especially the tolerance and honesty that embodied the positive energy and the central theme of the era. In other words, what the scriptwriters and director wanted to show was exactly what people had lost today, thus they rewrote the history of suffering and showed the audience a new aesthetic notion with their passion and aspiration for art as well as their emotional and rational perspective. From this point of view, the opera couldn't win the success without the scriptwriters' ingenuity of combining the artistic advantages of Shaanxi Opera and Henan Opera and retaining the artistic subjectivity of Henan Opera.

The Vivid Performance : The Normalization and Personalization of Characters

In terms of the performance, the Henan Opera *The Friendship between the People of Shaanxi and Henan Provinces* made great breakthroughs in the design of singing and stage art, which was manifested in seeking peace in thrilling performance, simplicity in complicated plots, and reflection in plain lines. It was reported that the director Li Lihong made bold innovations on the basis of the fixed movements of traditional operas in rehearsal, and the scriptwriter added long librettos when the atmosphere of the story was getting more and more tense, which were naturally displayed on the stage through the artistic processing of director and composer and left an impression on the audience. Besides, the real elements full of strong regional color in that historical era evoked a strong echo in the audience. As far as the actors were concerned, Xu Junxia, a national first-class actor and winner of the 24th China Plum Performance Award, was a performing artist of Henan Opera with rich performance experience. She had a good understanding of the image of the protagonist Xiao Qin, and vividly played Xiao Qin with great performance and skillful movement. Her success was attributed to her understanding of the protagonist's emotions, thoughts and personalities, as well as the natural combination of movements in traditional opera with the stage art in contemporary opera. After watching the opera, it was worthwhile to ponder the protagonist's slightest facial expression and every gesture as well as the motion that combined the aesthetic implication of traditional opera with the innovative elements of modern Henan Opera.

Chen Duo, a famous theatre art educator and professor of Shanghai Theater Academy, said in the book *Aesthetics of Theatre* : "The movement and singing in the opera could express the emotion and personality of the characters and touch the hearts of the audience.", which was a brief summary of the aesthetic characteristics of theatre. Xu Junxia followed the above principle of shaping the image with sincere emotions and adjusted her tune in accordance with the atmosphere of the story. For instance, the plot depicted that Xiao Qin and Zhang Da fall in love with the passage of time after going through mutual resentment and understanding. The singing of Henan Opera with the charm of the Shaanxi Opera was resonant, and expressed the sincere emotions of the characters and touched the heart of the audience. The aria and spoken parts showed the candidness of Shaanxi people and the simplicity of those famine refugees of Henan, and struck a chord with the audience.

To compose a music in accordance with the keynote of the story and to show the vicissitudes of life with the music, it was undoubted that the Henan Opera *The Friendship between the People of Shaanxi and Henan Provinces* was artistic according to the distinction between commercial films and artistic films, because it recreated the history of Henan people fleeing from famine in a vivid and sincere way without political utility or the endless preaching for some idea. It was a modern tragedy without the existence of bad person in a strict sense. At the beginning of the opera, the stage scenery of the gray city gate of Chang'an suspended in the air brought the audience into a specific atmosphere of the times, and heightened the quiet, primitive, desolate and melancholy atmosphere implying the bitter experience that the protagonists suffered. Under the grand historical background, the work told the true and painful story of the people living at the bottom of society, conveyed the human feelings and nature across the times and regions, and shortened the psychological distance between the audience and the characters in the opera. On the whole, the Henan Opera *The Friendship between the People of Shaanxi and Henan Provinces* spread the much-needed positive energy of the society, imbued the audience with the beauty of humanity reflected in the characters rather than the patronizing preaching.

Conclusion

In a word, the Henan Opera *The Friendship between the People of Shaanxi and Henan Provinces* made a successful attempt in the script, music, stage scenery and performance. It was the reputation of Henan Opera as a national famous local opera in the era of Chang Xiangyu (1923-2004, a famous performing artist of Henan Opera) as well as the love and innovation of young scriptwriters such as Yang Lin, Lei Linjing and Zhen Ye, the director Li Lihong and actors such as Xu Junxia to the modern Henan Opera that promoted the artistic innovation. What's more, the success of the opera informed us that the development of Henan Opera was always rooted in life of Henan and other places, and its artistic vitality cannot be separated from everyone who loved it.

Bibliography:

[1] Zhang Congbo. The Friendship between the People of Shaanxi and Henan Provinces [N]. Dahe Daily, 2017 -08-30.(A1·16).

[2] Yang Lin, Lei Linjing, Zhen Ye. Henan People [J]. Script, 2016(8) : 32.

[3]Yang Lin, Lei Linjing, Zhen Ye. Henan People [J]. Script, 2016(8) : p33.

[4] Yang Lin, Lei Linjing, Zhen Ye. Henan People [J]. Script, 2016(8) : p33.

[5] Yang Lin, Lei Linjing, Zhen Ye. Henan People [J]. Script, 2016(8) : p36.

[6] Yang Lin, Lei Linjing, Zhen Ye. Henan People [J]. Script, 2016(8) : p36.

[7] Zhai Wencheng. On the Confucian Aesthetic Spirit Created by Wang Zengqi [J]. Journal of Theoretical Studies, 2010(8) : 124.

[8] Yang Lin. About Henan People [J]. Script, 2016(8) : 59.

[9] Li Yu. Casual Expressions of Idle Feeling [M].Shanghai: Shanghai Ancient Books Publishing House, 2000:25.

[10] Dai Ping. Life is always beyond Logic [J]. Shanghai Drama, 2014(12) :25.

[11] Yang Lin, Lei Linjing, Zhen Ye. Henan People [J]. Script, 2016(8) :42.

基于乐感美学理论的戏曲审美实践再认识

——由黄梅戏《仲夏夜之梦》说开来

摘要："乐感美学"的提出为当代戏曲艺术提供了一个更加契合审美实践的新美学视角。以"乐感"为基本特质和核心的美学理论建构是融中外、古今诸多美学理论，集具体审美实践经验而形成的。基于乐感美学理论来重新观照当代戏曲艺术的境况，审美实践基本呈现出三大特征，即传统与现代并举、形式与内涵兼顾、感受与思辨并重。由第八届中国（安庆）黄梅戏艺术节优秀黄梅戏展演剧目——《仲夏夜之梦》说开来，借此"解剖一只麻雀"来得以提升理论水准，为当代戏曲审美实践提供助益。

关键词：乐感；美学；黄梅戏；仲夏夜之梦

第八届中国（安庆）黄梅戏艺术节优秀黄梅戏展演剧目——《仲夏夜之梦》在安庆黄梅戏艺术中心的成功上演正是当代黄梅戏创作在西方名著改编方向所做的一次有益尝试。"任何成功的建构都是建立在对既有成果继承的基础之上的。"[1] 该剧改编自莎士比亚同名喜剧作品《仲夏夜之梦》，由上海戏剧学院副教授张泓执笔改编。在戏曲文本编创上，既具有中国传统戏曲的古典况味，又兼具当代语境的时代特色；在综合舞台呈现上，视觉、听觉和直觉意象的形式之美与情感、意蕴的内涵之美相辅相成；在戏曲艺术整体构成上，触发审美受众观剧体验的感受，并引导着审美受众进行积极地再度解读和思辨。基于"乐感美学"理论的认知来重新审视黄梅戏《仲夏夜之梦》，依傍戏曲审美实践进行再度理解和认识，进而探讨黄梅戏艺术审美实践中"美"的内核和实质。

在安庆黄梅戏艺术中心观看黄梅戏抒情喜剧《仲夏夜之梦》是一次相对完满的审美体验，这也为通过审美实践来探讨其"美"的实质提供了一个适宜的契机和切入点。"探讨'美'的语义，必须从审美实践出发，以美是'令人愉快的东西'这种审美经验为逻辑起点。"[2] 观看《仲夏夜之梦》而产生的审美认知与感受确实是做到了"令人愉快"。观剧的直观体验和观后感受都证明了《仲夏夜之梦》这部黄梅戏抒情喜剧在情节线索的处理、角色行当（尤其是丑角）的设置以及台词文化内蕴等方面呈现出了足够的层次性审美愉悦感。面对着莎士比亚经典喜剧《仲夏夜之梦》这样一部煌煌剧作，不同时代、不同民族、不同艺术门类的艺术家们都试图利用不同的艺术载体去诠释自己或是时代对《仲夏夜之梦》的认识与理解。当这样一部西方经典喜剧佳作碰撞上中国的黄梅戏艺术，对其进行本土化的移植和改编极其考验编剧对于整部戏剧故事脉络的把控能力和戏曲艺术细节的处理能力。正如马克思在其《1844年经济学哲学手稿》中谈及的一样，人类凭借"自觉自由"的"意识"，可以认识"美"的本质和规律，"按美的规律造型"。故而在观剧之余，惊叹这样一部由西方名著移植而来的黄梅戏剧目是出自一位谙熟传统戏曲编创的剧作者之手。

黄梅戏所能够带给审美受众的感官体验在我国浩繁的戏曲种类中绝对是独具美学价值的。黄梅戏传世时间虽远不及安徽本土的其他剧种，如徽剧、泗州戏、南陵目连戏等，却有着令人惊叹的旺盛艺术生命力，充分印证了"美就是由视觉和听觉产生的快感"[3]。黄梅戏兼收并蓄，如安徽省剧协王长安主席讲的：黄梅戏"吃百家奶，广采博纳"。可以说，黄梅戏形成、成熟的道路是自由的、轻松的、包容的。黄梅戏是"好学、好唱、好看、好玩"，这就奠定了其在安徽本土有着广泛的审美受众。《仲夏夜之梦》演出散场后，观众们都受到了比较强烈的艺术熏染，哼唱着剧中片段或旋律尽兴而回。通过阅读剧本、观看演出，增进了我们对黄梅戏与《仲夏夜之梦》创造性融合的立体化体悟。即当代戏曲实践如何在美学理论指引下前行，如何在审美实践中探寻更富多元、更具层次的戏曲美。"我们所从事的艺术以美为目标，我们的任务就在发现而且表现这种美。"[4] 据此观点，黄梅戏《仲夏夜之梦》在审美实践方面的艺术得失可以为我们当下戏曲审美实践活动提供参考范式和借鉴价值。

一、传统与现代并举

不能简单地、机械地将莎士比亚的《仲夏夜之梦》视为不会改变的、界定明晰的纯文学作品。每个时代都会有其时代性的解读和艺术性的再现，只是总有些内在的相对稳定的因素、特质氤氲其中。"要从所有形形色色称为'文学'的文本中，将某些内在的特征分离出来，并非易事。"[5] 张泓在对原著故事内核、情节主线的处理上是下了不少功夫的。将文本中最为本质的特征进行了时代性的艺术赋格，又合时宜地将更富于中国本土美学意蕴的传奇故事与莎士比亚的《仲夏夜之梦》故事进行糅合创作。呈现在我们眼前的，即是这部在整个第八届中国（安庆）黄梅戏艺术节优秀黄梅戏剧目展演活动上都十分亮眼的黄梅戏抒情喜剧《仲夏夜之梦》。将西方剧作原原本本、照抄照搬式地套入到黄梅戏艺术载体上，本土审美受众必然是不能够普遍接受的。剧作家张泓采取了传统、现代并举的创作手法，即以莎剧《仲夏夜之梦》的故事板和线索为创作轮廓，以传统戏曲才子佳人戏填入，使这样一部莎士比亚的煌煌剧作得以以比较柔和的形式本土化、戏曲化。初次观剧，听得唱词写得很见传统戏曲文学底蕴，复又在张泓处讨得剧作文本。交谈中得知，该剧是从其执笔改编的越剧本《仲夏夜之梦》二次移植到黄梅戏的。唱词、念白所使用的戏曲语汇是极为契合中国传统戏曲美学意蕴的，这也平添了这部西方喜剧剧作移植黄梅戏的适配度。

就整部戏曲的结构和突破上来看，却也有着不尽如人意之处。尤其是在收尾上确实是留有遗憾的，不能够突破"神性"枷锁，显得像是小脚女人缩手缩脚的模样，让审美受众不能够直接感受"人性"突破"神性"，"现代性"在传统戏语境躯壳内的释放。这样一部与时代精神相契合的剧作，收尾时却未能突出人文情怀的敢于追求人性解放的精神主旨，没有将戏曲的"扣子"着力放在挣脱"神性"束缚的刻画和叙事上，未能跳脱清风神、明月神及一对精灵的"安排"，而是将这一系列的"胡作非为"都归罪于了一瓶"风月之水"。剧中预设的古典情境中，玲珑、鱼儿、高尚、吴铭皆是敢于追求自由恋爱的青年人，这在人物设定上虽说是古装戏曲，却也是具备着十分明显的人文主义思考的戏曲人物形象设置，在戏曲结束之时不能够一以贯之地突破"传统性""现代性"的躯壳束缚就显得在戏曲的呈现上是美中不足、功亏一篑的。

不论是西方剧作中国化（戏曲化）还是中国剧作西方化（话剧化），都是为了更好地借由本土（本色）语境诠释异域的文化审美体验。然而，放眼于当下的现代戏、新编历史戏的改编和创作实践，成功者少，失败者多。总体上，虽呈现出发展、前进的态势，可以视为当代戏曲审美实践的经验积累，但却缺乏热潮之中的冷静反思与总结。戏曲改编、创作实践活动的成败与否，都值得我们认真思考，理性总结，积极探索，勇于实践。我们不能偏执于一端，既要坚守传统戏曲美学意蕴的精髓，也应当理性地对待当代戏曲实践的转向。学有中西、古今，它们不过都是从某一文化视域去尝试接近、探寻"美"。不能简单地讲西方剧作就比中国戏曲高明，无数的西方剧作与中国戏曲在某些方面存在着异时空、无交集的同时期发生现象。黄梅戏《仲夏夜之梦》在对待传统、现代的平衡上，涵濡了剧作者的心力和美学积淀的迸发，为戏曲审美实践在对异域文化的本土化移植方面给予了一定的启迪作用。

二、形式与内涵兼顾

戏曲是形式与内涵的统一体。没有离开了形式仍可以独立存在的内涵，也没有离开了内涵可以独立展现的形式。但戏曲形式美与内涵美的关系则与戏曲的形式与内涵关系有所不同，两者具有一定的相对独立性，即能以单独的形式呈现其美质。黄梅戏《仲夏夜之梦》从戏曲文本到舞台演出，很好地兼顾了形式与内涵的关系，由此将戏曲的形式美与内涵美互为表里地发挥得淋漓尽致。

戏曲是一门综合艺术，灯光、舞美、音响、化妆等构成了其视听审美的整体，也就是我们所看到的戏曲"形态"。如果通过精细的舞台灯光和布景、精致的妆容和服饰、保真的音响设备、曼妙的戏曲动作引起审美受众的普遍愉悦，就可以视之为"形态之美"。那么，黄梅戏《仲夏夜之梦》在此方面一定是表现得甚是出色。整部戏由再芬黄梅艺术剧院的青年演员陈邦靓、谢军、潘柠静、王泽熙（均为"90后"黄梅戏演员）主演，在现场的舞台呈现上，其四位主要的生、旦角色的唱功、身段展现都显示出了青年演员所应具备的朝气和娴熟扎实的技艺,在对高尚、鱼儿、吴铭和玲珑相似而又不同的角色形象拿捏方面也诠释得恰如其分。四人都体现出了勇于打破封建枷锁、追求个人需求的精神旨趣,但同时由于家境、经历等的不同而又在具体的情节展现和细节处理上有着极大的不同。鱼儿与高尚互相爱恋;吴铭对鱼儿,玲珑对吴铭的爱是求而不得。又经过反转的剧情设计,造就了高尚、鱼儿、吴铭、玲珑,乃至清风神、明月神和戏班班主等角色的形象丰满可感。灯光、乐队和音响等的配合衔接也是十分连贯,这对整部戏的演出是多有助益的。戏曲正是通过演员发声、音响传导、乐队伴奏的若合符节才能够呈现出听觉之美;通过舞美设计、导演编排、演员发挥的得当,乃至超常发挥,才使得舞台上呈现出视觉之美;借由戏曲文本的深刻立意、导演和演员的再度解读与设计、审美受众的观感体会发散不拘,才能够使得一部戏曲迸发出直觉美感。黄梅戏《仲夏夜之梦》能够成功地立展现在舞台上,主要得益于从创编到演出各个环节的配合和发挥。黄梅戏给人的最为直观的听觉感受就是悦耳动听,鱼儿、玲珑的饰演者均是青年黄梅戏演员,有着扎实的演唱功底和纯熟的气息吐字技巧,呈献给观众悦耳动听的黄梅戏自然是不在话下的。

戏曲除却感官作用于审美主体的直接感受以外,还会经由神经发挥作用,促使中枢理解。因为戏曲所蕴含的内涵、意蕴、精神等不可感的形态使大脑产生令人精神愉悦的感觉,这就是戏曲意义的表征,也可以称作“意象”。它大致常见于悬念美、功利美、意蕴美和情感美几种形态。观剧评论者众多,却多是关注于物质的外化,精神的外化时常被忽略。相比较于华丽的服饰、高端的音响等,人们更容易受到演员、乐师等的精神外化的感染与熏陶,也就是中国古典美学中经常谈及的“意蕴生动”。《仲夏夜之梦》在服装、舞台设计和演员的扮相等方面给了审美受众一个最为直观的感受,即“美”。然而,真正最为震撼人心的则是乐师将乐谱酣畅淋漓地演奏,以及这些青年演员们倾力专注于角色饰演的演唱和身法表演所带给人们的“美”的体验。开场鱼儿的一段唱“汗淋淋,慌不择路往前奔——(两人上);步匆匆,违逆父命离家门;乱纷纷,发松鬓散脚不稳……”三句配合着演员的身法,既表现出了富有层次性的戏曲“美”,也交代清楚了两人的现状、背景和样貌。戏曲艺术是基于演出人员和观剧人员双方的一种互动。

戏曲演员在偌大的排练厅中对着镜子练习而无观众,这并不能称之为戏曲表演;观众坐在舒适的剧场当中,对着空空荡荡的舞台而没有演员演出、乐师伴奏,这也不构成戏曲表演的严整形态。同时,演员会因为观众的赞扬而有更好的表演发挥,观众也会因演员投入的表演产生愉悦的心情。在现场观看了黄梅戏《仲夏夜之梦》,安庆市的戏曲观众对于这样一部戏曲的掌声和支持是对整部戏曲演员、乐师等呈现的一个极大精神鼓励。同时,演员、乐师的倾情诠释也为审美受众提供了一场完满的戏曲作品。"艺术表现的价值和意义在于理念和形象两方面的协调和统一。"[6]缺少任何一方都不能够构成严整的戏曲表演艺术。"鱼儿多次跳崖",采用了电影"闪回"的手法进行剧情铺展,化用电影艺术的形式将鱼儿此刻绝望的情感宣泄而出。与鱼儿情投意合的高尚此刻向玲珑百般迎合,玲珑向鱼儿的解释也令鱼儿误以为是炫耀,究其根本却将所有的矛盾归咎于"清风神、明月神"胡闹而引起的一出闹剧。这样的情感表达都得益于电影"闪回"手法在《仲夏夜之梦》中的巧用,既宣泄了戏曲中人物的情感,同时也增添了喜剧色彩。"美的艺术用意在于引起情感,说得更确切一点,引起适合我们的那种情感,即快感。"[7]演员和观众的倾情投入也会使戏曲在整体的叙事和表现过程中产生和引导观众与演员体会到更为深刻的意蕴美和情感美。

莎士比亚《仲夏夜之梦》是"双生双旦"的人物设置,这与李渔《风筝误》的人物设置不谋而合,其戏剧文本具形式美感。黄梅戏《仲夏夜之梦》是"双生双旦"的戏曲角色设置。在整部戏曲的谋篇布局中,至真与戏谑、爱情与玩笑等凸显出了尤为"对称"的形式美感,符合艺术鉴赏中理性化审美实践的常态。当德国学者齐美尔指出"一切美学的动机最初都是对称……"[8]时,那些不规则、不对称,甚至说存有差异性的审美诱惑力才引起了人们的关注,成为一种能够对抗"对称"审美体验所带来的疲劳感的新形式。长久以来,在中国传统戏曲中,人们对于美的追求都偏执于"过分"的"对称",而忽略掉了错综缠绕的"对称"同样也具有形式美感。它在相互错落、激荡和消磨间同样也构成了和谐、合度,《仲夏夜之梦》这样错落有致的剧情设计带给人们一种消解审美疲劳的新体验。

戏曲的形式美是内涵意蕴的迸发。无论是善的主旨,还是真和美的内核借由戏曲形式转化为美,必然都是要蕴藉于合适的感性形象之中。中国古典美学中讲究"立象以尽意"的意象化大致要表达的就是这样的意思。鱼儿、玲珑两位旦角在整部戏曲中就是真与善的化身,在这样一个至美的情境之中将她们的美呈现出来。戏曲意蕴生动,内涵必须要借助舞台情境和人物关系才能够有所外化和展现。美"不是一个抽象的理念世界,而是一个完整的、充满意蕴、充满情趣的感性世界"[9]。它需要有功法卓绝的演员借助身段、步法等基本功自出机杼地化用来诠释和再创作;也需要灯光、舞美通过不同色调、风格化服装等来助益和推动。完全脱离于形式化的理念并不能构成"美",戏曲化抽象为形象的动作范式和故事情节错落的生动意蕴恰是形式美与内涵美的有机糅合。

"'理念'是普泛的、一般的,而给'理念'赋予的美的'形象'则不能是普适的、唯一的,而是千差万别、富有个性的。"[10] 这就是讲,我们基于对某种戏曲的谙熟所进行的审美实践是各不相同的。不仅仅是观看不同剧目、不同人观看同一剧目,即使是同一人观看同一剧目多次所感触到的戏曲形象、情节主旨等都会存有各不相同的可能性。而剧作者和导演在进行戏曲编导演的过程中,不应当将关注点过分集中于它们的普遍性,而是必须转向形象丰满、性格独立的戏曲人物形象和曲折动人的事件。如果仅是通过戏曲的语言去表述它们的普遍性,那只能算作是抽象观念的复述,不属于艺术作品的范畴。

三、感受与思辨并重

戏曲审美实践的最后一环,是受众在观剧结束之后的反响。人,作为一种感官动物,"与美关系最密切的感官是视觉和听觉,都是与认识关系最密切的、为理智服务的感官"[11]。戏曲表演通过视觉、听觉的刺激不仅是在表述故事,更为重要的是通过"中枢"所引起的思辨。倘若是观众看完黄梅戏《仲夏夜之梦》萌生了向往爱情的憧憬而并没关注到在预设的封建社会背景下,鱼儿、玲珑、高尚、吴铭四位男女主人公身上所具备的那种人文主义精神以及抗击封建礼教束缚的勇气及其他剧作者和导演等所欲留给审美受众在观剧过程中的"心思"。如此,则我们可以说这部戏曲是不够成功的。将大量的戏曲关注点聚焦于对四人爱情误会与矛盾的处理上,而不进行足够的拔高或者是放大"人本"的追求,会使得戏曲的思辨教育功能有所弱化。"艺术作品给予我们最大的愉悦,也许是人类本性能够感受的最为持久的和最为强烈的愉悦。"[12]这份欢愉不能仅仅停留在戏曲表演过程中戏班班主、东奔、西跑丑角形象的逗趣,以及戏曲对白中几句看似"时髦"实则突兀的语汇所引发的欢笑上。戏曲的最终成功必然是要在审美受众的观剧实践中产生足够深远而长久的影响的,其中也包含着充满着人文主义情怀的爱情自由的完满结局所带给观众们的精神愉悦和满足感。理念蕴藉于戏曲之中,通过演员、导演和乐师等的感性表露使得这藏匿于剧情、唱词等之后的意蕴得以显露头角,为细心的观者所发现。

戏曲是对生活的高度凝练和艺术表达。纯粹地讲"男欢女爱",若是戏,固然是俗不可耐;若是实,则动人心魄。剧中清风神、明月神登场与戏班班主的对白充满着生活的艺术审美体会与思辨精神。如下:

明月:谁要你说! 咱家是明月神,主持人间男欢女爱。

清风:贤妻,这戏还看得过眼?

明月:老里老套,俗里俗气……我不喜欢,要他们退钱!

　　　[戏班班主冲上。]

班主:谁叫退钱?

明月:你是谁?

班主:我嘛……管戏班吃喝拉撒,任漂泊四海为家,着急了也能上台耍,哈哈,咱是这戏班老大。

明月:哦,是班主呀。

班主:没收订金,如何退钱? 真不看,先付半天工钱。

明月:(要哭了)老公,他、他、他欺负人呐——

清风:(示意班主闭嘴)今日是夫人寿辰,大喜之日,不宜动怒。再说,此戏也并非胡编乱造,乃是下界正在发生的一桩真事!

明月:哦,倒是人间真事?

班主:人间真事。

明月:此刻二人正在梦乡?

清风:正在梦乡。

明月:没有骗我?

清风:夫人借我个胆子,我也不敢呀。

明月：那，（拍手）好！好！好！

清风：好什么好？

明月：（撒娇）夫君，你还不随我下界去呐。

清风：做什么？

明月：这事若是戏文，好不俗气；可倘是真事，倒怪有意思！我要去寻，我要去找，我要去现场看个热闹，你陪着人家嘛——

借这样一个情节，将《仲夏夜之梦》这样一个故事的艺术真实与生活真实的思考铺展开来，抛给了审美受众一个有趣味的问题。在感受这样一个充满逗趣、误会的故事中，思辨当代戏曲文本的创作在"俗"与"不俗"间的探讨。而在第二场戏中，清风神向往地说："还是人间好呀。"以及后来清风神哄骗明月神的"风月之水"时有一系列对白：

清风：将那风月之水，给吴铭滴上一滴，叫他恋上玲珑，好也不好？

（唱）你我神祇擅法术，

何不暗中助娉婷，

巧把冤家化鸳鸯，

锦上添花送人情！

明月：（唱）虽说神祇擅法术，

怎好卷入是非中？

滥施人情违仙道，

你打消此念少吭声！

清风：哦，哦，如此嘛……我倒忘了，几日来为夫人备下的寿辰之礼，还未曾奉上——（作法，摸出一个小小礼盒）

明月：（转怒为喜）这是什么？

清风：夫人亲自看来……（趁其不备偷走其腰上宝瓶）

明月：（打开，失望）又是金货！

清风：女人不是最爱这些东西吗？

明月：谁说的？

清风：夫人亲口所说。

明月：瞎讲！

清风：（从中掏出手机）哎哎哎，你看，我都留着底——壬辰年四月二十五日子时，夫人曰：金货不光好看，升值潜力无边，有钱就买，多多益善。

　　明月：你就买了？

　　清风：买了。

　　明月：你不知道金价刚刚大幅跳水吗？你，你——

　　清风：总比买股票强呀。（后悔失言，捆脸）

　　明月：你……你还买过股票！

　　清风：一些些。

　　明月：你——你又动了我的账户啦？（冲下）

　　清风：交点学费，小嘎把气！（看到手中宝瓶，一乐）来人呐！

　　上述为清风神与明月神对于是否能够施仙法帮助玲珑得取吴铭的爱情时的争论，其中用喜剧的形式进行了铺陈，同时也暗涵着对生活的艺术反映以及"人本"思想的思辨。首先便是"手机""股票""金货"等语汇的进入让观众们不免跳脱了这样一个传奇式的传统戏曲情境，转而引发审美受众对生活中"投资""理财"这样的思索和笑料，而后又是对"帮"与"不帮"的意见上。经由这些逗趣的情节的发展，清风神展现出其带有着明显"小男人"特性，究其根本，是"人"的思维和处事原则；而明月神则是有着相对清楚认知的"神"，认定了人间世事归于"人性"，并不是所谓的"仙道"可以肆意扰乱的。这也就构成了整部戏的最为深刻的矛盾所在。虽然最终仍然未能跳脱或是突破对于"人性"高于"神性"的扣子而着实让人诟病，但是整部戏所带有的当代剧作孕育于审美实践感受之中的思辨仍然是最大的亮点和特色。

　　人有区别于单细胞的生物，其最为明显的特质便是懂得"感受"之后的"思辨"。"文学批评、文学研究的出发点是美的体验、美的印象和美的感动，一切文学研究都应由此出发。"[13]出发并不意味着"终点"。多数的人停留在了表象、表征的关注与研究，而致使"思"和"辨"的弱化与消解。这也是当下戏曲作品风起云涌，佳作却鲜有的一个原因，过分地追求创作，而缺乏对现有新近创编剧目的打磨和深化，新作迭出，佳作鲜有。人们空喊"人本"的口号却始终未能关注到其"形而上"的层面。

　　戏曲审美实践即是将作为"乐感对象"的戏曲艺术作为美学探寻价值

的本体,探寻戏曲美学价值的范畴、实质和内核。这是一个由"感知"到"感受"再到"思辨"的两度转向。"如果我只简单地分析我们对于一个艺术作品的直接经验,而不去寻求一个关于美的形而上学的理论,那么我们几乎要失去目标。"[14] 戏曲的停滞不前,究其根本原因就在于"固步自封",或是不敢放开步子创新,有着这样或那样的隐忧。黄梅戏《仲夏夜之梦》的成功是当代戏曲审美实践做出的一次有益尝试。现象背后需要进行归纳、研究,究其本质与规律,这是任何一门具有科学精神的学科的基本品格。

参考文献:

[1] 祁志祥. 乐感美学 [M]. 北京:北京大学出版社,2016:9.

[2] 祁志祥. 乐感美学 [M]. 北京:北京大学出版社,2016:56.

[3] 柏拉图. 文艺对话集 [M]. 朱光潜译. 北京:人民文学出版社,1963:198.

[4] 北京大学哲学系美学教研室. 西方美学家论美和美感 [M]. 北京:商务印书馆,1982:116.

[5] 伊格尔顿. 文学原理引论 [M]. 刘峰、龚国杰,等译. 北京:文化艺术出版社,1987:11.

[6] 黑格尔. 美学(第一卷)[M]. 朱光潜译. 北京:商务印书馆,1981:90.

[7] 黑格尔. 美学(第一卷)[M]. 朱光潜译. 北京:商务印书馆,1981:40.

[8] 齐美尔. 桥与门:齐美尔随笔集 [M]. 涯鸿,宇声,等译. 上海:三联书店上海分店,1991:217.

[9] 叶朗. 美学原理 [M]. 北京:北京大学出版社,2009:82.

[10] 祁志祥. 乐感美学 [M]. 北京:北京大学出版社,2016:196.

[11] 北京大学哲学系美学教研室. 西方美学家论美和美感 [M]. 北京:商务印书馆,1982:167.

[12] 蒋孔阳主编. 二十世纪西方美学名著选(下)[M]. 上海:复

旦大学出版社，1987：19.

　　[13] 浜田正秀．文艺学概论 [M].陈秋峰,杨国华译．北京：中国戏
剧出版社，1985：9.

　　[14] 蒋孔阳主编．二十世纪西方美学名著选（下）[M].上海：复
旦大学出版社，1987：21.

Recognition of Opera Aesthetic Practice Based on Musical Sense Aesthetics Theory
—From Huangmei Opera "*A Midsummer Night's Dream*"

Abstract: the proposal of "musical aesthetics" provides a new aesthetic perspective for contemporary opera art that is more in line with aesthetic practice. The construction of aesthetic theory with "sense of music" as its basic characteristic and core is formed by integrating many aesthetic theories at home and abroad, ancient and modern, and integrating specific aesthetic practical experience. Based on the aesthetic theory of musical sense, the situation of contemporary opera art is reconsidered. The aesthetic practice basically presents three characteristics, namely, the combination of tradition and modernity, the combination of form and connotation, and the combination of feeling and speculation. From "*A Midsummer Night's Dream*", an excellent Huangmei Opera performance in the 8th China (Anqing) Huangmei Opera Arts Festival, we can analyze an example to raise the theoretical level and provide help for the aesthetic practice of contemporary operas.

Key words: Musical sense; Aesthetics; Huangmei Opera; A Midsummer Night's Dream

Recognition of Opera Aesthetic Practice Based on
Musical Sense Aesthetics Theory

The successful performance of "*A Midsummer Night's Dream*", an excellent Huangmei Opera performance in the 8th China (Anqing) Huangmei Opera Art Festival in the Anqing Huangmei Opera Art Center, is a useful attempt in the adaptation of western masterpieces by contemporary Huangmei Opera creation. "Any successful construction is based on the inheritance of existing achievements." [1] The play is adapted from Shakespeare's comedy "*A Midsummer Night's Dream*" of the same name, and is written and adapted by Zhang Hong, an associate professor of Shanghai Drama Institute. In the compilation and creation of opera texts, it not only has the classical flavor of traditional Chinese Opera, but also has the characteristics of the times in the contemporary context. On the comprehensive stage presentation, the formal beauty of visual, auditory and intuitive images and the connotation beauty of emotion and implication complement each other. On the overall composition of opera art, it triggers the aesthetic audience's feeling of viewing the opera's experience and guides the aesthetic audience to read and think again actively. Based on the cognition of the theory of "aesthetics of musical sense", this paper re-examines Huangmei Opera "*A Midsummer Night's Dream*" and relies on the aesthetic practice of the opera to understand and cognize it again, thus exploring the core and essence of "beauty" in Huangmei Opera's artistic aesthetic practice.

Watching Huangmei Opera lyric comedy "*A Midsummer Night's Dream*" in Anqing Huangmei Opera Art Center is a relatively perfect aesthetic experience, which also provides a suitable opportunity and breakthrough point for discussing the essence of "beauty" through aesthetic practice. "To explore the semantic meaning of 'beauty', one must start from aesthetic practice and take the aesthetic experience that beauty is a 'pleasant thing' as the logical starting point." [2] The aesthetic cognition and feelings generated by watching "*A Midsummer Night's Dream*" are indeed "pleasant". The intuitive experience of watching the drama and the feeling after watching both prove that "*A Midsummer Night's Dream*", a lyrical comedy of

Huangmei Opera, has a sufficient level of aesthetic pleasure in dealing with plot clues, setting up roles (especially clowns) and cultural connotation of lines. Facing Shakespeare's classic comedy "*A Midsummer Night's Dream*", which is a brilliant play, artists of different times, different nationalities and different artistic categories are trying to use different artistic carriers to interpret their own cognition and understanding of "*A Midsummer Night's Dream*". When such an excellent western classic comedy collides with Chinese Huangmei Opera art, the transplantation and adaptation of its localization will greatly test the screenwriter's ability to control the whole drama story and handle the details of opera art. Just as Marx talked about in his *Economic and Philosophical Manuscripts of 1844*, human beings, relying on their "consciousness" of "conscious freedom", can understand the essence and laws of "beauty" and "shape according to the laws of beauty". Therefore, while watching the opera, I marveled that such a Huangmei Opera repertoire transplanted from a famous western work was written by a playwright who was familiar with the compilation and creation of traditional operas.

The sensory experience Huangmei Opera can bring to the aesthetic audience definitely has its unique aesthetic value among the numerous types of Chinese operas. Huangmei Opera is far less handed down than other local operas in Anhui, such as Hui Opera, Sizhou Opera and Nanling Mulian Opera. However, it has amazing exuberant artistic vitality, which fully proves that "beauty is pleasure produced by sight and hearing" [3]. Huangmei Opera is eclectic, just like the Chairman Wang Changan of Anhui Opera Association said, Huangmei Opera "collects hundreds of opera styles and takes all the advantages as it learns", which can be said that the way of Huangmei Opera's formation and maturity is free, relaxed and inclusive. Huangmei Opera is "studious, easy to sing, good-looking and fun", which has established its extensive aesthetic audience in Anhui Province. After the performance of "*A Midsummer Night's Dream*" was over, the audience were strongly influenced by art, humming fragments or melodies of the play and returning after thoroughly enjoying themselves. Through reading the script and watching the performance, we have improved our comprehensive understanding of the creative integration of Huangmei Opera and "*A Midsummer Night's Dream*". That is, how can contemporary opera practice move forward under the guidance of aesthetic theory and how can it explore more diversified and higher-level opera beauty in aesthetic practice. "The art we are engaged in aims at beauty, and our task is to discover and express this beauty." [4] From this point of view, the artistic gains and losses of Huangmei Opera "*A Midsummer Night's Dream*" in aesthetic practice can provide us with reference paradigms and values for our current aesthetic practice of drama.

1. Combining Tradition with Modernity

Shakespeare's "*A Midsummer Night's Dream*" cannot be simply and mechanically regarded as an unalterable and clearly defined pure literary work. Every era has its own interpretation and artistic representation, but there are always some internal and relatively stable factors and characteristics. "It is not easy to separate some inherent characteristics from all kinds of texts called 'literature'." [5] Zhang Hong has done a lot of work in dealing with the core of the original story and the main plot line. The most essential and characteristic of the text has been given an artistic fugue of the times, and the legendary story with more Chinese local aesthetic implication has been combined with Shakespeare's "*A Midsummer Night's Dream*" story at the right time. What lies in front of our eyes is the lyrical comedy Huangmei Opera "*A Midsummer Night's Dream*", which is very brilliant in all the outstanding Huangmei Opera repertoire performances of the 8th China (Anqing) Huangmei Opera Art Festival. When western dramas are copied into Huangmei Opera art carrier, the local aesthetic audience cannot be generally accepted. Playwright Zhang Hong has adopted both traditional and modern; creation methods, namely, the storyboard and clues of Shakespeare's "*A Midsummer Night's Dream*" are taken as the creation outline, and the traditional opera drama of gifted scholars and beauties is filled in, thus enabling such a Shakespeare's brilliant play to be localized and dramatized in a softer form. The first time I watched the play, I heard the lyrics written very clearly in the traditional opera literature, and I got the text of the play from Zhang Hong, while from the conversation, I learned that the play was transplanted to Huangmei Opera from the Shaoxing Opera script "A Midsummer Night's Dream" written and adapted by Zhang Hong. The opera vocabulary used in the lyrics and chants is very consistent with the aesthetic implication of traditional Chinese opera, which also adds to the adaptation of this western comedy drama to Huangmei Opera.

Judging from the construction and breakthrough of the whole opera, it is not satisfactory. Especially in the ending, it is indeed regrettable that it cannot break through the shackles of "divinity" and appears a bit bound, which makes aesthetic audiences unable to directly feel the release of "humanity" breaking through "divinity" and "modernity" in the body of traditional drama context. Such a play, which is consistent with the spirit of the times, failed to highlight the spiritual theme of human feelings of daring to pursue the liberation of human nature at the end. It did not focus on the depiction and narration of breaking away from the shackles of "divinity" and failed to break away from the "arrangement" of Qingfeng God, Moon God and a pair of elves. Instead, it blamed a bottle of "Water of Wind and Moon" for this series of "misbehaviors". In the classical situation preset in the drama, Ling Long, Yuer, Gao Shang and Wu Ming are all young people who dare to pursue free love. Although the character setting is of an ancient costume drama, it is also a drama character image setting with obvious humanistic thinking. If the restraint of "tradition" and "modernity" cannot be consistently broken through at the end of the drama, it appears that the performance of the drama is deficient in beauty and falls short of success.

Both the sinicization of western plays (dramatization) and the westernization of Chinese plays (dramatization) are aimed at better interpreting foreign cultural aesthetic experience through local (natural) contexts. However, looking at the current adaptation and creation of modern drama and new historical drama, there are fewer winners and more losers. On the whole, although it shows a trend of development and advancement, which can be seen as the accumulation of experience in the aesthetic practice of contemporary operas, it lacks calm reflection and summary in the upsurge. The success or failure of opera adaptation and creative practice is worth our serious consideration, rational summary, active exploration and courageous practice. We should not be paranoid at one end and not only stick to the essence of traditional opera aesthetics, but also rationally treat the turn of contemporary opera practice. Learning includes being Chinese and western, ancient and modern, but they all try to approach and explore "beauty" from a certain cultural perspective. Western dramas cannot be simply said to be superior to Chinese operas. Numerous Western dramas and Chinese operas have different time and space in some aspects and occur at the same time without intersection. Huangmei Opera "*A Midsummer Night's Dream*" has imbued the author's heart and the generation of aesthetic accumulation in the balance between tradition and modernity, which has given some enlightenment to the aesthetic practice of opera in the localization of foreign cultures.

2. Combining Both Form and Connotation

Opera is the integration of form and connotation. There is no connotation that can exist independently without form, and there is no form that can be displayed independently without connotation. However, the relationship between formal beauty and connotative beauty of operas is different from the relationship between form and connotative of operas. They have certain relative independence, that is, they can present their beauty in a separate form. Huangmei Opera "*A Midsummer Night's Dream*" innovates the relationship between form and connotation from the opera text to the stage performance, thus giving full play to the beauty of form and connotation of the opera.

Opera is a comprehensive art; lights, stage art, acoustics, makeup and so on, all these elements constitute the whole of audio-visual aesthetics, which is what we see as the "form" of opera. It can be regarded as "the beauty of form" if it causes the general pleasure of the aesthetic audience through fine stage lights and scenery, delicate makeup and costumes, fidelity audio equipment and graceful opera movements. Then, Huangmei Opera "*A Midsummer Night*'s *Dream*" must have performed very well in this respect. The whole play is starred by young actors Chen Bangjing, Xie Jun, Pan Ningjing and Wang Zexi (all "post-90s generation" Huangmei Opera actors). On the scene, the singing skills and figure display of the four main actors show the youthful spirit and solid skills that young actors should possess, which is also appropriate for the similar but different role images interpretation of Gao Shang, Yuer, Wu Ming and Ling Long. The four persons all showed the spirit purport of bravely breaking the feudal restraints and pursuing personal needs, but at the same time they had great differences in specific plot display and details processing due to differences in family circumstances and experiences. Yuer and Gao Shang love each other and Wu Ming's love for Yuer and Ling Long's love for Wu Ming is in vain. After the reverse plot design, this also created Gao Shang, Yuer, Wu Ming, Ling Long, and even Qingfeng God, Moon God and the troupe leader and the other characters, we can feel the full images that have been created. The coordination and connection of lights, bands and acoustics are also very coherent, which is very helpful to the performance of the whole play. It is through actors' vocalization, sound transmission and orchestra accompaniment that operas can present the beauty of hearing. It is Through the design of stage art, the arrangement of directors, the proper performance of actors, and even extraordinary performance that the stage presents visual beauty. Through the profound conception of the opera text, the re-interpretation and design of the directors and actors, and the divergent perception of the aesthetic audience, an opera can generate intuitive beauty. Huangmei Opera *"A Midsummer Night's Dream"* can be successfully presented on the stage, mainly thanks to the cooperation and of every link from creation to performance. Huangmei Opera gives people the most intuitive sense of hearing which is sweet and pleasant, and the actors of Yuer and Ling Long are all young Huangmei Opera actors. Who have solid singing and breathing skills, to present sweet and pleasant sounds to the audience.

Apart from the direct feelings of the aesthetic subject, opera will also play a role through nerves to promote central understanding. Because the connotation, implication, spirit and other imperceptible forms contained in the opera make the brain produce a pleasant feeling, which is the representation of the meaning of the opera and can also be called "image". It is generally common in suspense, utility, implication and emotion. There are many critics watching the drama, but most of them focus on the externalization of material, and the externalization of spirit is often ignored. Compared with luxuriant costumes and high-end acoustics, people are more easily influenced and edified by the externalization of the spirits of actors and musicians, which is often referred to as "vivid implication" in Chinese classical aesthetics. *"A Midsummer Night's Dream"* gives the aesthetic audience a most intuitive feeling, namely "beauty", in terms of clothing, stage design and actor's appearance. However, the most shocking thing is that the musicians performed their music perfectly, and these young actors devoted themselves to the "beautiful" experience brought by the singing and posture performance played by the characters. At the beginning, Yuer sang "dripping with sweat, running forward without any choice but to panic- (on both sides) ; step in a hurry, against his father's orders to leave home; Chaos, hair loose, temples scattered, feet instability ..." The three sentences combined with the actors' posture showed the "beauty" of the opera with rich levels, and also explained the current situation, background and appearance of the two. Opera art is based on the interaction between performers and audience, while opera artists practice in the large rehearsal hall in front of a mirror without an audience, which cannot be called opera performance. The audience sat in a comfortable theater, facing the empty stage without actors and musicians accompanying it, which did not constitute a strict form of opera performance. At the same time, the actors will perform better because of the praise from the audience, and the audience will also feel happy because of the performance put in by the actors. I watched Huangmei Opera *"A Midsummer Night's Dream"* on the spot, the applause and support from the opera audience in Anqing City is a great spiritual encouragement to the actors and musicians of the whole opera. At the same time, the emotional interpretation of actors and musicians also provides a perfect drama work for the aesthetic audience. "The value and significance of artistic expression lies in the harmony and unity of concept and image." [6] The absence of either party cannot constitute a rigorous perform art of opera. "Yuer Jumped Over Cliffs Many Times" uses the movie "flashback" to spread out the plot, and uses the movie art to express Yuer's desperate emotion at this moment. Gao Shang who is in love with Yuer caters to Ling Long in every way at the moment. Ling Long's explanation to Yuer also makes Yuer mistake it for showing off. However, all the contradictions are basically attributed to a farce caused by the nonsense of "Qingfeng God and Moon God". This kind of emotional expression benefits from the skillful use of the movie "Flashback" technique in *"A Midsummer Night's Dream"*, which not only gives vent to the emotions of the characters in the drama, but also adds comedy color. "The artistic purpose of beauty is to arouse emotions, to be more precise, the kind of emotions that suit us, namely pleasure." [7] The devotion of the actors and the audience will also make the opera produce and guide the audience and the actors to realize more profound beauty of meaning and emotion in the overall narrative and performance process.

Shakespeare's "*A Midsummer Night's Dream*" is the character set of "Twin Shuang Dan", which coincides with the character set of Li Yu's "*Kite Mistake*". The formal aesthetic feeling of his drama text is the drama character set of "Twin Shuang Dan" in Huangmei Opera "*A Midsummer Night's Dream*". In the layout of the whole drama, truth and banter, love and hurt, etc. highlight the formal aesthetic feeling of "symmetry", which is in line with the norm of rational aesthetic practice in art appreciation. When German scholar Zimmer pointed out that "all aesthetic motives are symmetrical at first ..." [8], the irregular, asymmetrical and even differentiated aesthetic allure attracted people's attention, becoming a new form that can resist fatigue brought by "symmetrical" aesthetic experience. For a long time, the pursuit of beauty in traditional Chinese operas has been paranoid about "excessive" symmetry, while ignoring the intricate "symmetry" which also has formal beauty. It also forms harmony among the scattered, stirring and killing of each other. The scattered plot design of "*A Midsummer Night's Dream*" brings people a new experience to relieve the aesthetic fatigue.

The formal beauty of opera is generating with connotation. Whether it is the theme of good or the core of truth and beauty transformed into beauty through opera forms, it must be embedded in appropriate perceptual images. This is roughly what the imagination of "setting up an image to fulfill one's meaning" in Chinese classical aesthetics should express. Yuer and Ling Long are the incarnations of truth and goodness in the whole opera, presenting beauty in such a beautiful situation. The connotation of opera is vivid, and the connotation must be externalized and displayed by means of stage situation and character relationship. "The beauty is not an abstract world of ideas, but a complete, meaningful and emotional world" [9]. It requires outstanding performers to interpret and re-create with the help of basic skills such as figure and footwork. Lighting and stage art are also needed to help and promote through different colors and stylized clothing. Completely divorced from the formal concept, it does not constitute "beauty". The dramatic action paradigm abstracted into images and the vivid implication of the story plot are just the organic combination of formal beauty and connotative beauty.

"'Idea' is universal and general, while the 'image' of beauty given to 'idea' cannot be universal and unique, but it is very different and full of individuality." [10] This means that our aesthetic practices based on our familiarity with certain operas are different. Not only watching different plays and watching the same play by different people, but even the drama images and plot themes that the same person feels many times when watching the same play have different possibilities. The author and director of the drama should not focus too much on their universality in the process of editing and directing the drama. Instead, they must turn into full-featured and independent drama characters and tortuous and moving events. If only the language of opera is used to express their universality, it can only be regarded as a retelling of abstract concepts and does not belong to the category of artistic works.

3. Combining Both Feeling and Thinking

As the last link in the aesthetic practice of opera, it is the audience's response after watching the opera. Human being, as a sensory animal, "the senses most closely related to beauty are vision and hearing, which are the senses most closely related to cognition and serve for reason". [11] The drama performance is not only expressing the story through visual and auditory stimulation, but also the speculation caused by the "center". If the audience saw Huangmei Opera "*A Midsummer Night's Dream*" and had a longing for love, they did not pay attention to the humanist spirit possessed by the four protagonists of Yuer, Ling Long, Gao Shang and Wu Ming, the courage to fight against the restraints of feudal ethics, and the "thoughts" that other playwrights and directors wanted to leave to the aesthetic audience in the process of watching the opera. In this way, we can say that this opera is not successful enough. A large number of opera concerns are focused on the treatment of misunderstanding and contradiction in the love of four people, without sufficient promotion or amplification of the pursuit of "humanism", which will weaken the speculative education function of opera. "Art works give us the greatest pleasure, perhaps the most lasting and strongest pleasure that human nature can feel." [12] This joy can not only rest on the amusing images of troupe leaders, buffoons running east and running west during the performance of traditional operas, as well as the laughter caused by a few seemingly "fashionable" but actually abrupt words in the dialogue of traditional operas. The ultimate success of opera must have a far-reaching and long-lasting impact on the audience's watching practice, which also includes the spiritual pleasure and satisfaction brought to the audience by the happy ending of love and freedom full of humanistic feelings. The idea is embedded in traditional operas. Through the emotional expression of actors, directors and musicians, the implication hidden behind the plot, lyrics and so on can be revealed and discovered by careful viewers.

Opera is a highly condensed and artistic expression of life. Pure "men and women love each other". If it is the play, it is so ordinary; if it is real, it is really fascinating. The dialogue between Qingfeng God and Moon God and the troupe leader in the play is full of artistic aesthetic experience and speculative spirit of life. As follows:

Moon God: Who wants you to say? I am Moon God, presiding over men's and women's love.

Qingfeng God: My darling, did you enjoy this play?

Moon God: Old-fashioned, vulgar, ... I don't like it, I want them to refund my ticket!

[The troupe leader rushed up]

Troupe leader: Who calls for a refund?

Moon God: Who are you?

Troupe leader: I'm in charge of the troupe ... I'm in charge of everything in people's daily life here, and I wander around the world and the whole universe can be regarded as my home. I can play on stage when there is vacancy of actors here. Hahaha, I'm the boss of this troupe.

Moon God: It's the troupe leader.

Troupe leader: Confiscated the deposit, how to refund it? I don't think so. I'll pay half a day's wages first.

Moon God: (to cry) My dear, did you see that? He, he, he bullies me —

Qingfeng God:(motioning the troupe leader to shut up) Today is the birthday of my sweety; it is not appropriate to be angry. Besides, this play is not a hoax, but a real thing happening in the lower world!

Moon God: Is it true?

Troupe leader: The real thing in the world.

Moon God: The two are asleep at the moment?

Qingfeng God: Yes, falling asleep.

Moon God: Did you lie to me?

Qingfeng God: Even though you lent me courage, I still dare not lie to you.

Moon God: (clap her hands) OK! OK! OK!

Qingfeng God: What's so good about?

Moon God: (coquetry) My dear, why don't you go down with me?

Qingfeng God: What are we going to do?

Moon God: If it is a drama, it is very tacky. But if it is true, it is very interesting! I want to find one. I want to find one. I want to go to the scene to see a lively drama. I want you to accompany with me, please —

Through such a plot, the artistic truth and real life of a story like "A Midsummer Night's Dream" are spread out, leaving an interesting question to the aesthetic audience. In the experience of such a funny and misunderstood story, the author ponders the discussion between "vulgar" and "not vulgar" in the creation of contemporary opera texts. In the second scene, Qingfeng God is yearning, "it is better to live in the world." And the following is a series of dialogues when Qingfeng God coaxed Moon God the

"Water of the Wind and Moon":

*Qingfeng God: We can drop a small drop of the romantic water on Wu
Ming to make him fall in love with Ling Long, okay?*

(singing)

You and I are all gods good at magic.

Why don't you help them secretly?

Turned enemies into friends,

The icing on the cake to send human feelings!

Moon God: (singing)

Although you and I are all gods good at magic,

How to get involved in right and wrong?

Abusing human feelings violates the immortal principles.

You give up this idea and keep quiet!

*Qingfeng God: Oh, oh, so ... I forgot it, several days to prepare for my
wife's birthday gift, which has not been presented — (pulled out a small gift
box)*

Moon God: What is this?

*Qingfeng God: My darling, please see it personally... (Stole the vase on
her waist when she was unprepared)*

Moon God: (open the box, disappointed) It is gold again!

Qingfeng God: Isn't this women's favorite?

Moon God: Who said that?

Qingfeng God: My dear, you told me that yourself.

Moon God: No, that is nonsense!

*Qingfeng God: (took out his cell phone) You see, I have the evidence —
my wife said, gold is not only good-looking, but also has great potential for
appreciation. If you have money, you can buy as much as possible.*

Moon God: Then you bought it as I said?

Qingfeng God: Yes, my dear.

Moon God: You don't know that gold price has just declined sharply?

You, you —

Qingfeng God: That is better than buying stocks. (regret his mistake and slap his face)

Moon God: You ... you bought stocks!

Qingfeng God: Only a little bit.

Moon God: You... you have moved my account again? (bushing down)

Qingfeng God: Come on! Don't be so mean, my dear. (see the treasure bottle in hand and enjoy it) Come on!

The dispute between Qingfeng God and Moon God over whether they can apply magic to help Ling Long win Wu Ming's love has been elaborated in the form of comedy, which also implies the artistic reflection of life and the speculation of "humanism". First of all, the utilizing of words such as "mobile phone", "stock" and "gold goods" makes the audience inevitably jump out of such a legendary traditional opera situation, which in turn triggers aesthetic audiences to think and laugh about "investment" and "financial management" in life. Then there is the opinion of "helping" and "not helping". Through the development of these amusing plots, Qingfeng God has obvious characteristics of being a "little man", which is basically the thinking and principle of being a "man". On the other hand, Moon God is a "god" with relatively clear cognition, which confirms that the human world belongs to "human nature" and is not arbitrarily disturbed by the so-called "immortal Tao", which also constitutes the most profound contradiction of the whole play. Although it is still criticized for failing to break through the button that "human nature" is higher than "divinity", the whole play is still the biggest bright spot and feature with the speculation that contemporary plays are pregnant with aesthetic experience.

Human beings are different from single-celled organisms, and their most obvious characteristic is "speculation" after understanding "feelings". "The starting point of literary criticism and research is the experience of beauty, the impression of beauty and the touch of beauty. All literary research should start from this." [13] Departure does not mean "destination". Most people stay in the attention and research of appearances and representations, resulting in the weakening and dissolution of "thinking" and "distinguishing", which is also one of the reasons why the current dramatic works are blasting but excellent works are rare. People are so fully engaged in creation, and lack the polishing and deepening of the existing newly created repertoire and new works, resulting in few excellent works existing. People's empty slogan of "people-oriented" has always failed to pay attention to its "metaphysical" level.

The aesthetic practice of traditional opera is to regard traditional opera art as the noumenon of aesthetic value, and to explore the category, essence and core of traditional opera aesthetic value, which is a two-time turn from "perception" to "feeling" and then to "speculation". "If I simply analyze our direct experience of a work of art without seeking a metaphysical theory of beauty, then we will almost lose our goal." [14] The fundamental reason for the stagnation of opera lies in its "self-denial" or its unwillingness to open up and innovate. With some hidden worries, the success of Huangmei Opera "*A Midsummer Night's Dream*" is a beneficial attempt in the aesthetic practice of contemporary operas. The phenomenon needs to be induced and studied, and its essence and laws are the basic character of any discipline with scientific spirit.

Reference:

[1] Qi Zhixiang. Musical Aesthetics [M]. Beijing : Peking University Press. 2016:9.

[2] Qi Zhixiang. Musical Aesthetics [M]. Beijing : Peking University Press. 2016:56.

[3] Plato, Collection of Literary Dialogues [M]. Translated by Zhu

Guangqian. Beijing : People's Literature Publishing House, 1963:198.

[4] Aesthetic Teaching and Research Office. Department of Philosophy, Peking University. Western aestheticians on beauty and aesthetic feeling [M]. Beijing : The Commercial Press, 1982:116.

[5] Eagleton. Translated by Introduction to Literary Principles [M]. Beijing : Liu Feng, Gong Guojie, et al. Culture and Art Publishing House, 1987:11.

[6] Hegel. Aesthetics (vol. 1) [M]. Beijing Translated by Zhu Guangqian. The Commercial Press. 1981 90.

[7] Hegel. Aesthetics (vol. 1) [M]. Beijing : Translated by Zhu Guangqian. The Translated by Zhu Guangqian. The Commercial Press, 1981:40.

[8] Simmel. Bridge and gate: essays of Simmel [M]. Shanghai : Translated by Ya Hong, Yu Sheng, et al. Shanghai : Shanghai Branch of Joint Publishing, 1991:217.

[9] Ye Lang. Aesthetic Principles [M]. Beijing : Peking University Press, 2009 :82.

[10] Qi Zhixiang. Musical Aesthetics [M]. Beijing : Peking University Press, 2016:196.

[11] Aesthetics Teaching and Research Office. Department of Philosophy, Peking University. Western aestheticians on beauty and aesthetic feeling [M]. Beijing : The Commercial Press, 1982:167.

[12] Jiang Kongyang, editor-in-chief. Selected Works of Western Aesthetics in the 20th Century (II) [M]. Shanghai : Fudan University Press, 1987:19.

[13] Masayoshi Hamada. An Introduction to Literature and Art [M]. Translated by Chen Qiufeng and Yang Guohua. Beijing : China Drama Publishing House, 1985 : 9.

[14] Jiang Kongyang, editor-in-chief. Selected Works of Western Aesthetics in the 20th Century (II) [M]. Shanghai : Fudan University Press, 1987 : 21.

历史真实与艺术真实的完美结合

——评历史题材豫剧《玄奘》

摘要：历史题材豫剧《玄奘》从历史维度观照当下，兼具了历史真实性与艺术真实性，以豫剧艺术的形式，讴歌玄奘为终身追求"普度众生"的宏愿，奋斗不止、百折不挠的坚韧毅力，赞颂对信仰至死不渝的传统美德；在客观地还原历史本来面目的同时，对弘扬社会主义核心价值观，呼唤精神文明回归，起到了巨大的促进作用；就历史题材艺术创作在历史真实与艺术真实的取舍问题上，以实践成果的形式进行了有益探索，为我们提供了有效案例。

关键词：豫剧；玄奘；历史真实；信仰

历史题材戏曲在创作和演出阶段的争执点在于历史真实性与艺术真实性的拿捏上。历史是真实的、不可欺的，艺术则是要给审美受众以一定的遐想空间。历史题材戏曲的编创往往是基于大量的史料文献的搜集、整理与甄别，然后通过剧作者进行艺术性的还原与加工。散布于文献史料中的只言片语会引导着编创者建构出一个历史上真实的情境。但，历史终归是吝于笔墨去过分描述，而力求其客观真实的记录与表述。字里行间的线索仅能够建构出一个历史上真实存在的时代背景和人物模样，但却是模糊的、扁平的。编剧要依据史料书籍上只言片语的描绘来还原与重塑一个有血有肉的、形象可感的历史人物，就必然要在正史、野史的记载之上添加一定的艺术性虚构。如何通过简要凝练的史料话语叙述来重新建构起当时的时代背景、人物关系以及艺术性地塑造曲折生动的故事情节和立体的人物形象，这是摆在剧作者面前的最大难题。由河南豫剧院青年团主演、孟华编剧、李利宏导演的大型历史题材原创豫剧《玄奘》，就此"难题"，以实践成果的形式似乎给出了一份令专家学人都相当满意的答卷。

一、在历史真实中展现艺术真实

国人对"玄奘"其人的认知偏颇主要是基于长篇浪漫主义小说《西游记》及由小说《西游记》改编的影视剧作等。历史上真实存在的"玄奘"其人其事急需正本清源。玄奘是一位在佛学界有着崇高声望的高大僧德、优秀的经学翻译家，同时，他也是中原的一张文化名牌。他历经十七年，孤身西行印度求法。一路上，越荒漠，忍饥渴，斗盗贼，历千辛，尽万苦，用坚韧的毅力和行动开拓出了由中国至西域天竺的佛法济世之路。为求取佛教祖庭经书，挽大唐"经幢不全，缺乏善本"之危，一路西行"血足终濯印度河"。然而，受《西游记》话本小说和影视作品的影响，在多数国人眼中的"玄奘"却是一个敌我不分、懦弱无能的僧人形象。显然，这是不符合历史真实的。面对着艺术加工后的"唐僧"形象逐步成为国民的普遍认知，还原历史上真实的"玄奘"、端本正源就变得刻不容缓。值得欣喜的是，孟华先生执笔创作的历史题材豫剧《玄奘》应时而作，遵循着历史的真实评述，兼顾艺术性与真实性，极大限度地还原了这位视"信仰如同生命灯"的玄奘大师。豫剧《玄奘》所蕴含其中的那份为求真理而坚韧不屈的精神品格，以及对真、善、美矢志不渝追寻的那份笃定，都是对历史上玄奘的最为妥帖和中肯的呈现。这不仅是在大力弘扬中华优秀传统文化的背景下将国民的文化关注点和普遍认知由《西游记》溯源至《大唐西域记》，更为玄奘做了历史文化层面最为真实生动的正名！

豫剧《玄奘》中的"玄奘"形象塑造基本是遵照着文献史料上"玄奘"原型进行的，历史细节不尽详述之处恰是留给编剧进行艺术加工和再创造的丰腴沃土。第一、二场，通过玄奘与丹阳公主、石磐陀、慧净等人物的对唱、道白来交代剧情、塑造人物形象，凸显出了玄奘的无私信仰。正因玄奘秉承着对济世的极大信仰，在一路西行的道途中才会展现出刚毅笃定、自强不息、奋力前行的伟岸形象。剧作既是以玄奘西去取经、为佛教正统教义的传播和济世而做出极大牺牲与奉献的故事为创作素材，同时也契合了当下国家"一带一路"时代背景之下文化多元共融、交流互动的主题，借助中原"玄奘"这一历史人物作为河南的一张文化名片，以豫剧艺术表演的形式来弘扬和扩大中国文化、中原文明的影响及软实力。

斯坦尼斯拉夫斯基说："实际上，在世界上没有一个人没有他自己独具的性格特征，正如在世界上没有像两滴水那样完全相同的两个人，甚至没有个性的人，也有他毫无个性这个特征。"[1] 基于"玄奘西行求法"这样一个宏大历史事件为叙事题材的豫剧《玄奘》，其情节构思的巧妙安排，舞美动作的用心展现，以及唱腔念白的精心设计，真实还原了玄奘十七载艰辛异常的"寻佛陀"历程。其中，既有宽广的文化视野，又有对人物个性细节的钩沉。它通过玄奘一路西行、献身佛教文化事业的坎坷经历，使许多转瞬即逝的珍贵历史瞬间不再藏匿，静置于历史书卷中。通过豫剧艺术的形式，使真实的"玄奘"得以重新呈现在世人眼前。玄奘三年跋涉"苦绝历尽"，只为能够来到印度那烂陀寺投拜戒贤大师。为求佛法，谢绝丹阳公主、高昌国王、蔻儿公主的再三挽留，虔诚礼佛；舌战五印外道，义正词严，对答如流，显示了高深的学识、卓越的智慧和大度的品格；面对印度国王的各种奖赏，玄奘始终坚定执着于回归东土大唐。之后，他鞠躬尽瘁，报效唐朝，译经 47 部，共 1337 卷，开创了佛教史上"法相宗"的文化新纪元。应该说，玄奘的这份爱国济世之心借由豫剧《玄奘》所呈现给世人，是跨越任何时代都具有极为强烈的现实意义的教育典型，符合我们从历史记载中得到的史料书写。

豫剧《玄奘》开场即直接切入主线叙事，玄奘"市南买得千里驹"，和慧净、石磐陀商定"提前行期，连夜启程"。当此时，丹阳公主自知一道懿旨留不下玄奘，便亲自前去挽留，又许之以高官厚禄、金钱真情，但终究动摇不了玄奘求佛取经的虔诚之心。一波未平，一波又起。师徒三人途经八百里荒漠，风沙肆虐，极度缺水，严重危及生命；慧净前往烽火台"偷水"时不幸中了毒箭，生命垂危，玄奘宁愿被渴死，也要用水为慧净冲洗伤口，以挽救爱徒的生命。在这里，信仰，是玄奘身上"至坚、至净、至纯、至真"的悲悯之心，是不远万里求真经、为求佛法济世人的动力源泉，是危难困苦中迸射出来的人性最为质朴的生命原色。换言之，不管是文学小说、影视剧作中的玄奘,还是豫剧《玄奘》真实还原的玄奘,这种耐得住寂寞、禁得住诱惑的共性特点正是源自玄奘内心之中有着一份笃定的信仰。这信仰正是一盏指引前行的明灯,是吴承恩、刘镇伟、孟华等都不能够轻描淡写、一笔带过的。

就豫剧《玄奘》的剧本创作来讲,编剧孟华游刃有余地把握了历史题材戏曲编创的真实性与艺术性的二元对立统一。"历史剧既然具有历史与艺术的双重身份,这就要求历史剧的创作者应具备历史学家和艺术家的双重品格,既尊重艺术规律,也尊重历史规律,既要求历史真实,也要求艺术真实。"[2] 通过孟华的塑造,剧中人物形象是真实可感且个性鲜明的。这一点,既符合戏曲艺术程式化和历史史料真实性的特征,也迎合了当下审美受众追求戏剧矛盾冲突的审美需求。在人物形象的塑造和人物关系的处理上,孟华恪守着历史的真实性,是带着对历史的尊重和理性审视来执笔创作的。同时,他又将历史叙事的不尽之处大胆添加,制造戏剧性、矛盾性和曲折性。一部历史宏大叙事的剧作搬演到舞台之上必然是基于一部绘声绘色的戏剧文本。豫剧《玄奘》在对历史进行戏剧化的表述之外,还加入了艺术虚构的成分与时代语境的思考。例如,将风沙等幻化为魔障;沙漠昏迷时玄奘幻化出的丹阳公主;河畔遇险时的天雷滚滚,借愚昧人之口将其归于上天惩戒;等等。这正是豫剧《玄奘》导演李利宏基于文化根由的舞台艺术性调度和导演阐发。

影视剧作《西游记》在人民群众当中流传甚广,源出于明代吴承恩所著长篇小说。其人物与情节都是浪漫的、奇幻的,甚至说带有着很强烈的虚构性。但,正因为虚构与演义的比例太重,突破了历史的底线,从而使玄奘的人物形象失真而完全艺术化。既如此,它即便是已经"并且产生了广泛的、世界性的影响"[3] 的经典名著,其所塑造的人物形象再真实可感,如果以历史观审视,也不免留下一丝遗憾。以郭沫若"失事求似"的历史题材文艺创作原则来观照豫剧《玄奘》这部大戏,它无疑是兼具了戏剧艺术性与历史真实性的时代佳作。在这里,编剧孟华以一种近乎传记的笔法,在兼顾了对历史人物的理解与尊重的同时,又创造性地、极大地丰富了戏曲艺术,收到了震撼人心的艺术效果。

二、用艺术形象还原历史形象

历史题材戏剧的创作决不能凭空杜撰,在塑造人物形象方面必须尊重历史,尊重历史真实。豫剧《玄奘》在情节的构思方面是花费不少心思的,以现代剧作法为指导,使这样一部反映历史、再现历史人物的戏曲作品能够满足当下人民日益提升的审美追求。同时,也确实是在主线和历史细节处理上做到了历史性与艺术性的统一,颇具匠心。以此为基础,让真实的历史与佛教济世精神相结合,把玄奘形象与时代精神相融为一体。从历史的维度拂照现实,以当代语境解读历史,所创作的这部鸿篇巨制无疑是兼具着历史的厚重与艺术的魅力,大气磅礴而振聋发聩。剧中无时无刻不凸显着美,形象美、情感美、意蕴美……蕴藏着一种催人振奋的动力,这种"美"是一种饱满、积极、健康、向上的正能量。虽然,剧作《玄奘》中援引了不少佛教原典和语汇,让剧作在欣赏过程中显得晦涩难懂了些。但孟华把剧中的人物关系始终置于矛盾波澜之中,引导着审美受众去体悟、思考世事,又不失为对诘屈难懂语汇的一种生动诠释。紧凑的情节处理集中烘托和渲染了故事的曲折和复杂,终了又不忘记将人物的道德境界进行拔高。譬如,佛家是不轻易发誓的,然而当石磐陀诉说家有可怜的母亲子女时,玄奘便有了怜悯之心,开始为石磐陀起誓。在恒河边,玄奘遭到突伽匪徒袭击时,差点丢掉性命,得救后还恳请援救的将官开恩,放他们一条生路等。从玄奘这一宽容大度和与人为善的举止里,展现出剧作者孟华深刻体悟和把握到了佛教的悲天悯人与参透人生的平静与豁达。同时,豫剧《玄奘》让数百年的风雨沧桑、枝枝蔓蔓、离合悲欢、辉煌困顿,由远而近;让创造盛唐佛教文化奇迹的玄奘渐渐清晰而鲜活起来,从而为观众呈现出最为"正牌"的玄奘形象。

一部能够让人民咋舌称赞的历史题材戏曲定然不是将历史事件串联之后严整地叙述下来这样简单和机械。创作出一部好的历史剧,其关键就在于如何讲述故事,如何塑造人物。一部戏能不能够在舞台上立得住,首要就是看它的故事情节和人物形象是否能够吸引观众。玄奘这样一位为中印文化交流传播做出卓越贡献的人物,关于他的大多记载都保存在史学典籍之中。但历史的记录是概要性的、要言不烦的,因此这就需要剧作者对所要叙述的历史故事进行巧妙地设置安排，并赋予这些事情以典型的人物形象和意义，贯穿剧作始终。这是极为考验剧作家对于历史题材剧作编创的掌控能力以及对情节安排、人物塑造的艺术创作功力的。孟华将玄奘这一剧中男主人公置身在真实的历史背景和复杂的戏剧情境之中，使得这一人物形象变得有血有肉了起来，而不再是以往影视剧作中那样不食人间烟火、高高在上。玄奘是一位虔诚的佛家信徒，但首先他是一位有着极大善意的人。显然，孟华是清醒地意识到这一点的。于是，《玄奘》开篇即将情节背景设置在了玄奘西行之前丹阳公主竭力挽留，而后又接连写了西行路上丹阳公主的百般阻挠、窘境之中石磐陀的妥协软弱和高昌国王的强硬挽留等，这些情节设置都并不是完全落脚在玄奘对于西行求佛法的笃定与坚决。相反的，这些是剧作者所欲以表现的一部分，其中也掺杂着玄奘作为一个肉体凡胎的人的思想纠结与人文情怀。导演李利宏又以极其细腻的导演艺术为我们描绘了唐朝与外邦的生活场景和衣着习俗，这都应该归功于主创团队为创作这样一部剧作而搜集与查阅资料下的那一番真功夫。同时，以孟华、李利宏的戏剧艺术风格让受众做了一次心灵皈依的体验，回归到生命本质和人性纯真。孟华、李利宏用当下的审美视域去重新审视与解读历史，见人之所未见，闻人之所未闻，力求耳目一新，力求振聋发聩；或者通过某个人物的塑造，让审美受众为之动容。既如此，豫剧《玄奘》就不再是单纯地叙述历史，更不是机械地道德说教，而是借助这最具有艺术感召力的戏曲形式进行潜移默化的教育，这也令观者丝毫没有反感的情绪掺杂。而这一切，正是《玄奘》取得成功的重要基础。

　　"豫剧《玄奘》以历史上真实的唐玄奘西行取经故事为基础，复原了玄奘一路遭遇种种磨难而不忘初心、现身佛法的故事"。[4] 剧本创作不能被真实的历史背景所局限和约束，同时也应当更多地关注于在这样一个背景下的"人"，以及"人"所蕴藉的情感与思想。一个个鲜活立体的人物形象交织构成了戏曲的曲折情节，曲折情节非线性的交叠构成了一部完整的戏剧而呈现于舞台之上。这就好似立体几何中的"点线面"原理一般无二，面是由无数线构成，线是由无数点构成。因为人物的命运、情感、思想才是历史题材戏曲创作的导向和根由，写出舞台上立得住、观剧后忘不掉的人物形象和故事情节是戏曲艺术创作者孜孜以求的。孟华关于《玄奘》的创作是带有着佛家弘法济世与当下弘扬真、善、美相统一的旨趣的。他既从玄奘生活过的地方获得创作灵感，又从明、清、民国初年以来的大量通俗文学中汲取创作营养，从而增强了剧作的艺术性与情节张力，让故事和人物在戏曲舞台上多面性地展开。然而，历史题材戏曲是真实历史的艺术再现，仅有宏大叙事的历史架构是远远不够的，必须写出"典型环境中的典型人物"。卢卡契在评论莎士比亚的特殊之处时说："古往今来，从来没有一个人像他那样描写没有被分割的人和人的不可分割性，人的核心甚至对他的一切客观表现来说也具有不可取消的优先地位。"[5] 从这个意义上讲，实证主义精神从来都应该贯穿于剧作者所有的创作中。一些质量上乘的古装剧、历史剧，比如《包青天》《海瑞罢官》等，无一不具有强烈鲜明的人物个性和现实意义。毕竟，所有的历史书写都是为当下服务的，一切历史都是为了观照当下。从这个角度说，豫剧《玄奘》别具匠心、独辟蹊径。随着剧情的展开，那环环相扣、跌宕起伏的情节设置，让恩、怨、情、仇伴随着玄奘的西行之路，逐渐融化在了佛家普度众生的宽阔情怀之中，讴歌了民族信仰的主旋律，传递了积极、健康、向上的正能量。

三、以舞台艺术播撒时代精神

豫剧《玄奘》中玄奘的饰演者孟祥礼是一位豫剧界戏曲功底深厚的青年演员。早在豫剧《香魂女》中，他就已经凭借着任忠实这一人物角色给观众留下了不俗的印象。孟祥礼"扮相英俊洒脱，唱腔高亢挺拔，做派稳健豪放[6]。"在豫剧《玄奘》中，那些经过豫剧声腔大师耿玉卿精心打磨设计的大段唱词给观众以荡气回肠、痛快淋漓的艺术美感。一段段宽厚、深邃、饱满的唱腔里蕴藏着对历史和世事的洞察，听得观众如痴如醉。徐俊霞（剧中饰蔻儿公主）出场亮相大气端庄，奔放而不轻浮，细腻而不琐碎。正如李利宏导演所言："（徐俊霞）她在她主攻的青衣、花旦及刀马旦行当里有着先天的优势，又有着后天扎实的'童子功'对'四功'、'五法'的拿捏……"[7] 关于《玄奘》中的人物设计，一方面他们有历史的大义和信仰，有不畏苦难的英雄气概；另一方面在面临生死考验关头时，又有着居心叵测和贪生怕死的小人（如石磐陀、外道），对比强烈、扣人心弦。总之，不管是主角、配角，每一个演员都扎扎实实地去塑造，一招一式，行腔唱词，都有可圈可点之处。

"以歌舞演故事"[8] 这是王国维概括的戏曲基本表征之一。借此，足可见歌舞表演也是戏曲艺术的有机组成部分。在我国古代，戏曲演出中或多或少都穿插着各种舞蹈形式，这也是其表演丰富多样的原因之一。豫剧《玄奘》在力求舞台干净的基础上，取舍得当地多次穿插了数人集体舞蹈的片段，无论是表现喜庆气氛抑或是悲痛情绪，如西行途中风沙阻挠、高昌国国王挽留玄奘和为戒贤大师祝寿，都准确到位、恰到好处。这样的编排，显然改变了过去多年我国戏曲艺术停滞不前、缺乏灵活性和创新意识的现状。豫剧《玄奘》的导演李利宏也是铸就这部历史剧作能够为世人认可和喜爱的豫剧功臣，正是由他对于戏曲艺术和豫剧的谙熟，才能够如此得心应手地编排和导演。同时，孟祥礼及其河南豫剧青年团的演员们也向观众呈现了专业的戏曲表演功底。演员们动作娴熟流畅、举止得体，将《玄奘》里的每一个人物表演得都惟妙惟肖、栩栩如生。

豫剧《玄奘》拒绝因循守旧，从戏曲文本创作到演出编排都取得了累累硕果。从历史层面上看，它写得真实而可信；从文学艺术层面上看，写得波澜壮阔、荡气回肠；在表演艺术层面上，唱、念、做、打的基本功扎实，达到了相当高的艺术水准。基于此，我们有理由相信豫剧《玄奘》是完全可以作为豫剧的一部经典剧目而被观众铭记于心的。

参考文献：

[1] 斯坦尼斯拉夫斯基. 斯坦尼斯拉夫斯基论文讲演谈话书信集 [M]. 郑雪来等译. 北京：中国电影出版社，1981：501.

[2] 卫厚生. 历史剧与历史真实性 [J]. 文艺理论与批评，2004（3）：59-61.

[3] 任广宣主编. 俄罗斯文学简史 [M]. 北京：北京大学出版社，2006：536.

[4] 焦波.《玄奘》走进台湾：打造河南文化交流新名片 [N]. 中国文化报，2015-06-11（4）.

[5]卢卡契.戏剧和戏剧创作中艺术中有关历史主义发展的概述.莎士比亚评论汇编(下)[M].北京:中国社会科学出版社,1981:490.

[6]谭静波.粗犷与细腻的完美结合——简评孟祥礼的舞台艺术[J].东方艺术,2014(S2):46-47.

[7]李利宏.梅花绽放 色浓任风霜——说说优秀豫剧演员徐俊霞[J].中国戏剧,2009(6):26-28.

[8]王国维.王国维戏曲论文集[M].北京:中国戏曲出版社,1984:163.

A Combination of Historical and Artistic Authenticity —An Analysis of the Historical-themed Henan Opera *Xuan Zang*

Abstract: In an artistic form of Henan Opera, the historical-themed Henan Opera *Xuan Zang* (602—664 known as Tang Monk, a famous monk of Tang Dynasty and translator of Buddhist sutra) combines the historical and artistic authenticity from the conception of history. The work praises Xuan Zang for his ambition of delivering all living creatures from torment, his spirit of perseverance and his eternal faith. Apart form restoring the history in an objective way, the work also plays an important role in promoting the core values of socialism and spiritual civilization. What's more, the work makes an exploration on the choice of historical and artistic authenticity, which provides us with effective cases.

Key Words: Henan Opera, Xuan Zang, historical authenticity, faith

Historical-themed operas need to make a choice of historical and artistic authenticity in the process of creation and performance, because history is real and cannot be deceived, while art aims to provide imagination space for the audience. The creation of historical-themed operas is often based on the collection, collation and screening of a large number of historical materials, and then makes an artistic restoration and processing by the creators. A few words that are scattered in the historical materials will guide the creators to construct a real situation in the history. Nevertheless, the history strives for an objective and true record of the situation rather than lengthy depiction. The clues between lines can only construct a real historical background and figures that are vague. The creators need to combine certain artistic fiction with the records of official and unofficial history to create a flesh-and-blood historical figure based on a few words in the historical materials. Therefore, what the biggest problem the creators face is how to re-construct the historical background, the relationship of the figures, and the complicated plots and vivid figures in an artistic way through the concise discourse. The large-scale, historical-themed and original Henan Opera *Xuan Zang* played by the Youth League of Henan Opera Theatre, created by Meng Hua(the national first-level scriptwriter) and directed by Li Lihong(the national first-level scriptwriter and director) seems to solve the above problem.

1. The Expression of Artistic Authenticity through Historical Authenticity

Chinese people's cognitive bias towards Xuan Zang is mainly influenced by the long romantic novel *Journey to the West* as well as the films and teleplays adapted from the novel, thus we need to make a detailed analysis of the real historical figure Xuan Zang. Xuan Zang was an eminent monk, an excellent translator of Buddhist sutra and a cultural celebrity of the Central Plains. He spent 17 years on going to India alone to seek Buddhist scriptures. To obtain Buddhist scriptures and rid Tang Dynasty of the situation that lacks complete and good Buddhist scriptures, Xuan Zang walked through the deserts, endured the hunger and thirst and grappled with the bandits on his way to India, and finally promoted the communication of Buddhism between China and India after innumerable hardships. However, influenced by the films and teleplays adapted from the novel Journey to the West, most Chinese people think Xuan Zang is a spineless monk who fails to tell friend from foe, which is inconsistent with the real historical narratives. Thus, it is urgent to restore the real image of Xuan Zang in the history. Complying with the trend of cultural creations, the historical-themed Henan Opera *Xuan Zang* created by Meng Hua follows the true records of history, combine the artistry and authenticity, and greatly restores the image of Xuan Zang who would sacrifice his life for the faith. The work praises Xuan Zang for his indomitable spirit in seeking for truth, goodness and beauty, and makes an appropriate and pertinent description of the image of Xuan Zang in history, which not only transforms the national cultural concerns and cognition from *Journey to the West* to *Records of Western World in Great Tang Dynasty* (also known as *Records of Western World*), but also makes a real and vivid depiction of Xuan Zang from the aspects of cultural and history.

The image of Xuan Zang in the Henan Opera *Xuan Zang* is basically in accordance with the prototype of Xuan Zang in the historical materials, thus the records of the historical materials that fails to give a complete and detailed depiction offer creators opportunities to process and recreate the image of the figure. In the first and second scenes of the opera, creators explain the plots, shape the images of characters, and highlights Xuan Zang's eternal faith through the antiphonal singing and spoken parts among Xuan Zang, Princess Dan Yang(the daughter of Emperor Gaozu of Tang Dynasty), Shi Pantuo(the real archetype of Monkey King in the novel *Journey To the West*) and Hui Jing(a disciple of Xuan Zang and a great monk of Tang Dynasty). It was Xuan Zang's belief of delivering all living creatures from torment that he showed the image of resolute determination and perseverance on the way to India. The opera draws material from the story that Xuan Zang devoted himself to propagating the doctrines of Buddhism and delivering all living creatures from torment, and accords with the theme of cultural diversity and exchange under "the Belt and Road Initiative". What's more, the Henan Opera *Xuan Zang* shows us a flesh-and-blood Xuan Zang, promotes the Chinese culture and expands the influence and soft power of Central Plains.

Stanislavsky (1863—1938, a famous Russian theorist of theatre and performance) once said : "In fact, there is no one in the world who doesn't have his own unique characters, just as there are no such two people in the world who are exactly same as two drops of water, or even people who have no personality are also characterized by no personality." Based on the story that Xuan Zang went to India alone to seek Buddhist scriptures, the Henan Opera Xuan Zang restores the hardships and dangers that Xuan Zang had encountered during his 17 years' travel by the ingenious arrangement of the conception and plots, the elaborate display of the acting and acrobatics, and the careful design of the antiphonal singing and spoken parts, and shows broad cultural vision as well as the personalities of the characters. Besides, the opera presents us the real image of Xuan Zang and many precious historical moments that are hidden in the historical materials by depicting the difficulties and hazards that Xuan Zang had went through on his way to India. According to the historical materials, Xuan Zang spend three years and overcame numerous difficulties and obstacles to become a student of Shīlabhadra (528—651, the abbot of Nalanda Monastery of ancient India); Princess Dan Yang, the king of Gao Chang Dynasty and his daughter Princess Kou Er repeatedly urge Xuan Zang to quit his visit to India, but Xuan Zang refused and remained steadfast in his determination to seek Buddhist scriptures; besides, Xuan Zang once answered fluently in the debate with five Indian Buddhists, which showed his profound knowledge, quick wit and generous heart. What's more, facing the various rewards of the King of India, Xuan Zang was strongly determined to return to the Tang Dynasty. Finally, Xuan Zang returned to the Tang Dynasty with numerous precious Buddhist scriptures, and he exerted his utmost to translate 47 sets of Buddhist scriptures (amounted to, 1337 volumes), which created a new era of Dharma in the history of Buddhism. Thus, the Henan Opera Xuan Zang presents us a patriotic image of Xuan Zang, sets an educational example full of strong practical significance across any era, and corresponds to the records of historical materials.

The opening of Henan Opera Xuan Zang introduced that Xuan Zang bought a thousand-li colt in the south of the market, and talked to Shi Pantuo and Hui Jing that they would set out for India that very night. At this time, Princess Dan Yang knew that her decree could not make Xuan Zang quit his plan, thus she personally persuaded Xuan Zang to stay, and promised that he would be given a high position and good pay as well as a lot of money, while Xuan Zang refused and remained steadfast in his determination to seek Buddhist scriptures. On their way to India, Xuan Zang and his two disciples passed through a 800-li desert where it was so windy and dry that seriously threatened their lives. Hui Jing hung between life and death because he was shot by poisonous arrows when he went to the beacon tower to steal water, while Xuan Zang was dying of thirst, but he still flushed Hui Jing's wound with water, which shows Xuan Zang's great sympathy for others and his determination for delivering all living creatures from torment. In other words, it is Xuan Zang's eternal faith that makes him remain steadfast in his determination to seek Buddhist scriptures when he faces hardships and temptations, which also has been showed in the novel *Journey to the West* written by Wu Chengen (1501—1582, the famous novelist of Ming Dynasty), films directed by Liu Zhenwei(a famous director of China) and the Henan Opera created by Meng Hua.

As far as the creation of the historical-themed Henan Opera Xuan Zang is concerned, the scriptwriter Meng Hua has succeed in combining the authenticity and artistry. Since the historical play has the dual identity of history and art, which requires that the creator should have the dual personality of historian and artist, respect the laws of art and history, and seek for historical and artistic authenticity. The characters are vivid with different personalities in Meng Hua's play, which is not only in line with the stylization of opera and the authenticity of historical materials, but also meets the aesthetic needs of the current audience in pursuit of dramatic conflicts. Meng Hua abides by the principle of historical authenticity, and depicts the characters and their relationships with respect and rational cognition about history. What's more, he boldly added dramatic and contradictory plots to the vague parts of historical materials. A great dramatic text is an essential precondition for the show of a play with a grand historical narratives. In addition to dramatizing the history, Meng Hua also incorporates the elements of artistic fabrication and the thinking of the context into the creation of the Henan Opera *Xuan Zang*. For example, the sandstorm is the sign of evil spirit; Xuan Zang suffered hallucinations caused by hydropenia and he saw the Princess Dan Yang when he fainted in the desert; the fools thought the thunder was heaven's punishment to Xuan Zang and his two disciples when they fall into danger by the river, and so on. This is exactly what the Director Li Lihong wants to elucidate through stage art from the perspective of traditional culture.

The films and teleplays adapted from the long novel *Journey to the West* written by Wu Chengen has been circulated widely among the people. The characters and plots are romantic and fantastic with a strong fiction. However, the novel devotes so good deal of space to fiction and romance that deviates from the records of historical materials, and makes the image of Xuan Zang completely distorted. Thus, it is still a great pity to appreciate the novel *Journey to the West* from a historical perspective no matter how classic and popular the novel is and how really and vividly the characters are shaped. If we analyze the Henan Opera *Xuan Zang* with Guo Moruo's principle of seeking the likeness and abandoning the authenticity in the historical-themed creation, it is undoubtedly that the opera is an excellent work combining theatrical artistry and historical authenticity. In the work, the screenwriter Meng Hua shows his understandings and respect for historical figures, greatly enriches the forms of opera art in a creative way, and realizes wonderful artistic effects by a kind of style of writing close to biography.

2. The Expression of Historical Image through Artistic Image

The historical-themed opera must not be created without foundation, and we must respect the history and historical truth in shaping the characters. Meng Hua has spent a lot of efforts in designing the plots of the Henan Opera Xuan Zang. Guided by the writing techniques of the modern drama, the opera reflecting history and reproducing historical figures can meet the increasing aesthetic pursuit of the contemporary people. Besides, the opera also achieves the unity of historical and artistic quality in handling the main line and historical details. On this basis, the opera combines the real history with Buddhism's spirit of delivering all living creatures from torment, and integrates the image of Xuan Zang with the spirit of the times. Demonstrating the truth from the historical perspective and interpreting the history from the contemporary context, it is undoubtedly that this monumental work shows the long history and the artistic charm. The opera is majestic and impressive, manifests beauty in form, feeling, meaning and so on, and contains a kind of motivation that inspires us to keep positive and energetic. It is maybe a little difficult to appreciate the opera, for there are many obscure allusion and words from the Buddhist scriptures, while Meng Hua dramatizes the relationship between the characters in the opera, and guides the audience to think about the world, which is also a vivid interpretation of the obscure language. The well-knit plots highlights the complexity of the story and demonstrates the ideological level of the characters. For instance, Xuan Zang and Shi Pantuo needed crossed the border of Tang Dynasty illegally, for they had no legal permit, and they would be safe as long as they crossed the five beacon towers without being noticed. At that morning, Shi Pantuo begged Xuan Zang not to go any further, for he worried that they would be killed if they were found near the beacon towers. Xuan Zang let Shi Pantuo go home lonely, but Shi Pantuo was worried that Xuan Zang would betray him after being captured. A Buddhist does not take a vow easily, while Xuan Zang swore that he would never betray Shi Pantuo when he heard that Shi Pantuo had elderly mother and young children to support. Besides, Xuan Zang almost died when he was attacked by bandits of Durga by the Ganges River, but he begged the soldiers to give these bandits a chance to live after he was saved. From the above story, we could find that the scriptwriter Meng Hua has a deep understanding of Buddhist's compassionate feelings for the masses and peaceful attitudes towards life. Furthermore, the opera shows audience the vicissitudes of life, joys and sorrows as well as successes and failures, and presents the audience with the most real image of Xuan Zang—who created the Buddhist cultural miracle in the prosperous Tang Dynasty.

A historical-themed opera that widely praised is certainly not as a simple and mechanical narrative of historical events. To create a good historical play, the key lies in how to tell the story and how to shape the characters. Whether a play is popular or not depends primarily on whether its story and characters can attract the audience. Xuan Zang is a figure who has made outstanding contributions to the cultural communication between China and India, and most of his records are kept in historical materials. However, the historical record is brief and concise, which means that the scriptwriter needs to arrange the historical stories subtly, and endows these stories with typical characters and meanings throughout the play. This is a test of the scriptwriter's control over the creation of historical plays, and the artistic creativity of plot arrangement and characterization. The scriptwriter Meng Hua put the protagonist Xuan Zang in the real historical background and complicated opera situation, making the character become flesh-and-blood rather than being far removed from the masses and reality as in previous movie and teleplays. Xuan Zang is a devout Buddhist, but firstly he is a man of great kindness, which Meng Hua has realized and tried to express. Thus, at the beginning, the Henan Opera *Xuan Zang* narrates that Princess

Dan Yang tried her best to persuade Xuan Zang to quit his plan before Xuan Zang set out for India, then the princess obstructed Xuan Zang by all means on his way to India, and Shi Pantuo's compromise and weakness when they were in the dilemma as well as the coercive means of the king of Gao Chang Dynasty. All these plots are not completely used to highlight Xuan Zang's strong determination to seek Buddhist scriptures. On the contrary, these are part of what the scriptwriter used to show Xuan Zang's ideological struggle and basic decency as an ordinary mortal. Furthermore, the director Li Lihong depicts the life style and dress customs of Tang Dynasty and foreign countries with extremely exquisite directing art, which is attributed to the great efforts of the creative team in collecting and consulting materials for the creation of the play. At the same time, the audience has the opportunity to cleanse one's soul and appreciate the essence of life and innocence of human nature. All in all, the scriptwriter Meng Hua and the director Li Lihong re-examine and interpret the history from the current aesthetic perspective, try to show something new and refreshing and enlighten the audience's ignorance, and impress the audience with the shaping of a certain character. Therefore, the Henan Opera *Xuan Zang* is no longer simply a narrative of history, nor is it a mechanical moral sermon, but it exerts an imperceptible influence on the audience through the most artistic and inspiring form of opera, which establishes a firm basis for the success of the work.

Based on the true historical story of Xuan Zang who went India to seek the Buddhist scriptures, the Henan Opera *Xuan Zang* restores the hardships and difficulties that Xuan Zang had encountered on his way to India. The creation of opera should focus on the protagonist and his emotions and thoughts rather than being confined by the real historical background. The vivid images of characters form a part of the complicated plots, and the complicated plots form a complete play, which is just like the principle of geometry: innumerable points constitute the line, and innumerable lines constitute the surface. Similarly, the fate, emotion and thought of the characters are the main points of the creation of historical-themed opera, thus the creator strives to depict the characters and plots that can impress the audience after watching the opera. In terms of the creation of Henan Opera *Xuan Zang*, the scriptwriter Meng Hua combines Buddhist's belief of delivering all living creatures from torment and the spirit of truth, goodness and beauty. He derives inspiration from the places where Xuan Zang lived, and obtains intellectual nutrition from numerous popular literature of Ming Dynasty, Qing Dynasty and the early years of Republic of China, thus enhances the artistic quality of the opera and represents the story and characters in various aspects on the stage. However, the historical-themed opera is an artistic representation of real history; which means that a grand narration is largely insufficient to present history, thus it is necessary to depict typical characters in a typical environment. Georg Lukacs (1885— 1971, the modern Hungarian aesthetician, literary critic and philosopher) once said when he commented on Shakespeare's unique features : "No one has ever described the indivisibility of people and people who have not been divided like Shakespeare did throughout the ages, and he even gave high priority to the core of a person rather than objective manifestations."In this sense, positivism spirit should always run through all the works of the scriptwriter. Some high-quality costume dramas and historical dramas, such as *Bao Qingtian* (an upright and incorruptible official of Northern Song Dynasty) and *Hai Rui Dismissed from Office*, have distinct personalities and practical significance. In essence, all writing of history intends to serve the contemporary era. From this point of view, the Henan Opera *Xuan Zang* shows originality in conception. With the evolution of the play, the intricately woven plot integrates the gratitude, resentment, love and hate into the Buddhist's belief of delivering all living creatures from torment on Xuan Zang's way to India, eulogizes the national belief and spreads positive energy.

3. The Expression of the Spirit of the Times through Stagecraft

Meng Xiangli (the head of the the Youth League of Henan Opera Theatre, a national class-A actor and a member of Chinese Dramatists Association), who played Xuan Zang in the opera, is a good actor with profound knowledge of Henan Opera. As early as in Henan Opera *The Women from the Lake of Scented Souls*, he had impressed the audience with the character of Ren Zhongshi. Meng Xiangli looks handsome when in costume and makeup, has a loud and sonorous voice, and acts in a stable and natural way. In the Henan Opera *Xuan Zang*, the long lines designed by Geng Yuqing, a national class-A composer, contain insight into the history and the vicissitude of life, and offer the audience an opportunity to appreciate the artistic beauty. Xu Junxia (a national class-A actor), who played Princess Kou Er in the opera, appeared in a dignified and graceful way. As the director Li Lihong said, "Xu Junxia has innate advantages and acquired foundation in the career of the opera." In terms of the design of characters in the Henan Opera *Xuan Zang*, there are decent persons who have a profound understanding of what is righteous and a heroic spirit that defies hardship and danger, while there are also villains who have ulterior motives and cowards who are mortally afraid of death at the critical moment of life and death, such as Shi Pantuo and Wai Dao, which constitutes a striking contrast. In a word, every actor tries his best to play no matter he is the leading role or the supporting role and receive unanimously praise.

Wang Guowei (a famous scholar in modern China) once summarized that one of the basic characteristics of opera is to tell a story in forms of singing and dancing. From this point of view, we could find that singing and dancing performance is also a part of opera. In ancient China, opera performances were more or less interspersed with various dance forms, which is one of the reasons for its rich and varied performances. The Henan Opera *Xuan Zang* intersperses the show with several group dancing on the basis of managing to keep the stage clean, which exactly heightens the atmosphere of the story, such as the grief atmosphere when Xuan Zang confronted with the sandstorms and the coercive means of the king of Gao Chang Dynasty, and the joyful atmosphere at the birthday party of Master Jie Xian. This kind of performance obviously changes the situation that the Chinese opera art has stagnated for many years and lacks innovation consciousness. Li Lihong, the director of Henan Opera *Xuan Zang*, makes great contribution to the success of the work, and it is his proficiency with the art of opera and Henan Opera that enables him to arrange the show flexibly. What's more, Meng Xiangli and the actors of the Youth League of Henan Opera Theatre show the audience their high proficiency in performance and play every character of the opera *Xuan Zang* in a vivid way.

The Henan Opera *Xuan Zang* refused to follow the beaten tract and achieved great success in the creation and the performance. From the perspective of history, the story is a true record of the history. From the perspective of literature and art, the scriptwriter creates the opera with exquisite and elegant language. From the perspective of performing arts, the actors have high proficiency in singing, recitation, acting and acrobatics (four elements of the art of singing and acting in Chinese opera). Based on this, we believe that the Henan Opera *Xuan Zang* can be engraved on the audience's memory.

Bibliography:

[1] Stanislavski. Papers, Lectures, Conversations and Letters of Stanislavski [M].Translated by Zheng Xuelai, et al. Beijing: China Film Publishing House, 1981: 501.

[2] Wei Housheng. Historical Drama and Historical Authenticity [J]. Literary Theory and Criticism, 2004 (3): 59-61.

[3] Ren Guangxuan. A Brief History of Russian Literature [M].Beijing: Peking University Press, 2006: 536.

[4] Jiao Bo. *Xuan Zang* Entering Taiwan: Creating a New Business Card for Cultural Exchange in Henan [N]. China Culture Daily, June 11, 2015 (4).

[5] Luacs. Overview of Historicism in Drama and Art in Dramatic Creation. Shakespeare Review Collection (Part II) [M].Beijing: China Social Sciences Press, 1981: 490.

[6] Tan Jingbo. Perfect Combination of Roughness and Delicacy—A Brief Comment on Meng Xiangli's Stage Art [J]. Oriental Art, 2014 (S2): 46-47.

[7] Li Lihong. Talk about Outstanding Henan Opera Actor Xu Junxia [J]. Chinese Drama, 2009 (6): 26-28.

[8] Wang Guowei. Wang Guowei's Essays on Drama [M].Beijing: China Drama Publishing House, 1984: 163.

论当代语境下戏剧中的"乡愁"美学意蕴

——以现代戏《丹水情深》为例

摘要：戏曲作为乡音、乡韵的一种传播媒介,承载着浓厚的"乡愁"美学内蕴。豫剧现代戏《丹水情深》在宏大历史事件背景下展开叙事,是一次对传统豫剧艺术超越的尝试。这种"乡愁"美学内蕴主要表现在戏剧题材的选择、情节结构的设置、人物形象的塑造、本色化的戏剧语言运用以及饱含传统意义和现代精神的思想意蕴等,为当代戏剧的创作提供了一种新的审美范式。其文本创作和舞台排演既开拓了对豫剧的发展思路,又丰富了豫剧表演的内涵,具有较强的借鉴意义。

关键词：豫剧现代戏；《丹水情深》；乡愁；美学意蕴

一曲丹江水冲不开"安土重迁"的浓浓乡愁,一棵小槐树见证了半个多世纪以来几代人的血泪心酸。陈涌泉编剧、李利宏导演的豫剧现代戏《丹水情深》以"南水北调""搬迁移民"这一宏大历史事件为背景,以"民族团结""舍小家为大家"的精神为思想内核,讲述了一村人两次离乡背土、历经三代的辛酸委屈与牺牲奉献。故事发生在丹江库区,是"修建丹江水库""建设南水北调工程"的移民迁徙发生地。一个自然村的村民们,20 世纪 50 年代,由于修建丹江水库,他们第一次进行了移民搬迁。在新的村落里他们历尽艰难生存发展,在党和政府的关怀与支持下,终于建起了一个皂素厂,在朝着幸福美好的新生活迈进的时候,由于举世瞩目的"南水北调"工程,村子要再一次搬迁,刚建起的皂素厂也要停产拆迁。何去何从？村支书李丹霞和村民们必须做出艰难的抉择，那就是服从大局，再次搬迁到距离家乡遥远的地方。这个剧作有许多可圈可点的成功之处，比如它的主旋律题材、折射出当代中国农村现代化的历程以及着力渲染了移民无私奉献的思想境界等，但是从乡愁这一美学意蕴角度来解读，更能发现它的艺术价值。

传统乡愁是一个文化哲学概念，是人类故园情愫的表达，现代意义上的文化乡愁所指的则是一种具有人文意味、历史情怀的文化象征。这种情感或文化结构是丰富复杂的，具有具体的历史内容和文学表现形式。具体在这一戏剧中，这种乡愁所包含的美学涵蕴，主要体现在地域之美、安土重迁的人物之美、富于本土特色的戏剧语言美以及深厚的思想意蕴美几个方面。

首先，题材所呈现的地域之美。

传统村落是民族文化的根，是中华文明的源头。乡村始终是中国人的出发点和心灵的最终归宿，而对于移民来讲，是他们背井离乡时和离去后最难割舍的乡愁情思。《丹水情深》把戏剧的发生地置放在河南南阳伏牛山下的一个小山村里，这里原来依山面水、风景如画，全村在修建水库的时候整体搬迁到更高的一个地方，但依然是依水而居，世世代代的耕作生息使他们对这里产生了深深的感情，而先辈们的坟茔则是他们生命之根所在。剧作者把人物放在这样的戏剧环境中，让他们去面对又一次的迁徙。美丽的乡村风光无疑加重了人们的乡愁。故乡是一个时代、一群人的集体记忆，树高千丈，叶落归根，对于每个人而言，都期盼留存充满着乡愁乡情的村庄、田野、房舍、一草一木。因而在这里，戏剧作为"乡愁"美学的一种载体，承载着乡音乡韵，使羁旅漂泊、离乡背井的人听之动容。

豫剧现代戏《丹水情深》讲述一个时代、一个群体的故事，通过个体人物叙述模式展现宏大历史事件的戏剧舞台尝试无疑是成功的。"许多观众在看完演出后仍津津乐道，认为《丹水情深》整个剧情跌宕起伏，饱含深情，具有浓郁的中原特色和鲜明的时代精神。"[1]但不可否认，这里所说的"中原特色"，地域特色是其主要元素，戏剧环境所提供的地域之美是整个剧作的基础，它奠定了这一乡愁美学意蕴的基本底色。

其次，安土重迁的人物之美。

论当代语境下戏剧中的"乡愁"美学意蕴

随着生活节奏的不断加快，人们对于审美需求日趋高涨，审美能力也不断提高。传统戏曲的脸谱化、程式化显然已经不能满足现代人的感官追求和审美需要，而豫剧现代戏已有跳脱传统戏曲人物形象脸谱化标记的趋势，让舞台上的角色更立体化和层次化。《丹水情深》在创作中不落窠臼，突破了传统戏曲的局限。剧作家深刻剖析了市井乡野里形形色色的人物的共同特征，深入地挖掘了矛盾对立面人物的产生根源，分寸拿捏得恰如其分，同时又兼有舞台人物形象塑造的真实感。

陈涌泉在创作《丹水情深》时曾做过这样的感想："比丹江口水库更宽广的是移民的胸怀，比伏牛山更挺拔的是移民的脊梁，比南水北调大渠更悠长的是移民的真情。"[2] 为了传达这样的胸怀、脊梁和真情，剧作塑造了以移民村党支部书记李丹霞为代表的一代基层青年形象，展现出中原人大海一般的广阔胸襟和百折不挠的坚毅品格。尽管李丹霞为建造皂素厂付出了巨大的牺牲与贡献，甚至她的丈夫为保护生产设备而牺牲了宝贵的生命；尽管她时刻盼望移民村能够早日走上一条致富的道路，且愿景即将实现；尽管搬迁和停产的事情令她左右为难，然而，当国家利益与个人利益、发展经济和保护环境之间发生冲突的时候，她毅然决然地坚持原则，大局为重，晓之以理，动之以情，说服和教育了村民们。剧作生动地塑造了一个有血有肉、胸襟坦荡，忧国忧民的共产党员形象。

除她之外，正直而率性自然的马玉林，单纯而真诚痴情的方小荷，老练而历经沧桑的老贵爷，阳光而充满朝气的夏小满等一个个鲜活而立体的剧中人物形象。正如贺宝林先生所评价的一般："他们位卑而不失尊严，贫穷而不改气节，身小而不渺小，处下而不低下，体现出一种平凡中的伟大，一种平常中的刚强，一种平淡中的崇高"，[3] 这是戏剧艺术在舞台上表现欲的充分释放。此外，阻碍女儿与马玉林自由恋爱的方大伯虽自私狭隘而专制，但也不失真诚坦率。他第一次追着打骂马玉林，表面是嫌他纠缠自己的女儿，根源是在于移民村贫苦落后；第二次又追着打骂马玉林是嫌他疏远自己的女儿，其实质是移民村已开始靠自己的力量建厂而要富裕起来了。同是打骂，两次却有着迥异的区别，深刻反映了方大伯的心理骤然变化轨迹。还有对马玉林是喊"大伯"还是"爹"这一称呼的细节刻画，深刻地表现了方大伯老练而又机敏的处世智慧，使得人物形象真实而丰满。

再次，传达离愁别绪的情节之美。

剧作《丹水情深》情节极有层次感和真实感，环环相扣，对戏剧矛盾转化处理得妥帖得当。全剧分为两个大的故事：第一个故事讲述为了修建丹江水库第一次搬迁，在新的家园建厂致富；第二个故事是第二次搬迁，这次要拆迁工厂，迁徙到更远的地方。在两个大的故事中衔套了不少小故事，但都围绕着"离乡"这一戏剧矛盾展开。不同人物的态度、前后变化的原因处理等，都比较到位。毫无疑问，《丹水情深》对修丹江水库和南水北调大背景下人民所经受的艰难困苦的情状及村民对故土眷恋的生动描写，以及矛盾对立面人物的刻画，不仅使剧情波澜曲折、扣人心弦，而且提供了现代剧作关注底层人民话语与揭示人生哲理的审美新范式，用真切的笔触将移民的故事以及那段属于一代人、一个地域、一个民族的记忆完整地记录了下来。

值得一提的是，在抢救设备时，李丹霞的丈夫秋生不幸遇难，李丹霞悲痛欲绝，回忆起与丈夫患难与共的岁月，此时在情节与场面调度的安排上，让已经牺牲的秋生出现在前台和她对唱，逝者与生者将丹江水所蕴含的悠悠深情演绎得更加深化而奔放，增强了催人泪下的艺术感染力。这样穿越式的处理，显然是剧作者与导演的良苦用心，从侧面揭示了李丹霞百感交集的内心世界，为以后的矛盾转化埋下了伏笔。

又次，渲染氛围、表达乡愿的本色语言之美。

《丹水情深》表现了豫剧以唱见长，唱腔铿锵有力，质朴通俗、本色自然，紧贴老百姓生活的特点。关键剧情上的大板唱腔，节奏流畅鲜明、极具口语化，易被观众听清，显示出特有的艺术魅力。剧作不假雕饰，没有丝毫的浮夸之气，引领着每一位欣赏者去聆听剧中人通过个性化的戏曲语言来畅谈他们的故事，体悟生命最原汁原味的感动。编剧陈涌泉先生把自己多年以来的农村生活经历、记忆、乡野传说、奇人异事以及个人对人生的体验式感悟，浇铸在那质朴唱腔的字里行间，沁润在文学创作之中。剧作在序幕震撼人心的演出场面里，尽情用肢体动作与语言诠释了库区底层农民对故土难离的眷恋和离乡背井的愁绪，他们骨子里流淌着乡愁的血脉，绵延不绝。

"哭罢还要接着干，天亮又是新一天。""山茫茫，水茫茫，故土难舍痛断肠。登上高岗回头望,再看一眼沉没的故乡。"这些唱词以及对于小槐树、老娘土等平实的道白等,无一不是本乡本土的方言俚语,充满着乡愁,而正是在这些最具表达力的艺术语言中,深深地蕴含着戏剧语言之美。

最后,剧作的多层意蕴之美。

这是最能体现乡愁美学蕴含的部分,而且,这种意蕴之美是多层次的。第一,它创造了具有乡愁审美意义的意象。《丹水情深》里"小槐树""一抔土""一瓶水"三个审美意象,自始至终暗含于剧情故事发展的脉络之中,草蛇灰线,若隐若现,牵动着观众的喜怒哀乐。"这棵小槐树栽到哪里,哪里就是我们的家!"剧本中,剧作者借丹霞爹之口对乡愁乡情作出的这一阐述,质朴纯真、振聋发聩!同时,"小槐树"贯穿全剧,前后呼应,恰如其分地和剧作文本构成了一种互文现义的关系,两者相互映衬,烘云托月;但更重要的是,它们不仅使《丹水情深》获得了整体性的隐喻特征,也构成了对于文本之外的戏曲表演场域的一种精神内涵象征。阿多诺说:"如果哲学有任何定义的话,那就是一种努力,努力说出不可说的事物,努力表述不可界定的东西。"[4] 在此意义上,《丹水情深》在现实和虚构之间的界限渐渐消融,呈现出一种诗意浪漫的美好意境。"美毕竟是人们日常生活中的一个现实因素,审美也构成了人们日常生活追求的一个特殊的精神维度"。[5] 在这样一个横跨半个多世纪的宏大历史事件之下,每一个人都有着自己的"故事",陈涌泉先生正是将这些充满了乡土气息的"美"进行了艺术创造,以"一剧之本"的载体进行比较完美的呈现。

在剧作所建构的隐喻世界里,以"小槐树"作为喻体,这是极典型的,也是极普通的。它是一种高度形象化的、充满寓意的意象,是对"乡愁"情感的浓缩和折射,犹如一张多姿多彩的油画,让现实的离乡背井比之升华至精神层面的背井离乡的愁思显得更真实和触目可及,自然乡愁的内涵也更显深刻和广阔。《丹水情深》中一棵小槐树三次出现:"这棵小槐树栽到哪里,哪里就是我们的家!"这就让人们想起洪洞县大槐树这一中原地区居民共同拥有的根,"乡愁"借此得以深化。

第二,对于人情、人性的关注和家国情怀的寄托。剧作充分挖掘了移民村的农民失去故土家园之后的思想恐慌,"关注人性、人心,关注民生,关注底层话语",[6] 触摸到当前社会最敏感的神经中枢。它带给人的绝不仅仅是感动，更多的是对自我灵魂的认知与救赎。"迷途的焦虑感在审美文化上形成一种留恋往昔的'集体乡愁'"，[7] 尽管是离愁别恨，但却哀而不伤，平淡从容之中显露出一种豁达和超然。"我们的祖先一直在漂泊，在寻找美好的家园，现在咱们算是找到了美好的家园。"在戏曲接近尾声的时候，海阿訇那意味深长的话告诉观众：移民村的人们对苦难的抗争、对困境的突围、对出路的探寻、对希望的憧憬、对幸福的追求与向往，不仅是故土家园的重建，更是一次心灵重建的过程。正是这样的艰苦磨难和挫折，激发了人们对生存的渴望和对美好幸福生活的憧憬与向往，呼唤着一个和谐新时代的来临。同时，剧作编导成功地避开了主旋律题材最容易陷入的"概念化""肤浅化"误区，以小故事小人物来叙述宏大历史事件，其对丹江库区人民"舍小家顾大家、牺牲小我成就大爱"的美好情操这一思想意蕴的呈现也是明确的、成功的。

著名华文文学家王鼎钧先生曾直言"乡愁是美学"，[8] 这当然是一种文学表达，应该说，乡愁里包含着丰富的美学意蕴。这种"乡愁美学"正是孕育在这个有着五千年文明的国家中，有关"乡愁"的文化概念在历史发展的长河中从不曾缺席，更似生生不息的血液流淌于每一个人的命脉之中。换言之，乡土情结是中华文化的一种组成元素，是人们内心深处最难以割舍的浓浓情愫，浸润着道德人心，激励中原儿女用具体行动去实现富强的生活愿景。

总之，《丹水情深》所呈现出来的这种"乡愁"美学内蕴为当代戏剧的创作提供了一种新的审美范式。其文本创作和舞台排演既开拓了豫剧的发展思路，又丰富了表演内涵，具有较强的艺术价值和借鉴意义。

参考文献：

[1][2] 米根孝. 创作过程就是被平民英雄感动的过程 [N]. 中国民族报，2012-07-03(3).

[3] 贺宝林. 扎根中原沃土的创作者 [N]. 中国文化报，2014-12-11(6).

[4] 迈克尔·伍德著. 顾钧译. 沉默之子——论当代小说 [M]. 北京：生活·读书·新知三联书店, 2003：11.

[5] 谭好哲. 语境意识与美学问题 [M]. 北京：人民出版社, 2012：138.

[6] 吴新斌. 新语境下的话语重构——当代戏剧丛论 [M]. 北京：中国文联出版社, 2015：7.

[7] 周斌. 电视戏曲节庆晚会与当代文化的"乡愁"意识 [J]. 平顶山学院学报, 2010, 25（4）：100.

[8] 王鼎钧. 在心房漩涡·脚印 [M]. 台北：台北尔雅出版社有限公司, 1988：201.

On the Aesthetic Implication of "Homesickness" in Drama in Contemporary Context
—The Perspective of the Modern Play *Deep Love for the Danjiang River.*

Abstract: As the media of local accent and rhyme, opera boasts a strong aesthetic connotation of "homesickness". The modern play *"Deep Love for the Danjiang River"* of Henan modern opera narrates the story under the background of historical events, which becomes an attempt to transcend the traditional Henan Opera. On the one hand, the connotation of "homesickness" has provided a new aesthetic pattern for the contemporary drama. It also consists of the different drama themes, the setting of plots, the shaping of characters, the application of natural drama language and the ideological implication full of traditional and modern spirit. On the other hand, its play creation and stage arrangement not only stimulate new perspectives for the development of Henan Opera, but also enrich the connotation of Henan Opera performance, which has a strong significance for the future development.

Key words: modern drama of Henan Opera; *Deep Love for the Danjiang River*; nostalgia; aesthetic implication

The Danjiang River flows day after day with the deep homesickness of those immigrants "moving to the other land". A small locust tree has witnessed the hard work of generations for more than half a century. Written by Chen Yongquan and directed by Li Lihong, the modern drama "*Deep Love for the Danjiang River*" is based on the historical events of "South-to-North Water Diversion" and "Relocation of Immigrants" while taking the spirit of "national unity" and "responsibility for the community" as its essence. The story unfolds with the villagers who left their hometown twice and suffered bitterness and sacrifice by three generations. It is in the Danjiang Reservoir area that the story takes place—the area where immigrants need to be relocated for "the Danjiang Reservoir" and "the South-to-North Water Diversion" projects. People of a natural village migrated for the first time in the 1950s due to the construction of Danjiang Reservoir. In the new village, they went through hardships to survive and develop. However, with the help of the Party and the government, they finally built a saponin factory. As they aimed for a better new life, the villagers had to be relocated again because of the world-renowned "South-to-North Water Diversion" project, and the newly built saponin factory had to stop production for demolition. What should they do? The village secretary Li Danxia and the villagers have to make a difficult decision, that is, obeying the community and moving to a place far away from their hometown again. In conclusion, this play shows many remarkable advantages, such as its main theme, mirroring the process of modernization in contemporary rural areas, and reflecting the selfless dedication of immigrants. However, its artistic value will be found if we interpret it from the view of homesickness.

As one of the concepts of cultural philosophy, traditional homesickness is an expression of the feelings towards hometown. However, homesickness in the modern times refers to a cultural symbol with humanistic and historical feelings. This kind of emotional or cultural structure is much more complex and it has practical historical content and literary forms. In the "*Deep Love for the Danjiang River"*, the aesthetic significance of this homesickness is mainly expressed in the four aspects. They are the beauty of the region, the beauty of the characters who left their hometown twice, the beauty of the language in the drama with local characteristics and profound cultural connotation.

First of all, the regional beauty of the theme.

Traditional villages have been considered as the root of national culture and the origin of Chinese civilization. What's more, the countryside has always been the starting point and the spiritual homeland of Chinese people. Thus, for the immigrants, it has already become the most bitter feeling—homesickness; the emotions caught them all the times when they left their homes. The drama *"Deep Love for the Danjiang River"* took place in a small mountain village under Funiu Mountain in Nanyang, Henan Province. It was a place surrounded by water and picturesque scenery. While the whole village moved to a higher place for the building of the reservoir, they still lived by water. Generations of farming and living here have formed their deep love for this place, and the tombs of the ancestors are the symbols of their roots. The playwright put the characters in such a beautiful environment and let them face another migration. In that circumstance, people's homesickness was strengthened by the beautiful rural scenery. Besides, hometown is the shared memory of an era and a group of people. Though the trees grow by times, the leaves still fall to the ground. For each of us, we expect to preserve the villages, fields, houses and trees filled with our deep love and homesickness. Therefore, as a carrier of "homesickness" aesthetics, the drama takes the local accent and charm, touching people's heart, especially those who uprooted themselves from their homes.

The modern drama *"Deep Love for the Danjiang River"* of Henan Opera describes the story of an era and a group. It is undoubtedly a successful attempt in stage drama through the narrative mode of individual characters. "Many audiences, after the performance, have been talking about it thoughtfully. They observed that the whole plot of the drama was full of ups and downs with deep feelings, reflecting central plains characteristics and distinctive spirit of the times." [1] But undoubtedly, regional characteristic is its main element of the "central plains characteristics" mentioned here. The beauty of the region provided by the drama environment is fundamental to the whole play, and it makes the basic background of the homesickness aesthetic implication.

Secondly, the beauty of the characters who had to relocate twice far from home.

Since the pace of life has developed rapidly, at the same time, people's aesthetic demand for art performance is rising day by day, and their aesthetic ability is also improving. The facial makeup and certain procedures of traditional operas have obviously failed to meet modern people's sensory pursuit and aesthetic needs. However, the modern drama of Henan Opera managed to make the roles on the stage more dimensional and vivid by trying to break away from the makeup marks of traditional opera characters. Instead of being confined in the conventional pattern in its creation, this play has broken through the limitations of traditional operas. What's more, the playwright analyzed the common characteristics of people in the city thoroughly and explored the root of the contradictory characters. The development of the story has been appropriately dealt with. The reality of stage characters to the audience is thus formed.

When he wrote the play, Chen Yongquan once held that : "What is broader than Danjiangkou Reservoir is the mind of immigrants; what is stronger than Funiu Mountain is the backbone of immigrants, and what is longer than the big canal of South-to-North Water Diversion is the true feelings of immigrants." [2] In order to convey such feelings, the play portrays the figure of a grass-roots youth represented by Li Danxia, secretary of the Party branch of the immigrant village. It shows the broad mind like the sea and perseverance character of the Central Plains people. In addition,

Li Danxia has made great contributions to the construction of the saponin factory, even her husband sacrificed his life to protect the production equipment. She always hopes that the immigrant village can have a wealthy life as soon as possible, and her vision will soon be realized. Although she was in a dilemma between the relocation and the shutdown, she was still committed to the principle that the overall community was the most important, especially when there was a conflict between the national and personal interests, economic development and environmental protection. Besides, she explained the situation reasonably to convince and educate the villagers. The play vividly describes a CPC member who is flesh-and-blood, broad-minded and concerned about the country and the people.

In addition to her, there are many other vivid and dimensional characters in the play. For example, Ma Yulin, who is honest and straightforward; Fang Xiaohe, who is simple and sincere; Lao Gui Ye, the senior who experienced so many events; Xia Xiaoman, who is sunny and energetic. Just as Mr. He Baolin commented : "They are humble without losing dignity, poor but do not change their integrity. They are the grass-roots in the society with their distinctive strength so that they expressed a kind of greatness in ordinary, firmness in ordinary, and loftiness in daily life." [3] This is the full expression of theatrical art's desire to show on the stage. In addition, Uncle Fang, who is selfish and autocratic, but also honest and straightforward, once hinders his daughter's free love with Ma Yulin. For the first time, he chased and beat Ma Yulin. The reason seems to be that he was upset about Ma Yulin pestering his daughter. In fact, it lies in the poverty and backwardness in the immigrant village. The second time he ran after Ma Yulin beating him was because Ma did not connect with his daughter. The truth was that the immigrant village had started to build factory on its own and gradually become rich. The same beating and scolding, but the two were quite different, which deeply reflected the sudden psychological change of Uncle Fang. There is also a detailed depiction of whether Ma Yulin calls Fang his "uncle" or "father", which profoundly shows Uncle Fang's sophisticated and acute wisdom in life and makes the figure real and lively.

Thirdly, the beauty of the plot of sorrow in immigration from homeland twice.

It was because the plots are closely linked that the transformation of dramatic contradictions is handled properly. Therefore, the plot of the play *"Deep Love for the Danjiang River"* becomes very vivid and realistic. The whole play is divided into two stories. The first relocation was conducted in order to build Danjiang Reservoir and develop a factory in a new home to become rich. The second story happened later. This time, the villagers would be relocated to a further place. It can be noticed that the two big stories contain many small ones, but they all serve for the whole contradiction of "leaving one's hometown". The attitudes of different characters and the reasons for the changes before and after are properly dealt with.

Definitely, this play practically describes the hardships suffered by the people and their attachment to the native land under the background of the construction of the Danjiang Reservoir and the South-to-North Water Diversion Project. Besides, contradictory people's personalities not only make the plot changing smoothly and exciting, but also provide a new aesthetic example for modern dramas, which emphasizes the situation of the people at the bottom and reveals the truth of life. With the memory of a generation, a region and a nation, the story of immigrants is completely recorded by practical writing style.

It is worth mentioning that Li Danxia was desperate for her husband Qiusheng's death when protecting the factory's equipment. Besides, as she was lost herself in the years of sharing happiness and hardship with her husband, it was arranged in plot and scene scheduling that the sacrificed Qiusheng reappeared at the stage to sing with her. The dead and the living further deepened affection and memory with the Danjiang River, strengthening the artistic appeal that makes people cry. It is obvious that the author and the director of the play have made the stage singing for both of them arranged carefully, revealing Li Danxia's bitter feelings from the side and foreshadowing for future contradictions.

Next, the beauty of the natural language that strengthens the atmosphere and expresses the immigration's affection for the hometown.

The play shows five characteristics of Henan Opera. They are : being good at singing, being powerful in singing, being simple and popular, being natural and close to the life of ordinary people. The play has shown unique artistic charm, for example, vocal music in Chinese operas on the key plot is with distinctive Henan features, having smooth and clear rhythm, being highly colloquial and being easy to be heard by the audience and other attractions. Furthermore, the play is based on the immigrant's real life experiences, without any exaggeration. It guides every audience to enjoy the story of the immigrant through the personalized drama language and makes them realize the most original touching moments of life. In addition, Screenwriter Mr. Chen Yongquan combined his years of rural life experience, memory, rural legends, gifted people and events, and personal understanding of life into the plain singing words, blended in the play creation. The play makes the most use of body movements and language to interpret the nostalgia of the grass-roots farmers for their hometown and the sadness of movements in the dramatic prologue performance. The homesickness for the immigrants is like a flowing river with deep memory.

"You have to go on working though crying for missing home. Tomorrow is another day." "The mountains are boundless, the water is still, and the homeland is hard to leave. Climbing the mountain and looking back, once more look at the sunken hometown. " These are lyrics for the locust tree and hometown by using the plain, clear and sincere words and expressions, which are all local dialect, full of homesickness. Moreover, it is these most expressive artistic languages that reflect the beauty of the play.

Finally, the beauty of the multi-level implication of the images in the play.

This is the essential part reflecting the aesthetic implication of homesickness, and the beauty of it is multilateral. First, it creates images with homesickness aesthetic significance. The three images of "little locust tree", "a small mound of earth" and "a bottle of water" in *Deep Love for the Danjiang River*" are used in the development of the story from beginning to end, which are hidden and clear, affecting the audience's feelings. "Where this little locust tree is planted, it is our home!" In the script, the author of the play uses Danxia's father's words to express his homesickness, which is simple, pure and powerful. At the same time, the "little locust tree" connects the whole play and echoes for the beginning to the end, appropriately forming an inter-textual relationship with the text of the play. The two together create a beautiful atmosphere. But more importantly, these images not only make the play obtain the overall metaphorical characteristics, but also constitute a spiritual connotation symbol for the drama performance beyond the text. In addition, Adorno said : "If philosophy has any definition, it is an effort to say what cannot be said and to express what cannot be defined." [4] In this aspect, the boundary between reality and fiction gradually has a connection in *Deep Love for the Danjiang River*", presenting a artistic conception of poetic romance. "After all, beauty is a realistic factor in daily life, and aesthetics has also become a special spiritual pursuit for people in their daily life." [5] For more than half a century, everyone has his/her own "story" under such a historical event. Mr. Chen Yongquan created these beautiful stories full of local characteristics and presented them perfectly with the carrier of the play script.

Moreover, it is very typical and common to use "little locust tree"as metaphor in the metaphorical expressions constructed by the plays. It is a highly visual and full of sensitivity, while it is also the concentration and reflection of the "homesickness", just like a colorful oil painting, which makes the practical situation more real and visible than the spiritual homesickness does. Thus the connotation of immigrants' homesickness is deeper and broader. A small locust tree appeared three times in the play, "Where this small locust tree is planted, it is our home!" This reminds people of the root—the big locust tree in Hongdong County—Shared by residents of the Central Plains region, through which "homesickness" is deepened.

Second, it shows concern for human feelings and humanity and the affection of their family and country. The play fully observes the panic of the immigrant farmers after leaving their homeland. "Paying attention to human nature, people's mind, their livelihood and their discourse." [6] Thus it touches the most sensitive and concerned part in the current society. Thus what it brings to people is not only touching, but more recognition and redemption of self-soul. "The relocation anxiety forms a kind of 'collective homesickness' for the past in aesthetic culture." [7] Although sorrow of parting from homeland exists, it does not hurt, which shows a kind of open-mindedness and understanding in plain and calm expressions. "Our ancestors have been moving and looking for a beautiful home. Now we have built one." At the end of the play, Imam Hai said meaningful words to the audience : it is meaning for the immigrant villagers' to struggling against hardships, their solutions for difficulties, their search for a way out, their longing for hope, and their pursuit for happiness. It is not only the reconstruction of their homeland, but also the process of spiritual reconstruction. Furthermore, such hardships and setbacks have stimulated people's desire for survival and a better life, calling for a new era of harmony. In the meanwhile, the playwright and director successfully avoided the misunderstanding of "conceptualization" and "superficiality" that this kind of subject expressing the main theme is most likely to end with. Most importantly, they narrated the historical events with small stories of small people. It is also clear and successful in presenting the ideological implication of the people in the Danjiang Reservoir to sacrifice their small families to care for the community and their great affection for the motherland.

Mr. Wang Dingjun, a famous writer studying Chinese culture abroad, once said that "homesickness is aesthetics". [8] This is, of course, a literary expression. To some extent, homesickness contains rich aesthetic implications. This "homesickness aesthetics" was cultivated in China with a civilization of 5,000 years. The concept of "homesickness" has always been there in the long period of historical development, which seems to have become the blood flowing in everyone's life. In other words, the homeland memory is an element of Chinese culture, also the most difficult to forget in People's minds. It affects the moral development, and encourages the Central Plains people to take actions to realize the rich and strong life.

In conclusion, the aesthetic connotation of "homesickness" in *Deep Love for the Danjiang River*" provides a new aesthetic reference for the contemporary drama. Moreover, its text creation and stage performance have not only provide new ideas for the Henan Opera, but also enrichs the content of performance, which has profound artistic value and reference significance.

References:

[1][2] Mi Genxiao. The creative process is the process of being touched by civilian heroes [N]. China Ethnic News, 2012-07-03 (3).

[3] He Baolin. Creator Rooted in The Central Plains [N]. China Culture Daily, 2014-12-11 (6).

[4] Michael Wood. Translated by Gu Jun. Son of Silence — On Contemporary Fiction [M].Beijing: Joint Publishing of Life, Reading and New Knowledge, 2003 : 11.

[5] Tan Haozhe. Context Awareness and Aesthetics [M].Beijing: People's Publishing House, 2012 : 138.

[6] Wu Xinbin. Discourse Reconstruction in the New Context — A Review of Contemporary Drama [M].Beijing: China Association of Literature and Art Publishing House, 2015 : 7.

[7] Zhou Bin. TV Drama Festival Gala and Contemporary Culture's "Nostalgia" Consciousness [J]. Journal of Pingdingshan University, 2010, 25 (4) : 100.

[8] Wang Dingjun. Mixture and Footprint in Heart [M].Taipei: Taipei Er Ya Publishing House Co. Ltd., 1988 : 201.

艺术美学视域下的廉政题材豫剧研究

——以河南豫剧院"廉政文化三部曲"为例

摘要：近年来,由河南豫剧院编排的豫剧《张伯行》《全家福》和《九品巡检暴式昭》合称为"廉政文化三部曲",受到了广泛的群众好评,引起了深刻的社会反响。这三部新创排的豫剧作品深植于时代环境的土壤,明确了文艺的政治导向,亦体现了中华文化的优良传承；实现了戏曲形式与内容的和谐统一,表现了丰富的意蕴内涵；通过具有层次感和逻辑性的叙述方式,展现了艺术审美特点,具有深厚的美学价值。本文以艺术美学的相关理论（叙事美学、接受美学等）为视角,以"廉政文化三部曲"为范本分析与研究剧作文本、舞台形式、观众接受度等综合美感,旨在挖掘"廉政文化三部曲"的艺术特色、美学价值,为当代豫剧的编创提供一种新的美学范式。

关键词：艺术美学；豫剧；廉政；意蕴

日趋多元化的当代艺术审美格局逐步形成,豫剧等中国传统艺术所独具的美在其中日益凸显,为专家学者所关注。豫剧以其通俗生动的叙事风格和丰厚的内涵意蕴在戏曲百花竞艳中表现不俗。近年来,河南豫剧院编排的豫剧"廉政文化三部曲"（《张伯行》《全家福》和《九品巡检暴式昭》）,既体现了习近平新时代文艺思想,响应了党反腐倡廉的号召,又兼顾了中华传统文化传承；实现了戏曲程式美与意蕴丰富性的和谐统一；通过具有层次感的叙述方式,给予观众独特的美学体验。

时代导向性和文化传承性兼顾

丹纳在《艺术哲学》中提出：影响艺术的三个要素分别为：种族、时代与环境[1]。好的文艺作品必然是在三者的土壤中孕育的奇葩,并深刻反映了三者的风貌。"廉政文化三部曲"的出现正是中华民族对时代与环境的回应,兼顾了时代导向性和文化传承性。

2014年,习近平总书记在文艺工作座谈会上谈道："衡量一个时代的文艺成就最终要看作品。推动文艺繁荣发展,最根本的是要创作生产出无愧于我们这个伟大民族、伟大时代的优秀作品。"面对习总书记的号召,在"廉政建设"的时代背景下,河南豫剧院创排了《张伯行》《全家福》《九品巡检暴式昭》三部廉政题材豫剧作品,引起了广泛的社会反响和群众好评,合称为"廉政文化三部曲"。《张伯行》删繁就简,选取江南科考案作为核心事件,讲述了清朝清官张伯行的廉洁故事,赞扬其崇高的精神品质和思想境界。《全家福》以韩家三代为叙述核心,讲述了官员韩英杰的贪腐行为给家人和自己带来的巨大伤害,讨论贪腐行为对人伦亲情的破坏。《九品巡行暴式昭》讲述了暴式昭为官一方,关心民生,清正廉洁,得罪权贵致使丢官却赢得百姓爱戴的故事。这三部作品贯穿古今,亦正亦反,从正面为为官者树立廉政榜样,真正造福百姓;从反面表现贪腐对家庭造成的巨大破坏,敲响"警示"之钟。这三部作品均体现了鲜明的时代导向性,体现了从严治党、拒绝贪腐的政治风向标。将张伯行作为典型人物更是源于习近平总书记的想法。2014年,习总书记在河南省兰考县的讲话中指出："兰考历史上出了一个有名的清官张伯行。他历任福建巡抚、江苏巡抚、礼部尚书,为谢绝各方馈赠,专门写了一篇《却赠檄文》。其中说道：'一丝一粒,我之名节;一厘一毫,民之脂膏。宽一分,民受赐不止一分;取一文,我为人不值一文。谁云交际之常,廉耻实伤;倘非不义之财,此物何来？'我看,这也可以作为一面镜子。"

除了鲜明的时代导向之外,"廉政文化三部曲"还体现了一种"精神气质",即丹纳所说的"风俗习惯与时代精神",也就是中华民族的文化传承。其一是《张伯行》《九品巡检暴式昭》中的两位主人公张伯行与暴式昭两人本身就是中原历史文化星河中璀璨的星辰,他们在历史上是真实存在的,本身就隶属于历史文化的一部分。事实上,明德仁爱、清正廉洁本身就是古代文化的一部分,是中国传统文化对士大夫的要求。儒家思想鼓励士大夫"为天地立心,为生民立命",正直廉洁,责任担当,傲然于天地之间,心系天下百姓。这种思想不仅影响了古代士大夫的价值取向,至今也潜移默化地影响着当代官员的思想境界和行为方式。"廉政文化三部曲"正是继承了中华文化的儒家士大夫传统,砥砺当代官员秉承廉洁清正操守。其二,豫剧是中华戏曲文化中重要的组成部分,其风格为大板行腔,奏演酣畅。豫剧亦是河南地方特色文化的一部分,真实自然,淳朴率真,贴近百姓生活。"廉政文化三部曲"将中原历史文化人物代表(张伯行、暴式昭)和古代士大夫传统价值观念(政治清廉,关心民生)做了全新的时代阐释,搬上现代舞台;同时借助豫剧来书写一部现代人物韩英杰在官场上一步步走向贪腐的深渊、给家庭造成巨大伤害的新"官场现形记"。"廉政文化三部曲"体现了对优秀传统文化的传承,贯通古今,将传统与现代艺术美熔于一炉,同时也契合了时代特色,体现了鲜明的文艺政治导向。歌德曾说过:"艺术要通过一个完整体向世界说话。"[2]"廉政文化三部曲"正是代表了由古至今延续的中华文化完整体向世界说话、向时代呼唤。

戏曲程式美和意蕴丰富性同一

戏曲不同于其他门类的舞台表演艺术,讲求戏曲程式美与意蕴内涵美的共融。戏曲有着程式性的表演动作和脸谱化的人物设定,加之受到近代西方戏剧思潮的影响,更是束缚于标准化的演出时长。苏珊·朗格在《形式与情感》中强调,艺术形式和艺术情感的配合,要求创作者选取最适宜表达情感态度的艺术形式,同时根据不同的形式表达不同的情感,两者之间相辅相成,存在和谐共生而又充满拗怒的张力。在此观点上,豫剧"廉政文化三部曲"做到了戏曲程式性与情感表现的紧密结合。例如《全家福》中,音乐节奏的停顿与人物感受、态度的变化一致,起到了渲染气氛的作用,最鲜明的便是韩英杰见到两位省委工作人员时,态度由热情得意(以为自己要升官)到慌张心虚(得知两位同事是纪委人员)、强作镇定(要求纪委拿出证据,要求见柳书记)再到绝望颓丧(得知自己已经完全暴露）的过程。这场戏中，每一种情绪、心态的转变都伴随着器乐伴奏的停顿和突转，加之演员的神色变化，简直精彩绝伦。又如在母亲提议留下上海的房子时，韩琳琳唱道："我知道高档房产好，也知道爸妈怜女把心操。贪欲膨胀迷心窍，不义之财是毒药。你说这房子是个宝，我看它来路不明是危巢。"该唱段一气呵成，振聋发聩，全部押"ao"尾韵，且是"开口呼"音节。"开口呼"声音更为洪亮雄浑有气势，符合韩琳琳表达归还房子的坚决意愿、大义凛然和剧作"反腐败"的正义主题。再如在韩英杰妻听到保姆说韩英杰有情妇、要判死刑之后疯癫状态的戏中，唱词全部押"i"韵，"i"韵具有萎靡凄楚的声音特点，符合韩妻此刻的忧愁凄恻的情绪特点。同时，《全家福》在舞台上方加了电子大屏幕，依次放映了旧全家福（韩父、韩及韩姐三人）照片、给韩琳琳的生日礼物大别墅的照片以及韩英杰父亲在病床之上的心电图等，这些图片的放映弥补了以往戏曲舞台上"介质"的缺乏，运用现代媒体技术化虚为实，既追溯家史、展现了韩家三代人的命运跌宕，同时又便于表达人物的情绪，以达到更好的演出效果。正是这种形式（台本文字、表情神色、音乐伴奏、道具、服装等）与情感内容的紧密结合，使"廉政文化三部曲"成了著名艺术理论家克莱夫·贝尔在《艺术》一书中所提出的"有意味的形式"，即"艺术品中必定存在着某种特性：离开它，艺术品就不能作为艺术品而存在"[3]。

除戏曲程式美以外，"廉政文化三部曲"也具有丰富的意蕴。黑格尔在《美学》一书中谈到"意蕴总是比直接显现的形象更为深远的一种东西。艺术作品应该具有意蕴。"[4]"廉政文化三部曲"紧紧围绕着"廉政"这一主题展开，契合时代风貌，但绝不仅仅是政治教化剧，它在人性的挖掘以及主体和世界的关系的问题上也有着深入的探讨。"艺术作品作为艺术生产的产品，具有更加复杂丰富的内涵。"[5]法国思想家布朗肖曾指出："人文艺术的主要特点在模仿中或更在它对人的关注中。"[6]创造者（作者）对创作对象（文本各要素，包括人物）的关注体现了自我再认识，正表明了人的强大意志和真正本质。因而，艺术本质是在模仿中实现对人的重新省察。"廉政文化三部曲"在此意义上是富有创新意义的时代戏曲。一方面契合了党风廉政建设的时代需要，体现了党在反腐建设上"从严治党""壮士断腕"的信念和决心；另一方面人物均突破了原本政治戏曲中主人公的"模式化"脸谱，正如《全家福》中的韩英杰，不再是绝对恶的贪腐分子。他在生活中也是个孝敬父亲、呵护女儿的人。他从贫困的山村走出来，一路至副市长，勤奋学习、努力工作，真正做了许多改善民生的实事。从以上两个层面来说，韩英杰是一个复杂的人物，是福斯特笔下的"圆形人物"。其性格的多面性在作品中充分体现，是戏曲对人物探索的一个进步。事实上，在美国思想家洛夫乔伊的《存在巨链——对一个观念的历史的研究》一书中，已经锁定了人的序列，即在动物与上帝之间[7]，是兽性和神性的混合体。因而不必过分要求每个人都是圣人神人，每个人都有利己的一面。因而观众能对韩英杰这个人物形象产生共情，尤其是以家庭人伦亲情为突破口，更使得观众将日常经验和审美经验相融合，产生移情效应，因而更能理解"贪腐"对家庭情感的巨大破坏。但洛夫乔伊也指出，人与其他生命体最为不同之处便是人一直在向上爬，不甘在存在的巨链中苟且偷生，攀爬着存在的巨梯向神性靠拢。因此，张伯行才能在面对灾区百姓流离失所、哀鸿遍野之时，声讨两江总督噶礼为母过寿的奢靡铺张；暴式昭才能一次次拒绝许虎姐的金银贿赂和上级官员的威逼，依照法令办事，更拿自家的钱修桥，衣衫尽当、无米为炊。正是因为人对神性的向往，凭借独立精神和自由意志修炼品格，才有"廉政文化三部曲"中的"天下清官第一"张伯行和不顾威逼利诱最终被革职的暴式昭。再加上反衬廉洁形象的"韩英杰"，这三个人物形象共同形成了对人性深度的探讨，挖掘了人的内心世界。"廉政文化三部曲"不仅探索个体的内心世界，也探讨人和世界（社会、他人等）之间的关系。一如韩英杰的"双规"不仅是自己未坚守住底线，也有官场的一些灰色地带的影响（如韩英杰隐晦地向韩琳琳提起做什么都行，就是不要从政），有党各部门之间监督的疏漏（柳书记在韩被双规后的深刻反省），也有社会整体大风气的原因。韩英杰的家庭悲剧是内外因共同作用的结果，当然自身内因仍占主要部分。一如九品廉吏暴式昭对妻子始终生活在贫困中的愧疚；面对贪官上级通判的刁难最终丢了官职的无奈；时刻为百姓着想，尽得民心，留下"两袖清风朝天去，不带江南一片锦"的佳话。这些错综复杂的方方面面，塑造了立体的人物，也探索了人与外部世界（社会、他人）的关系。

叙述层次感与艺术审美性并举

戏曲相较于其他艺术门类更为活泼生动、通俗易懂,便于创作者传达思想,也利于观看者理解和接受,故而戏曲艺术在民间文艺中深受人民喜爱。"廉政三部曲"的三位编剧姚金成、陈涌泉和李学庭均是戏曲编剧方面造诣颇高的名家,通过有层次感的叙述和有逻辑性的情节安排,充分发挥了戏曲艺术的生动活泼、通俗易懂的特点。

《全家福》中,韩英杰妻等待韩英杰父到来的第一个场景交代了韩英杰妻的身份和态度(韩妻,对韩父孝顺;收礼,因韩是副市长而产生的骄傲),韩英杰的身份和地位(副市长,即将升任市长),韩琳琳的身份(从国外留学归来)。开篇已然交代了人物各自的身份,从中能看出韩英杰腐败的小苗头,即韩妻不知道是谁送的就敢收礼的行为和骄横傲慢的态度。随着剧情的深入,情节依次铺展开来,追溯韩英杰从贫困到飞黄腾达的奋斗历程,韩英杰被双规,柳书记自责检讨,韩琳琳找柳书记问说法,韩琳琳与韩妻决心将赃物全数归还,韩妻疯癫,韩父住院,韩英杰狱中深刻检讨,韩父责骂韩英杰,韩父去世。就这样一步一步,从人物到情节到主旨,层层递进,逻辑清晰。《九品巡检暴式昭》亦是如此。开篇演绎乌烟瘴气的逍遥馆的许虎姐为讨好魁大人将民女荷花绑架,要送给魁大人。描述了许虎姐的嚣张气焰,以及许虎姐讨好衙门皂隶、权色交易的丑恶行径。随后围绕讨要荷花、永宁桥造桥等情节,表现了暴式昭不畏强权、廉洁奉公、为百姓做实事的工作作风,结尾处众多山民送米的场景升华了主题。《张伯行》一剧第一幕便是鲜明的对比,一边是噶礼为母贺寿张灯结彩、铺张奢靡,一边是灾民哀鸿遍地、流离失所。"朱门酒肉臭,路有冻死骨",张伯行顾念百姓的疾苦,给噶礼母亲送白菜作为贺礼,用以教诲噶礼清正廉洁。这个情节点明了冲突双方,也表现了张伯行正直廉洁的人物性格。这种以冲突为开篇的情节设计能够让观众迅速进入设定的戏剧情境之中。而后,进入到中心情节江南科考案的叙述中,张伯行面对诱惑始终能够不忘初心、清正廉洁,从而升华了主旨。

"廉政文化三部曲"不仅体现了叙述的层次感,也兼顾了艺术审美性。《全家福》虽然有着喜庆欢乐的剧目名称,却是一出令人痛心疾首的悲剧。鲁迅先生在《再论雷峰塔的倒掉》中说过，"悲剧就是将人生有价值的东西毁灭给人看"。《全家福》将一个完整的家庭毁灭了，妻子疯癫，老人离世，昔日的温情不复存在，而这一切的罪魁祸首正是贪腐行为。编剧姚金成未像以往的政治剧详细讲述贪官腐化的进程和给人民造成的巨大灾难，而是另辟蹊径，从贪腐给家庭造成的伤害入手，最大限度地引发观众的"共情"。为了家人和自己过上好生活而贪腐，贪腐却给予家人和自己沉痛的悲剧。事实上，贪腐毁灭的不只是一个韩英杰的家庭，更是韩英杰心中的道德感。韩英杰将内心的正直清廉销毁殆尽，这本身就是巨大的悲剧了。不同于《全家福》给予观众的悲剧感，《张伯行》和《九品巡检暴式昭》给观众以崇高感的审美体验。"有一种超乎一切之上的动力，就是爱，因为爱的目的是促成另外一个人的幸福，把自己隶属于另一个人，为了增进他的幸福而竭忠尽智……爱的对象越广大，我们越觉得崇高。因为爱的益处随着应用的范围而扩张。"[8] 愿为毫不相关的人的幸福而奉献终生，必是源于责任的大爱。正是在这样的大爱之下，暴式昭舍弃了对自己和家人的小爱；张伯行始终坚持本心，清廉如初。这些源于大爱的行为给予观众深切的崇高感。古罗马时期希腊修辞学家朗吉弩斯认为，"崇高的风格是一颗伟大心灵的回声"。康德认为，"崇高提高了我们的精神力量超过平常的尺度，而让我们在内心里发现另一种抵抗的能力，这赋予我们勇气。"[9] 他所说的"另一种抵抗的能力"就是指主体的超越精神。当观众（审美主体）在观看具有崇高的超越精神的戏剧时，审美主体不再是"日常的实用的自我"而是"观照的自我"[10]，观众会自我观照、审视，得到净化；审美对象也不再是对象本身，而是审美主体灌注生命体验的形象，是主体生命的另一种存在形式。因而，"廉政文化三部曲"的崇高感净化了观众的心灵，使之重新审视自我，有勇气成为具有超越精神的人，即有崇高道德感的人。

小　结

豫剧"廉政文化三部曲"在时代的土壤中孕育，是"反腐倡廉"建设的果实，既汲取了中华传统文化的养分，又结合时代有了新的发展。它将戏曲程式化形式与丰富的戏曲美学意蕴紧密结合，形成了"有意味的形式"。三部豫剧由人物到情节再到主旨的叙述具有层次感和逻辑性，便于观众理解和把握戏曲内容,层层渲染,烘托主题,更让观众获得悲剧感和崇高感的多重审美体验,起到了宣泄和净化的作用。它"既是内容与形式的统一,又是感性与理性的统一"[11],具有深厚的美学价值。

参考文献:

[1] 丹纳. 艺术哲学 [M]. 傅雷译. 南京:江苏文艺出版社,2012:3.

[2] 爱克曼辑录. 歌德谈话录 [M]. 朱光潜译. 北京:人民文学出版社,1978:137.

[3] 克莱夫·贝尔. 艺术 [M]. 薛华译. 南京:江苏教育出版社,1984:4.

[4] 黑格尔. 美学(第一卷) [M]. 朱光潜译. 北京:商务印书馆,1979:59.

[5] 彭吉象. 艺术学概论 [M]. 北京:北京大学出版社,2006:321.

[6] 莫里斯·布朗肖. 文学空间 [M]. 顾嘉琛译. 北京:商务印书馆,2003:221.

[7] 洛夫乔伊. 存在巨链——对一个观念的历史的研究 [M]. 张传有,高秉江译,北京:商务印书馆,2015:164.

[8] 丹纳. 艺术哲学 [M]. 傅雷译. 南京:江苏文艺出版社,2012:370.

[9] 康德. 判断力批判 [M]. 邓晓芒译,北京:商务印书馆,1985:101.

[10] 朱光潜. 西方美学史 [M]. 北京:人民文学出版社,1964:261.

[11] 彭吉象. 艺术学概论 [M]. 北京:北京大学出版社,2006:321.

Research on the Incorruptness-themed Henan Opera from the Perspective of Art Aesthetics —Taking the Incorruptness Trilogy of Henan Opera Theatre as an Example

Abstract: In recent years, the "incorruptness trilogy" including *Zhang Boxing* (an incorruptible official of Qing Dynasty), *A Family Photo* and *Bao Shizhao* (an honest and upright inspector of Qing Dynasty) created by Henan Opera Theatre has been well received by the masses and has aroused profound social repercussions. Based on the reality, three new works of Henan Opera clarify the political orientation of literature and art, and reflect the noble traditions of Chinese culture, realizing the harmony between the form and content, and expressing the profound connotations. Besides, the three works show the aesthetic characteristics of art and profound aesthetic value through a logical narrative. Based on the relevant theories of art aesthetics including narrative aesthetics and acceptance aesthetics, this thesis will analyze the script, stage forms and audience acceptation of the incorruptness trilogy, aiming to explore the artistic characteristics and aesthetic value of the incorruptness trilogy and provide a new aesthetic paradigm for the creation of contemporary Henan Opera.

Key Words: Art Aesthetics, Henan Opera, incorruptness, connotations

With the contemporary art aesthetic becoming more diversified, the unique aesthetic of traditional Chinese arts such as Henan Opera is becoming more and more prominent, which attracts the attention of experts and scholars. Henan Opera stands out among various traditional Chinese operas on its vividly narrative style and profound connotations. In recent years, the "incorruptness trilogy" including *Zhang Boxing, A Family Photo* and *Bao Shizha*o created by Henan Opera Theatre embodies the literary and artistic thought of President Xi in the new era, responds to the call of the CPC to combat corruption, builds a clean government, and also takes into account the inheritance of traditional Chinese culture. What's more, the "incorruptness trilogy" realizes the harmony between the beauty of form and the richness of connotations of operas, and gives audiences a unique aesthetic experience through a logical narrative.

The Unity of the Mainstream of Era and the Inheritance of Culture

In *Philosophie De L'Art*, Hippolyte Adolphe Taine puts forward that race, era and environment are three elements that influence art [1]. And good literary and artistic works are inevitably bred in the soil of the three elements, and deeply reflect the style of the three elements. Thus, the "incorruptness trilogy" is the response of the Chinese nation to the backgrounds of era, which realizes the unity of the mainstream of era and the inheritance of culture.

In 2014, President Xi said at the seminar in literature and art : "The literary and artistic achievements of an era will ultimately depend on the works. To promote the prosperity and development of literature and art, what we should do is to create excellent works that correspond to our great nation and era." Facing the call of President Xi, Henan Opera Theatre creates the "incorruptness trilogy" under the backgrounds of anti-corruption and clean governance, including *Zhang Boxing, A Family Photo* and *Bao Shizhao*, which has been well received by the masses and has aroused profound social repercussions. The work *Zhang Boxing* simplifies the case of imperial competitive examination of Qing Dynasty, which tells the story of an incorruptible official called Zhang Boxing, and praises his lofty quality and ideological level. The work *A Family Photo* focuses on the three generations of the Han family, which tells the great harm that the corrupted official Han Yingjie has brought to the family and himself, and discusses the damage of the kinship caused by the corruption. The work *Bao Shizhao* tells the story of Bao Shizhao—an honest and upright inspector of Qing Dynasty, who cared about people's livelihood and enjoyed the respect of people, and lost his position after offending bigwigs. The three works link the past to the present. For one thing, they set an example for the officials and truly benefit the people. For another, they show the great damage caused by corruption to the family and ring the bell of "warning". What's more, the three works embody the distinctive orientation of the era, and reflect the political vane of strictly administering the party and rejecting corruption. It is worth mentioning that taking Zhang Boxing as a typical figure is derived from the idea of President Xi. In 2014, President Xi delivered a speech during his visit to Lankao County of Henan : "Zhang Boxing, a well-known honest and upright official of Qing Dynasty born in Lankao, he has served successively as the Governor of Fujian and Governor of Jiangsu and Minister of Rituals, and he has wrote a proclamation in order to decline gifts of others. Thus, I think that the honest and upright official Zhang Boxing sets a good example for our contemporary officials."

In addition to the distinctive orientation of the era, the "incorruptness trilogy" also embodies a kind of spiritual temperament, that is Taine's "customs and the spirit of the times", and also known as the cultural heritage of the Chinese nation, which could be found in the "incorruptness trilogy" from two aspects. For one thing, the two protagonists of Zhang Boxing and Bao Shizhao are real in history and belong to the part of culture. In fact, traditional Chinese culture required the scholar-officials in feudal China to be virtuous, benevolent, clean and upright. Confucianism encourage scholar-officials to be clean, honest and serve for the masses. This kind of thought not only affected the value of ancient scholar-officials, but also imperceptibly influenced the ideological realm and behavior of contemporary officials. Thus, the "incorruptness trilogy" inherits the noble traditions of Confucian scholar-officials, and encourages contemporary officials to be clean and honest. For another, as an important part of Chinese Opera culture, whose style is sturdy and elegant. And as a part of the local culture of Henan, which is realistic performance and is close to the lives of common people. The two works *Zhang Boxing* and *Bao Shizhao* centred on two historical figures of the Central Plains and represented the traditional values of the ancient scholar-officials. And the work *A Family Photo* tells the great harm that contemporary corrupted official Han Yingjie has brought to the family. All in all, the "incorruptness trilogy" embodies the inheritance of excellent traditional culture, combines the beauty of traditional and modern art, meets the characteristics of the era, and reflects the distinct literary and political orientations. As Goethe once said : "Art must speak to the world through a complete body" [2], thus, the "incorruptness trilogy" represents that the Chinese culture throughout the history speaks to the world and calls to the era.

The Unity of the Formal Beauty and Rich Connotations of Opera

Unlike other categories of performing arts, opera stresses the unity of the beauty of form and the richness of connotations. Besides, opera has prescriptive acting and various characters who wear different facial makeups, and it is constrained by the specified show time under the influence of modern western drama. In *Feeling and Form*, Susanne K. Langer says that the creator needs to select the art form that is the most suitable for expressing feelings in order to realize the unity of artistic form and feeling, and express different feelings according to different art forms at the same time, which means that the form and feeling complement each other and co-exist harmoniously. From this point of view, the "incorruptness trilogy" has realized the unity of the form and feeling of opera. Taking *A Family Photo* for example, the pause of music is consistent with the changes of the characters' feelings and attitudes, which heightens the atmosphere. What most striking is that the shifts in mentalities of Han Yingjie when he was seeing two provincial staff; he was firstly enthusiastic for he thought that he would be promoted, then he was nervous when he learned that the two staff came from the Commission For Discipline Inspection, but he tried to keep calm and asked them to show evidence and he wanted to see Secretary Liu, eventually he became despair when he learned that his crime had been completely exposed. The show is marvelous, for the changes of emotion and mentality are accompanied by the pause and shift of instrumental accompaniment as well as the changes of characters' looks. For another example, when Han Yingjie's wife proposed to leave the house in Shanghai, Han Linlin (the daughter of Han Yingjie) sang : "I know that a high-end house is valuable, and what my parents have done is good for me. However, my father has been blinded by greed, and this is a house bought by ill-gotten wealth." This aria is enlightening, smooth and rhymed with "ao" in every last word. Besides, this aria is resonant for adopting the syllables of vowels at the beginning of each line, which not only expressed Han Lin Lin's strong will to return to the house, but also conformed to the theme "anti-corruption". What's more, Han Yingjie's wife became crazy when she heard that Han Yingjie not only had lover, but also were sentenced to death; in this play her lines all rhymed with "i", which sounded mournful, and it was in line with the sadness of Han Yingjie's wife. At the same time, the play *A Family Photo* used the large electronic screen to show the old family photo, the photo of villa as Han Linlin's birthday gift and the electrocardiogram of Han Yingjie's father on the hospital bed, etc, which made up for lack of media in the previous plays, used the modern media technology to retrospect the family history, showed the fate of three generations of Han's family, and expressed the moods of the characters to achieve a better performance effect. It is the unity of feeling and form (including playscript with stage directions, looks, music, stage property and clothing) that makes the "incorruptness trilogy" become the "meaningful form" proposed by the famous art theorist Clive Bell in the book *Art*, which means that there must be special properties in art, otherwise, works of art can't exist without it. " [3]

In addition to the beauty of form, the "incorruptness trilogy" also has rich connotations. Hegel said in the book *Aesthetics* that "connotation is always a more profound thing than the form that appears directly. Works of art should have connotations." [4] The "incorruptness trilogy" centers on the theme of "clean governance", fits the style of the era, which is not only emphasizes the political civilization, also delves deeper into human nature and the relationship between the subject and the world. [5] The French thinker Maurice Blanchot once said : "As a product of art, works of art have more complex and rich connotations. The main characteristics of the humanities art lie in imitation or its concern for people." [6] The creators' (namely authors) attention to the creation object (various elements of the text including the characters) reflects self-recognition, which indicates the strong will and essence of humanity. Therefore, the essence of art is to realize the examination of conscience of humanity in imitation. In this sense, the "incorruptness trilogy" is an innovative play. On the one hand, it meets the needs of building a clean government, and reflects the CPC's belief and determination to strictly rule the party in the anti-corruption construction; on the other hand, the characters differ from the stereotyped facial makeup of the protagonist in the previous political plays. For instance, the character Han Yingjie in *A Family Photo* was no longer an absolute evil corrupt official. In daily life, he was also a dutiful son and a father who cared for his daughter. In the transformation of a little child born in the poor mountain village to deputy mayor, he was diligent and worked hard, and really did a lot of things to improve people's livelihood. From the above two levels, Han Yingjie is a complex figure, who is a "circular figure" written by Foster. His complicated characters are fully reflected in the play, which remarks an improvement in the exploration of characters for the play which describes how an ambitious, clean and upright official became corrupt, and how to choose when humanity faces temptation. In fact, in *The Great Chain of Being—A Study of the History of a Concept* written by American thinker Arthur Oncken Lovejoy, he believed that the sequence of human beings has been locked. In other words, the status of human beings is between animals and god, which is the combination of animals and divinity. [7] There is no reason to require everyone to be a saint, for everyone has his own interests. Therefore, audiences can easily be affected through the character of Han Yingjie, especially the family's relationship as a breakthrough.Besides, the audience could combine daily and aesthetic experience to produce empathy effect for a better understanding of the damage of the kinship caused by the corruption. However, Lovejoy also pointed out that the most distinguished difference between human beings and other living beings is that people have some motivations. They are not willing to sneak in the existing chains, and to climb the giant ladders that close to the divine. Therefore, in the face of the displacement and sorrow of the people in the disaster area, Zhang Boxing condemned Gali, the Governor General of Jiangnan and Jiangxi Provinces, of wasting money on his mother's birthday celebration. Bao Shizhao refused Xu Hujie's gold and silver bribes and the intimidation of superiors again and again, and acted in accordance with the law. Besides, he even took his own money to repair the bridge, and finally he had no clothes to wear and no rice to eat. There are "the first honest and upright official in the world" Zhang Boxing, Bao Shizhao who disregarded the threat of coercion and was eventually dismissed, precisely because of the yearning for divinity and the spirit of independence and free will, and Han Yingjie, whose image contrasts the image of integrity. These three figures discuss together, the depth of human nature and analyze the inner world of people. "Incorruptness trilogy" not only explores the inner world of the individual, but also discusses the relationship between human and the world (the society and others). Just as Han Yingjie, his behavior implicates that he has not adhered to the bottom line of the integrity, which shows the influence of the officialdom (for example, Han Yingjie vaguely talked to Han Linlin that she could do whatever she wants to do, except to do political working) and supervision omissions among various departments of the party (Secretary Liu reflected deeply after Han Yingjie being investigated) under the influence of the overall social atmosphere. Han Yingjie's family tragedy is the result of internal and external factors, and certainly the internal factors still account for the main part; just like Bao Shizhao, who was guilty about his wife lived in poverty, lost his position facing the spites from the corrupt superiors' magistrate, cared for people's life and won their approvals and respects, and left a historic story. These intricate aspects have shaped three-dimensional figures and explored the relationship between people and the outside world (the society and others).

The Unity of Narrative Layering and Artistic Aesthetics

Compared with other art categories, the images of opera become livelier and richer for creators to convey ideas, and also for viewers to understand and accept it. Therefore, opera in folk art is deeply loved by people. The three screenwriters of "Incorruptness trilogy" Yao Jincheng, Chen Yongquan and Li Xueting are famous masters among opera writers. Through their layered narrative and logical plot arrangement, the vivid and understandable characteristics of the art opera have been fully showed.

In *A Family Photo*, the first scene is that Han Yingjie's wife was waiting the arrival of Han Yingjie's father to explain the identity and attitude of Han Yingjie's wife (Han's wife has filial piety to Han's father, received gifts because of the pride of Han's status of deputy mayor), Han Yingjie's identity (as a deputy mayor, he will be promoted to the mayor by and by), and his daughter Han Linlin's identity (she has came back from studying abroad). The beginning of the article has already explained the respective identities of the characters, through which we can see the small sign of Han Yingjie's corruption, that is, Han's wife does not know who sends the presents but she accepts them with imperious and arrogance. With the development of the plot, the plot was unfolded in turn, which dated Han Yingjie's struggle from poverty to success. Since Han Yingjie was investigated, Secretary Liu blamed himself. Then Han Linlin asked Secretary Liu to give a explanation, and finally Han Linlin and Han's wife decided to return all the received presents. Shortly afterwards, Han's wife became mad and Han's father was hospitalized. During this process, Han Yingjie made a profound review in prison. Han's father scolded Han Yingjie for his corruption and his father died before long. In this way, characters, plots and theme were logically clear. So is *Bao Shizhao*. At the beginning, the character Xu Hujie in the Xiaoyao Pavilion abducted the girl Hehua to flatter the officer Kui, which described the ugly act of trading in power of Xu Hujie. Then the plot such as saving the girl Hehua, constructing Yongning Bridge and other plots all reflected the Bao's working style of doing practical things for people and fighting against the powerful superiors. In the end, the scenes of many people sending rice to him have sublimated the theme. The first act of *Zhang Boxing* is a stark contrast. On the one hand, Gali's mother's birthday celebration is lavish, and on the other hand, the homeless people are moaning with sorrow. As the saying goes, "While the rich wine and dine, the poor die of cold by the roadside", *Zhang Boxing* cared about the suffering of people and gave Gali mother a Chinese cabbage as a birthday gift to teach him to be honest. This plot clearly points out that the conflict of two sides, and also shows Zhang Boxing's integrity, through which the conflict-based plot design allows audience to quickly enter the set drama situation. Then in the narrative of the main plot of Jiangnan Science Examination Case, Zhang Boxing always sticks to his heart and keeps integrity when facing the temptation, which finally sublimates the subject.

The "incorruptness trilogy" not only reflects the layering of the narrative, but also takes into Artistic aesthetics. Although *A Family Photo* has a happy and joyful repertoire name, it is really a tragedy. Mr. Lu Xun said in *The Reconsideration of the Falling of Leifeng Pagoda* that "tragedy is to destroy people's valuable things in life." *A Family Photo* has destroyed a completely happy family. Han' wife is mad and Han's father has passed away. The main culprit of all is corruption. The screenwriter Yao Jincheng does not pay great attention to deteriorating process of corrupt officials and the disaster caused to the people, but starts with the harm caused by corruption to the family and maximizes the "compassion" of the audience by a new way. Han Yingjie was gradually addicted to corruption for his family and he wanted to live a good life, but finally what he did brought the ending of the happy life, of his family. In fact, the corruption behavior not only destroys Han Yingjie's family, but also the moral sense in Han Yingjie's heart. It is a huge tragedy in itself when Han Yingjie ruined his inner integrity. Being different from the tragic feelings expressed by *A Family Photo*, *Zhang Boxing* and *Bao Shizhao* give the audience a sublime aesthetic experience. "There is a kind of power that is above all else, and that is love, because the purpose of love is to promote the happiness of another person, subordinate to another person, and be loyal to the promotion of his happiness... The wider the object of love is, the more we feel sublime, because the benefits of love expand with the scope of the application." [8] Being willing to sacrifice his life for the happiness of others is from responsible love. It is in such great love that Bao Shizhao has abandoned the little love for himself and his family; Zhang Boxing always adheres to his heart which is honest as ever. These behaviors stem from the great love, which give audiences a deep sense of sublimity. Greek rhetorician in ancient Rome Longinus believes that the sublime style is the echo of a great soul. Immanuel Kant believes that sublimity enhances our spiritual strength beyond the usual standards and discovers another resistance capability in our hearts, which gives us courage.[9] What he calls "another resistance capability" refers to the transcendental spirit of the subject. When audiences (aesthetic subject) are watching a drama with a noble spirit of transcendence, the aesthetic subject is no longer a "daily and practical self" but a "self-reflection" [10], and audiences will get purified by self-view. The aesthetic object is no longer object itself, but combination of the aesthetic subject with life experience, which is another existence form of the subject's life. Therefore, the lofty sense of the "incorruptness trilogy" purifies audiences' minds, which makes them re-examine themselves, and encourages them to become a person with transcendence spirit and high moral sense.

Conclusion

Bred in the soil of the era, the Henan Opera "incorruptness trilogy" is the fruit of the "anti-corruption" construction, absorbs traditional Chinese culture, and has a new development in accordance with the era. It combines the stylized form with the rich aesthetics of the opera, and forms a "meaningful form". From the characters, plots to the theme, the narratives of the three Henan Operas are logical, which make the audience understand and grasp the content of the opera, and highlight the theme. Besides, it also gives audience a multi-aesthetic experience of tragic and sublime feelings, plays the roles of the publicity and purification. Thus, it is "not only the unity of content and form, but also the unity of sensibility and rationality" [11], and has profound aesthetic value.

Bibliography:

[1] Hippolyte Adolphe Taine. Philosophie De L' Art [M]. Translated by

Fu Lei. Nanjing: Jiangsu Literature and Art Publishing Press, 2012:3.

[2] Ekman's Record. Gesprache mit Goethe [M]. Translated by Zhu Guangqian. Beijing: People's Literature Publishing Press, 1978:137.

[3] Clive Bell. Art [M]. Translated by Xue Hua. Nanjing: Jiangsu Education Press, 1984:4.

[4] Hegel. Aesthetics Vol.1. [M]. Translated by Zhu Guangqian. Beijing: The Commercial Press, 1979:59.

[5] Peng Jixiang. Introduction to Art [M]. Beijing: Peking University Press, 2006:321 .

[6] Morris Brownshaw. Literature Space [M]. Translated by Gu Jiayu. Beijing: The Commercial Press2003:221.

[7] Lovejoy. The Great Chain of Being — A Study of the History of a Concept [M]. Translated by Zhang Chuanyou, Gao Bingjiang. Beijing: The Commercial Press, 2015:164.

[8] Hippolyte Adolphe Taine. In Philosophie De L'Art [M]. Translated by Fu Lei. Nanjing: Jiangsu Literature and Art Publishing Press, 2012:370.

[9] Immanuel Kant. Critical Criticism [M]. Translated by Deng Xiaomang. Beijing: The Commercial Press, 1985:101.

[10] Zhu Guangqian. History of Western Aesthetics [M]. Beijing: People's Literature Publishing House, 1964:261.

[11] Peng Jixiang. Introduction to Art [M]. Beijing: Peking University Press, 2006:321 .

云路招邀回彩凤

——谈曲剧《信仰》的艺术创获

摘要：河南省曲剧艺术保护传承中心用富于时代感的笔触尝试改编话剧《共产党宣言》，创排了大型现代曲剧《信仰》。曲剧《信仰》在文本改编与唱腔设计上进行继承与创新，借助曲剧艺术的载体为观众描绘了白色恐怖年代里共产主义信仰者不屈抗争、英勇牺牲的故事，讴歌和颂扬了共产主义者为了党性信仰和民族大义勇于牺牲小我、成就大我的信仰力量和令人为之动容的情感抉择，对曲剧传统的传承和声腔设计的突破以及新时期曲剧艺术的发展做出了有益的尝试与实践。曲剧《信仰》是一部具有较高艺术成就和较强时代意义的佳作。

关键词：《信仰》；曲剧；改编；编曲

河南省曲剧艺术保护传承中心创排的大型现代曲剧《信仰》是王明山先生根据唐栋、蒲逊的话剧《共产党宣言》改编而来，由耿玉卿、李全生谱曲，黄在敏导演，方素珍、杨帅学等曲剧名家联袂主演。《信仰》在刚刚落幕的"天中杯"第八届黄河戏剧节主会场——驻马店市会展中心又一次（2018年8月24日在河南艺术中心首演）成功上演，并一举斩获大赛金奖。该剧用细腻悠扬的曲剧艺术为观众描绘了一幅战火硝烟中革命志士信仰熔铸的壮丽画卷。戏曲使思想性变得形象化。曲剧《信仰》从戏曲文本、导演编排、演员诠释再到灯光、舞美、音响乐队的配合上来讲都是一次效果上乘的形象性呈现，这其中都蕴涵着艺术创作者（改编者、导演、乐师、演员等)对于《信仰》思想性的一次深挖、升华、凝练和释放。曲剧《信仰》在文本移植与编创方面做出了一次有益的尝试；唱腔设计方面更是剧种意识的一次加强与突破；主题意旨层面达到了"母爱——人性——信仰"的高度。《信仰》一剧从创排到上演，以艺术实践的形式提出了不少令人深思的问题，是新时期河南曲剧发展的优秀成果。

戏曲文本：人物、情节与艺术技法的完美融合

根据话剧《共产党宣言》改编而来的曲剧《信仰》为新时期河南戏曲文本移植所进行的一次有益尝试。剧作家王明山有着清晰而笃定的历史题材戏曲创作操守，即务求真实还原历史情境，并在真实的历史情境中有的放矢地进行艺术创作。一部化历史本真为戏曲情境、借艺术创作发时代呐喊的剧作，绝不是历史事件的堆叠和情感意象的重复所拼凑成的扁平人物形象和简单故事框架。曲剧《信仰》是融合了剧作者(原作编剧与改编作者)心头热血、脑中思考和平生阅历的艺术喷发，是融涉历史本真与艺术创作的新时期河南戏曲佳作。

曲剧《信仰》讲述的是历史背景之下的真实、简单而不落俗套的故事。王明山在话剧《共产党宣言》故事脉络的基础之上，挣脱原作人物形象、故事情节的束缚与限制，大胆而细腻地对《信仰》中人物的形象与情节矛盾进行了重新解读与编排，使得曲剧《信仰》与话剧《共产党宣言》既相像却又完全不同。该剧对历史情境的营造力求真、实，用极富年代感、画面感的笔触还原、再现了共产党人在1927年大革命低潮时仍矢志不渝、坚守信仰的时代背景。曲剧《信仰》所讲述的故事正是在这样的时代背景之下所发生的。大革命失败，蒋介石背叛革命，阴谋大肆屠杀共产党人。女共产党员林雨洁(方素珍饰演)在躲避国民党军警追捕时被女大学生况梅(晋红娟饰演)救下，并带回家中藏身。救下林雨洁的正是自己前夫况兆年(张转社饰演)的小女儿。之后，林雨洁不幸被捕入狱。审讯她的国民党稽查队队长则是自己十五年未曾见过面的儿子——况为(常向克饰演)。特务头子沈卓(杨帅学饰演)等对林雨洁软硬兼施，最后甚至阴谋让林雨洁牵连况兆年一家人。林雨洁为信仰，被沈卓等反革命者残忍杀害。

戏曲要发挥它的功用，必须具有生动可感的人物形象。王明山对人物

形象的塑造与刻画拿捏得恰到好处。曲剧《信仰》中的人物关系与矛盾冲突是相互羁绊在一起的，并不能简单、机械地将该剧的人物形象一分为二地看作是正面人物形象和反面人物形象。王明山将人物的形象从三民主义进行了辩证性的区分，使人物形象更为微妙和丰满。同样是三民主义的效法者，林雨洁、沈卓、况为却在面对信仰时作出了不同的选择。林雨洁早年参加革命党，是三民主义的效法者，而后参加共产党，是共产主义的信仰者。作为《信仰》中的主人公，她是那个动荡岁月中难以计数的共产党员的一个缩影，是为救民族于危亡的仁人志士中的一员。她信仰三民主义，信仰共产主义，相信它们能够挽救人民于水火，林雨洁信仰了三民主义和共产主义的精神内核。沈卓作为《信仰》中最为阴鸷狠毒的反面角色，同样也有自己的"信仰"，他信仰一份"死"了的三民主义。沈卓奉为圭臬的三民主义如蒋介石一样的排外、不包容，这与孙中山先生所提出的三民主义精神实质是相背离的。沈卓也是背叛革命的蒋介石之流的一个缩影，故而在剧中开篇，潘队长率人搜查况兆年宅邸时，沈卓唱道：

"先生啊！现如今要清除乱党共匪，

蒋校长有号召上下紧跟随。

错杀一千不为罪，

放过一人悔难追。

情势紧更需要谨小慎微，

万不可拿鸡蛋去碰铁锤。"

这本就是与三民主义精神背道而驰，却偏要信这"蒋校长"的信仰，上行下效。沈卓信仰的仅仅是"蒋校长"口中的三民主义，一个背叛革命者遮羞的"幌子"。况为与林雨洁、沈卓的大是大非相比有着明显的不同，其自身对信仰的思考就是一个由纠结、矛盾、迷惘转向萌动、希冀和赤诚的历程。况为自认为自己的信仰是最为"纯粹"的三民主义，却在审讯过程中被林雨洁的一番话惊醒，唱道：

"林雨洁一番话搅人心扉，

啥力量能让她视死如归？

在黄埔接受过多少教诲，

早已把三民主义刻在骨髓。

共产党与先生教诲没有相悖，

看不出他们哪里像罪魁。

到底是谁的错来谁的对，

顿迷茫难分辨孰是孰非。"

林雨洁对信仰的虔诚和面对死亡威胁的大义凛然都让况为打心底里生出敬佩之心。纵然是嘴上讲着林雨洁是"共党要犯"，却是在心里叩问着自己的信仰。有别于沈卓的"信仰"，况为的信仰是处在迷茫中的。甚至他有些机械地相信"三民主义"，但他的信仰却绝不是虚伪的、虚假的。同时，况为的信仰又是有别于林雨洁的，况为的信仰远没有林雨洁对共产主义信仰笃定与坚信，但况为却在一系列的情节矛盾冲突中产生了对共产主义信仰的萌动与向往。

情感、意象必然要附着于具体的戏剧人物关系和情节矛盾之上，通过事件和感觉表现出来，而不能是简单地塑造扁平人物、罗织俗套故事。由王明山改编的曲剧《信仰》在人物关系与情节矛盾的设置与安排上是独具匠心的。主要人物之间的关系、主次人物之间的关系等都是互有关联、互有羁绊、互有矛盾的，且是层层相套、环环相扣的。林雨洁与沈卓之间是信仰的矛盾、党派的矛盾、生死的矛盾和正义与强权的矛盾；林雨洁与况为之间是信仰的矛盾、相认与诀别的矛盾、民族大义与母子亲情的矛盾等。林雨洁在监牢里要来白纸、线绳和竹篾制作出蝴蝶风筝让况为倍感亲切，这是林雨洁与况为母子亲情的呼唤与呐喊。林雨洁面对着审问自己的儿子况为，想相认却又担心、害怕而不敢相认的矛盾；况为被林雨洁质问信仰，看到蝴蝶风筝想到自己母亲的那份情思，这些都令两人的关系变得极富戏剧性的焦灼与矛盾。剧作者对于剧中小人物的刻画与设置是删繁就简的。况兆年、谢婉云夫妇两人从一开始担心林雨洁的到来会给这个家庭带来不幸，到后来受到林雨洁凛然大义的感化和共产主义信仰的震撼而钦佩和支持共产主义事业的情感变化。况梅更是在这样阴郁的反革命斗争环境中似革命希望之火般存在，她在学堂接受教育，思想和情感都向往着进步，纵然是在沈卓等反革命之徒的威胁下也保持着一颗坚定而勇敢的心。剧中况为稽查队的"好兄弟"李副官搭救林雨洁一出戏的安排更使情节矛盾陡然紧张，同时也赋予了李副官人物身份的一种开放性的假设，为况为信仰由动摇到彻悟的转向提供了一个外在的动因。莱辛在《拉奥孔》中曾指出："替人类情感定普遍规律从来就是最虚幻难凭的。情感和激情的网是既精微而又繁复的,连最严谨的思辨也很难从其中很清楚地理出一条线索来。"[1] 曲剧《信仰》在人物关系的处理上做到了既复杂又清晰,仅从戏曲文本来看足见剧作者对于戏曲人物形象、关系和情节矛盾处理的深厚功力。因为戏曲人物形象从来都不是能够简单定义的,是无法通过寥寥言语就能准确说明的。戏曲人物形象需要情节、故事去表达与阐述,情节、故事又需要冲突与矛盾去激化和推动。这就需要剧作者能够将复杂的人类情感体验和低级简单的感性认知规律化,用以进行戏曲创作实践。

作为一部仍在不断改进、完善中的作品,曲剧《信仰》在背景叙述和情感铺陈上稍显冗长、拖沓,使戏曲情节推进与矛盾激化变得缓慢、乏力。剧作在对整个故事的背景和人物关系进行严整交代时,大致用了两场戏的时间,这显然会让观众的审美期待因前期的大篇幅铺陈而有所消磨。耗费过多的笔墨进行背景的叙述和情感铺陈让《信仰》开篇故事叙述进入主题、审美受众进入戏曲情境显得迟滞。卡西尔曾讲道："无人能否认:艺术作品给予我们最大的愉悦,也许是人类本性能够感受的最为持久的和最为强烈的愉悦。"[2] 这也是审美受众对于戏曲艺术的一种期待性心理。在进行戏曲创作过程中应当设法兼顾戏曲情节的紧凑程度,让人物关系、矛盾冲突变得激烈,这样也许能够使《信仰》在观看过程中的体验更为酣畅和过瘾。

唱腔设计:传统曲剧唱腔艺术的继承与创新

曲剧《信仰》的唱腔设计是剧种意识的一次加强和突破。在唱腔方面由国家一级作曲耿玉卿、国家三级作曲李全生亲自操刀,在对传统曲剧唱腔继承与发扬的基础上,大胆地进行"自出机杼"式的融合与创新。时白林先生曾在《时白林黄梅戏音乐的唱腔选集》中提道:"一、尽量地发扬传统声腔的特长与优势,二、尽最大可能把人物的思想感情、内心世界展示给观(听)众,三、不重复自己,努力做到自我超越。"[3] 戏曲发展进入新时期以来,观众对戏曲的审美需求日益提高。曲剧唱腔如果循规蹈矩、一成不变,必然难以吸纳与发展年龄层次更富多元的戏曲受众;但如果一味地求新求变,则必然要损失掉不少的原有的戏曲受众。值得欣慰的是,耿玉卿、李全生在遵循章法的基础上,大胆地对曲剧《信仰》的唱腔进行创造性的化用与尝试,结合该剧中方素珍、杨帅学等演员的声腔特点进行编曲与设计,这是新时期曲剧声腔创作,甚至是剧种意识的一次加强与突破。曲剧《信仰》在唱腔上从各方面都做出了极大的尝试和实践:

其一,在曲剧《信仰》中大胆地使用两个宫调。C宫调与D宫调的使用,妥善地解决了男、女演员在演唱过程中因"同宫同调"所产生的一系列问题:女声感到低,男声顶不上去。曲剧《信仰》中,男声用C宫调、女声使用D宫调。男、女演员在演唱过程中都能够舒展自如,发挥各自音域的个性特长。这也需要演员和乐手都能够与时俱进、敢于突破,尤其是自我突破。值得注意的是,乐队在伴奏过程中使用了两把曲胡(一把C宫调、一把D宫调),在演出过程中轮换使用进行演(伴)奏;古筝在整场演出中反复多次进行变调调整。这些在唱腔、伴奏等方面的创造性变革对于演员与乐队无疑是极具挑战性的,在曲剧演奏史上更是前人所未敢轻易尝试的。该剧的演员,以杨帅学为主的男声,以方素珍、刘艳丽为主的女声,还有古筝乐手王健不断地在实践中摸索,在摸索中调整,在调整中完善。作为曲剧《信仰》演出的关键,只有演员与乐队伴奏之间搭配无间,乐队各乐器演奏配合、衔接得当才能够称得上是真正意义上的成功。就首演以来的多场演出实践来看,同时使用两个宫调的演奏和演唱得到了观剧专家学者和曲剧戏迷的认可与赞许。

其二,创造性地使用曲剧【摇板书韵】。【书韵】是曲剧艺术中使用率极高的曲牌,表现力强、旋律美,如《卷席筒》中的"小仓娃"、《寇准背靴》中的"下朝来"、《风雪配》中的"今日是"等唱段。因为【书韵】的旋律性极强,故而在编曲过程中可塑性也是极强的。曲剧《信仰》中要同时去表现林雨洁、沈卓、况兆年和谢婉云四人的博弈与心理,并渲染出令人心悸的肃杀氛围,最好的办法就是将这一段演出整体的节奏加快、提高。然而,在此之前的众多曲剧演出都是循于曲剧传统,未有任何可供套用和借鉴的办法。国家一级作曲耿玉卿敢为人先,在与剧作者、演员和乐队多次沟通后,数易其稿,直至第五稿时才确定成稿。其中最大的难度是要保持【书韵】的调式特点、主音与骨干音,同时又要自出机杼地化用新的节奏,这就极为考验方素珍、杨帅学、张转社和刘艳丽四位演员的配合默契与曲剧功底了。此间，还有男、女演员不同唱腔的问题。这难度虽然不小，但是方素珍、杨帅学等几位曲剧名角的演唱功底是十分深厚的，经过难以计数的练习、磨合与衔接，最终还是克服了这样的困难并在实际演出中达到了预期的艺术效果。在此过程中，也为新时期的曲剧艺术创造了一个【摇板书韵】的新唱法，这对曲剧音乐创作的发展具有深远的现实意义，为当代曲剧编曲提供了一个全新的范式。

其三，用属调演唱【老剪剪花】。耿玉卿将 C 调的 35235 下调四度，改为 72672。

图：C 调的 35235 与下调四度的 72672

首先，是为了解决男声的音域问题；其次，是为了突出人物的个性特点，让唱腔设计更适宜于每一位演员，量体裁衣，使演员的演唱既符合戏曲角色的情态，同时也不必担忧音域不适应所带来的演唱压力。经此一变，沈卓的唱腔部分就完全地融于反动特务头子阴阳怪气、狡诈阴险的身份与情态。这个改动，在排演之初大家都感到了不适应，但经过与剧中饰演警察局局长的杨帅学反复磋商和磨合，几经调整和修改、提升，使这个最初并不被看好的唱段获得满堂喝彩，被观剧专家给予了高度评价，称其为"最有曲剧味"。

其四，用 F 调演唱【边关】。林雨洁在狱中的唱段，配合着女声伴唱来渲染牢狱中压抑沉闷的氛围，而不转调进入【诗篇】去抒发主人公林雨洁的革命情怀与思儿、念儿而不得相认的母爱，通过提高商调式的女声旋律来达到烘托气氛的艺术效用。继承中有创新，创新中有继承。曲剧《信仰》采用曲剧传统曲牌【边关】来表现戏曲内容，而河南省曲剧艺术保护传承中心在此之前是极少使用曲牌【边关】的。曲剧《信仰》在这次唱腔设计中再度使用曲牌【边关】，并经过耿玉卿、李全生与乐队乐师们的反复磨合和修改，才最大限度地表现了剧情和刻画了人物形象。

由此可见，耿玉卿等在曲剧《信仰》的唱腔设计方面，始终坚守曲剧曲牌体的基本规律，保持了曲剧质朴、自然、婉转、柔美的特性，旋律悠扬缠绵、抒情性强、生活气息浓郁的风格，融合了新的音乐语汇和素材，包括调式、骨干音、板眼位置、腔体结构等。就整部曲剧《信仰》来讲，每一处的革新与改动都不是空中楼阁、空穴来风，都是有本之木、有源之水，都是遵循于曲剧艺术传统基础之上的改革与创新。"循破皆由我，方得妙曲出。"曲剧《信仰》真正做到了植根于曲剧艺术本体，在保持曲剧艺术特色的前提下进行借鉴、创新与化用，使观众在观看《信仰》时，能够真正做到"演员一亮嗓，便知是曲剧"，同时也极富时代性地对一些情节的唱腔进行创新设计，使之更贴切于情节、人物。曲剧《信仰》在唱腔设计方面遵于传统，又敢于突破与创新，为新时期曲剧艺术的发展做出了积极的尝试与实践。

主题内容：当代情境下历史事件叙述的升格

戏曲并不是简单的、机械的模仿与扮演，它更是对生活深刻的思考。一味地偏执于戏曲艺术的舞台效果和乐感体验，会使戏曲本体所蕴含的主题意指产生弱化与消解。"艺术给予我们的是一个丰富得多的更为生动的和色彩绚丽的现实的形象，是一种对现实的形式构造更为深刻的洞察。"[4]曲剧《信仰》落笔于宏大历史背景之下的具体人物与故事，着眼于对当下时代情境的思考与呼唤。戏曲是生动可感的。它不是一个抽象的概念，而是一个完整的、感性与理性共同驱动的乐感世界的形式化显现。曲剧《信仰》不仅仅是对林雨洁这样一个革命志士慷慨赴死故事的描绘与书写，更是对当下时代的一种观照、思考与启迪。审美受众通过戏曲表演的审美体验来感悟其中所蕴含的思考与内涵。这是一个不断深挖人物形象、情节矛盾的过程，更是一个不断深化、提升戏曲主题意指的过程。

"云含笑，风悄悄，纸鸢蓝天飘，迎着朝阳飞呀飞，尽情唱歌谣……"曲剧《信仰》以独特的艺术视角，讴歌、颂扬信仰的强大力量，展现共产党人为民族大义矢志不渝、不怕牺牲的悲壮情怀。演出过程中，作为背景音乐时常萦绕于情节故事推进过程中的，一首是恬淡自然的童谣，另一首则是气势雄浑的国际歌。刚柔相济的背景音乐所传达出的情感张力,烘托、渲染着一种至真至善的审美追求。危险环境中,林雨洁完成了"母爱——人性——信仰"的不断升华。林雨洁在面对着审问自己的稽查队队长就是自己多年未曾谋面的儿子时,与况为在牢狱中一番关于信仰的对唱与表演层次尤为鲜明。林雨洁作为人母,作为千千万万劳苦大众中的一员,作为一位共产主义信仰者,她的情感有着担忧况为处境的母爱,有着对幸福生活憧憬的人性,更有着要带领最广大劳苦人民过上好日子的党性。"母爱——人性——信仰"条理清晰且层层递进。这样的主要人物情感的极大丰富使得整部剧作也变得饱满,富有艺术张力和感染力。白色恐怖下的亲情和党性、严刑拷打里的抉择和考验,都凭借着演员扎实而娴熟的唱腔、考究而投入的动作被呈现出来,从而将《信仰》的主题旨趣在戏剧舞台上进行阐释和颂扬。林雨洁在生死与信仰面前选择了信仰;况兆年、谢婉云夫妇在安逸生活与民族大义间选择了民族大义;况为、况梅在黑暗与光明中选择了光明……剧作中,林雨洁、况兆年、谢婉云、况为、况梅,还有李副官等,代表着不同阶层、不同身份的有着共同信仰追求的人。正是这些人用信仰烛照这世界,映照出了那些背叛革命者的猥琐与阴险,也映照出了未来的希望与美好。

曲剧《信仰》通过"毁灭"的悲剧感以及"超越"的崇高感,给予观众更为深层的净化,从而自我省察,熔铸信仰。剧作将白色恐怖下的千千万万革命者中的一个缩影——林雨洁的故事画卷式地铺展开来,娓娓道来的不仅仅是这样一个故事,这其中更是氤氲着改编者、编曲者和导演者等助益这部曲剧《信仰》展示给世人的艺术家们的思考。《信仰》有着极为崇高的语汇命名,其所演绎的却是一出令人心胸激荡的悲剧。鲁迅先生在《再论雷峰塔的倒掉》中说过,"悲剧就是将人生有价值的东西毁灭给人看"。[5]《信仰》将一个共产主义者"毁灭"了,但是她所代表的崇高的信仰却真真正正地活了过来,更是唤醒了群众(况兆年、谢婉云夫妇等)的觉醒。王明山未像以往的政治题材戏曲那样详细讲述主人公是如何成为英雄人物的过程以及周围环境的帮助,另辟蹊径地将戏曲的开端设置成一位有着崇高信仰的女子面对母子亲情与党性信仰而选择牺牲小我、成就大我的"毁灭"过程进行叙事,最大限度地引发观众的"共情"。用革命最低潮时的崇高信仰和人物故事去警醒当下社会的信仰缺失问题,引人深思。一个人的死亡并不是最悲哀的,最悲哀的莫过于信仰的死亡。《信仰》带给审美受众以崇高感的审美体验。一位共产主义者母亲愿意为了普罗大众的未来而革命,愿意为此诀别自己刚刚相认的儿子,愿意舍弃自己宝贵的生命,必是源于最为崇高的信仰。朗吉弩斯认为:"崇高的风格是一颗伟大心灵的回声"。[6]康德认为,"崇高提高了我们的精神力量超过平常的尺度,而让我们在内心里发现另一种抵抗的能力,这赋予我们勇气。"[7]他所说的"另一种抵抗的能力"就是指主体的超越精神。当审美受众在观看曲剧《信仰》这样一部具有崇高的超越精神的戏曲时,审美主体不再是"日常的实用的自我"而是"观照的自我"[8],观众会自我观照、审视,得到净化;审美对象也不再是对象本身,而是审美主体灌注生命体验的形象,是主体生命的另一种存在形式。因而,曲剧《信仰》的崇高感能够更为深层次地净化观众的心灵,使之重新审视自我,重新熔铸信仰,有勇气成为具有超越精神的人,即有崇高信仰的人。

结　语

曲剧《信仰》在改编、音乐、导演、舞美等各方面做了全方位的探索与实践,取得了不俗的艺术成就。戏曲文本方面,角色形象丰满,情节矛盾激烈;唱腔设计方面,重拾属调【老剪剪花】,突破创造【摇板书韵】;主题意指方面,故事主题清晰,戏曲内涵深刻。《信仰》可以说是在传承传统曲剧艺术的基础上,又带有一股明媚的戏曲改良春风,剧作思维方式、唱腔设计技巧和戏曲主题内蕴等都较传统曲剧艺术有所突破与创新,甚至是在一些方面做到了重新定义曲剧艺术编创方法与技艺的程度。戏曲艺术是发展着的艺术,传统并不意味着一成不变,用僵化的戏曲编创思维对待观众,令其不习惯、不喜欢,甚至是反感都实属正常。在曲剧《信仰》每一次演出过后进行调整与修改的过程中,可以看到该剧的主创团队是抱着对审美受众负责、对曲剧艺术负责的崇高艺术信仰在做尝试和努力。曲剧《信仰》也绝不仅仅是讲了一个革命故事、告诉观众一个道理那样简单。《信仰》真正做到了让审美受众在该剧的情境中自我引导、自我投入、自我重塑信仰。这样的《信仰》不仅是一个戏曲故事,更是一部呼应时代、重铸信仰的佳作。正如彭吉象所言,好的艺术作品"既是内容与形式的统一,又是感性与理性的统一",在这个意义上,曲剧《信仰》无疑是优秀的艺术作品,具有深厚的艺术价值和借鉴意义。

参考文献:

[1] 莱辛. 拉奥孔 [M]. 朱光潜译. 北京:人民文学出版社,1997:28.

[2] 蒋孔阳主编. 二十世纪西方美学名著选(下册)[M]. 上海:复旦大学出版社,1987:19.

[3] 时白林. 黄梅戏音乐发展历程辨析 [J]. 星海音乐学院学报,2014(4):4.

[4] 蒋孔阳主编. 二十世纪西方美学名著选(下册)[M]. 上海:复旦大学出版社,1987:24.

[5] 鲁迅. 鲁迅全集(第一卷)[M]. 北京:人民文学出版社,1956:297.

[6] 朗吉弩斯. 论崇高 [M]// 缪灵珠. 缪灵珠美学译文集(第一卷). 北京:中国人民大学出版社,1998:184.

[7] 康德. 判断力批判 [M]. 邓晓芒译. 北京:商务印书馆,1985:101.

[8] 朱光潜. 西方美学史 [M]. 北京:人民文学出版社,1964:261.

Be Staying, Be Together
—On the Artistic Creation of the Opera *"Belief"*

Abstract: The Henan Opera Art Protection and Heritage Center tried to adapt the drama *"Communist Manifesto"* with a brushstroke of the times, creating a large-scale modern opera *"Belief"*. The *"Belief"* of Quju Opera inherits and innovates in the text adaptation and vocal design. With the carrier of the art of the opera, the story of the communist believers in the white terror era is unyielding and heroic, which praises the communists for their party-based beliefs and national ethics to sacrifice the self-creation and the emotional choices that make them moving. The breakthrough of the tradition of the opera and the design of the sound chamber also made a useful attempt and practice for the development of the art in the new era. The *"Belief"* of Quju Opera is an excellent work with high artistic achievements and strong contemporary significance.

Key Words: *"Belief"*; Quju Opera; adaptation; arrangement

Created by Henan Opera Art Protection and Inheritance Center, the large-scale modern Quju Opera "*Belief*" is an adaptation of Tang Dong's and Pu Xun's drama "*Communist Manifesto*", composed by Geng Yuqing and Li Quansheng, directed by Huang Zaimin, and costarred by Fang Suzhen, Yang Shuaixue and other famous artists. "*Belief*" was successfully staged in Zhumadian Convention and Exhibition Center, the main venue of the 8th Yellow River Drama Festival, which just ended (the premiere was in Henan Art Center on August 24, 2018), and won the gold medal in the competition. The opera depicted a magnificent picture of the belief cast by revolutionary soldiers in the era of war using exquisite and melodious opera art. The opera makes ideological content visualized. From the opera text, director's arrangement, actor's interpretation to the coordination of lighting, stage design and sound band, the Quju "*Belief*" is an image presentation with excellent effect, which contains a deep excavation, sublimation, condensation and release of the ideological content of "*Belief*" by the artistic creators (adaptors, directors, musicians, actors, etc.). The "*Belief*" has made a beneficial attempt in text transplantation and editing. The singing style design is a strengthening and breakthrough of opera consciousness. Meanwhile, the level of theme meaning has reached the height of "maternal love— humanity—belief". And it has raised many thought-provoking questions in the form of artistic practice from creation to performance, which is an outstanding achievement in the development of Henan Opera in the new era.

Opera Text: Perfect Integration of Characters, Plot and Artistic Techniques

The opera "*Belief*" adapted from the drama "*Communist Manifesto*" is a useful attempt to transplant Henan Opera texts in the new era. Wang Mingshan, the playwright of the opera, has a clear and definite integrity in the creation of traditional operas with historical themes, that is, to restore the historical situation and create art in a targeted manner in the real historical situation. A play that turns history into a drama situation and makes the era whoop through artistic creation is by no means a flat character image and a simple story frame pieced together by stacking historical events and repeating emotional images. *"Belief"* is an artistic eruption that combines the passion and life experience of the playwright (the original writer and the adaptation writer). It is a masterpiece of Henan Opera in the new era that integrates the true nature of history and artistic creation.

The opera *"Belief"* tells a true, simple and unconventional story under the background of history. On the basis of the story line of the drama *"Communist Manifesto"*, Wang Mingshan broke free from the shackles and restrictions of the original characters and plot, boldly and delicately reinterpreted and arranged the contradictions between the characters and plot in *"Belief"*, which makes it and the drama *"Communist Manifesto"* similar but completely different. The opera strives to create a true and realistic historical situation, restoring and reappearing the historical background of the communists' unswerving determination and belief in the low tide of the 1927 revolution with extremely chronological and pictorial strokes. The story told in *"Belief"* takes place under such a background of the era. After the Great Revolution failed, Jiang Jieshi betrayed the revolution and plotted to massacre communists. Lin Yujie (played by Fang Suzhen), a female Communist Party member, was rescued by Kuang Mei (played by Jin Hongjuan), a female college student, and brought back to her home to hide when she escaped capture by the Kuomintang military police. Lin Yujie was saved by the girl whose father was Kuang Zhaonian (played by Zhang Zhuanshe), the ex-husband of Lin Yujie. After that, Lin Yujie was unfortunately arrested and imprisoned. What is unexpected is that the head of the Kuomintang inspection team who interrogated her was her son, Kuang Wei (played by Chang Xiangke), whom she had not seen for 15 years. The spy chief Shen Zhuo (played by Yang Shuaixue) and others used kinds of cruel methods against Lin Yujie. Finally, they even conspired to implicate Lin

Yujie in Kuang Zhaonian's family. Lin Yujie, a believer, was brutally killed by counter-revolutionaries such as Shen Zhuo.

To play its role, opera must have vivid and sensible characters. The portrayal of characters from Wang Mingshan really hit the spot. The relationship between the characters and conflicts in "*Belief*" are bound up with each other, and the characters in the opera cannot be simply and mechanically divided into two parts as positive characters and negative characters. Wang Mingshan dialectically distinguished the characters from the Three Principles of the People, making the characters more subtle and full. Lin Yujie, Shen Zhuo and Kuang Wei, who are also imitators of the Three Principles of the People, made different choices when facing their beliefs. Lin Yujie, who joined the revolutionary party in her early years, was an imitator of the Three Principles of the People and later joined the Communist Party, being a believer in Communism. As the hero in "*Belief*", she is a microcosm of the countless communists in those turbulent years and one of the people with lofty ideals who are trying to save the nation from danger. She believes in the Three Principles of the People and Communism. She believes that they can save the nation from danger and the people from the plight. Lin Yujie believes in the spiritual core of the Three Principles of the People and Communism. As the most vicious villain in "*Belief*", Shen Zhuo has his own "belief" and believes in a "dead" Three Principles of the People. The Three Principles of the People, which Shen Zhuo held as a principle, are as exclusive and intolerant as Jiang Jieshi, which is contrary to the spirit of the Three Principles of the People put forward by Dr. Sun Yat-sen. Shen Zhuo is also a microcosm of Jiang Jieshi's betrayal of the revolution, and when Captain Pan led a search of Kuang Zhaonian's mansion at the beginning of the opera, Shen Zhuo sang:

> *"Sir! Now, we need to eliminate the rebels and communists,*
> *President Jiang has called on all sides to follow him.*
> *It is not a crime to kill a thousand people wrongly.*

If you let one go, you will regret it.

The tight situation calls for more caution.

And never touch a hammer with an egg. "

This is contrary to the spirit of the Three Principles of the People, but it is determined to believe in the belief of "President Jiang" and act in both ways. Shen Zhuo only believed in the "Three Principles of the People" told by "President Jiang", a "cover" for betraying revolutionaries to hide the shame. Besides, it is obviously different from Lin Yujie's and Shen Zhuo's right and wrong. His own thinking on belief is a process from tangle, contradiction and perplexity to sprouting, hope and sincerity. Besides, Kuang Wei thought his belief is the most "pure" for Three Principles of the People, but he was awakened by Lin Yujie's words in the interrogation process and sang:

"Lin Yujie's words stirred people's hearts,

What power can make her turn her back on death?

How many teachings have I received in the Huangpu Military Academy?

The Three Principle of the People have been engraved in my heart deeply.

The Communist Party does not run counter to Mr. Wang's teachings.

I don't see any resemblance between them.

Whose fault is it and whose right is it?

It's hard to tell the truth. "

Lin Yujie's devotion to belief and her righteously facing the death threat both made Kuang Wei feel a sense of admiration from the bottom of his heart. Even though he said Lin Yujie was a "communist fugitive", he felt doubt about his beliefs. Being different from Shen Zhuo's, Kuang Wei's belief is in confusion, even a bit being mechanical in the "Three Principles of the People", but is by no means hypocritical or false. At the same time, there are some differences about beliefs between Kuang Wei and Lin YuJie. Kuang

Wei's belief is far from Lin Yujie's belief in Communism. However, Kuang Wei has sprouted and yearned for Communism belief in some plot conflicts.

Emotions and images should be attached to specific dramatic character relationships and plot contradictions and expressed through events and feelings, rather than simply shaping flat characters and fabricating conventional stories. The opera "*Belief*" adapted by Wang Mingshan is unique in the arrangement of the contradiction between the character relationship and the plot. The relationship is interrelated, fettered and contradictory among the main characters, the primary and secondary characters, etc. Besides, the relationship between Lin Yujie and Shen Zhuo is the contradictions of belief, parties, life and death, justice and power. On the contrary, the contradiction between Lin Yujie and Kuang Wei is the contradiction of belief, mutual recognition and farewell, the nation's sense of honor and mother-child affection, etc. In prison, Lin Yujie wants white paper, string and bamboo sticks to make a butterfly kite, which makes Kuang Wei feel more friendly. This is the call and cry for mother-child bonding between them. LinYujie is contradictory when she faced her son was interrogating her but feared to recognize him. Kuang Wei was questioned by Lin Yujie about his belief and saw butterfly kites thinking of his mother's thoughts, which made the relationship between them become extremely dramatic anxiety and contradiction. The author's depiction and setting of the characters in the play is simple. At the beginning, Kuang Zhaonian and Xie Wanyun feared that Lin Yujie's arrival would bring misfortune to the family, but later they were influenced by her awe-inspiring righteousness and shocked by the communist belief, and admired and supported the emotional changes of the communist cause. Kuang Mei is just like a fire of revolutionary hope in such a gloomy counter-revolutionary struggle environment. She is educated in school and yearns for progress in thought and emotion. Even under the threat of counter-revolutionaries such as Shen Zhuo, she still keeps a firm and brave heart. The situation in the opera makes the plot conflict suddenly tense because of the arrangement of the "brother" Aide Li who served on the inspection team to rescue Lin Yujie. At the same time, it also endows Aide Li with an open assumption of the identity of the character, and provides an external motivation for the change of belief from wavering to thorough understanding. Lessing once pointed out in *Laocoon* : "It is always the most illusory and difficult to establish universal laws for human emotions. The network of emotions and passions is subtle and complicated, and even the most rigorous speculation is difficult to clearly draw a clue from it." [1] The handling of the relationship between the characters in the opera is both complex and clear. From the opera text we can see the profound skills of the author in handling the conflicts among the characters, relationships and plots in it. That is because the images of opera characters have never been defined simply and cannot be explained accurately in a few words. The images of opera characters need plots and stories to express and elaborate, and plots and stories also need conflicts and contradictions to intensify and promote. This requires the playwright to regularize the complex human emotional experience and low-level simple perceptual cognition for opera creation practice.

As a work that is still being continuously improved and perfected, the opera "*Belief* " is somewhat lengthy and tardy in its background narration and emotional elaboration, slowing down the progress of plot and intensification of contradiction. While giving a thorough account of the background and character relationship of the whole story, the play takes roughly two scenes, which obviously makes the audience's aesthetic expectation eroded by the previous large-scale elaboration. Taking too much time to narrate the background and elaborate the emotion makes the narrative of the opening story's entering the theme and the audience's entering the drama appear sluggish. Cassirer once said : "No one can deny that artistic works can give us the greatest pleasure, perhaps the most lasting and strongest pleasure that human nature can feel." [2] This is also a kind of expectant psychology of the audience for opera arts. In the process of opera creation, attention should be paid to the compactness of the plot, so that the relationship between the characters and the conflicts becomes fierce, which may make the watching experience of "*Belief*" more enjoyable.

Vocal Design: Inheritance and Innovation of Traditional Opera Vocal Art

The vocal design of Quju "*Belief*" is a strengthening and breakthrough of drama consciousness. Geng Yuqing, a national first-class composer, and Li Quansheng, a national third-class composer, personally conducted the "spontaneous" fusion and innovation on the basis of inheriting and developing the singing style of traditional operas. Shi Bailin once mentioned in *Selected Vocal Tunes of Shi Bailin's Huangmei Opera Music*: "First, try to develop the special features and advantages of traditional vocal tunes; second, try to show the characters' thoughts, feelings and inner world to the audience; third, do not repeat yourself and strive to surpass yourself." [3] The demand of audience's aesthetic for opera has been increasing gradually since the development of opera entered the new era. If the singing style of opera follows the rules and remains the same, it will inevitably be difficult to absorb and develop audience with more diversified ages. However, if we are blindly seeking new things and changes, we will inevitably lose a lot of the original audience. It is gratifying to note that Geng Yuqing and Li Quansheng boldly made creative use and attempt in the aria of "*Belief*" on the basis of following the rules of composition, and combined the aria characteristics of the actors such as Fang Suzhen and Yang Shuaixue in the opera to make up and design. This is a strengthening and breakthrough in the creation of the aria of the opera in the new era. The opera "*Belief*" has made great attempts and practices in all aspects in singing:

One is to boldly use Gong Diao in the opera "*Belief*". The use of the C and D tones has properly solved a series of problems caused by the "same tone" of the male and female actors in the singing process: female voice can reach it easily and male voice cannot reach the top. In the Quju Opera, the male voice uses the C tone and the female voice uses the D tone. Both male and female actors can stretch freely in the singing process and give full play to their respective vocal range's individual characteristics. This also requires actors and musicians to keep pace with the times and dare to break through, especially self-breaking. It is worth noting that in the accompaniment process, the band used two Quhu (a C tone and a D tone) to perform (accompany) on a rotating basis during the performance. During the whole performance, the zither changed its tone several times. Undoubtedly, these creative changes in singing and accompaniment are extremely challenging for actors and bands, and have never been easily tried before in the history of opera performance. The actors of the play, mainly male vocalists from Yang Shuaixue, female vocalists from Fang Suzhen and Liu Yanli, and Guzheng musician Wang Jian, are perfecting and adjusting constantly. As the key to the performance of the opera, only when the actors and the orchestra accompany each other perfectly, and the orchestra's various musical instruments are properly performed and connected, can it be regarded as real success. From the practice of many performances since the premiere, the performance and singing using the two Gong Diao at the same time have been recognized and praised by opera experts and scholars and opera fans.

Second, the creative use of Quju [Yao Ban Shu Yun]. [Shu Yun] is a highly used piece of music in the art of opera, with strong expressive force and beautiful melody, such as the aria in "*Roll Mat Drum*" (Xiao Cang Wa), "*Kou Zhun Bei Xue*" (Xia Chao Lai), "*With the Snow*" (Jin Ri Shi) and so on. Because the melody of [Shu Yun] is very strong, it is also very flexible in the process of composing music. In Quju "*Belief*", it shows the game and psychology of Lin Yujie, Shen Zhuo, Kuang Zhaonian and Xie Wanyun at the same time, and renders a chilling atmosphere of silence. So the best way is to speed up and improve the overall rhythm of the performance. However, many musical performances before this followed the tradition of musical drama, and there was no way to apply and learn from it. Geng Yuqing, a national first-class composer, dared to be a pioneer. After many communications with the playwright, actors and bands, he changed his draft several times and didn't bring it to completion until the fifth draft. Among them, the biggest difficulty is to maintain the mode characteristics, main tone and key tone of [Shu Yun], and at the same time, to use a new rhythm for self-creation, which will greatly test the tacit cooperation and musical skills of the four actors, Fang Suzhen, Yang Shuaixue, Zhang Zhuanshe and Liu Yanli. There is also a question about different tones of male and female actors. Although the difficulty truly exists, the singing skills of several famous opera stars, such as Fang Suzhen and Yang Shuaixue, are very profound. After countless exercises, running-in and connection, they finally overcame such difficulties and achieved the expected artistic effect in the actual performance. During the process, it also created a new singing method for Quju art in the new era, which has far-reaching practical significance for the development of Quju music creation and provides a new paradigm for the compilation of contemporary Quju.

Third, singing in the tune of genus [Lao Jian Jian Hua], Geng Yuqing lowered the C key 35235 by four degrees to 72672.

Figure: 35235 for C and 72672 for 4 lower degrees

First of all, it is to solve the problem of male voice range. Secondly, it is to highlight the personality characteristics of the characters. Let the singing style design be more suitable for each actor and suit his own circumstances. The singing of actors should not only conform to the mood of the opera role, but also not need to worry about the singing pressure caused by the inappropriate range. After this change, the part of singing for Shen Zhuo was completely integrated with the sinister identity and modality of the reactionary spy chief. At the beginning of the rehearsal, everybody felt uncomfortable with this change, but after repeated negotiation and running with Yang Shuaixue, who played the police chief in the play, and after adjustments, modifications and promotions, this aria was highly praised by the opera experts.

Fourth, sing [Bian Guan] in F key. The aria sung by Lin Yujie in prison, accompanied by female singing, plays up the depressing atmosphere in prison, instead of transferring to [Shi Pian] to express the revolutionary feelings of protagonist Lin Yujie and the maternal love that can't be recognized with the longing for her son. The artistic effect of setting off the atmosphere is achieved by improving the female melody in commercial mode. Inheritance and innovation are integrated into each other. The traditional Qupai (Border Pass) of Quju is used to express the content of the opera, while the Henan Quju Art Protection and Inheritance Center seldom used it before that. However, after repeatedly adjusted and revised by Geng Yuqing, Li Quansheng and the musicians of the band, the opera "*Belief*" used it again in this aria design, showing the plot and portraying the characters greatly.

From this, we can see that Geng Yuqing and others have always adhered to the basic rules of the style of "*Belief*" in its aria design. They have maintained the simple, natural, tactful and gentle characteristics of the Quju Opera, with melodious and lingering melodies, strong lyricism and flavor of life. They have integrated new musical vocabulary and materials, including modes, key notes, blackboard positions, cavity structure, etc. Actually, every innovation and change for the opera "*Belief*" is meaningful, and it is a reform and innovation based on the artistic tradition of opera. "I am the one who follows the path of destruction, and I will be the one who makes the most of it." "*Belief*" is truly rooted in the artistic noumenon of Quju, and it can be used for reference, innovation and application on the premise of maintaining the artistic characteristics of Quju. When watching it, the audience can truly know that the opera is a musical play as soon as the actor sings. At the same time, the "*Belief*" also innovates the singing style of some plots with the characteristics of the times so as to make them more appropriate to the plots and characters. It follows the tradition in its aria design and dares to break through and innovate, making positive attempts and practices for the development of Quju art in the new era.

Subject Content: Upgrade of Historical Event Narration in Contemporary Context

Opera is not a simple, mechanical imitation and play, it is a profound reflection on life. If we blindly cling to the stage effect and musical experience of opera art, we will weaken and dissolve the theme implied in opera itself. "Art gives us a much richer, more vivid and colorful image of reality, and it is a deeper insight into the formal structure of reality." [4] The opera "*Belief*" is written with specific characters and stories under a grand historical background, focusing on thinking and calling for the current situation of the times. The opera is vivid and sensible. It is not an abstract concept, but a formal manifestation of a complete, sensual and rational world of music. "*Belief*" is not only a description of the story of Lin Yujie, a revolutionary who went to die generously, but also a reflection, thinking and enlightenment of the era. The audience understands the thinking and connotation contained in opera performance through its aesthetic experience. This is a process of continuously digging up the contradictions between the characters and plots, and it is also a process of continuously deepening and upgrading the meaning of the theme of opera.

"The clouds are smiling, the wind is quiet, the kite is flying in the blue sky, flying under the rising sun, singing and singing ..." The opera "*Belief*" eulogizes and praises the powerful force of belief with a unique artistic perspective, showing the solemn and stirring feelings of the communists, who are unswerving in their national sense of honor and are not afraid of sacrifice. There are two songs as the background music during the performance, one is a serene and natural nursery rhyme while the other is a forceful international song. The emotional tension conveyed by the hard and soft background music exaggerates a kind of aesthetic pursuit that is true and perfect. In the dangerous environment, Lin Yujie completed the continuous sublimation of "maternal love—humanity—belief". When Lin Yujie was confronted with the captain of the inspection team who interrogated her—the son whom she had not met for many years, the emotion between them, by the antiphonal singing and performance about belief in prison, reached a distinctive level. As a mother, a member of the absolutely toiling masses, and a communist believer, Lin Yujie has many different feelings, including a mother's love of worrying about the situation, a human nature of longing for a happy life, and a party spirit of leading the most toiling people to live a good life. The relationship among "maternal love—humanity-belief" is clear and progressive. This kind of main character's emotion is extremely rich, making the play full of artistic tension and appeal. The affection and party spirit under the white terror, and the choice and test in the torture all rely on the actors' solid and skillful singing, exquisite and devoted actions to interpret and celebrate the theme and purport of "*Belief*" on the stage. Lin Yujie chose belief firmly among different choices. Kuang Zhaonian and Xie Wanyun chose the second one between their comfortable life and the national sense of honor. Kuang Wei and Kuang Mei chose light in darkness and light... In this play, Lin Yujie, Kuang Zhaonian, Xie Wanyun, Kuang Wei, Kuang Mei and Aide Li, et al. represent the people of different classes and identities who share common beliefs and pursuits. It is these people who illuminate the world with belief, reflecting the lewdness and insidiousness of those who betrayed revolutionaries, as well as the hope and beauty of the future.

The Quju Opera "*Belief*" gives the audience a deeper purification through the tragic sense of "destruction" and the lofty sense of "transcendence", thus self-examining and casting belief. The story of Lin Yujie, an epitome of revolutionaries under the white panic, unfolds in a scroll style, telling not only such a story, but also the thoughts of the artists (the adaptor, arranger and director, etc.) that help this play to be shown to the world. "*Belief*" is a lofty name, but what it deduces is a stirring tragedy. In *Re-discussing the Fall of Leifeng Pagoda*, Lu Xun once said that "tragedy is the destruction of valuable things in life for people to see" [5] *Belief* "destroyed" a communist, but the noble belief she represented really came to life and aroused the awakening of the masses (Kuang Zhaonian, Xie Wanyun, et al.). Wang Mingshan did not elaborate on how the protagonist became a hero and how the surrounding environment helped her. In a different way, the beginning of the opera is set up as a woman with lofty belief who chooses to sacrifice her ego to achieve greater self to narrate the process of "destruction" in the face of mother-son bonding and party spirit belief, thus arousing the audience's "empathy" to the greatest extent. With the lofty belief and character stories at the lowest ebb of the revolution to alert the lack of belief in the present society and make people think deeply. A person who loses his belief is the saddest thing. "*Belief*" brings aesthetic experience with lofty feeling to the audience. A communist mother's willingness to make a revolution for the future of the general public, to bid farewell to her son whom she had just recognized, and to give up her precious life must be rooted in the most noble belief. Longinus argued that "noble is the echo of a great heart". [6] Kant believes that, "Sublimity improves our spiritual strength beyond the normal standard, and allows us to find another resistance in our hearts, which gives us courage." [7] What he said was "another kind of resistance" refers to the transcendence of the subject. When the audience watches a drama with lofty transcendence spirit, such as the Quju Opera "*Belief*", the aesthetic subject is no longer the "daily practical self" but the "contemplative self" [8], and the audience will observe, examine and purify themselves. The aesthetic object is no longer the object itself, but the image in which the aesthetic subject infuses life experience, which is another form of existence of the subject's life. Therefore, the lofty feeling of the opera "*Belief*" can purify the hearts of the audience in a deeper level, so that they can re-examine themselves, recast their beliefs, and have the courage to become the people with transcendent spirit.

Conclusion

The opera "*Belief*" has made all-round exploration and practice in adaptation, music, direction, stage design and other aspects, and has achieved great artistic achievements. In terms of drama texts, the characters are full of images and the plot is contradictory. In the aspect of singing design, it has regained its original tune of "Lao Jian Jian Hua" and broken through the creation of "Yao Ban Shu Yun". In terms of theme meaning, the story has a clear theme and the opera has profound connotation. Based on the inheritance of traditional opera art, "*Belief*" is also with a bright and beautiful spring breeze for opera improvement at the same time. Its thinking mode, singing design skills and theme connotation of opera have made breakthroughs and innovations compared with traditional opera art, and even have redefined the editing methods and skills of opera art in some aspects. Tradition does not mean invariability; opera art is a developing art. During adjusting and revising the opera "*Belief*" after each performance, we can see that the main creative team of "*Belief*" is trying and making efforts with the lofty artistic belief of being responsible for the audience and the art of the opera. And it is not just a revolutionary story, telling the audience a truth as simple as that. The opera "*Belief*" truly enables the audience to guide, devote to themselves and reshape their beliefs. It is not only a drama story, but also a masterpiece that echoes the times and recasts belief. As Peng Jixiang said, a good work of art "is not only the unity of content and form, but also the unity of sensibility and rationality". Undoubtedly, in this sense, "*Belief* " is an excellent work of art with profound artistic value and reference significance.

References:

[1] Lessing. Laocoon [M]. Translated by Zhu Guangqian. Beijing: People's Literature Publishing House, 1997:28.

[2] Jiang Kongyang, Editor-in-Chief. Selected Works of Western Aesthetics in the 20th Century [M]. Shanghai: Fudan University Press, 1987:19.

[3] Shi bailin. Differentiation and analysis of the development process of Huangmei Opera music [J]. Journal of Xinghai Conservatory of Music, 2014(4):4.

[4] Jiang Kongyang, Editor-in-Chief. Selected Works of Western Aesthetics in the 20th Century [M]. Shanghai: Fudan University Press, 1987:24.

[5] Lu Xun. Lu Xun's complete works (Vol. 1) [M]. Beijing: People's Literature Publishing House, 1956:297.

[6] Longinus. On Sublime [M]// Miao Lingzhu. Volume 1 of Miao Lingzhu's Aesthetic Translation Collection [M]. Beijing: Renmin University of China Press, 1998:184.

[7] Kant. Critique of Judgment [M]. Translated by Deng Xiaomang. Beijing: The Commercial Press, 1985:101.

[8] Zhu Guangqian. History of Western Aesthetics [M].Beijing: People's Literature Publishing House, 1964:261.

在融摄中西美学思想中超越本土传统

——论樊粹庭剧作的美学成就

摘要：樊粹庭先生被誉为"现代豫剧之父"。他的戏剧创作成熟于"五四"新文化思潮之中，融涉中西美学思想，逐渐形成了独具特色的戏剧艺术思想并付诸于自己的创作实践中。其所编创的豫剧《麻风女》正是这一艺术实践的代表作。该剧作博采众家之长，构思奇巧，意蕴深刻，是超越传统豫剧艺术的一次成功尝试。《麻风女》的艺术之美主要表现在对西方文艺思想的兼收并蓄之美、选题构思的镂冰雕琼之美和剧作况味的兴发感动之美，为当代戏剧创作提供了一种新的审美范式。其关于戏剧的创想和实践开拓了现代豫剧的发展道路，丰富了豫剧艺术美的内涵，具有较强的理论价值和现实借鉴意义。

关键词：樊粹庭戏剧；中西美学思想；《麻风女》；融涉超越

二十世纪初期，是中西文化交融、碰撞最为激烈的时期。著名豫剧作家樊粹庭的学习和成长阶段正处在这个变动激荡的时代。传统文化的熏陶、西方文化的影响交互发生作用，造就了樊粹庭多元的文化积淀和先进的文艺理念他融涉中西美学思想，逐渐形成了独具特色的戏剧美学思想。他所创作的一批构思巧妙、主题鲜明、意蕴丰富的"现代豫剧"，体现了他这种新颖独特的思想。综观樊粹庭的戏剧创作，其美学成就大致可以概括为对西方文艺思想的兼收并蓄之美、选题构思的镂冰雕琼之美和剧作况味的兴发感动之美，而这些特点在他的代表作《麻风女》中尤显突出。

一、对西方文艺美学思想的兼收并蓄之美

樊粹庭的剧作《麻风女》（又名《女贞花》,剧本文稿出自河南大学张大新教授编校的《樊粹庭文集·创作剧目》）大意讲了如此一个故事：粤西邱员外之女原本生得国色天香,却不幸染上当地人常患的一种"百药无效"的"麻风病症"。当地传说若诱得外乡男子成婚"冲喜",将病"传"给男方,女子即可痊愈。于是,邱员外便暗合司空浑诱骗了淮南落难书生陈绿琴,假意许他与邱家小姐成婚。岂料想,邱丽玉心地善良,不忍染病给陈绿琴,新婚夜以诚相待,将事情原委和盘托出并为陈绿琴制造染病假象,助陈绿琴逃脱邱府。事后,得知真相的邱员外夫妇一怒之下将病重的邱丽玉逐出家门,送进了麻风院。淳朴厚道的落难书生陈绿琴回到家中拜见老父陈懋,遵从父命"垂帷苦读盼功名",怎料得"时见丽玉在书中"。邱丽玉逃出了麻风院千里寻夫,沿途受尽苦楚,陈绿琴拔得头筹仍不忘丽玉的恩情,曲折之中有情人遂终成眷属。

"从历史发展来看,一种文化对他种文化的吸收总是通过自己的文化眼光和文化框架来进行,也就是要通过自身文化屏幕的过滤,很少会全盘照搬而多半是取其所需。"[1]7 樊粹庭先生在进行戏剧创作之时,正是充分地建立在对传统豫剧的成熟思考之上,批判地借鉴、吸收和融合的一种戏剧美学新尝试。这与樊粹庭先生的个人成长经历和所经受过的戏剧教育有着潜移默化而又深远持久的关系。俄国思想家别林斯基在《文学的幻想》一文中说过："只有遵循不同的道路,人类才能够达到共同的目标",樊粹庭先生对东西方戏剧和传统、现代戏曲兼收并蓄的经历就是一部河南豫剧改良与发展的缩影和简史。多元文化的接受和教育,让樊粹庭先生在学习和实践过程中接触到了更为丰富的戏剧艺术,对河南传统地方戏曲赓续得力,对话剧、京剧等戏剧也是博采众家之长。眼界较以往的剧作者更加开阔,思维更加开放。

樊粹庭幼年即喜爱戏剧,14岁考入开封留欧美预备学校（即现在的河南大学）。他爱戏之心浓烈,常组织同学从事戏剧活动。毕业后曾担任河南省教育厅社会教育推广部主任,足迹遍及全省三分之二以上的城镇和乡村,并深入到各县的豫剧班社,结识了不少名扬一方的艺人。在欣赏和钦佩

他们演唱才能的同时，也看到了他们凄惨的生活境遇和在演出方面存在的诸多问题。至 1934 年，他不顾家庭的反对，毅然弃官从艺，组织陈素真、赵义庭、张子林等豫剧精英，在相国寺创建了"豫声剧院"。从剧场设施到剧团管理、文化教育、编剧导演等方面践行自己"破除陈规，改良豫剧"的初衷，进行了全方位的改革和创新。自从 1935 年 3 月他的处女作《凌云志》，一炮打响之后，他又接连编导上演了《义烈风》《柳绿云》《三拂袖》《涤耻血》《麻风女》《霄壤恨》等。

樊粹庭的戏剧创作思想主要源于其受教育阶段对多元戏剧文化和美学思想的熏染，这深刻影响了他的人生观和世界观。首先是本土文化。樊粹庭在河南这片戏剧的沃土里浸润，河南的话语以及所构成的语境使得他的创作深深地打上了本土文化的印记。其次是对于西方思想的接受与认同，更是"五四"时期新文化运动背景下的广泛影响。义烈的情怀、爱国的精神，乃至题材、故事情节上的承续，樊粹庭所创的剧作中有不少剧目是对中国戏剧优秀传统的延续。但同时，他在"五四"新文化运动的影响下对豫剧的创作也进行了大量的改造。超越传统忠爱主题，樊粹庭剧作的内容更为丰富、主题更为多元、手法也更加多样。得天独厚的艺术成长经历令他可以轻松自如地在文化规训中打开缺口，不断地引入怀疑、探索、创新、否定与认同，兼收并蓄地发展樊粹庭式豫剧美学，从而使他的豫剧剧目创作进入了一个全新的时代。

二、选题构思的镂冰雕琼之美

"由不同传播媒介构成的不同的艺术门类之间就必然存在一种共同性或交融性。"[2]9 樊粹庭剧作《麻风女》取材于晚清小说家宣鼎写的短篇小说《麻风女邱丽玉》，1936 年由他改编成豫剧并成功上演。这绝不仅仅是一部剧作的成功，更是"五四"新文化思潮涌动之下人民的呼唤与剧作者选材构思的"相通共契"。该剧作着笔于旧社会中最无话语权的两类人物形象，使之立为主角，一是"邱丽玉"这类封建社会中的女性角色，纵是富贵员外家的千金小姐，面对"大家长"的安排本应是沉默不语或是苟且认同的，却在不断的压迫和规训下向往着自由、平等，主动地追求自己的爱情；二是"陈绿琴"这类落魄书生的男性角色，遵从其父陈懋的规训，读书谋取功名,在县考中夺了"案首"后,周、刘两家前来提媒,陈绿琴不忘恩情地守住了最后的道德底线和爱情追求,守护着邱丽玉。剧作中打破以往简单的"金榜题名,洞房花烛"草草收尾的套路,着重刻画了邱丽玉和陈绿琴两人对爱情的忠贞不渝。豫剧《麻风女》的上演,由樊粹庭先生运用戏曲综合性展现的方式去描摹、再现和再创造小说家宣鼎笔下的麻风女邱丽玉,所呈现的正是一场同故事原型跨艺术门类的对话。田汉于1919年写给郭沫若的信中曾明确提出"生活艺术化":

"我如是以为我们做艺术家的,一面应把人生的黑暗面暴露出来,排斥世间一切虚伪,立定人生的基本。一方面更当引人入于一种艺术的境界,使生活艺术化。即把人生美化,使人家忘现实生活的苦痛而入于一种陶醉法悦浑然一致之境,才算能尽其能事。"[3]265

这段信摘自宗白华先生的文集,尽管没有细致地展开论述,但其大致的精神旨趣跨越时空地契合了樊粹庭先生对豫剧《麻风女》创作的理念。该剧作将邱员外夫妇等主配角人物形象刻画得丰满、真实而意蕴生动。为人父母者,皆盼望女儿能够嫁得一"门当户对"的人家,无可厚非。邱员外夫妇二人为救女儿听从司空浑的言说诱骗外地青年"冲喜""传病",显尽了封建社会愚昧、迷信的可笑风气;得知女儿并没有痊愈,便将其逐出家门送进麻风院去,其狠心可见一斑。可叹、可笑、可气、可悲。邱丽玉来到陈家庄见到了公爹陈懋,老先生因绿琴投考未归而令家中保童送邱丽玉到女庵暂住。其后从陈懋言辞"真乃怪事!"和保童"俺爷嫌她肮脏,把她送到尼姑庵里啦!"等细节可推断出陈绿琴之父陈懋此刻可谓是五味杂陈,究其症结莫不源自怜惜家中这颗独苗。再说到"邱丽玉",既不似杜丽娘一般的刚烈不屈,又不像戏曲中常见的闺阁小姐枯守绣楼而不敢追求,既温婉、识大体,同时又有着向往自由、爱情的一些早期新文化思潮的萌芽于其中。这些丰满而真实的人物形象必然得益于剧作者樊粹庭先生深厚的艺术积累,将生活艺术化,并将之再现于戏剧舞台之上。"有限、偶然的具体形象里灌注充满了那生活本质的无限、必然的内容。"[2]143艺术化地塑造人物形象,使之从千千万万人中脱胎而成;艺术化地设定故事情节,使之将千千万万的不幸归拢化合成了同感共鸣。"以艺术的理想境界为标准去把现实的人生美化。"[2]43这种艺术创作观念造就了樊粹庭先生戏剧的优美、丰富、有条理、有意义。

"巧借中国本土戏曲的美学样式去推演西方式社会革命精神,以便唤醒沉睡的中国普通民众,已然成为一种跨文化交融的艺术选择。"[2]19《麻风女》不同于以往豫剧的"才子佳人"戏,构思巧妙独特,情节裁云剪水。在樊粹庭先生创作的诸多剧作中,才子与佳人均经受了挫折,而不再是一方经受挫折,另一方痴情守候这样的故事架构。《麻风女》的创排虽未完全地跳脱明清以来"才子佳人"戏的大框架和大团圆结局,但诚然是豫剧选题构思创作的一次大的进步。樊粹庭先生纵览漫长的戏剧发展历程中那些留存下来的"才子佳人"戏,又与自己对于戏剧美学的观念交融、分析,最终铸就了这部具有鲜明的"樊式"美学特色,不同寻常的"才子佳人"戏。

陈绿琴险些染病而幸得良缘,郎有情,妾有意;陈绿琴遵从父命考取功名仍不忘邱丽玉的恩情;邱丽玉染病在先,其后又经历了被父母逐出家门、他乡寻夫却遭尽世人冷眼。该剧一反以往才子多磨难而佳人空守候的剧情,将剧情矛盾与挫折更多地向女方倾斜,侧面显露出"五四"以来女性"平等"观念的觉醒。尝试横跨以"五四"为时代界限的传统戏曲文化与新多元戏曲文化这两种异质文化,探讨"新旧"异质文化接触、碰撞时河南豫剧创排的变异情况。显然,假借陈绿琴、邱丽玉二人之口呈现的大段唱词与念白表述了一个伫立在时代变革之际的戏剧人的质朴心愿,对美好情感的向往和追求,对封建社会的蔑视与批判。就此一点,樊粹庭先生对于戏剧的精妙构思和选题无疑是发时代之先声的。

世界上不存在"一种绝对属于本土的、未经任何'污染'的话语"[1]56,樊粹庭戏剧将故事发展脉络梳理并经过精巧的构思,使情节更为曲折和动人,如同苏州园林一般,构思奇巧,曲径通幽。戏剧,本身就是在不同文学、艺术元素所构成的文化场域中生长、滋生的产物。全然隔绝,只能加速这样的艺术走向消亡。樊粹庭先生则是以一种开明的心态和开放的思维进行戏剧创作,悦纳并尝试着融涉不同的价值观和新思想于自己的戏剧创作之中,通过交融或消解的方式让剧作故事发展脉络简洁明了,情节曲折动人。在这样的脉络树下延展开的脉络无疑是扣人心弦、引人入胜的。

三、剧作况味的兴发感动之美

　　"心里印着美的意象，常受美的意象浸润，自然也可以少存些浊念。"[4]25 切合着朱光潜先生无功利审美"意象"论观点来看，更多的人喜欢以道德层面的评判标准来谈论文艺作品，强拉硬拽地想要把艺术作品的审美归置到现实世界里去。观剧者是将现实的道德规范化用到了戏剧观演的生态场域之中，而忽视或迷失了艺术与现实存在的间离性。审美体验的直接目的绝不仅是令身处其中者受到教育或陶冶，但陶冶情操却是通过其过程中的戏剧教育性而得以体现的。樊粹庭先生所创排的豫剧《麻风女》中，邱丽玉、陈绿琴等人物形象充分体现了梁启超先生的"仁者不忧"，其根源便是儒家、道家等本土哲学思想。观众在审美体验过程中，虽沉浸其中，却也经由剧作者巧思安排的"梗"而间离出化境，使观者既保持一种身临其境、身经其事的感官体验，同时也具有一种道德与艺术双重标榜的戏剧观演间离效果。观剧者既悲悯邱丽玉、陈绿琴二人的悲惨曲折遭遇，同时也为邱员外夫妇、陈父的可笑行径感到不耻。其中，邱员外夫妇与陈父的初衷与本质又有着些许微妙的区别，更有层次蕴含其中。"逐女"一场"邱丽玉在秀阁泪流满面"一出中，邱员外夫妇逐女儿出家门，其父唱道：

　　"喝住丫头好大胆，

　　讲出此言真疯癫。

　　我今送你麻风院，

　　父女从此断了缘。"[5]230

毅然决然地要将女儿逐出家门送去麻风院。而樊粹庭先生在《麻风女》"探病"一场则写下了其母催舟前去麻风院探望女儿的唱词：

　　"叫家院你与我将身催动，

　　背员外探女儿走上一程。

　　实可叹小女儿真太薄命，

　　身染了麻风病赶出门庭。"[5]232

纵然是高门大户，父亲与母亲的对待与处理总还是有着层次的变化和差别，邱员外恼自己的女儿邱丽玉不懂得爹娘一份好心，为救她性命不惜重金诱骗陈绿琴进府，一怒之下将自己的女儿逐出家门，断绝关系，自然是发乎情理的。邱夫人不好违逆邱员外的意思，顺从了他将女儿逐出家门的决定；而后背着邱员外唤家丁陪着去麻风院探望女儿，女儿的逃脱使得她"赶快回去派人寻找，回去我与这个老东西吵，与这老东西闹，家院回去！女儿啦！（哭）"[5]233。邱夫人先是作为封建家庭的女性，所表现的顺从无可厚非，后在女儿逃走时展现的那份母爱却着实是世间无二的。就此一出细节亦足以见得樊粹庭先生深刻的生活体悟和高超的艺术拿捏。樊粹庭先生"弄清每代对话者各自的发言背景、动机和意图"[2]133，深刻而细致地把握了每一组人物关系间的关联与矛盾，对话的背景、动机和意图，这是极考验剧作者对生活人物细致观察和戏剧形象生动刻画的功力的。

樊粹庭先生对豫剧创作的自出机杼是豫剧跨时代发展的先声，是源自对豫剧艺术热爱的初心。其创排的《麻风女》产生了一种综合性艺术审美新范式，营造了一个颇具时代性的审美"意境"。正如李泽厚在《"意境"杂谈》一文中所谈及的：

"读一首诗，看一幅画，总之，欣赏艺术，常常是通过眼前的有限形象不自觉地捕捉和领会到某种更深远的东西，而获得美感享受。齐白石的画，在还不懂事的小孩眼中，不过是几只不像样的虫、虾；……然而，也就在这虫、虾、音响之中，却似乎深藏着某种更多的东西，藏着某种超越这些外部形象本身固有意义的'象外之旨'、'弦外之音'。"[6]138

在同时期的戏曲创作中该剧作率先运用了辩证的思维来编创剧本，排演戏剧，令原本重复冗长的豫剧在承袭豫剧优良传统的基础上，更加积极地焕发出新的艺术魅力。樊粹庭在对封建文化的批判上是旗帜鲜明的，批判封建礼教、批判愚昧与迷信，这些均是"五四"以来新思想的萌芽。然而，樊粹庭先生对才子佳人的相恋又不同于旧时候戏曲创作的那样简单，让相恋的过程颇受阻挠，来自自身病痛的滞阻，来自父母家庭那种延续香火、门当户对思想的阻挠，这些都让最后邱丽玉和陈绿琴的爱情修成正果给观者以不同以往的观剧震撼感。"五四"以来，女性主体的突出使得樊粹庭在进行戏剧创作之时，无不透露出那种对爱情的向往与追求，对男女平等和对自由向往的精神主旨。他将精神主旨化作故事和情节，经由矛盾的产生、激化和化解，让精神主旨成为戏剧人物的意象指代，让观众在欣赏剧作的同时得到"五四"新文化思潮的熏陶和滋润,那就是民主与平等。

以传统豫剧创作为视角,有很多专家学人从不同理论视域对樊粹庭编创的豫剧《麻风女》进行解读与阐释。但在全球化语境中,我们从中西方文化的角度重新审视,对其戏剧艺术美质进行总结,就显得更为必要,这对当下戏剧如何传承与创新具有启发意义。"任何文化都可以超越自己,为其他文化提供新的思考和可能。"[1]33 樊粹庭的豫剧艺术美学成就会对戏剧特别是当代豫剧的发展产生的普适性的借鉴经验。我们探讨他的戏剧美学在异质文化环境中产生的对话与交流,明确指证其剧作自身的美学旨趣和审美追求的当下价值,这对于进一步复兴繁荣中国戏剧,特别是河南豫剧艺术的创作提供了更为广阔的思路。

参考文献:

[1] 乐黛云. 跨文化方法论初探 [M]. 北京:中国大百科全书出版社, 2016.

[2] 王一川. 跨文化艺术美学 [M]. 北京:中国大百科全书出版社, 2017.

[3] 宗白华. 宗白华全集 [M]. 合肥:安徽教育出版社, 1996.

[4] 朱光潜. 谈美 [M]. 合肥:安徽教育出版社, 1987.

[5] 樊粹庭. 女贞花 [M]// 樊粹庭. 张大新,编校. 樊粹庭文集·创作剧目. 开封:河南大学出版社, 2013.

[6] 李泽厚. 门外集 [M]. 武汉:长江文艺出版社, 1957.

Improvements from Local Traditions by Integrating Chinese and Western Aesthetics
— On the Aesthetic Achievements of Fan Cuiting's Plays

Abstract: Fan Cuiting is known as "the father of modern Henan Opera". His drama works became mature during trend of thoughts of the May 4th New Culture Movement, integrating Chinese and Western aesthetic thoughts, and gradually formed a unique drama thought and put it into his own play practice. What's more, the Henan Opera *Leprosy Woman* created by him, is the representative work of this practice. The play is a successful attempt to break through the traditional Henan Opera with its rich experience, distinctive conception and profound implication. Besides, the artistic beauty of *Leprosy Woman* is mainly reflected in three aspects: its integration of Western artistic thoughts, the design for the selected themes, and the touching and exciting plots of the play, which provides a new aesthetic reference for contemporary drama works. His ideas and practice on drama have opened up the development path of modern Henan Opera, enriched the connotation of the beauty of Henan Opera. Thus it has profound theoretical value and practical reference significance.

Key words: Fan Cuiting's drama; Chinese and Western aesthetic thoughts; *Leprosy Woman*; integrationg and surpassing

At the beginning of the 20th century, it is a period that the Chinese and Western cultures communicated a lot. Fan Cuiting, a well-known Henan Opera writer, learned knowledge and grew up in this changing era. Therefore, the interaction of traditional culture and Western culture created Fan Cuiting's diverse cultural accumulation and improved artistic ideas. He absorbed himself in Chinese and Western aesthetic thoughts and gradually formed his unique dramatic thoughts. A group of "modern Henan Opera" were created by him with his creative ideas, distinct themes and rich implication, which reflects his creative and unique ideas. In conclusion, Fan Cuiting's aesthetic achievements of his drama can be summarized as: the beauty of integrating Western literary thoughts, the beauty of the design of the theme selection, and the beauty of moving and exciting plots of the drama. These characteristics are clearly expressed in his representative work *Leprosy Woman*.

1. The Beauty of Integration with the Western Literary Aesthetics

Fan Cuiting's play *Leprosy Woman* (also known as *Privet Flower*; the script is compiled and edited by Professor Zhang Daxin of Henan University from *Fan Cuiting's Collected Works and Creation Plays*) tells a story to the readers. It is said that in the eastern part of Guangdong, Mr. Qiu's young child, originally a beautiful girl, unfortunately had a common disease in this area—"leper disease"—that is often suffered from "the ineffectiveness of all drugs". According to local legend, if a man from another county is induced to marry her, the disease is "passed on" to the man, and the woman will recover. Therefore, Mr. Qiu conspired with Sikong Hun to lure Chen Lvqin, a scholar in need from Huainan and pretended to allow him to marry Miss Qiu. It is unexpected that Qiu Liyu was kind-hearted, unwilling to infect Chen Lvqin. She treated Chen Lvqin honestly on the wedding night, told the whole story and made the false impression of illness for Chen Lvqin, helping him escape from Qiu's house. After knowing the truth, the couple expelled their seriously-ill daughter, and sent her to the leprosy hospital. Chen Lvqin, an honest scholar in distress, went home to visit his old father Chen Mao. He followed his father's orders to "study hard for fame", only to find "and see Liyu in the book". Qiu Liyu escaped from the leprosy hospital and suffered a lot on the way to find her husband. Chen Lvqin passed the exam and won the first, still not forgetting Liyu's kindness. After the twists and turns, lovers eventually got married.

"From the perspective of historical development, one culture's absorption of other cultures is always continued through its own cultural vision and framework; that is, through the filtering of one's own culture, it seldom copies completely but mostly it takes what it needs." Fan Cuiting's drama work was a new attempt of drama aesthetics based on comprehensive thinking towards traditional Henan Opera, critically drawing lessons from, absorbing and integrating it. This has a subtle but lasting relationship with Mr. Fan Cuiting's personal growth and education experiences. Moreover, Russian thinker Belinsky said in his article *Fantasy in Literary* that "only by following different paths can human beings achieve common goals." Mr. Fan's experience of combining Eastern and Western drama with traditional and modern drama is a brief history of the improvement of Henan Opera. The acceptance and education of multi-culture enabled Mr. Fan to come into contact with more abundant drama arts in the process of learning and practice, which has been a great help to the traditional local operas in Henan. He has also absorbed the strengths of many schools such as Peking Opera and other dramas. Compared with previous playwrights, he has a wider horizon and more open thinking ways.

Fan Cuiting loved drama from a young age. At the age of 14, he was admitted to Kaifeng European and American Preparatory School (now Henan University). He absorbed himself in drama and often organized his classmates to take part in drama activities. After graduation, he served as the director of the social education promotion department of Henan Province, visiting more than two-thirds of the cities and villages in the province. What's more, he connected with the Henan Opera troupes in various counties, where he met many famous artists. While admiring their singing ability, Mr. Fan also noticed their miserable living conditions and many problems in performance. By 1934, in spite of the opposition of his family, he still gave up his official position and chose the art career. Moreover, Chen Suzhen, Zhao Yiting, Zhang Zilin and other Henan Opera elites were organized to set up the "Henan Opera Theater" in Xiangguo Temple. They have carried out all-round reforms and innovations to fulfill their intention of "breaking away from stereotypes and improving Henan Opera", from theater facilities to troupe management, culture and education, screenwriter and director, etc. Since he made his successful debut "Ling Yunzhi" in March 1935, he continually directed "Yi Lie Feng" (《义烈风》), "Liu Lv Yun" (《柳绿云》), "San Fu Xiu" (《三拂袖》), "Di Chi Xue" (《涤耻血》), "Leprosy Woman" (《麻风女》) and "Xiao Rang Hate" (《霄壤恨》).

Fan Cuiting's drama creation mainly comes from the influence of differing drama culture and aesthetic thought during his education stage, which deeply influenced his outlook on life and world. The first is the local culture. Fan Cuiting grew up in Henan, where the drama performance is popular. Henan's words and the context made his creation deeply marked by local culture. The second is the acceptance and agreement of Western thoughts. Besides, it also comes from the influence under the background of the New Culture Movement during the May 4th periods. Furthermore, many of Fan Cuiting's plays are the development of the tradition of Chinese drama, such as, the strong affection, love for the motherland, even the continuation of the story plot. But at the same time, under the influence of the "May 4th" New Culture Movement, he also made a lot of changes in the creation of Henan Opera. Apart from the traditional theme of loyalty and love, Mr. Fan's plays are diversified in content, more rich in themes and more varied in techniques. Finally, with his unique artistic experience, he can easily make breakthroughs in culture tradition, constantly introducing doubts, exploration, innovation, negation and identification so that he was able to develop Fan Cuiting-style Henan Opera aesthetics, thus bringing his Henan Opera repertoire creation into a new stage.

2. The Beauty of Carefully Selected Themes and Play Construction

"There must be common or blending characters between different artistic categories based on different media." [2]9 Fan Cuiting's play *Leprosy Woman* was adapted according to the short story *Leprosy Woman Qiu Liyu* written by late Qing novelist Xuan Ding, which was written into Henan Opera in 1936 and successfully performed. This is not only the success of a play, but also the "mutual agreement" between the people's call and the writer's conception under the trend of the May 4th New Cultural Movement. In other words, the two most grass-rooted types of characters in the old society were written to make them the main characters. On the one hand, the female characters in feudal society such as Qiu Liyu, a darling daughter from a wealthy family. She was supposed to be silent or agreed facing the arrangement of "her parents in charge", while she longed for freedom, equality and actively pursued her love under constant oppression and discipline. On the other hand, male characters such as "Chen Lvqin", who followed his father Chen Mao's instructions to study hard and seek fame, and came to be promoted with the match after winning "the prize" in the county examination. Chen Lvqin kept kindness and the moral discipline and love pursuit to protect Qiu Liyu. Accordingly, the play breaks traditional ending of "to be No.1, wedding and celebration". But it focuses on describing Qiu Liyu and Chen Lvqin's unswerving loyalty of love. Fan Cuiting directed the performance of Henan Opera *Leprosy Woman*. He used a comprehensive way of drama to reproduce and recreate Qiu Liyu, a leprous woman once written by novelist Xuan Ding, which presents a communication with the same prototype of the story across different art categories. Tian Han clearly put forward "the artistry of life" in his 1919 letter to Guo Moruo:

"I think we artists, on the one hand, we should expose the dark side of life, reject all hypocrisy in the world, and establish the foundation of life. On the other hand, are should instruct people towards art to make life artistic. That is, to beautify one's life and make one forget the pain of real life and enter into a state of harmony. Only then can one do his/her best. " [3]265

This letter is taken from the collected works of Mr. Zong Baihua. Although it is not discussed in detail, its general spiritual pursuit beyond time conforms to Mr. Fan's idea of creating Henan Opera *Leprosy Woman*. The main and supporting characters, such as Mr. Qiu and his wife, are described in a full, practical and vivid images. Parents all hope that their daughter can marry a "suitable" family, which is understandable. In order to save their daughter, Mr. Qiu and his wife believed Sikong Hun's words to cheat the young man from other place to "arrange a wedding to counteract the bad luck" and "spread diseases", which showed the ridiculous thoughts of ignorance and superstition in feudal society. Her parents expelled her after knowing that she had not recovered and sent her to the leprosy hospital, which showed their cruelty. The story's plot here is ridiculous, upsetting and pathetic. Additionally, Qiu Liyu made her way to Chenjiazhuang to meet her husband's father Chen Mao. The old man ordered the servant in his family to send Qiu Liyu to the nunnery to stay temporarily because Chen Lvqin failed to return for the examination. After that, Chen Mao said, "It's really strange!" and the servant said. "Mr. Chen thinks she is dirty, and I have sent her to the nunnery." It can be inferred from these details that Chen Mao, the father of Chen Lvqin, is confused at the moment. The key reason of the problem lies in the pity for the only child in his family. Moreover, "Qiu Liyu" is neither as strong and tough as Du Liniang, nor as the common lady in traditional operas who only stays in home and dares not pursue happiness. On the contrary, Qiu Liyu is gentle and broad-minded, at the same time she has cultivated some early new cultural thoughts longing for freedom and love. In other words, these practical and real figures are sure to benefit from the profound artistic accumulation of the playwright Mr. Fan, who skillfully turned life into a piece of art and reproduced it on the stage. "Limited and accidental concrete images are filled with infinite and certain contents of the essence of life." [2]143 Artistically making of the characters makes it possible that it was born out of millions upon millions of people; the artistic plot setting has combined together total misfortunes and shared with them. "To beautify the real life with the ideal state of art as the standard." [2]43 This concept of art has made Mr. Fan's plays elegant, rich, organized and meaningful.

"Skillfully absorbing the aesthetic style of Chinese local operas to perform the revolutionary spirit of the Western society in order to awaken the silent ordinary Chinese people. This has become an artistic choice for cross-cultural communication." [2]19 *Leprosy Woman* is different from the traditional "scholar and beauty" drama in Henan Opera, with ingenious and unique conception and plots. In many plays written by Mr. Fan Cuiting, both gifted scholars and beauties have suffered difficulties, rather than the plot in which one suffered and the other did nothing but passionately waiting. Although the plot and arrangement of *Leprosy Woman* did not completely break away from the framework and happy ending of the drama "gifted scholars and beauties" since the Ming and Qing dynasties, it was undoubtedly a great progress in the theme selection and design of Henan Opera. Mr. Fan's survey of the "scholars and beauties" plays, which have survived in the long development of drama, as well as his integration and analysis of the aesthetic concepts of drama certainly created this unusual "gifted scholars and beautifes" play with distinctive "Fan style" aesthetic characteristics.

Chen Lvqin nearly fell ill and was fortunate enough to have a good relationship. Both of them have feelings for each other. On the one hand, Chen Lvqin still remembers Qiu Liyu's kindness though obeying his father to obtain fame. On the other hand, Qiu Liyu suffered from the disease, and then she experienced being expelled from her home by her parents and finding her husband in another county unfortunately. In contrast to the past, men suffered many hardships and beautiful women were waiting for them; the plot conflicts and setbacks were more inclined to the women. Thus the awakening of woman concept of "equality" since the May 4th Movement was also revealed accordingly. This paper attempts to cross the boundary between the traditional opera culture and the new multi-cultural opera culture which takes the May 4th Movement as the breaking part. It also discusses the variation of Henan Opera creation and arrangement when the "old and new" cultures contact and collide. Obviously, under the performance of Chen Lvqin and Qiu Liyu, the long lyrics and chants expressed the simple expectation of a dramatist who experienced the changes in this period. It is also reflected in his yearning for and pursuit of ideal emotions, as well as his contempt and criticism of feudal society. In this aspect, Mr. Fan Cuiting's conception and theme selection of drama have been undoubtedly the forerunner of the times.

There is no "kind of absolutely pure local discourse without any integration" [1]56. Fan's drama polishes the development of the story and makes the plot more vivid and moving, just like Suzhou Gardens, with ingenious ideas and plots leading to the ending. What's more, drama itself is the product of artistic creation in the culture formed by different literary and artistic elements. If we completely isolated it, the art will easily die. Fan Cuiting, on the other hand, created the drama with an open mind. He accepted and tried to incorporate different values and new ideas into his own drama creation. This approach makes the development of the drama story concise and clear and the plot touching by ways of integration or adaption. Instructed by such methods, the unfolding context development is undoubtedly exciting and fascinating.

3. The Beauty of the Touching Plot in the Drama

"The image of beauty is kept in my heart, and I am often touched by the beauty. Naturally, I will have more pure thoughts." [4]25 According to Mr. Zhu Guangqian's non-utilitarian aesthetic "image" theory, more and more people tend to talk about literary and artistic works based on moral standards. What's more, they want to put the aesthetics of artistic works into the real world. Additionally, viewers take the moral standardization of reality into the field of drama viewing, ignoring or losting the separation between art and reality. However, the direct purpose of aesthetic experience is not only to educate or edify those who are in it, but edifying personality is strengthened through the dramatic education in the process. Mr. Fan's Henan Opera *Leprosy Woman*, featuring Qiu Liyu, Chen Lvqin and other figures, fully reflects Liang Qichao's idea of "benevolent person is not worried". Its root lies in the local philosophical thoughts of Confucianism and Taoism. In the process of appreciation drama experience, the audience, though immersed in it, is also independent from the scene through the "plot techniques" designed by the playwright in a creative way. Therefore, it makes the viewers not only enjoy an immersive and experienced sensory experience, but also have an effect of independence from performance of drama, which is based on both morality and art. In this play, viewers can express their sympathy for Qiu Liyu and Chen Lvqin's tragic and tortuous experiences. They are also ashamed of the ridiculous acts of Mr. and Mrs.Qiu, and Chen Lvqin's father. Among them, the original intention and essence of The Qius and Mr. Chen have some subtle differences, containing complex feelings in it. In the performance of "expelling" containing the act of "Qiu Liyu crying in pavilion", in which Mr. Qiu and his wife expelled his daughter out of the house, his father says :

"You are so bold,

This is insane.

I send you to leprosy hospital today,

Father and daughter have since broken up." [5]230

He decided to expel his daughter and send her to the leprosy hospital. While Mr. Fan wrote down her mother's lyrics urging the servant to visit her daughter in the leprosy hospital during the performance of "Visit to the leper daughter",

"Here in the home courtyard you and I will do something,

Hiding from Mr. Qiu to visit my daughter and taking a ride.

It is regrettable that the younger daughter is so miserable.

She was cast out of the home for leprosy." [5]232

Even in a wealthy family, the treatment of father and mother always have changes and differences. Mr. Qiu had anger with his daughter Qiu Liyu, who did not understand the kindness of her parents even though they did not hesitate to spend a lot of money to cheat Chen Lvqin into the house to save her life. It is understandable that he expelled his daughter out of rage and broke the relationship. For Mrs. Qiu , it is inconvenient for her to disobey his decision to expel their daughter. After that, she sent the servant to accompany her to visit her daughter in the leprosy hospital. Her daughter's escape made her "hurry back home and send someone to look for her. Once I get home, I will quarrel with Qiu and talk to him. Go home! My poor daughter! (Crying) ". [5]233 As a woman from a feudal family, Mrs. Qiu naturally showed obedience first. After finding her daughter run away, her love was second to none in the world. This detail is also enough to show Mr. Fan's profound understanding of life and skillful artistic application ability. In other words, Mr. Fan "makes clear the background, motivation and intention of each generation of speech".[2]133 He has grasped the relationship and contradiction between each group of characters in a deep and careful way. What's more, the background, motivation and intention of the dialogue, these three factors provide a objective test of the playwright's ability to observe life characters and make drama images vividly.

Fan Cuiting's self-creation of Henan Opera is the precursor of the differing development in times. It also comes from his love for the art of Henan Opera. *Leperosy Woman* created by him, has produced a new comprehensive aesthetic reference and created a new "artistic conception" of the times. As Li Zehou observed in his article *Talks on Artistic Conception,*

"*When reading a poem or watching a painting, in short, you are appreciating art often through the limited image in front of you, unconsciously capturing and comprehending something profound so that you gain aesthetic enjoyment. Qi Baishi's paintings are just a few improper worms and shrimps in the eyes of children who still don't understand....However, even among these insects, shrimps and sound, there seems to be something hidden, something with the intrinsic meaning beyond these external images, such as 'the purpose and the implication in the image'.*"

In the same period of drama creation, the dialectical approach was first used to create scripts and rehearse dramas. It enables the originally repetitive and lengthy Henan Opera to be more active and full of new charm on the basis of inheriting the traditional Henan Opera. Fan Cuiting has a clear attitude towards the feudal culture, especially in criticizing the feudal ethics, ignorance and superstition, all of which are the development of new ideas since the May 4th Movement. However, Mr. Fan's love story with gifted scholars and beauties is different from that of the opera in the old days. The process in pursuing love is obstructed. It comes from the stagnation of her own illness and the obstruction of parents for the idea of the family continuity. All these difficulties make the happy ending of Qiu Liyu's love with Chen Lvqin give viewers a different amazed feeling from the previous drama. Additionally, since the May 4th Movement, the prominence of female has made Fan Cuiting reveal his yearning for love and pursuit in his drama, with the theme of equality between men and women and freedom. The theme is turned into stories and plots. Through the intensification and dissolution of contradictions between different generations, the aspiration is turned into the image reference of dramatic characters. The audience is nurtured by the May 4th new cultural trend while enjoying the drama, which is democracy and equality.

From the perspective of traditional Henan Opera creation, the Henan

Opera *Leprosy Woman* edited by Fan Cuiting has been interpreted by many scholars from different theoretical perspectives. However, in the context of globalization, it is necessary for us to re-examine these plays from the perspective of Chinese and Western cultures and to summarize the beauty of them. It is also instructive for how to inherit and innovate the current drama. Moreover, "any culture can improve itself and provide new reference and possibilities for other cultures." [1]33 Fan Cuiting's achievements in Henan Opera will provide common experience for the development of drama, especially for contemporary Henan Opera. We observe the dialogue and communication of his drama aesthetics in the different cultural environment, and testify his own aesthetic pursuit and the current values, which provides broader approaches for further revival and prosperity of Chinese drama, especially the development of Henan Opera.

References:

[1] Le Daiyun. A Preliminary Study of Intercultural Methodology [M]. Beijing: China Encyclopedia Publishing House, 2016.

[2] Wang Yichuan. Intercultural Art Aesthetics [M].Beijing: China Encyclopedia Publishing House, 2017.

[3] Zong Baihua. Works of Zong Baihua [M].Hefei: Anhui Education Press, 1996.

[4] Zhu Guangqian. On the Beauty [M].Hefei: Anhui Education Press, 1987.

[5] Fan Cuiting. Privet Flower [M]// Fan Cuiting. Zhang Daxin, Edit. Fan Cuiting's Collected Works. Creation Plays. Kaifeng: Henan University Press, 2013.

[6] Li Zehou. Outdoor Collection [M]. Wuhan: Changjiang Literature and Art Publishing House, 1957.

"楚河汉界——象棋文化的传说"
调查研究

摘要：广武山是象棋文化的滥觞源头，象棋文化使广武山壮丽辉煌。荥阳在中国象棋文化发展史上有着不可替代的重要作用和历史地位。象棋文化可溯源至公元前203年。荥阳北部的广武山上，项羽和刘邦以鸿沟为界虎虎相峙，两军屯兵多垒，相持经年，留下了不少脍炙人口的故事。汉霸二王城遗址所在地，对研究中国古代军事斗争史具有重要价值。中国古代象棋，包括棋盘结构（如楚河汉界）、棋子颜色、博弈格局的设定等，从汉霸二王城刘、项双方对垒争战的成败得失里汲取了丰富的营养之后，逐步得到发展和完善。

关键词：河南荥阳；象棋；楚河汉界

一、广武山是象棋文化的滥觞之地

象棋文化历史悠久，源远流长。汉高祖四年（公元前203年）十月（秦历），汉军破曹咎取成皋后，"汉军方围钟离眛于荥阳（古荥）东，项羽至。汉军畏楚，尽走险阻"[1]209，"军广武，就敖仓食"[1]179。项羽"与汉俱临广武而军，相守数月"[1]209。即：汉据西广武城，楚据东广武城，中间隔着鸿沟。最后，"项王乃与汉约，中分天下，割鸿沟以西者为汉，鸿沟而东者为楚"[1]180，鸿沟成了楚汉河界（即象棋博弈双方的隔离空间），此是象棋的雏形状态。

如果向更早的年代追溯，依然能寻觅到象棋在那不同的历史阶段不同的形态和制作工艺所存在的足迹。象棋最早萌芽于极为古老原始的年代，表现形式是祭祀与占卜。到了周代，有了"六博"的形态和制作工艺，最早见诸文字，是在屈原的《招魂》一诗中。诗中写道："菎蔽象棋，有六簙些。分曹并进，遒相迫些。成枭而牟，呼五白些。"[2]211-212 到了汉代，又有重大演进，不再掷"琼"行步而出现"塞戏"的制作工艺。到了南北朝的北周武帝宇文邕天和四年（即公元 569 年），已出现《象经》这样的文字典籍，而王褒的《象经序》则指出象棋是以《易学》为核心理念的。庾信的《象戏赋》中的句子"马丽千金之马，符明六甲之符"，则表明"马"已是"双子"，象棋中六种棋子也各有名目。到了唐代，则依据牛僧孺描述的象棋中的传奇，展现出"宝应象戏"的基本形态。有金属棋盘，"金铜而形"的棋子，棋子的名目已有"将""车""马""卒""物包"和"矢石"。传奇中虽然没有标明棋盘，但在稍后的北宋初年，苏绣名家的"琴棋书画"作品中，可看出棋盘乃"八八六十四格""黑白相间"（与今日国际象棋棋盘完全相同），以"四象"搏斗为核心内容。

唐末，五代到北宋初的百余年间，象棋又经历了一次脱胎换骨的演进，由《易学》的"八卦成列，象在其中"的"四象之博"，完全演进到楚河汉界象棋。即：在棋盘的中部增一横线，作"河界"，棋子分黑红双方，隔"河界"对峙，且从格子里博"易象丕变"转为两组隔"河"相对地在"竖九横五"的纵横线上相争。象棋新演进而形成的态势，完全秉承楚汉隔鸿沟在广武山对峙的历史内蕴。当然，也有与时俱进的象棋制艺揉进其中，如增添一个名目"炮"，变古代象棋的六个名目为七个。但，这并不影响"楚河汉界象棋"的文化底蕴。故而北宋学者程颢在《象戏》一诗中写道："中军八面将军重，河外尖斜步卒轻。却凭纹楸聊自笑，雄如刘项亦闲争"。[3]134 比程颢更早，北宋初年的政治家、军事家、文学家范仲淹在《赠棋者》一诗中写道："入险汉将危，奇兵翻背水"[3]132。还有宋人郑谟也在诗中写道："二士终朝默运筹，纷纷兵卒度鸿沟"。[3]134 可见在宋代，就有诸多文学作品已十分明确地表明，新演进成形的象棋制作工艺从楚汉隔鸿沟的对峙中受到启迪。

宋代之后出现的带"河界"的象棋制作工艺（即楚河汉界象棋），同样也源于楚汉隔鸿沟对峙的历史典故。明初的状元曾启在《棋》的诗句中写道："两军对敌立双营，坐运神机决死生。千里封疆驰铁马，一川波浪动金兵。虞姬歌舞悲垓下，汉将旌旗逼楚城"，[3]136 这一首诗被人们普遍尊为咏象棋的代表作。另有明人毛伯温作咏棋诗："马行二步鸿沟渡，将守三宫细柳营"；[3]137 清人叶燕《看象棋赠赵寿山》作诗："居然刘汉划鸿沟，车马纵横杀气浮"[3]137 等都说明楚河汉界象棋在千百年的传承、普及中，而早已被文学家所瞩目的广武山之鸿沟，也因其精彩的描述而日益深入人心。

象棋运动的真谛"斗智不斗力"闪烁出辩证法的光芒。事实上，楚河汉界象棋制作工艺的深厚文化内蕴亦源于楚汉隔鸿沟的对峙。其间，项王曾约汉王隔鸿沟对话，要和汉王单打独斗，刘邦笑着谢绝："吾宁斗智，不能斗力"[1]179。再者，项王约汉王对话，预设了伏弩，话不投机，即发伏弩射伤刘邦。（俗语"两王相见，必有一伤"，即源于此）显然，象棋棋规里的"两王不能相见，后来之王见先到之王为负"应该与此有着一种密不可分的关系。此外，象棋棋子分红黑，更为明确地源之于汉、楚。史载汉刘邦宣称自己是"赤帝子"，起兵反秦时以"帜皆赤，由所杀蛇白帝子，杀者赤帝子，故上赤"[1]198，称炎汉，崇火德，尚红。项王随其叔父项梁压会稽之兵起事，袭用秦制；又得东阳陈婴"苍头特起"之兵，崇水德，尚黑。楚河汉界象棋红方喻汉，黑方喻楚，而对峙于鸿沟两边。在象棋制作工艺中，更为重要的是，楚汉相约："中分天下，割鸿沟以西者为汉，鸿沟而东者为楚"[1]180，展现到棋盘上，形成"楚河汉界"为中分线。正是这一最基本的演进，使楚河汉界象棋完全区别于古代（唐代以前）的"象（棋）"。楚汉相约，"鸿沟为界，中分天下"之后，"项羽解而东归，汉王欲引而西归，用留侯、陈平计，乃进兵追项羽"[1]211。这样，便产生了关于象棋开局的俗语："红先黑后，输了不臭"，也在民间形成象棋开局"红先"——红方先行子的惯例。

楚河汉界象棋的"中线"就是指鸿沟。《史记》明确记载："荥阳下引河东南为鸿沟，以通宋、郑、陈、蔡、曹、卫，与济、汝、淮、泗会"[1]1020，说明鸿沟首流，源自荥阳。到明代，嘉靖年间的《荥阳县志》仍写明："鸿沟，旧治西北二十里。即汉楚分界处"，[4]7 "汴水（鸿沟）从广武涧中东南流，今涸。"[4]8 这些表述详尽的史料在极大程度上都佐证了鸿沟的确是楚汉对峙广武山时的界河，之后便与象棋发生了交集。

荥阳还有许多关于象棋的传说,至今仍保留着古代的一些象棋制艺。例如开局摆放棋子,"将(帅)"不是摆在底线,而是摆在九宫格的中心。再如,开局的第一步,必须走帅与将,先把它走到八格的中心,这叫作"将军升帐",又叫作"先礼后兵"。民间"头一步不能先走当头炮"的说法,大概来源于此。

荥阳,特别是广武山区一带保存着遗留千百年的象棋实物,既有宋代铜铸象棋,也有元代、明代的铜铸象棋,还有明代楚河汉界象棋的丝织棋盘。宋代铜铸象棋,棋子的大小似制钱而稍大、稍厚,32个棋子一个不少,棋子正面,阳文楷书各自的名目,背面乃相对应的图像,妙在红黑双方的铜质不一样,分别以红铜和青铜铸成;红黑双方的名目皆为"将""士""卒""车""马""炮",无"帅""相""兵"("士"无"亻"偏旁)。元代铜铸象棋的棋子大小和宋代铜铸棋子差不多,但已经有了"帅""相""兵",而且红方的"车""马"另外加上了一个单人旁。明代丝织棋盘,除多绣出棋盘边沿的花边外,"楚河汉界"居中,分别绣出了两组"竖九横五"的纵横线,与现今的棋盘制艺完全相同。1999年4月,宋代铜铸象棋和明代丝织棋盘被荥阳市文物保护管理所收藏。

二、象棋文化涵盖着人生的哲理和智慧

"人生如棋,棋如人生。"博大精深的象棋内容,主要是围绕着"鸿沟"而展开,文化底蕴里涵盖着人生的智慧。

1. 楚汉在广武山隔鸿沟对峙,相约以鸿沟为界,使鸿沟成为楚汉河界,产生楚河汉界象棋。

2. 楚汉以鸿沟为界的核心内容是"中分天下",象棋棋盘秉承这一观念,而鸿沟的"楚河汉界"位于棋盘的正中间,正是此理念的体现。

3. 楚尚黑,汉尚红,黑红棋子分别表示双方以鸿沟(楚河汉界)为界,对峙于"河"两边。

4. 楚汉对峙是为了夺取天下、夺取政权,"楚河汉界"于棋盘上的两边,各由"竖九横五"的纵横线组成,喻指"九五之争"。

5. "竖九横五"纵横线所表示的"九五"内涵,加上"楚河汉界"中分天下共同组成的棋盘,十分清晰地表明象棋双方的博弈是源于楚汉对峙

的核心理念：夺取天下。

6. 项王与汉王隔鸿沟对话中，项王约汉王单打独斗，汉王表示"吾宁斗智，不能斗力"。其中的"斗智不斗力"成为象棋运动的精髓。

7. 项王约汉王隔鸿沟相见，话不投机，以伏弩射伤刘邦，产生了"两王相见，必有一伤"的俗语；也形成了"两王不能相见，后来之王见先到之王为负"的象棋棋规。

8. 楚汉相约，以鸿沟为界"中分天下"之后，项王引兵东归，原本汉王也准备置鸿沟于背后而西归，但听从张良、陈平之计，出奇兵，渡鸿沟，追歼楚军。这既是范仲淹诗句"奇兵翻背水"的出处，也是民间行棋的俗语"红先黑后，输了不臭"的由来。行棋的开局，由红方先行，源自"中分天下"，汉军（红方）率先进攻。

9. 宋代铜铸象棋之实物为楚河汉界象棋发展的追根溯源提供了极为有力的佐证。楚河汉界象棋在演进定型之初，黑红双方都是"将""象""卒"，无"帅""兵""相"，其中的"炮"铸为"砲"的字样，背后的图像为"抛石机"，表示"军事游戏化"当时是以石块为驽弹的。

10. 广武山一带还在民间传说中保存了昔日象棋制艺的一些内容。如摆棋时，"将（帅）"摆在九宫格中心，开局的第一步应"将军升帐"、应"先礼后兵"，走动"帅（将）"到八格中间。

三、象棋文化的科学性、竞技性、艺术性

1. 象棋的科学性。首先，象棋自身构成是红黑两方对垒。7个兵种有直走的，有斜走的；有长腿的，有短足的；有独自发威的，有借子使力的；子力间相互制约；32枚棋子，90个交叉落点，搭配协调有致。其次，双方的博弈是公平、公正、合理的，胜负的结果取决于对弈者对局势的把握；不像牌类项目存在着运气和偶然的因素。另外，象棋棋艺的提高需要理论与实践相结合，需要学习者纵观全局，深思熟虑，谨慎选择，或进或退；一着不慎，全盘皆输，而这一些就具备了明显的科学性。

2. 象棋的竞技性。对弈双方按照规则行棋，每时每刻都在角力制胜。"斗智不斗力"既是象棋运动的特征，又是象棋运动的精髓和象棋艺术发展的原动力。二人对局，按照规定的位置，在棋盘上各放棋子十六枚，将

（帅）、士（仕）、象（相）、车、马、炮、卒（兵）等兵种,各子走法不同。棋盘系由九根纵线和十根横线组成,中间划定河界,共有九十个据点,双方各占其半,先后交替走子,以把对方"将死"为分胜负,互相不能"将"死则为和棋。博弈过程中,双方"斗智不斗力",则分明是象棋竞技性的鲜明体现,此乃象棋运动的思想精髓。

3. 象棋的艺术性。譬如在象棋中,同是一个"马"或者是"炮"等,却因为下棋者的使用水平而产生很大的不同,这就是艺术性的明显体现。还有下棋古有别名"手谈",同样是艺术性的体现。同时,从一千多年前流传下的棋谱和在实践与排演中不断形成的棋谱中（也有残局）,我们能看得出它是一种艺术形式、美的载体；而对弈者以自己的思维和创造表达着自己的思想与风格,也让象棋具有的艺术性的多元化审美被淋漓尽致地表现出来。

四、象棋文化的历史价值、军事价值和娱乐价值

象棋是中华民族传统文化的一部分,是文化多元化、多样性不容小觑的一部分,不仅能够娱乐休闲,更是一门开发人的智慧、锻炼人的思维、提高人的心智水平的综合艺术,具有很高的文化价值和社会价值,具有多方面的功能。

1. 历史价值

司马迁在《史记》里详细而明确地记载,荥阳"楚河汉界"（象棋棋盘中间位置谓之此名称）依托于楚霸王项羽和汉王刘邦在广武山隔鸿沟对峙长达近四年的历史遗址（霸王城、汉王城、中间隔开两城的鸿沟）,证实了象棋深厚的历史内涵与此联系密切,也表明了象棋文化深厚的内涵源于此。

从北宋范仲淹《赠棋者》一诗起（从现存资料来看）,经程颢的《象戏》、南宋郑谟的《咏画中围棋》,到明代曾启的《棋》、毛伯温的《咏棋》等,莫不表达出了荥阳"楚河汉界"（楚汉在广武山对峙）是象棋文化的核心,而"楚河汉界"醒目地置于棋盘之上,着实证明了"中分天下""鸿沟为界"的固有的历史价值。象棋作为中华民族贡献于人类的瑰宝,益神润智,蕴含深厚哲理,启迪辩证思维,陶冶高雅情操,实是中华民族历史进

程中至为宝贵的精华。

2. 军事思想价值

象棋是"智慧的体操"。象棋对弈是一种智力竞技,可以锻炼人们的思维能力。棋局变化多端,下棋时每盘棋的走法各不相同,每一招棋都不可能有现成的样式供你去模仿,都需要对弈者去发明、去创造、去实战演练。每一步棋都是对弈双方智力的比拼、才情的博弈。同时,棋局发展又遵循特有的规律,要求人们具备严谨的逻辑思维,否则一着不慎,满盘皆输。棋战两军对垒,要讲究谋略战术,又可培养人们的博弈思维与方法。而且,棋场斗智之时,对弈双方的思维异常集中,大脑皮层处于高度亢奋状态。换句话说,下棋时人们并不是静止地坐着只靠大脑进行思索的。人的全身是一个统一体,身体各部分互相联系、互相制约。正如进行各种体力锻炼活动有益于大脑一样,下棋时大脑的活动也对身体其他部分起一定的积极作用。因此,人们把象棋称为"智慧的试金石""聪明人的游戏"。

在象棋古谱中,排局占了很大的地位。一个奥妙的排局,常常是表面看来一方已处于绝对劣势,却有一系列"起死回生"的妙着可以解救,在演变中,双方都是危机四伏、草木皆兵,形势变幻、反复无常。一步绝招,可以置对方于死地;倘若一着不慎,难免会造成"一失足成千古恨"的结局。从这一点来说,与其说是下棋,还不如说是在打仗;换言之,它体现了一定的军事思想和策略,是孙子兵法的再版;事实上,一些优秀的军事家之所以能运筹帷幄,都是从象棋中汲取了丰富的营养。

3. 娱乐价值

象棋作为一种高雅的娱乐珍品,得到了人们的普遍喜爱。

无论对弈全盘,还是下残局、排局,象棋都毫无疑问是充满魅力、引人入胜的。下棋,儿童作为游戏,青年作为斗智,老人作为消遣,品品其中奥妙,其乐无穷。男女老幼,都可成为对弈者。"棋艺"就是人们对象棋奥秘和象棋文化的集中高度凝练。

以棋会友,共同提高。象棋这项让大家喜闻乐见的文化活动,无愧是中华民族贡献于人类的瑰宝。在净化心灵、蕴含深厚哲理、启迪辩证思维、陶冶变易认知的同时,其娱乐价值也充分得到了发挥和展示。

五、象棋文化薪火相、传生生不息

楚河汉界象棋文化的传承,有其广泛性、复杂性和民间自发性。它经过千百年的传承与发展,已普及到全国各地和海外,受到社会各阶层人民的喜爱。在当下,荥阳,特别是楚河汉界原生态所在的广武山区一带,民间对象棋文化的钻研和传承千百年来延续不衰,许多棋谱和象棋文化的著作与传说世代相传、生生不息。清末的秀才陈云彩(民国初年,担任过河阴劝学所所长),多次结合历史,实地考察汉霸二王城,特别是考察作为"楚河汉界"的鸿沟,把自己对象棋文化的认识融入千百年来的民间相关传说,升华和丰富象棋文化的思想境界。其中一些内容,包括关于"黑红"双方代表"楚汉";刘邦"斗智不斗力"的制胜真谛;"象棋中开局'红先黑后'缘起于鸿沟为界'中分天下',刘邦先出手,后起兵攻楚"等。这些讲述,都为其喜爱文史的教师儿媳赵佑甫和许多人所接受,并迅速地向四面八方传播。

其长子陈玮,从小跟母亲学下象棋,并受到象棋文化的知识熏陶,更焕发其致力于象棋的探讨和研究的热烈兴趣。他把探讨发现的成果,编撰成了《荥阳,象棋文化策源地》《象棋文化寻根游》《象棋文化的底蕴》等专著,还编撰了小学《象棋》课本(10册),且培训荥阳市各小学的象棋教师。他最重要的研究成果有二:一是国际象棋的文化基因在河洛;二是象棋棋盘"楚河汉界"两边的两组纵横线,隐喻"九五",整体棋盘和棋盘上行棋,表达着"九五之争"。其在《中国象棋文化论坛》发表"象棋的核心意识是九五之争"的观点,得到中国棋院前院长陈祖德、王汝南以及象棋文化专家韩宽、王品璋、董其亮等先生的认可和赞赏,还多次在中央电视台、河南电视台,讲述《楚河汉界象棋》故事和历史,产生了很大的影响。

最引人瞩目的是荥阳实施的"1123"工程,即:抓好一个载体,以楚河汉界文化产业园为载体;开展两项工程,象棋渊源工程和楚河汉界象棋棋士精神与象棋对弈礼仪文化研究推广工程;搞好三个合作,与中国象棋协会、亚洲象棋联合会、世界象棋联合会长期稳定的战略合作。这些都对象棋文化的传承和推广起到了有益的促进作用。取得以上诸多战略成果的强有力推手便是荥阳市人民政府原市长王新亭。

2017年G20峰会于7月7日—8日在德国汉堡举行。河南荥阳"中国楚河汉界象棋文化展"作为国家形象推广活动内容,被中宣部纳入汉堡G20峰会"感知中国"系列活动,并在汉堡大学孔子学院举行。荥阳6岁的象棋神童杨圣煊亮相德国。人们对中国象棋打入G20、进入全球视野倍感兴奋,对促成此举的"幕后总导演"王新亭更是万分感激。一位了解他的学者告诉笔者:"人民利益在王新亭心中永远置于首位;他深知没有国家文化储备的处境将十分危险,因而他想把象棋文化发扬光大;他懂得人们高举着在古希腊赫拉神庙前点燃的奥运火炬的深远意义,因而,他想让鸿沟侧畔广武山上的圣火也越过喜马拉雅山远渡重洋抵达每一个举办象棋大赛的城市,来播撒棋士精神,传递荥阳文明;他想向前迈出意义非凡的一步,把荥阳打造成世界象棋之都、象棋圣地,进而增强荥阳在世界大棋盘中'法则'制定的主动权和话语权;他和荥阳人民同样期待荥阳能够成为一个受世界尊重的城市……"

六、关于做大做强象棋文化之对策

荥阳是象棋文化的策源地,也孕育衍生出荥阳广泛的象棋文化基础和别具一格的棋风棋俗。在荥阳的街头巷尾、家宅民户、校园课堂、绿地游园,随处可见精彩的棋局,下棋对弈早已融入荥阳人的日常生活。近年来,荥阳一系列象棋赛事活动的开展,进一步浓厚了象棋文化的氛围,使其走出了国门,走向了世界,成为家乡传统文化的一张金光闪闪的名片。但是通过调查走访,笔者认为要做实做大做强象棋文化,还有一段路要走,还需要从以下几方面努力。

一是做好楚河汉界策源地鸿沟的保护、开发、提升工作。截至目前,与象棋文化息息相关的楚汉战争地——汉霸二王城,由于两千多年来黄河的不断冲刷,大部分已沦入河中。东边的霸王城,除建有霸王举鼎、战马嘶鸣两处大型雕塑外,再没有其他表现当时战争形势的文化建筑。西边的汉王城更是凄凉凋零,没有任何标志。游人到此,根本看不到两军对峙的战争场面,难免会弱化象棋文化的艺术感染力。因此,要把汉霸二王城打造成既有观赏性又有文化内涵的旅游胜地,就需要我们进行认真考察,提出方案,进行论证,搞好设计,付之行动,建成一个主题鲜明、有文化内涵、环保的"汉霸二王城"主题公园。

二是加强对散落在民间的鸿沟（象棋）历史文物的搜集,如陶器及铜镞、铁镞之类的古代兵器,收集民间传说里对楚汉争战中的人物（如刘邦、项羽、周苛、曹咎、钟离眛、韩信等）的故事。完成如纪公庙、周苛庙等与楚汉文化相关的附属建筑,在市区主要街道增设象棋文化元素,研制象棋文化工艺品、纪念品,让荥阳的象棋文化之乡流淌出浓浓的艺术氛围,让每个游人心灵得到净化,情操受到熏陶。

三是加强对象棋文化的科学探讨和理论研究。象棋文化深厚的内涵和象棋文化独具特色的社会意义的弘扬,已经落后于象棋技艺的发展,作为象棋文化策源地,必须清醒地认识到这一点,把象棋文化的科学探讨和理论研究放在重要地位。要建立完整的象棋资料档案,开展象棋人才普查,走访象棋前辈,挖掘和抢救濒临失传的文史资料,将它们以文字、音像等方式记录存档。要对象棋文化的历史演变、文化内涵和科学价值等内容,组织专门人才分类进行深入研究,形成专著,并出版发行。要有计划、有重点地培养传承人,做好象棋进学校工作,在普及的同时搞好提高,使象棋文化的研究和象棋技艺后继有人。

四是建立"楚河汉界象棋文化"保障机制。要成立常设的"楚河汉界象棋文化"保护领导小组,负责研究制定保护措施,落实保护资金,监督各项保护工作的落实,层层分工,落实责任,形成合力；建立各项规章制度,共同搞好"楚河汉界象棋文化"的保护工作；编写有关影、视、戏剧本,编辑传奇故事和民间传说,加大象棋文化宣传力度,使其家喻户晓、深入民心。

楚河汉界象棋文化是中国特色的文化资源库里的一枚瑰宝。打造"世界象棋文化之都",这是融遗址保护、国学传承、旅游休闲、艺术表演为一体的大型综合工程,还有一段遥远的路程要走。万里征途,任重道远。近年来,在荥阳上下的共同努力下,楚河汉界"中国象棋文化之乡"的品牌具有了一定的知名度和影响力,但还需要我们抓实抓细、下大功夫,才能为荥阳这张文化名片增光添彩,为荥阳的经济建设和文化建设做出卓越的贡献。

参考文献：

[1] 司马迁. 史记 [M]. 西安：三秦出版社，1988.

[2] 屈原. 楚辞 [M]. 北京：中华书局，1983.

[3] 陈玮，韩露. 中国象棋文化之乡 [M]. 北京：中国文联出版社，2015.

[4] 陈万卿. 嘉靖荥阳县志 [M]. 扬州：广陵书社，2006.

Investigation and Research on the Legend of the Chu River and Han Boundary Chinese Chess Culture

Abstract: The Guangwu Mountain is the origin of chess culture, which makes Guangwu Mountain magnificent and glorious. Xingyang City has an irreplaceable important role and historical status in the development history of Chinese Chess culture.

The origin of chess culture can be traced back to the Guangwu Mountain in the north of Xingyang City in 203 BC where Xiang Yu and Liu Bang were facing each other by the gap between them and locked in a stalemate for many years,leaving numerous stories which enjoyed a great popularity. The historic site of the Han-Ba Er Wang City is of great value to the study of ancient Chinese war history.

Chinese ancient chess has been gradually developed and improved after absorbing abundant nutrients from the success and failure of the battle between the two Kings of Han and Ba, Liu and Xiang, including the structure of the board (such as the border of two opposing powers), the color of the chess pieces and the setting of game pattern, etc.

Keywords: Xingyang of Henan; chess; the border of two opposing powers

1.Guangwu Mountain Is the Birthland of Chinese Chess Culture

Chinese chess culture has a long and rich history. In the fourth year of emperor Gaozu of the Han Dynasty (203 BC), October (qin calendar), after the Han army defeated Cao Jiu and took Chenggao city that "the Han army encircled Zhongli Mei in the east of Xingyang City (ancient Xing), Xiang Yu arrived. Han army was afraid of Chu, so they took the steep road for marching". [1]209 and they "garrisoned in Guangwu City and ate food in a famous granary called Cangshi". [1]179 About Xiang Yu, "he garrisoned in Guangwu like the Han army did, and both of the two sides hanged there for several months. " [1]209 Aka, Han occupied the west area of Guangwu and Chu occupied the east area of Guangwu,with a gap between them. At the end, Xiang Yu and Liu Bang have reached an agreement that they divided the country equally. Thus, they set the west part of the gap as Han and the east part of the gap as Chu. [1]180 In this way, the gap became the original state of Chinese chess and was called the Chu River and Han Boundary (a seperated space for two player in Chinese chess).

If you go back further in time, you can still find traces of different forms and techniques of chess at different times in history. The earliest form of chess is about sacrifice and divination in primitive times.

In the Zhou Dynasty, a game called Liu Bo appeared according to the poem *Evocation* by Qu Yuan.This poem says : "Using jade to make a chess, it's called Liu Bo. Playing this game needs many skills and tactics and when the game goes to the key-point,it's called Five White, then the offensive side could kill any powerful army in the opposite side". In the Han Dynasty; there was a significant evolution of Chinese chess that no longer throwing away "Qiong" and the production technology of "Saixi" appeared. By the time of the Southern and Northern Dynasties (AD 569), such texts as *Chess Scripture* appeared, while Wang Bao's *Preface of Chess Scripture* pointed out that chess was based on yi-ology. The sentence "A horse of gold, a symbol of six armour" from Yu Xin's poem *About the Play of Chess* indicatesd that the chess pieces horse was double pieces and all six kinds of chess pieces in chess got its own names. In the Tang Dynasty, the basic form of "Baoying Xiangxi" was demonstrated by the legends which Niu Sengru described about the game of chess. Chess pieces made by gold and copper with metal chessboard. The names of the chess pieces include "general", "chariot", "horse", "pawn", "package" and "stoned".Legend does not mark the board, but later in the early years of the Northern Song Dynasty, it can be seen from Suzhou embroidery master's "Poetry and painting" works that the board has 64 grids with the color of black and white (exactly like today's chess board). Meanwhile, it centered around the gaming of four images.

In the late Tang Dynasty when the Five Dynasties and the early Northern Song Dynasty, Chinese chess underwent a completely new evolution. It means transforming the four images of gaming of trigram being into a column with images in *Yixue* into the Chinese chess of the border of two opposing. Namely: the middle of the chessboard is added a horizontal line as the river, and the pieces are divided into black and red sides, crossing the river for confrontations.And the grid is turned into two groups across the river in the vertical and horizontal line competition.

The situation formed by the new evolution of Chinese chess fully inherits the historical connotation of the confrontation between Chu and Han at Guangwu Mountain.Of course, there are advancing with the times of the chess system into it, such as the addition of a name "cannon", which changed the ancient chess of six items into seven.However, this does not affect the cultural deposits of Chinese chess.

Cheng Hao, a great scholar of the Northern Song Dynasty, wrote in his poem *"The Play of Chess"*: "The general of the eight sides of the Chinese army was a high-ranking general, while the pawn outside of the river was a low-ranking one. But having a rather leisure time with the Chinese chess board, even powerful person like Xiang Yu and Liu Bang would fight with trivial matters". Earlier than Cheng Hao did, in the early Northern Song Dynasty, the great statesman, strategist and litterateur Fan Zhongyan wrote a poem named *For Chess Play*, it says : "The risk of Han generals will be in danger, and the raider turned back water" .

Another poet named *Zheng Mo from Song Dynasty* also wrote in his poem : "The two scholars had a long history of silent strategy, and their soldiers had to overcome the gap." [3]134 It can be seen that in the Song Dynasty, there were a lot of literature works which clearly indicated that the newly evolved chess-making process was enlightened from the confrontation between Chu and Han.

After the Song Dynasty, the chess-making techniques with "river" also originated from the historical allusions that Chu and Han with confrontation across the gap. Zeng Qi, the top scholar in the early Ming Dynasty, wrote in a verse *Chess*: "The two armies set up a pair of camps against the enemy and decided to die or live by a crafty plan. Thousands of miles to the frontier the war horses were galloping, and waves swept Jin soldiers, Yu Ji sang and danced sadly, and Han army approached the walls of Chu City ". [3]136 This poem is generally respected as the representative of chess-ode. Another one named Mao Bo Wen in Ming Dynasty wrote poem to praise chess: "the horse will cross the gap with two steps, and the general keeps three palace with slim willow camp"; [3]137 One person named Ye Yan in Qing Dynasty wrote a poem named *Watching the Chinese Chess and Sending It to Zhao Shoushan* : " It's surprising that Liu in Han Dynasty drew a line for the gap, so as leading the fierce war all over the land." all of which indicates that the chess of Chu River and Han Boundary has been inherited and popularized for thousands of years because of wonderful description of Guangwu Mountain which attracts litterateurs' attention.

The essence of Chinese chess shining with the light of dialectics is that "fight a battle of wits,not of limbs". As a matter of fact, the profound cultural connotation of the chess-making field of Chu and Han also stems from the confrontation from the gap between the Chu and Han.

During this period, Xiang Yu once made an agreement with Liu Bang to have a dialogue across the gap, and he wanted to fight with him alone. Liu Bang declined with a smile: "I would rather fight with my wits than with my strength". [1]179 In addition, Xiang Yu had a dialogue with the Liu Bang, and he shot Liu Bang with a prepared crossbow when their negotiation didn't went very well. (the saying "when two Kings meet, there will be a wound" comes from this stroy.) Obviously, the rules of chess, "two Kings cannot meet, and the later king will lose the game the moment he saw the first king", should have an inseparable relationship with this story. In addition, the colors of chess pieces are black and red, more clearly from the Han and Chu. According to the history, Liu Bang declared that he was the son of the red emperor. When he launched his army against the Qin Dynasty, his army flag was red which means the superior color according to an ancient story. He called himself burning Han, admiring the virtue of flam and red. On the other hand, Xiang Yu and his army worships the color of black and the virtue of water, meanwhile, using Qin's regime. Thus, in Chinese chess, the red part means Han and the black part means Chu which are seperated on the two side of the gap. In the process of chess-making, it is more important that Chu and Han make an agreement: "The country is divided from the middle; Han is to the west of the gap, and Chu is to the east of the gap" [1]180 which is displayed on the chessboard, forming the boundary between Chu and Han as the Central Line. It is this most basic evolution that makes chess in the Han and Chu completely different from "Xiang (chess)" in ancient times (before Tang Dynasty). After the agreement between Chu and Han that the gap was the boundary, and the world was divided in the middle, Xiang Yu came back to the east, and Liu Bang wanted to lead him back to the west, so he used Liu Hou and Chen Ping's stratagem to attack "Xiang Yu" [1]211. In this way, there is a saying about the opening of chess that " the red goes first, and the one losing is not shamed ", and also formed a routine during the chess game in the folk that " the red party goes first ".

The middle line of Chinese chessboard refers to the gap. The Historical records clearly record that Xing yang under the river southeast as a gap connected Song, Zheng, Chen, Cai, Cao, Wei and met Ji, Ru, Huai, Si[1]1020, which means the origin of the gap is Xingyang.By the Ming Dynasty, *Xingyang County Records* written in Jiajing years still stated that " the gap is 10 kilometers northwest of the old administration.namely,at the boundary between Han and Chu. [4]7 " Bianshui (gap) flows from the southeastern part of the Guangwu River, which is now dry.[4]8 To a large extent, these detailed historical data all prove that the gap is indeed the boundary river between Chu and Han dynasties when they confronted each other in Guangwu Mountain and intersected with chess later.

Xingyang also has many legends about chess, and still retains some ancient chess-making techniques.For example, when we put the chess pieces in the beginning, general (leader) is not placed in the bottom line, but in the center of the grid. For another example, in the first step of the opening, we must take the lead of the general and the leader and move them to the center of the eight grids, which is so-called "general rises his curtain" or "force after courtesy". In the folk, people usually do not take the cannon as the first step, and it's probably from this.

Xingyang, especially around the Guangwu Mountain area, being a heritage of thousands of years of physical chess, not only has the Song Dynasty bronze chess, but also has the bronze chess from Yuan Dynasty and the Ming Dynasty, and the Ming Dynasty chessboard. The size of the chessmen from Song Dynasty bronze chess are slightly larger and thicker than bronze coins.The total 32 chess pieces all get its names on the front and get the corresponding images.The names on the front are general, guard, pawn, chariot, horse, cannon, without leader, chancellor and soldier.

The size of copper chessmen in Yuan Dynasty is similar to that in Song Dynasty, but there were general, chancellor and soldier in it.Besides, the chariot and horse in the red side were added with a Chinese character component. Ming Dynasty silk-woven chessboard, in addition to embroidering the edge of the chessboard lace with Chu River and Han Boundary in the center, respectively embroidered two groups of vertical and horizontal lines, and exactly like the present chessboard making system. In April 1999, Song Dynasty bronze chessboard and Ming Dynasty silk chessboard were collected by Xingyang Heritage Protection and Management Institute.

2. Chess Culture Contains the Philosophy and Wisdom of Life

Life is like chess, chess is like life.The extensive and profound content of chess is mainly developed around the gap, and the cultural deposits contain the intelligence and wisdom of life.

1.Chu and Han confront each other in Guangwu Mountain across the chasm, make a pact by taking the chasm as the boundary, the chasm into the Chu-Han river boundary, Chu-Han chess.

2.The core that Chu and Han take the chasm as adividing line is dividing the country from the middle. The chessboard adheres to this concept, and the "Chu River and Han Boundary" is located in the middle of the chessboard, which is the embodiment of this concept.

3.Chu is admiring the color of black, while Han is admiring the color of red.The black and red chess pieces respectively indicate that the two sides are facing each other on both sides of the river with the gap (Chu River and Han Boundary) as the boundary.

4.The confrontation of Chu and Han is to seize the world and power; Chu River and Han Boundary are on the two sides of the chessboard, each composed of nine vertical five horizontal lines, referring to the battle of imperial throne.

5.The meaning of nine and five represented by the vertical and horizontal lines of nine and five, together with the division of the world in the boundary between Chu and Han, constitute the chessboard, which clearly shows that the game between the two sides of chess is derived from the core idea of the confrontation between Chu and Han—to seize the world.

6.In the negotiation between Xiang Yu and Liu Bang across the gap, Xiang Yu decided to fight with Liu Bang alone. But Liu Bang claimed that he would rather compete in wits than in strength.Thus,the battle of wits became the essence of Chinese chess.

7.Xiang Yu shot Liu Bang on account of failing to agree with him when he made an appointment to meet Liu Bang across the gap. An old saying that "two Kings meet, there will be a wound" came into being.At the same time,a Chinese chess rule that "two Kings can not meet, the later king will lose the game the moment he sees the first king" also came into being.

8.After Chu and Han made an agreement that the gap should be the middle line of the world, Xiang Yu led troops to the east, meantime, Liu Bang decided to lead troops to the west without looking back the gap, but he listened to a stratagem from Zhang Liang which suggested crossing the gap and making a surprising attack to the army of Chu.

This is not only the source of Fan Zhongyan's verse "surprising attack by crossing the water ", but also the origin of the folk saying "red first, black lost not smelly". The opening of the game should be the red side first which originated from the story "divide the world by the gap", and Han army (red side) first attacked.

9.The physical objects of bronze casting chess in the Song Dynasty provided extremely powerful evidence for the development of Chu River and Han Boundary chess. At the beginning of the evolution of Chu River and Han Boundary chess, black and red sides have general, elephant, pawn, and don't have leader, soldier and chancellor. Among them, cannon was cast as the word kannon, and the image behind it was a stone-tossing machine, which indicated that military gamification at that time used stone as a refueling pellet.

10.The Guangwu Mountain area also preserves some of the old chess-making techniques in folklore. Such as when we place the chess pieces, the general (leader) should be in the center of the Nine Palaces and the first step of the opening should be "general rises his curtain" and "force after courtesy", walking the general (leader) to the middle of the eight grids.

3. Scientific, Competitive and Artistic Nature of Chinese Chess Culture

1.The science of Chinese chess.First of all, the two sides of red and black have formed the Chinese chess.7 kinds of arm of the services have their own way to move, such as being straight or oblique, with long legs or short feet,making a threat on its own or borrowing force from others, and there is mutual restriction between chess pieces. All in all, 32 pieces and 90 cross points coordinated perfectly.Secondly, the game between the two sides is fair, just and reasonable.Unlike some card games with elements of luck and chance.In addition, the improvement of chess skill requires the combination of theory and practice, which requires learners to look at the whole situation, deliberate with careful choices to decide advancing or retreating; one careless move will lose all, and these factors have obvious scientific nature inside.

2.The competitiveness of chess.The two sides try their most effort to win the game at every second according to the rules. "Rather fight with wits than with strength" is not only the characteristic of Chinese chess, but also the essence of Chinese chess and the motive force of the development of Chinese chess art. When two people play the Chinese chess, they need to put 16 pieces on the board based on the prescribed position with the different way of using general, guard, chancellor, chariot, horse, cannon and pawn.The chessboard is composed of nine vertical lines and ten horizontal lines, with the river boundary demarcated in the middle. There are 90 points, with each side taking half of them and playing the chess pieces by turn. Anyone who checkmates will be the victory, otherwise it would be even.In the process of the game, the two sides rather fight with wits than with strength,which is clearly a reflection of the competitive chess and the essence of the chess activity.

3.The artistry of chess. For example, a Chinese chess pieces, like a horse or a cannon, can have a great difference of power due to the player's level of use, which is an obvious manifestation of artistry. Playing chess was called hand talk in ancient time, which is the embodiment of artistic quality likewise. At the same time, from the chess manual handed down from more than a thousand years ago and the chess manual continually formed in practice and rehearsal (there are also endgame), it can be seen that it is an art form, the carrier of beauty. The players express their own thoughts and styles with their own thinking and creation, and the diversified aesthetic of the artistic nature of chess is also demonstrated incisively and vividly.

4. The Historical Value, Military Value and Entertainment Value of Chinese chess Culture

Chinese chess is a part of the traditional culture of the Chinese nation, and it is a part of cultural diversity that shouldn't be underestimated. It is not only for entertainment, but also for a comprehensive art of developing people's wisdom, exercising people's thinking and improving people's mental level. It has high cultural value and social value with many functions.

1.Historical value.

Historical records written by Sima Qian has a clear and detailed record that Xingyang Chu River and Han Boundary (a chessboard in the middle position of the name) depends on the history site where the Hegemon King Xiang Yu and King of Han Liu Bang confronted for four years (the Hegemon King Fortress, the King of Han Fortress, the gap separating between the two city), which confirms that The Chinese chess is closely related to the profound historical connotation, and also suggests that the chess culture due to the profound connotation.

From the poem *For The Chinese Chess Player* written by Fan Zhongyan in Northern Song Dynasty (from the existing data), *Game of Chinese Chess* written by Cheng Hao and *Chanting Go of Picture* written by Zheng Mo in Southern Song Dynasty to *The Chinese Chess* written by Zeng Qi in Ming Dynasty and *Chanting the Chinese Chess* written by Mao Bowen and so on. All of that express that the Xingyang Chu River and Han Boundary (the confrontation between Chu and Han is in Guangwu Mountain) is the core of the Chinese Chess Culture; while Chu River and Han Boundary is glaringly in the chess board, it proves that the intrinsic value of dividing ingthe world into two parts and drawing a middle line of the gap. As a treasure contributed by the Chinese nation to mankind, Chinese chess is the most precious essence in the history of the Chinese nation.

2.ideological value of military

Chess is the gymnastics of wisdom.Chess is a kind of intellectual competition of which can exercise people's thinking ability.The game of Chinese chess is varied and the moves of each round are different. There is no ready-made pattern for you to imitate on every move, and it is necessary for players to invent, create and practice.Every move is a game of intelligence and talent between two players.

At the same time, development of Chinese chess has followed the unique rules, requiring people to have rigorous logical thinking, otherwise they will lose the game with one single incorrect move. Strategy and tactics should be paid attention to in chess battle between two armies. It can also cultivate people's game thinking and methods. Moreover, when the player fights with their wisdom, the thought of both sides of the Chinese chess is abnormally concentrated and the cerebral cortex is in high excited state.

In other words, people don't just sit still and think with their brains; the whole body is a unity and its parts are interconnected and conditioned. Just as physical activity is good for the brain, it is also good for the body. Therefore, people call chess the touchstone of wisdom or the game of smart people.

In the ancient Chinese chess manual, the arrangement of chess occupied a great position.A brilliant arrangement is often a situation in which one party appears to be at an absolute disadvantage, but can be rescued by a series of "coming back from the dead" brilliant ideas.Both sides are full of dangers and threats and the situation is capricious in the change of the arrangement. One success move can kill the opponent. One careless move will inevitably lead to a irreversible defeat.In this respect, it is more a battle than a game of Chinese chess. In other words, it reflects a certain military thought and strategy, and it is a re-version of *Sun Tzu's Art of War*. In fact, some excellent strategists draw rich nutrition from the chess so that they are able to strategize skillfully.

3.Entertainment value.

As an elegant entertainment treasure, chess is widely loved.No matter playing Chinese chess overall, in the endgame or the arranged one, Chinese chess is undoubtedly full of charm and fascination. Children would take Chinese chess as a game, the youth take it as a battle of wits and it is an entertainment for the elderly. You will find endless joy when you savor the Chinese chess. Everyone can play Chinese chess. Chess skill means people's deep summary on the secret and culture of chess.

Meet friends in chess and improve together.As a popular cultural activity, Chinese chess is worthy of the Chinese nation's contribution to the human treasure. It purifies the mind,contains the profound philosophy, enlightens the dialectical thinking and edifies the cognitive change. At the same time, its entertainment value has also been fully developed and demonstrated.

5.The Inheritance of Chess Culture is from Generation to Generation

The inheritance of Chu River and Han Boundary chess culture has its extensiveness, complexity and spontaneity. It has been popular all over the country and abroad after thousands of years of inheritance and development by the people of all social strata.At present, in Xingyang City, especially in the Guangwu Mountain area where the original ecology of Chu River and

Han Boundary exists, the folk has been studying and inheriting the Chinese chess culture for thousands of years, and many works and legends of chess manual and culture have been passed down from generation to generation and have been growing continuously.

A scholar named Chen Yuncai in the late Qing Dynasty (in the early republican period, served as the director of the Department of Inducement in Heyin), has made many field visits to the Han-Ba Er Wang City, especially the gap between the Chu River and Han Boundary. He integrated his understanding of the chess culture into the related folk legends for thousands of years and sublimated and enriched the ideological realm of the Chinese chess culture, some of which include the black and red sides on behalf of the two sides of Chu and Han; Liu Bang's secret of winning a war with "rather fighting in wits than in strength"; In the opening game of chess, the rule that red side goes firstly and the black side goes secondly originated from the division of the world. Liu Bang started first and then attacked Chu and so on. These stories were accepted by many people and Zhao Youfu, his daughter-in-law as a teacher who loved literature and history.

His eldest son Chen wei learned chess from his mother when he was young and was influenced by the knowledge of chess culture, showing his keen interest in the discussion and research of Chinese chess.

He compiled books named *Xingyang*, *The Origin of Chess Culture*, *Chess Culture Roots Tour* and *The Heritage of Chess Culture* and other monographs with the findings he explored. He also compiled primary school textbook *Chess* (10 volumes) and trained chess teachers in many primary schools in Xingyang. His most important research results are as below: The first one is that the cultural gene of the chess is in Heluo and the second one is the two groups of vertical and horizontal lines on both sides of the Chu River and Han Boundary chessboard, which is a metaphor for "Jiu Wu". The moves on the chessboard express the battle of imperial power.

His view that the core consciousness of chess is the contention of the battle of imperial power was published in *Chinese Chess Culture Forum*, which was recognized and appreciated by Chen Zude, former President of Chinese Chess Academy, Wang Runan and Mr. Han Kuan, Wang Pinzhang, Dong Qiliang and other experts of chess culture.He also told the story and history of *Chess Between the Han Boundary and the Chu River* in CCTV and Henan TV for many times which had a great influence.

The most attractive example is the Project 1123 implemented by Xingyang City. "1" stands for taking a good grasp of the Chu River and Han Boundary Cultural Industrial Park as a carrier; "2" stands for popularizing the projects about the origin of Chinese chees and the spirit of Chu River and Han Boundary Chinese chess and the cultural research of the courtesy in playing Chinese chess; "3" stands for forming a long-term and stable strategic cooperation between Chinese Chess Association, Asian Chess Federation and World Chess Federation.All of these have played a beneficial role in promoting the inheritance and promotion of chess culture. A powerful promoter of these strategic achievements is Wang Xinting, the former mayor of Xingyang City.

Chinese Chess Culture Exhibition of Xingyang,Henan Province was brought into Hamburg G20 Summit "perception of China" series which was held at the Confucius Institute of Hamburg University as a national image promotion activity. And a 6-year-old chess prodigy Yang Shengxuan from Xingyang was present in Germany when the 2017 G20 Summit was held in Hamburg, Germany from July 7 to 8.

People are excited about Chinese chess's entry into the G20's global vision and Wang Xinting who is the general director behind the event especially feels grateful for it.A scholar who knows him told the author that Wang Xinting put people's interest beyond everything. He knew that it would be very dangerous to have no national cultural reserves, so he wanted to make chess culture as magnificent as possible.He understood the profound significance of the Olympic torch lit in front of the temple of Hera in ancient Greece. Therefore, he wanted the flame on Guangwu Mountain travels across the Himalayas to every city holding a chess competition, so as to spread the spirit of chess players and pass on Xingyang civilization. Wang Xinting wants to take a significant step forward to build Xingyang into the world Chinese chess capital and holy place of Chinese chess to enhance Xingyang's initiative and right of speech in the making of rules in the world Chinese chessboard. Both he and the people in Xingyang look forward to seeing Xingyang become a world respected city..."

6.The Countermeasure of Making Chinese Chess Culture Bigger and Stronger

Xingyang is the origin of Chinese chess culture and has developed a foundation of wide Chinese chess culture and a unique Chinese chess with Xingyang style .There are many wonderful chess games in places like the streets, homes,families, school classes and green parks of Xingyang City and it has long been integrated into Xingyang people's daily life.In recent years, with the development of a series of chess activities in Xingyang, it has further enhanced the atmosphere of chess culture and pushed it out of the country to the world and to become a glittering gold card of hometown's traditional culture.However, by doing some investigation and visit,the author believes that there is still a long way to go and efforts should be made about the Chinese chess.We should do what suggested in the following aspects to make the chess culture bigger and stronger .

Firstly, we are required to do a good job in protecting, developing and improving the gap in the source areas of the Chu River and Han Boundary.

Up to now, the two king cities of Han and Chu which are closely related to the chess culture have fallen into the river due to the constant erosion of the Yellow River for more than two thousand years.

In the Hegemon King Fortress which is in the east, there are no other cultural buildings to express the situation of the war at that time except for two large sculptures of Baowang Raising the Ding and Warhorse Neighing. To the west, the king of Han Fortress is even more desolate without any signs. Visitors can not see the confrontation historica site between the two military battle scenes which will inevitably weaken the artistic appeal of chess culture.

Therefore, in order to build Han-Ba Er Wang City into a tourist resort with both ornamental value and cultural connotation, we need to make a detailed research and plan to put the design into practice. We need to build a Han-Ba Er Wang theme park with distinct theme, cultural connotation and environmental protection.

Secondly, we should strength the collection of historical relics scattered in the folk (Chinese chess), such as ancient weapons, pottery and bronze or iron arrowheads. We also need to collect the stories about the figures in the Chu-Han War in the folk legends, such as Liu Bang, Xiang Yu, Zhou ke, Cao Jiu, Zhongli mei, Han Xin and so on. We should complete such as Ji Gong Temple, Zhou Ke Temple and other attached buildings related to Chu and Han Culture' add chess cultural elements and develop chess cultural artifacts or souvenirs in the main streets of the urban so that Xingyang can flow out of the thick artistic atmosphere and purify each tourist's mind and edify his sentiment .

Thirdly, we are required to strengthen scientific discussion and the theory research of the Chinese chess culture. The profound connotation of the Chinese chess culture and the promotion of the unique social significance of the Chinese chess culture have lagged behind the development of the Chinese chess skills. As the origin of the chess culture, we must clearly realize this and put the scientific discussion and theoretical research of the chess culture in an important position. We need to establish a complete chess information file by carrying out the general survey of Chinese chess talents, visiting the predecessors of Chinese chess and excavating and rescuing the literature and history data that are on the verge of being lost, and record and archive them by text, audio and video.

The historical evolution, cultural connotation and scientific value of chess culture should be studied in depth by professional personnel and a monograph should be formed and published. We should train successors in a planned and focused way and do a good job in introducing Chinese chess into schools. Thus, we can do a good job in improving it while popularizing it, so that there will be successors in the study of Chinese Chess Culture and Chinese chess skills.

Fourthly, establish the safeguard mechanism of chess-playing culture between Chu River and Han Boundary. A permanent leading group for the protection of chess culture in Chu River and Han Boundary shoule be formed, being in duty of studying and formulating protection measures and making sure implement protection funds on position and supervising the implementation of various protection works. Only when we do our own job well,can we work more effectively. We will establish rules and regulations to protect the Chinese Chess Culture of the Han River and Chu Boundary. We should compile the scripts of film, TV and drama, edit legends and folklore and intensify the publicity of chess culture to make it a household name and deeply rooted in the hearts and minds of the people.

Chu River and Han Boundary Chess Culture is a treasure in the cultural resources with Chinese characteristics.There is a long way to build the world chess culture capital which is a comprehensive project integrating the protection of ancient sites, inheritance of traditional Chinese culture, tourism and leisure and artistic performance. The journey is long and arduous.In recent years, under the joint efforts of the whole Xingyang City, the brand of Chu River and Han Boundary as "Hometown of Chinese Chess Culture" has made a big success with certain fame and influence. But it still requires us to make great efforts and contribution for the cultural card of Xingyang; what's more,we need to make contribution to the economic construction and cultural construction of Xingyang City.

References:

[1] Sima Qian. Historical Records [M]. Xi' an: Sanqin Press, 1988.

[2] Qu Yuan. The Songs of Chu [M]. Beijing: Zhonghua Publishing House, 1983.

[3] Chen Wei, Han Lu. Hometown of Chinese Chess Culture [M]. Beijing: China Federation of Literary and Art Publishing House, 2015.

[4] Chen Wanqing. Jiajing Xingyang County Chronicles [M].Yangzhou: Guangling Publishing House, 2006.

河南荥阳民间舞蹈"笑伞"调查研究

　　摘要：笑伞是流行在河南荥阳一带的民间舞蹈。据传,它起源于隋末瓦岗军攻打荥阳城时装扮成花伞表演队的故事。笑伞表演由五人构成,分别扮程咬金、侠客、武旦等,进行舞蹈、演唱、说快板交替表演,表演程序为"转——唱——转——唱——说"。笑伞作为中华文化多样性的重要构成部分,具有较高的历史价值、文化价值和审美价值,是当地民众的重要精神食粮。笑伞的唱词内容丰富、文学性强,尤其值得研究。笑伞在清代和民国时期最为兴盛,"文革"后迅速衰败,今天仅剩个别表演队还在坚持。笑伞的保护和抢救已迫在眉睫。我们应该尽快优化其文化生态环境,加强传承人的培养,运用现代科学技术手段和传播方式等对其进行有效的保护。

　　关键词：河南荥阳；民间舞蹈；笑伞

　　河南省荥阳市一带流行着一种极富地域特色的民间舞蹈——笑伞。据艺人讲述,"文革"前笑伞在当地曾流传很广,许多村镇都有笑伞表演队。"文革"开始后笑伞迅速沉寂,至今表演队已所剩无几,只有个别表演队能勉强演出。2016年秋,作者就笑伞问题在荥阳市进行了调查,先后到豫龙镇关帝庙村、龙泉寺村等地采访了李同中等艺人和村民,现将有关情况报告如下。

一、笑伞的起源及其发展

　　笑伞的历史比较悠久。据传,"笑伞"之名起源于隋末瓦岗军攻打荥阳城的历史故事。隋末,隋炀帝骄奢淫逸、横征暴敛,致使民怨沸腾、义军四起。公元 616 年，瓦岗军挥师中原，欲攻打战略要塞荥阳城。荥阳城池坚固，隋兵拼命抵抗，城池久攻不下。瓦岗义军首领翟让采用谋士李密之计，委派程咬金率部下乘正月十五闹元宵之机，扮作滑稽老夫，打着花伞、敲着鼓混进城内，最后与城外义军里应外合一举攻下了荥阳城。后来，人们就以该故事为原型，创造了"笑伞"这一独特的民间艺术。笑伞产生后逐步受到了当地群众的喜爱，并不断扩散，一直流传到了今天。笑伞发展到清代达到鼎盛，清康熙年间笑伞已在当地遍地开花。民国时期，荥阳很多村都有笑伞，并有艺人走乡串户表演，其已成为当地社火中的主要节目。新中国成立初期，笑伞作为群众喜闻乐见的文艺形式得到了进一步发展。"'文化大革命'中，基本销声匿迹。"[1]731 "文革"后，部分笑伞表演队恢复活动。但由于受多种因素影响，部分恢复活动的笑伞表演队又逐渐归于沉寂。根据调查，目前荥阳还在活动的笑伞表演队只剩下关帝庙村李同中一个队了。

二、笑伞的表演特点

笑伞是荥阳地区社火活动中的重要表演节目。"在原始时代，任何一种艺术文化现象，设若没有一种宗教作基础，那它能否产生和维持下去就很值得怀疑。"[2]232 在过去，荥阳的火神祭祀活动非常兴盛，多村都有火神庙。我们调查的豫龙镇关帝庙村过去就有火神庙。据该村笑伞老艺人李同中（79 岁）介绍，"关帝庙村过去的火神祭祀活动相当隆重，祭祀活动的主要内容是文艺表演。"为满足火神祭祀的需要，该村成立了九个文艺表演队，有狮子鼓、笑伞、龙灯、高跷、小车、旱船、独杆轿、确猴（蹦猴）、霸王鞭等。春节期间，初一到初七各路"故事"（表演队）要在村子各处演一下。"每年正月初七龙泉寺古庙会，军张、关帝庙、冯寨、寺后、马寨等地民间艺人大会师时，大都表演笑伞。"[1]730 每次出去演出，先要到本村的火神庙表演。豫龙镇龙泉寺（内供有火神像）的火神祭祀是当地规模最大、最有影响的活动。每年正月初七，这里都要举行隆重的火神祭祀活动。周边多个村子的文艺队都要到此进行表演。据艺人介绍，以龙泉寺为中心，以西的几个村叫"西大会"，以东包括关帝庙村在内的七、八个村叫"东大会"。"东大会"的文艺节目中有笑伞，节目精彩，地位很高。"东大会"每年要上"头会"，即第一个进庙演出。"东大会"演过，其他会的"故事"才能进庙演出。关帝庙村的"故事"在沿途各村一路演过去,到达龙泉寺时一般都到中午十二点了。即便如此,其他的村的"故事"也要在外候着,一定让"东大会"的"故事"进庙演过,他们才能进庙演出。同时,据当地文化学者陈玮介绍说,笑伞过去是整个社火表演的中心,其他文艺队都是围绕笑伞进行表演的。可见笑伞在当地文艺表演中的地位确实是比较高的。

笑伞表演时共有五个角色。主角是"程咬金",他头戴红白相间的花毡帽,面部化妆成黑白颜色的丑角模样,戴红色冉须,上身着古代宽袖宽摆的黄色长袍,下穿宽松白色长裤,着黑色牛鼻子布鞋,腰系又宽又厚的白色丝带,左手拿一破蒲扇,右手执一米多高花伞。其余四人,两个扮作侠客模样,两个作武旦扮相。五个人在乐器的伴奏下进行表演,伴奏乐器为手鼓和小锣。所用道具包括扇子、花伞(装饰得很漂亮)等。笑伞的表演通常是选一平地,五个人依次排成圆圈,先转两三圈,然后唱,再转,再唱。一般唱两遍、转两次,最后说一段快板,即按照"转——唱——转——唱——说"的程序进行表演。

笑伞的舞蹈步伐并不复杂,基本是围圈而舞,节奏缓慢,间有摇摆及舞伞等动作。演唱内容相对丰富,唱调属民间小调。唱词通俗易懂,内容丰富,表达的多是生活故事以及百姓对人生和未来的憧憬。如《四季谣》:

正月里来正月正,长坂坡前赵子龙。

怀中抱定皇太子,杀退曹操百万兵。

二月二来龙抬头,千金小姐抛绣球。

绣球单打吕蒙正,寒瓦窑里出诸侯。

三月三来三月三,昭君娘娘和北番。

思念父母泪涟涟,眼望南方好辛酸。

四月四来四月八,奶奶庙里把香插。

婶子大娘都跪下,祈祷神灵把雨下。

五月五来是端阳,大麦小麦齐上场。

牛板把式都上地,放滚打趔吼几嗓。

六月六来热难当,二妹独坐象牙床。

手拿罗扇还显热,想起相公拱麦秸。

七月有个七月七,天上牛郎会织女。

织女会把牛郎见,双双相见泪涟涟……

这段唱词从一月唱到十二月,谈古论今,内涵丰富,既有对历史人物的颂扬赞叹,又有对庄户农民辛苦劳作的讴歌,更有神话故事的浮想联翩,体现了劳动人民的聪明智慧和极强的创造力。

还有一些唱词风趣可人、寓庄于谐,充满生活气息,如《哄儿小调》:

闲言无事下北坡,新坟没有旧坟多。

新坟头上顶白纸,旧坟头上蒺藜窝。

赤抹肚孩儿逮蛐子,蒺藜扎住他的脚。

这手薅、那手摸,疾疾扎得就那么多。

往西看、日头落,蛤蟆叫唤鬼吆喝。

山上跑下来一群狼,好似饿虎找干粮。

有一些唱词是表现劳动生活以及劳动者的向往与憧憬的,如《锄地歌》:

清早起来背张锄,我到南湖锄蜀黍。

锄了一遭又一遭,肚子饿得直咕噜。

抬头往北看一眼,那边来了我媳妇。

迎上前去看一看,媳妇担着小担担。

一头挑的是黑窝窝,一头挑的是糠糊涂。

媳妇啊,我让你给我烙油馍、打鸡蛋,谁叫你做这糠糊涂!

媳妇说:想吃油馍也不难,等到五月麦上镰。

早上给你烙油馍、打鸡蛋,上午给你擀蒜面。

夜里咱俩一头睡,你的胳臂我枕住……

可见,笑伞的唱词内容丰富、充满生活情调,反映了劳动者的生活和理想。流传在当地的笑伞唱词除了以上所列外,还有《火烧战船》《闯王进北京》《四辈上工》等三十多首。这些多是一代代口传而来。也有少数唱词是现在的表演者即兴编创的,反映的是当代民众的生活和理想。

三、笑伞的价值、现状及其保护设想

笑伞历史悠久、形式独特,是中华文化大观园中的一朵奇葩。从非物质文化遗产保护的视角来说,它是中华文化多样性的重要构成部分。其独特的表现形式和内容丰富了中华文化的内涵。其特殊的舞蹈形式使中原舞蹈的内容更加丰富。它是中华民族悠久历史的表征,也是当地民众的重要精神食粮。在漫长的历史生活中,笑伞为当地民众带来了欢笑、充实和快乐。同时,它也在多样文艺的共生和竞生中发挥了积极的作用。它在吸收其他艺术营养的同时,也为其他艺术的发展贡献了力量。特别是在民间社火活动中,笑伞作为核心表演队,为整个文艺队的协同表演发挥了积极的作用。在今天的生活中,笑伞仍然有着它的独特价值和作用。它在丰富我们的精神生活的同时,还能为当代艺术创造和文化产业发展提供资源。因此,我们应该珍视笑伞这一独特的文艺形式,加强其传承保护和创新发展。

不过,值得注意的是,笑伞当前的生存状况极令人担忧。原曾遍布各地的笑伞表演队现已所剩无几。我们调查时访问了很多人,都说现在已经没有笑伞表演队了。几经周折,最后我们在豫龙镇关帝庙村找到了笑伞表演老艺人李同中,他说逢年过节他们还要演一下笑伞,只是演员队伍已不是在全村挑选,而是由其几个子女和小外孙(十多岁)凑合着演。表演的水平和内容自然与过去也不一样了。总之,当前笑伞的发展面临着严重的危机。一是传承人缺乏。演员青黄不接、后继乏人。现仅知的一个演出队——关帝庙村笑伞演出队,主要演员李同中已年近 80 岁。过去和他同场演出的几位老弟兄张海山、李会有、李石头都已是 90 多岁的人了,不能再参加演出。为了使这一手艺不至于失传,李同中曾发动过几位年轻媳妇参加演出。后来,出于经济效益的顾虑,大家都纷纷表示不愿意干这项工作。李同中无奈之中动员老伴儿王秀枝(78 岁)参加演出,之后又动员自己的女儿、儿子、外孙参加演出。"过去演员最多时一个队有三十多人,现在只能由这老少五人勉强坚持了。笑伞本来是需要一定体力的舞蹈艺术,现在的演员老的老、小的小,怎么能保证演出水平和有效传承?"再者,当前的笑伞艺术运作机制不良,经费缺乏,生存艰难。过去的笑伞表演都是以神会为依托,由神会为其提供精神动力和物质支撑的。调查中我们了解到,笑伞的演出主要是在各种各样的社火祭祀活动中进行的。荥阳的各种祭祀活动(特别是春节祭祀)是笑伞表演最集中的时刻。应该说,民间信仰及其相关的祭祀活动为笑伞的发展发挥了重要作用。今天,在经历了"文革"的冲击及各种各样的破坏之后,笑伞原曾依托的生存基础崩溃,精神动力和物质支撑消失。现在的艺人完全是凭爱好或保护文化遗产的信念在艰难维持。这种维持还能支撑多长时间，谁也说不清楚。目前笑伞的活动是极为艰难的。购置服装、道具、乐器等没有钱，完全是靠艺人自掏腰包，或者是利用废物制作。外出演出也要自己找车、自己负担生活费。在谈到笑伞的发展时，李同中忧心忡忡地说："我想把笑伞传下去，可是巧妇难为无米之炊。好多事力不从心啊！"在这样的情况下，笑伞的生存怎能不令人担忧？

笑伞作为独具特色的民间艺术和重要的非物质文化遗产需要尽快保护，而当地保护工作却并不尽如人意。作者认为，在笑伞的保护上，政府和民间应该携起手来，共同努力，应积极采取以下措施：

（1）优化文艺的生态环境。建立有效的生态机制，促进笑伞及多样文艺的繁荣发展。"在更高的人文审美上回归传统，让悠悠历史更加精炼地浮现和融合于当代社会。"[3]37 需要政府支持和鼓励民间艺术研究，加强民间艺术保护，建立文化生态保护区，不断改善艺术的生态环境，给予艺术发展更宽广的空间；加大资金投入力度，为民间艺术的发展和保护创造更好的条件。

（2）加强传承人的培养。笑伞保护最重要的是传承人的培养。文学即人学，笑伞也是人学。"正如曹禺所言：'没有一个人可以说，我把人的问题说清楚了'。"[3]20 人是笑伞发展的核心和基础。没有传承人，一切的活动都谈不上了。政府和艺人应该携起手来，共同开展传承人的培养工作。为做好笑伞的宣传、营造传承氛围，可以开展笑伞进学校、进课堂活动。通过在当地小学、中学开展笑伞学习培训，激发孩子们对笑伞的兴趣，并逐步开展特色人才培养，有针对性地培养笑伞传承人。学校通过相关活动也可以达到既丰富同学们的课外生活，又弘扬传统文化的教育效果。同时，也可由老艺人开设专门的笑伞培训班，从社会上选择有兴趣的年轻人进行培养。当然，目前最大的问题是，很少有年轻人愿意学习这门艺术。这恐怕还要将思想工作和经济手段同时用上。即既要将笑伞的传承意义讲清楚，提高年轻人对笑伞传承的认识，还要在经济上让学习者觉得不吃亏、值得干。这当然是最难的。因为这需要有坚实的经济后盾，而当前笑伞发展最难的就是缺乏足够的资金。这除了政府的大力扶持外，也要仰仗社会各界的支持以及笑伞自身的产业化运作。

（3）运用科技手段加快笑伞的资料记录和传播。即运用录音、录像等手段对笑伞进行资料记录和保存，同时利用互联网、微信等现代手段进行传播和宣传，扩大笑伞的影响，吸引更多的人关心、支持笑伞发展。

总之，笑伞是中华文化的瑰宝。它形式独特、价值独具，曾在当地民众的诗意生活中发挥了积极的作用。今天笑伞的生存前景堪忧、急需保护，相信在政府的积极支持和社会各界的共同关心之下，笑伞这颗艺术明珠一定会再次闪射出绚丽的光芒！

参考文献：

[1] 杜之庆 . 荥阳市志 [M]. 北京：新华出版社，1996.

[2] 丁亚平 . 艺术文化学 [M]. 北京：文化艺术出版社，2005.

[3] 吴新斌 . 新语境下的话语重构——当代戏剧丛论 [M]. 北京：中国文联出版社，2015.

Research on "Xiaosan"

—A Kind of Folk Dance in Xingyang of Henan

Province

Abstract: Xiaosan is a popular folk dance in the area of Xingyang, Henan province. It is said that this dance originated in the late Sui Dynasty; in order to attack and occupy Xingyang City, Wagang Army dressed up as a Xiaosan troupe. Xiaosan needs five people in total to dress as Cheng Yaojin, swordsmen and soldiers respectively. They are dancing, singing, or telling allegro alternately; the order is "swinging—singing—swinging—singing—telling". As an important part of Chinese cultural diversity and nourishment for local people, Xiaosan has high historical value, cultural value and aesthetic value. The lyrics of Xiaosan are rich in content and strong in literariness. It is worth studying. The most prosperous period of Xiaosan was in the Qing Dynasty and it declined after "the Great Cultural Revolutio". And today, only several troupes persist in Xiaosan performance, therefore, its protection is imminent. We should optimize its cultural ecological environment as soon as possible, and pay great attention to the cultivation of its successors, and use modern scientific and technological means and transmission methods to protect it effectively.

Key words: Xingyang, Henan province; folk dance; Xiaosan

Xiaosan, a kind of folk dance with rich regional characteristics, is popular in Xingyang City, Henan Province. According to the artists, it was widely spread in the local before the Great Cultural Revolution, and many villages and towns in Xingyang have Xiaosan performance troupes. However, after the Great Cultural Revolution, Xiaosan quickly fell into decay. So far, there are only a few performing troupes can barely perform. In the autumn of 2016, the author interviewed Li Tongzhong and other performers and villagers in Guandimiao Village, and Longquansi Village, Yulong Town to investigate Xiaosan. The findings are as follows.

1.The origin and Development of Xiaosan

Xiaosan has a long history. It is said that the name of "Xiaosan" originated from a historical story that Wagang Army conquered Xingyang City at the end of the Sui Dynasty. At that time, Emperor Yang of Sui Dynasty was very extravagant and extorted excessive taxes and levies to his people so that people who boiled with resentment began to revolt. In 616, Wagang Army commanded their troops to conquer Xingyang City, the strategic fortress of Central China. However, Xingyang City was not easy to be captured due to the troops of Sui's desperate resistance. Using the tactics of Li Mi, a strategist, Zhai Rang, the leader of the Wagang Army, appointed Cheng Yaojin and his soldiers to dress up as funny old men, with flower umbrellas, striking the drums into the city at the Lantern Festival on the fifteenth day of the first lunar month. At last, thanks to their cooperation, Yingyang City was occupied successfully. Later, people created the unique folk dance of "Xiaosan" based on this story. This dance was gradually loved by the local people from its creation, and constantly spread to the rest area. Until today, we still can watch people doing Xiaosan. It reached their peak in the Qing Dynasty, especially during the reign of Emperor Kangxi of Qing Dynasty.

And during the period of the Republic of China, many villages in

Xingyang had Xiaosan performance, and the artists even perform Xiaosan from door to door; it had become the main programs at Shehuo activity (a kind of folk recreational activity in Xingyang at Spring Festival). In the early days of the founding of New China, Xiaosan, as a popular art form, was further developed. " In 'the Great Cultural Revolution', it basically disappeared." [1]731 After "the Great Cultural Revolution", some of Xiaosan troupes restored their performance. However, some of restored troupes gradually declined because of many influenced factors. According to the survey, at present, the performance troupes of Xiaosan in Xingyang only leave one troupe, led by Li Tongzhong at Guandimiao Village.

2.The Characteristics of Xiaosan's Performance

Xiaosan is an important program in Shehuo activity at Xingyang. "In primitive times, it is doubtful that one artistic culture can be created and inherited without a religion as its foundation." [2]232 In the past, Vulcan sacrificial activities in Xingyang were very popular, and many villages had Vulcan Temples. And these kinds of temples can be seen at Guandimiao Village in Yulong Town now. Li Tongzhong, a 79-year-old artist of Xiaosan in this village, said, "the sacrificial activities of Vulcan in Guandimiao Village used to be quite grand, and the main contents of these activities were artistic performances." Actually, in order to meet the needs of the activities, Guandimiao Village has set up nine performing troupes, namely Lion Drum, Xiaosan, Dragon Lantern, Stilts, Handcart, Land Boat, Single-pole Sedan, Quehou (jumping monkey) and Overlord whip. During the Spring Festival, from the first day to the seventh day, each "story" (performed by these troupes) will be played at the villages everywhere. "On the seventh day of the first lunar month, folk artists who come from Junzhang Village, Guandimiao Village, Fengzhai Village, Sihou Village and Mazhai Village will perform Xiaosan at Longquan Temple." [1]730 The first place of Xiaosan performance is at the Vulcan Temple in their villages. The Vulcan sacrifice of

Longquan Temple at Yulong Town is the largest and most influential activity in this area. Every year on the seventh day of the first month, a grand Vulcan sacrificial ceremony is held here. Art troupes from surrounding villages will perform here. According to the Xiaosan performers, the temple fair divides into two part: West Fair and East Fair. West Fair refers to the villages located in the west of Longquan Temple; East Fair includes Guandimiao Village and other seven or eight villages. East Fair has Xiaosan performance, which is great and wonderful. Every year, the East Fair would perform the first program at Longquan Temple. And after their performance, West Fair's programs can be performed. The performance of Guandimiao Village goes through each village on the way. It is usually twelve o'clock at noon when they arrive at Longquan Temple. Even so, the performers of the other villages have to wait outside; until East Fair's performance is over, they can begin their performance. At the same time, Chen Wei, a local cultural scholar, said that Xiaosan used to be the core of the whole Shehuo performance, and other art troupes' performances are just icing on the cake. Thus it can be seen that Xiaosan has very high standing in local art performances.

There are five roles in Xiaosan performance. The leading role is Cheng Yaojin, with a red and white felt hat on his head; he dresses himself up as a clown with black and white colors on his face. He wears a red beard and an ancient wide yellow robe, a pair of loose white pants and black cloth shoes like cow nose. Tying with wide thick white ribbon, he holds a dilapidated cattail fan in his left hand and an umbrella over a meter high in his right hand. The other four performers, two dress as swordsmen, and the rest as soldiers. Five people begin to perform accompanied by musical instruments such as tambourines and small gongs. Their performance props include cattail fans, umbrellas (beautifully decorated) and so on. The place of their performance is usually at a level ground; five people form a circle in turn. Firstly, they turn clockwise two or three times. Next they begin to sing. And then they turn again, and sing again. Generally speaking, they sing twice and turn twice. Finally there would be a paragraph of allegro. That is, it is performed according to the order of "turn — sing — turn — sing — say".

The dance step of Xiaosan is not complicated; it is basically a circle dance with a slow rhythm. And sometimes they swing or dance with umbrella. Its tune belongs to the folk minor. And its lyrics are proper rich, easy to understand, close to life, and express people's longing for their future's life. Such as "The Ballad of Four Seasons" :

In the first day of the first month of lunar year,
Zhao Zilong was at the place of Changbanpo.
In order to save the crown prince Liu Chan,
He retreated the troops of Cao Cao by himself.
In the second day of the second month of lunar year,
Young rich lady throw her hydrangea for a spouse.
The hydrangea fell directly into Lv Mengzheng's hand,
He was just a poor man and finally became a duke.
In the third day of the third month of lunar year,
Wang Zhaojun married into Beisai for national peace.
She missed her country and her family tearfully,
She often looked at the direction of her country.
In the fourth day of the fourth month of lunar year,
The old ladies often stick incense in the temple.
In order to pray to the gods for raining down,
People all knelt down at the front of temple.
In the fifth day of the fifth month of lunar year,
People are busy for harvesting wheat and barley.
Eventually, all harvest tools come in handy.
They sometimes harvest, sometimes play for fun.
In the sixth day of the sixth month of lunar year,
The younger sister sits at ivory bed alone for relaxing and shading.
She holds a fan in hand but still feels hot.

Suddenly think of her husband working under the sun.

In the seventh day of the seventh month of lunar year,

Niulang makes a date with Zhinv on the sky.

Zhinv will meet her husband on time,

They meet each other with tears in their eyes.

...

The lyrics have rich connotations that are from January to December, from ancient to modern. It not only extols and praises historical figures, but also eulogizes farmers' hard work, and it is full of imagination of fairy tales, which reflects the wisdom and creativity of the Chinese people.

Some of the lyrics are funny, humorous, and full of vitality, such as "Coax Children Tune":

One goes to Beipo at his spare time,

New graves are not as many as the old ones.

New graves have white paper;

While, old graves have briars.

A little child catches crickets.

His foot is caught by briars.

He touches and pulls them,

Again and again.

In the west, the sun is setting.

Croak of frogs can be heard.

A group of wolves run from the mountain,

Like hungry tigers looking for food.

Some of the lyrics express how the working life it is and reflect workers' yearning for future. Such as "The Hoe Song":

I carried a hoe in the morning, hoed the corn at South Lake.

I hoed again and again, until my stomach rumbled with hunger.

Looking north, I saw my wife shoulder a pole.

One side of the pole was black steamed corn bread.

Another was bran polenta.

Darling, you know that I just want to eat baked bun oil and eggs.

And I do not want to eat bran polenta at all

My wife said : "It is easy, but you have to wait until May."

At that time, you can eat baked bun oil and eggs in the morning.

And eat garlic noodles at noon.

At night we sleep together; I pillow your arm...

It can be seen that the lyrics of Xiaosan are rich in content and full of life sentiment and reflect people's life and ideal. Besides, there are more than 30 Xiaosan lyrics spread in the local, such as "The Burning Warship", "King Chuang Enters Beijing", "Four Generations' Work" and so on. They are often handed down orally from generation to generation. A few of the lyrics, which reflect the life and ideals of contemporary people, are improvised by contemporary performers.

3. The Value, Present situation and Protection Assumption of Xiaosan

With a long history and unique form, Xiaosan is a distinguished one in Chinese culture. From the perspective of intangible cultural heritage protection, it is an important part of the diversity of Chinese culture. Its unique form and content enrich the connotation of Chinese culture. Its special dance forms enrich the content of Central China's dance. It witnesses Chinese nation's long history and it is important pabulum for the local people. During the long history, Xiaosan brings laugh, fulfillment and happiness for local people. At the same time, it also plays an active role in the symbiosis and competition of diverse literature and art. While absorbing the nutrition of other arts, it also contributes to their development. Especially in Shehuo, as the core performance, Xiaosan plays a positive role in the whole activity. Nowadays, Xiaosan still has its unique value and functions. While enriching our spiritual life, it can also provide resources for the creation of contemporary art and the development of cultural industry. Therefore, we should pay much attention to its unique artistic form and attach great importance to its inheritance, protection and innovative development.

However, it is worth noting that the current situation of Xiaosan is extremely worrying. There are not many Xiaosan troupes left. We asked a lot of people when we did the survey, and they said that there was no more Xiaosan troupes. After several twists and turns, finally, we found Li Tongzhong at Guandimiao Village, Yulong Town. He said that they would play Xiaosan in each festival. But, it is a pity that the performers were not selected from all over the village, but from his children and young grandchildren (only in their teens). Thus, the level and content of the performance is certainly not as good as what it used to be. In a word, the development of Xiaosan is facing a serious crisis. One is the lack of bearers. There is no young people would like to inherit Xiaosan performance. Now, it is known that only one Xiaosan troupe, namely, Guandimiao Village Xiaosan Troupe. The main performer Li Tongzhong has nearly 80 years old. And other performers Zhang Haishan, Li Huiyou and Li Shitou who performed with Li Tongzhong in the past, are all over 90 years old. They all cannot participate in the performance any more for their old ages. In order to make this craft not lost, Li Tongzhong once launched several young ladies to learn Xiaosan performance. Later, they all were reluctant to do this for its low paid. Li Tongzhong had no choice but to persuade his wife Wang Xiuzhi (78 years old) to participate in the performance, and then mobilize his daughter, son, grandson to participate in the performance. "In the past, a Xiaosan troupe had more than 30 performers. Now, it only has five people. Xiaosan is originally a dance art that requires a certain amount of physical strength, but now the performers are old or small. How can we ensure the performance level and effective inheritance?" Moreover, the current Xiaosan art has poor operating mechanisms, funds, thus leading to difficult survival. In the past, all the Xiaosan performances were based on the spiritual power and material support provided by the God Committee. From the investigation, we know that the performance of Xiaosan is mainly at a variety of Shehuo sacrificial activities. Xingyang's various sacrificial activities (especially the Spring Festival sacrificial activity) are the most concentrated performance place of the Xiaosan. It can be seen that folk beliefs and some sacrificial activities play an important role in the development of Xiaosan. Today, after the impact of the "The Great Cultural Revolution" and all kinds of destruction, the survival foundation that the Xiaosan used to rely on has collapsed, and its spiritual power and material support have disappeared. Today's performers are struggling to survive only on the basis of their interests or a belief in preserving cultural heritage. It is hard to say how long they can persist in. The present activity of Xiaosan is extremely difficult to implement. There is no money to buy clothes, props, musical instruments, etc.; all these spending is entirely from the artists' own pockets, or the use of waste productions. Even if they perform out of the field, they also need to look for cars and burden living expenses by themselves. When talking about the development of Xiaosan, Li Tongzhong said anxiously, "I want to pass it on. But one cannot make bricks without straw. There are a lot of incompetent difficulties!" Under such circumstances, how can the survival of Xiaosan not be worrying?

As a unique folk art and important intangible cultural heritage, Xiaosan needs to be protected as soon as possible. However, local conservation efforts have been less perfect. In the light of Xiaosan protection, from the author's perspective, the government should join hands with the public together to make Xiaosan better. And measures should be taken actively as follows:

1.Optimizing the ecological environment of literature and art. Effective ecological mechanism needs to be established to promote the prosperity and development of Xiaosan and diverse literature and art. "We need to return to the tradition based on humanistic aesthetics at a higher degree, and let the long history more succinctly emerge and integrate into the contemporary society." [3]37 The government needs to support and encourage the research of folk art, pay great attention to its protection, establish cultural ecological protection areas so that the ecological environment of art can be constantly improved, and give wider space to its development; and funds need to be increased to create better conditions for the development and protection of folk art.

  2.Strengthening the cultivation of the inheritors. It is the most important thing for Xiaosan protection. Literature is human science, so does Xiaosan. "Just as Cao Yu goes: 'no one can confidently said that he had researched humanity clearly." [3]20 Human is the core and foundation of the development of Xiaosan. Without successors, all is an empty talk. The government and artists should join hands to train successors. In order to publicize Xiaosan and create an atmosphere of inheritance, it can be carried out into schools. We should build the targeted training of the successors by conducting class activities as the training method of Xiaosan in local primary schools and middle schools, so that children's interests in Xiaosan can be stimulated. Thus, characteristic talent can be trained gradually. In addition, through these kinds of activities, schools can not only enrich students' extracurricular life but promote our traditional culture. At the same time, old artists can set up a Xiaosan training course to attract young people who are interested in Xiaosan performance. The biggest problem, of course, is that few young people are willing to learn this art. We should adopt the methods of both ideology and economy. In other words, the significance of the inheritance of Xiaosan should be clearly explained to improve young people's understanding of Xiaosan's inheritance. In addition, economically speaking, learners should feel that it is worth doing. This must be the hardest part. Because this needs to have a solid economic backing, and the current development of Xiaosan is lack of funds. Apart from the government's strong support, its funds can also need to rely on the support of all sectors of the society and its own industrialization operation.

  3.Using scientific and technological means to accelerate the recording and dissemination of Xiaosan materials. In other words, to expand the influence of Xiaosan and attract more people to care about and support its development, we can use audio recording, video recording and other tools to record and save these materials. Meanwhile, we also can use the Internet, WeChat and other modern medias to spread and publicize Xiaosan.

To sum up, Xiaosan is the treasure of Chinese culture. It has played an active role in the idyllic life of the local people by its unique form and value. Today, the prospect of Xiaosan is worrying and Xiaosan needs urgently to be protected. The author believes that under the active support of the government and the common concern of all sectors in the society, Xiaosan, an artistic pearl, must be have a brilliant future.

Bibliography:

[1] Du Zhiqing. Xingyang Magazines [M].Beijing: Xinhua Publishing House, 1996.

[2] Ding Yaping. Art Culture [M].Beijing: Culture and Art Publishing House, 2005.

[3] Wu Xinbin. Discourse Reconstruction in the New Context: Contemporary Theatre Series [M]. Beijing: Chinese Federation Press, 2015.

戏剧人类学视域下的社火"故事"研究

——以河南民间歌舞小戏"笑伞"为例

摘要：流行于河南荥阳一带的歌舞小戏——笑伞，融音乐、舞蹈和戏曲于一体。作为中华文化多元构成的一部分，笑伞具有较高的文学价值、史学价值和审美功用。其唱词文本内容丰富、纪实性与文学性俱佳，尤值得研究。戏剧人类学研究近年来方兴未艾，其侧重于观察、比较和田野作业的方式方法不仅为笑伞研究提供了一个崭新的学术视角，更有助于抢救濒危文艺而获取第一手资料。笑伞由五人分饰角色进行表演，分别作程咬金、侠客、武旦等扮相，进行舞蹈、扮唱、说快板交替表演。通过实地考察，笑伞已经处于消亡殆尽的边缘，亟待专家学者研究和文化部门进行必要性的保护与抢救。其保护应当从优化其文艺生态环境、加强传承培养力度、提升演出节目质量、信息化处理和产业化运营等方面进行有效传承保护。

关键词：戏剧人类学；河南荥阳；歌舞小戏；笑伞

戏剧是一门兼具文学性、纪实性和艺术性等特质的总体性艺术，受时间、地域、文化等差异的影响而呈现出丰富多样的形态。河南荥阳一带孕育并流行着一种名叫"笑伞"的民间歌舞小戏。它融音乐、舞蹈和戏曲为一体，节奏明快，唱词打趣、动作滑稽，被看作是荥阳地域文化的代表之一。据当地艺人们讲，早在"文革"以前，笑伞在当地的流传度极广，荥阳一带几乎是村村镇镇都有自己的笑伞故事队；"文革"期间，笑伞作为封建文化残余，其所用戏箱、道具等纷纷被焚毁殆尽，演出队在荥阳一带几乎销声匿迹;"文革"结束以后,笑伞得以短暂恢复和繁荣;随着改革开放的到来,人们的审美娱乐选择得到极大丰富,笑伞等民间文艺逐渐衰败;如今,能够演出整场的笑伞故事的表演队已所剩无几,仅有个别笑伞艺人能够艰难地组织起小规模的表演,娱人娱己。对于戏剧的研究归根结底是研究"人"。戏剧人类学为我们带来了一个崭新的学术视野,将关注和研究的落脚点都落到了"人",包括艺人、观众等等。民间文艺的创造、传承和审美都离不开"人"的实践活动,尤其是审美必然是"演员"与"观众"的双向互动。2016 年至 2018 年间,笔者一行人就笑伞这一民间歌舞小戏在荥阳一带的村镇中开展了实地调研和走访活动,先后到豫龙镇关帝庙村、城关乡龙泉寺村等地采访了李同中等艺人和村民。与当地笑伞艺人的多次接触和实地调研使我们感受到,笑伞作为地方歌舞小戏已经与当地民众的生活融为一体。正如汪宁生在《文化人类学调查》一书中提到的,"艺术是人类运用想象力以象征手法表达思想和发泄感情的产物,是人类文化中最具有感染力那一部分"[1]。现将有关调查及思考报告如下。

一、"笑伞"的起源及发展

作为荥阳一带重要的社火故事——笑伞,在当地由来已久。据当地艺人们讲,"笑伞"源自隋末的瓦岗军攻打荥阳城这一历史事件。隋末,炀帝声色犬马,大肆搜刮民脂民膏、奴役百姓,致使民怨四起,地方叛乱不断。隋大业十二年(即公元 616 年),瓦岗军欲攻打中原历代兵家必争之地——荥阳城。荥阳城坚池固,加之遇到守城隋军负隅顽抗,瓦岗将士苦于鏖战,城池久攻不下。瓦岗统领翟让采纳谋士李密之计,正月十五闹元宵之际趁城中兵勇防务懈怠,遣程咬金率领部下,扮作舞花伞的滑稽老夫,在众人敲着锣鼓簇拥之下混入荥阳城内,最终与城外事先埋伏好的兵将里应外合一举攻下了荥阳城。后来,当地的民间艺人以该故事和形式为创作原型,创造了笑伞这样一门颇具特色的民间艺术门类。

笑伞自传演于荥阳一带以来,即深受当地民众的喜爱和追捧,并借此基础而不断得以散播于附近乡镇,一直流传到了今天。清代以来,笑伞表演进入了一个鼎盛阶段,尤其到了清康熙年间,笑伞更是在荥阳附近村镇遍地开花。民国时期,荥阳当地许多草台班子走街串巷地进行笑伞表演。乡镇节庆的庙会、社火活动为民间文艺提供了很好的展示平台和传播载体。"在原始时代,任何一种艺术文化现象,设若没有一种宗教作基础,那它能否产生和维持下去就很值得怀疑。"[2] 据了解,荥阳一带过去盛行着火神祭祀活动,几乎村村都有火神庙,村村都有火神会。我们进行实地走访调查的豫龙镇关帝庙村和城关乡龙泉寺村至今仍留存着部分火神庙的遗迹。过去,为了满足火神祭祀的基本需求,关帝庙村先后共成立了9个文艺表演队,分别是狮子鼓、笑伞、龙灯、高跷、小车、旱船、独杆轿、确猴(蹦猴)、霸王鞭。每逢农历新年,正月初一到初七各路"故事"都要在本村和附近的村镇各处演上一演。每次外出进行演出前,都务必要先到本村的火神庙前进行演出以酬谢神明,护佑故事队平安。位于城关乡的龙泉寺是荥阳当地香火十分鼎盛的一座佛教寺庙,其内的一处偏殿就供奉有火神像。龙泉寺的火神祭祀是当地规模最大、最有影响力的社火活动。每逢正月初七这一日,这里都要举行规模盛大的酬神祭祀仪式。附近几个村子的社火故事队都要到此地参加祭祀仪式并进行酬神表演。龙泉寺古庙会是以现今的龙泉寺旧址为中心,以西几个村落的表演队称作"西大会",以东的称作"东大会"。"东大会"的表演扣人心弦、引人入胜,在整个龙泉寺古庙会中地位最为崇高。在每一年的活动中都要上"头会",即第一个进庙参与敬神祭祀的演出。"东大会"各路"故事"演过之后,其他会首方能率领各自村镇的"故事"进庙演出。关帝庙村所在的"东大会"各路"故事"是顺着沿途各村一路演过去的,到达龙泉寺时一般都到中午了。即便是其他村的"故事"早于"东大会"到达龙泉寺,也必定在庙外候着,一定要等到"东大会"的各路"故事"依次进庙演过,他们才能进庙演出。同时,在与当地文化学者陈玮进行交谈中我们了解到,笑伞过去是整个龙泉寺社火表演活动的中心,其他"故事"都是围绕在笑伞的周围进行表演的。足可见笑伞在当地社火表演中的地位确实是高于其他"故事"的。

新中国成立初期,即"文革"开始前的一段时间里,笑伞作为当地群众所喜闻乐见的一种重要的文艺形式一度活跃于街头巷尾、田间地头。但随着社会意识形态更迭背景下大众审美发生嬗变,原始信仰抑或是封建信仰摧枯拉朽般地被颠覆、摧毁,而使得笑伞原生生态环境急剧衰变。"'文化大革命'中,基本销声匿迹。"[3] "文革"结束后,一部分笑伞故事队得以短暂恢复与发展,但由于受多种因素影响,不少经典唱词、唱段佚失,部分恢复活动的故事队经历过民众审美娱乐选择极大丰富的改革开放时期后,也终归于沉寂。

笑伞艺术的生存现况着实令人担忧,发展更是无从谈起。曾遍布荥阳一带的笑伞,随着岁月更迭、艺人衰老,又缺乏新生代力量的更替,技艺传承人现已所剩无几。目前,在荥阳市各项文艺汇演及民间社火活动中,还能够参与表演的笑伞故事队仅剩下关帝庙村李同中老人所在的一个队了。几经周折,最终我们通过当地文化管理部门的工作人员在豫龙镇关帝庙村找到了笑伞表演老艺人李同中。他说,现如今也只是在逢年过节时,他们才会在本村演一下笑伞。只是笑伞的表演成员仅仅依靠本村的乡民自发参与已然难以为继,李同中老先生只得或要求或动员其几个子女和小外孙(十多岁)凑合着来演。所呈现给审美受众的演出水准和内容自然不能够与过去相比了。总之,当前的笑伞艺术在生存与发展的问题上正面临着严重的危机,濒于消亡。

现已知在当地文化管理部门有登记信息的"仅有"的笑伞故事队——关帝庙村笑伞故事队,主要参演人员李同中已过了杖朝之年。昔日能够与他同场演出的"老伙计"张海山、李会有、李石头等人或亡故或疾病都已不能再参加演出。为了使这一门民间歌舞小戏不至于失传佚散,李同中可谓想尽了办法,甚至发动过村子里的几位年轻媳妇学习和参演笑伞。可后来,受制于经济效益方面的制约,大家纷纷表示不愿意参加这样徒有意义而无经济收益的活动。李同中在万般无奈之下动员自己的老伴儿王秀枝学习和参加笑伞演出,之后又陆续动员自己的儿女和外孙参加其中。过去的笑伞表演都是以神会为依托,村落中颇有威望的长者担任会首,由神会为其提供精神动力和物质支撑。在调查过程中,我们了解到过去的笑伞演出主要是在各种各样的社火庙会、酬神祭祀中进行的。过去,荥阳一带的各种祭祀活动(特别是春节期间大大小小的祭祀)是笑伞表演最集中的场合。民间信仰及其相关的祭祀仪式(活动)为包括笑伞在内的民间文艺提供了绝佳的展示平台和发展契机。今天,在经历了"文革"冲击及现代艺术形式的极大丰富之后,笑伞原本所依托的生存基础轰然崩塌,精神动力和物质支撑也随之难以为继。当下,像笑伞艺人李同中老人这样完全凭着个人爱好或保护文化遗产的责任感与信念精神,在艰难维持的绝不仅是他一人。在谈到笑伞的发展时,李同中忧心忡忡地说:"我想把笑伞传下去,可是巧妇难为无米之炊,好多事力不从心啊!"[4]

二、"笑伞"的基本形态

格尔兹曾讲到以行为(实践)作为研究文艺的切入点是可行的。"必须关注行为,而且要有某些精确性,因为文化形态正是在行为之流中得到表达的。"[5]笑伞表演由五人分饰不同角色共同完成。主角扮作"程咬金",头戴红白相间的花毡帽,面化黑白相间的丑角妆容,戴红髯须,上穿古代宽袖摆的黄色长袍,下穿宽松白色长裤,着黑色牛鼻子布鞋,腰系又宽又厚的白色丝带,左手拿一破蒲扇,右手执一米多高的花伞。余下四人,两个扮作侠客模样,两个作武旦扮相。五人在小锣、手鼓等乐器的伴奏下进行表演。所用道具包括蒲扇、花伞、绸带等。笑伞表演时通常要先选一块开阔地,五个人依次排成圆圈,先转两三圈,然后唱,再转,再唱。一般唱两遍、转两次,最后说一段快板,即依照"转→唱→转→唱→说"这样的程序进行表演。

"戏剧是以舞蹈、音乐、语言等形式反映社会生活、表达主观情感的艺术形式。"[6]笑伞的舞蹈步法基本就是围圈而舞,节奏缓慢和交叠,间有摇摆、蹲跳及舞伞等动作。唱词内容则比较多样丰富,唱词通俗易懂,内容兼具纪实性与文学性,表达的内容多是百姓农事、居家生活中的故事以及对未来质朴美好生活的憧憬。唱调属于民间戏曲小调与方言融合的变种。如《四季谣》:

> 正月里来正月正,长坂坡前赵子龙。
>
> 怀中抱定皇太子,杀退曹操百万兵。
>
> 二月二来龙抬头,千金小姐抛绣球。
>
> 绣球单打吕蒙正,寒瓦窑里出诸侯。
>
> 三月三来三月三,昭君娘娘和北番。
>
> 思念父母泪涟涟,眼望南方好辛酸。
>
> 四月四来四月八,奶奶庙里把香插。
>
> 婶子大娘都跪下,祈祷神灵把雨下。
>
> 五月五来是端阳,大麦小麦齐上场。

牛板把式都上地,放滚打趄吼几嗓。

六月六来热难当,二妹独坐象牙床。

手拿罗扇还嫌热,想起相公拱麦秸。

七月有个七月七,天上牛郎会织女。

织女会把牛郎见,双双相见泪涟涟……

这段唱词从一月唱到十二月,一气呵成,勾连不断,纵论古今,意蕴绵长。其中既有对历史上所涌现的英雄人物形象和事迹的颂扬赞叹,又有对现实农事生活中庄稼汉辛勤劳作、质朴生活的讴歌祈福,更兼有神话故事天马行空的心往神驰,体现了我国淳朴的劳动人民的聪颖智慧和艺术创造力。其更充分印证了普列汉诺夫"劳动先于艺术"的观点,即这样的唱词是在劳动人民日积月累的农事生活中积累、打磨,不断地再创造而形成的,远早于以"笑伞"为载体进行表演的形式的产生。

劳动人民既是民间文艺的创造主体,又是审美主体。笑伞作为一门形式独特的民间艺术门类,必然具备由创造主体和审美受众双向建构、互动的雏形,即演出主体是农民大众,同时受众主体也是农民大众。其中蕴含着我国劳动人民质朴的艺术追求。在流传至今的众多笑伞唱词中,还有一些唱段文辞风趣、寓庄于谐。劳动人民用自己的聪颖与智慧将自己朴素无华的生活进行艺术创造再加工,艺术地再现了劳动人民的日常生活场景之余,更着重于实现劳动人民实用性的诉求,如《哄儿小调》:

闲言无事下北坡,新坟没有旧坟多。

新坟头上顶白纸,旧坟头上蒺藜窝。

赤抹肚孩儿逮蛐子,蒺藜扎住他的脚。

这手蘑、那手摸,蒺藜扎得就那么多。

往西看、日头落,蛤蟆叫唤鬼吆喝。

山上跑下来一群狼,好似饿虎找干粮。

有一些唱词则是侧重于劳动人民劳作生活场景的复写和艺术还原,以及展现劳动者对于幸福美满生活的向往与憧憬,如《锄地歌》:

清早起来背张锄,我到南湖锄蜀黍。

锄了一遭又一遭,肚子饿得直咕噜。

抬头往北看一眼,那边来了我媳妇。

迎上前去看一看，媳妇担着小担担。

一头挑的是黑窝窝，一头挑的是糠糊涂。

媳妇啊，我让你给我烙油馍、打鸡蛋，谁叫你做这糠糊涂！

媳妇说：想吃油馍也不难，等到五月麦上镰。

早上给你烙油馍、打鸡蛋，上午给你擀蒜面。

夜里咱俩一头睡，你的胳臂我枕住……

"戏剧的艺术形态取决于文化土壤之差异。"[7]调研过程中所采集的笑伞唱词内容十分丰富、充满着生活情调，更反映了中原地区劳动人民千百年间辛勤耕作、土里刨食的生活写照和渴望庄稼丰收、家庭和满的质朴生活理想。笑伞不仅是民间社火庙会中的一种仪式，在扮演者、传承人看来，笑伞更是与生活和本体（人）需求息息相关的一项活动。笑伞表演使得扮演者借此获得充足的物质生活基础，表演也在酬神、娱人中给予了人们足够的精神食粮。这一切，充分契合了荥阳一带劳动人民的文化创造力和艺术生态环境。流传于当地的笑伞文本，除了以上摘取用作分析的片段外，还有《火烧战船》《闯王进北京》《四辈上工》等三十多首。由于旧时候民间艺人们大多没有接受过良好的文化教育，因此这些唱词大多是经由一代代传承艺人们口传心授而来的，其中不乏文辞有待勘误的情况存在。同时，也有不少唱词是历代笑伞艺人即兴编创的，反映的也多是劳动人民真实的生活境况和质朴的生活憧憬。

三、关于"笑伞"的戏剧人类学思考

笑伞形成由来已久、表演程式较其他戏曲门类也甚是独特，是流散于河南民间众多歌舞小戏中的一朵奇葩。从戏剧人类学视角来看，它是戏剧活态传承中受着时间变化、文化差异和地域区别等诸多动因影响下衍生出的多姿多彩的民间文艺形态之一。笑伞独具特色的表演形式和兼顾写意与写实的唱词内容，极大地丰富了中华优秀传统文化的内蕴和民族认同感。其特殊的戏剧表演形态不仅丰富了中原戏曲的门类，更为中华优秀传统文化的多样性贡献了自己的一分力量。它既是中华民族悠久文明的重要表征和艺术载体，更是当地百姓教育、文化、娱乐乃至自身发展所不可或缺的一部分。在漫长的人类发展演变进程中，笑伞为当地百姓们带来了精神上的愉悦和满足。同时,它也在地方文艺的共生和竞生中发挥着自身积极的功用。它在汲取其他艺术门类营养来谋取自身在不同时期新发展的同时,也在为戏剧艺术形态多样性的发展贡献着力量。特别是在荥阳的民间社火活动中,笑伞作为当地社火的核心节目,为整个乡野文艺活动中众多民间文艺表演形式的和谐共存发挥着积极的调和作用。在今天的生活中,虽然民间信仰的影响力不断削弱,从而制约着笑伞的生存与发展,但是笑伞仍然有着它独特的文学价值、历史价值和审美功用。在繁荣社会主义文化事业的背景下,发挥着、贡献着其自己的价值。

(一)"笑伞"的价值

笑伞在满足当地民众基本文艺审美需求的同时,还在地方经济、社会观念和艺术理论等多方面产生深远持久、潜移默化的影响。在经年累月的地方社火表演中,笑伞已经与当地民众的精神寄托和娱乐紧紧地联系在了一起,成了节庆庙会、社火祭祀等活动中民众精神寄托的重要组成部分。当下,笑伞等先后被列入不同级别的非物质文化遗产项目,正逐步摆脱"封建文化残余"的泥沼,国家对中华优秀传统文化的正名、扶持和推动力度不断加大。笑伞作为荥阳地域文化的代表之一,谋求自身发展,生逢其时、盛逢其世。笑伞的价值大致可以从以下几个方面理解。

第一,笑伞是当地民众的自发需求。根据戏剧人类学的观点,有什么样的审美受众,就会有什么样的戏剧形态;有什么样的文化生态,就会有什么样的艺术内蕴;有什么样的物质、非物质条件,就会有什么样的戏剧格调。笑伞作为荥阳一带独有的歌舞小戏且自形成之日始就经久不衰,其必然与地域文化和民众需求不可分割。笑伞唱词内容主要分为两个方面,其一便是历史故事、神话传说讲述;其二则是民众生活内容的再现。笑伞的唱词既是民众生活的真实写照和艺术反映,同时也是地域文化和民众本体需求的凝练表达。

第二,笑伞是丰富人民精神文化需求的重要组成部分。"戏剧艺术自发生以来,基本都要经过由娱神到娱人的发展过程。"[8] 笑伞滥觞于封建社会小农经济时代,主要活动在宗教庙会、社火祭祀等活动之中,发挥着其作为原始戏剧形态的酬神功用。在长期的历史发展过程中,民众逐渐活跃起来的审美学需求使得笑伞这类的民间歌舞小戏不再仅仅局限于娱神,而兼具娱人的功效。及至当下社会,民众物质需求得到了极大的满足,精神文化追求变得迫切。随着弘扬中华优秀传统文化热潮掀起,笑伞作为丰富人民精神文化需求的重要组成部分发挥着其不容小觑的作用。

第三,笑伞是繁荣中华文化的重要资源。人类文明的发展生生不息,其间所产生的文化更是层出迭起,赓续不断。"戏剧人类学视野中的戏剧是文化的重要组成部分"[9],笑伞则是戏剧当中颇具文化内蕴和艺术特色的一个门类。当下的中华优秀传统文化必然是在前代文化的底蕴和基奠之上经年累月形成的。完全地抛却前代文化避而不谈,只言当下我们所提倡的中华优秀传统文化,必然是空中楼阁、镜花水月。中华文化的博大精深就在于像笑伞这类形形色色的地域特色鲜明的文化资源共同架构起的历史硕果藤架。在当下艺术门类空前繁盛的今天,笑伞作为中华文化资源的重要组成部分,不仅仅要唤起人们的关注度和保护意识,更应当充分地利用这一重要资源构筑起中华优秀传统文化的框架。

(二)"笑伞"的传承保护

通过调查研究发现,笑伞作为河南省荥阳市一带极具地域特色的歌舞小戏,已经处在了消亡殆尽的边缘,急需发掘、整理、保护和传承。"由人类学材料所揭示出所有民族的共性,最终将为世界大同的实现做出贡献。"[10]笑伞作为丰富文化多样性的重要构成,理应得到尽早保护和传承,而当地保护工作却并不尽如人意。在市场经济、文化多元等趋势下,笑伞生存现况不容乐观,谈及发展更是举步维艰。艺人年龄趋于高龄且分布明显断层,演出团队难以为继,演出市场不断萎缩,这就使得对笑伞采取必要的措施进行保护显得尤为迫在眉睫。鉴于笑伞艺术濒于失传的危机,我们应当做好以下工作。

第一,适应文艺发展规律,改善文艺生态环境。笑伞长久以来的良好发展都得益于遵从文艺发展的科学规律所建立起的有效生态机制。同时,笑伞更是茁壮于荥阳一带的原生文艺生态环境。笑伞的文化内蕴、戏剧形态都随着社会形态的规律性、周期性嬗递。随着社会形态的兴替,民间信仰和思想发生了巨变,致使笑伞的原生文艺生态环境失衡而难以自我发展。笑伞的发展仍旧要遵循着科学的文艺发展规律,在多方的支持和努力下重新建构适宜笑伞发展的生态场。这就需要政府相关部门能够不遗余力地支持和鼓励非遗、民俗类民间组织活动,持续性加强对地方文艺的保护,建立文化生态保护区,不断改善笑伞等地方文艺的生态环境。

第二,加强传承力度,提升演出品质。民间文艺的主体是人,既指扮演者,又指观演者。在笑伞的传承问题上,要使传承有力度,必定要认清艺术主体——人,人是其传承与保护的着力点、落脚点。因此,讲笑伞的传承与保护,艺人、观众的发掘与培养居于首位。人是所有民间文艺生存、发展的核心和基础。没有人,一切活动都无从谈起。近年来,各级政府的有关部门从不同层面上都不断加大对传承人的资金、政策扶持力度,并不断通过政府送戏下基层等形式营造良好的戏曲生态,为的就是让笑伞这样的民间文艺能够重新活跃于文化多样性的舞台上。究其实效,甚微。原因莫过于政策转化为实践缺乏成功案例参考,各地方在实际工作中为避免失误而缩手缩脚。笑伞艺人和观众均趋于老龄化,缺乏青年力量接续,窥一斑而见全豹,这在民间文艺中绝不是个案。试想一群年过花甲的艺人们如何能够很好地适应当下民众的审美趋势和需求,编创出符合当下时代的新作品。就连经典剧目,以笑伞故事队现今的实力也很难保证其演出的完整度,质量更无从谈起。要改变艺术传承青黄不接,演出剧目质量不高的现状必须要双管齐下。其一,"进校园"。学生是中国审美需求的发展风向标和潜在受众群体,只有抓好校园这样的民间文艺宣传传播平台,营造、熏陶良好的传统优秀文化审美环境,才能够从根本去改善发展举步维艰的问题。其次,思想转变与经济手段两手抓、两手硬。既要让群众转变对学习笑伞等民间文艺的思想态度,也要予以一定的经济鼓励、补偿来满足传承人的基本生存问题。

第三,信息化处理,产业化经营。笑伞已属于濒于消亡的民间歌舞小戏,其戏剧文本作为文艺项目的重要构成,要充分借助当下数字化的录音、录像等手段进行记录和保存。与此同时,民间神祇信仰的崩塌和市场经济的开放使得笑伞要尝试着迎合市场发展需要,产业化经营。依托于高校的文化产业化,让笑伞在文艺演出、文化产品销售、互联网宣传等方面综合性运营。构建一个良好的运营机制,逐步使演出、文产盈利,以达到艺人生存、发展的平衡,甚至是由收支平衡转向盈利。

笑伞是中华优秀传统文化中风雨飘摇的一棵浮萍。我们坚信,通过我们的不懈努力,笑伞能够以自身的发展、政府的支持、文艺市场的繁荣迎来一个更好的明天。它形式独特、价值独具,曾是当地劳动人民质朴生活中的寄托和宣泄。今天,笑伞的生存和发展受到了一定的阻碍,但这都绝对不是制约和停滞不前的原因。古往今来,任何一项民间文艺的发展都必然不会是一帆风顺的,这将是一段有高低、有起伏的艰苦历程。这就需要社会各界能够共同努力,处理和把握好笑伞的生存、发展、保护、传承等各方面的关系。

参考文献:

[1] 汪宁生. 文化人类学调查 [M]. 北京:文物出版社,1996:188.

[2] 丁亚平. 艺术文化学 [M]. 北京:文化艺术出版社,2005:232.

[3] 杜之庆. 荥阳市志 [M]. 北京:新华出版社,1996:731.

[4] 2016 年 10 月 2 日作者在荥阳市豫龙镇关帝庙村对李同中的采访

[5] 格尔兹. 文化的解释 [M]. 上海:上海人民出版社,1999:20.

[6] 陈炎. 艺术本质的动态分析 [J]. 文艺理论研究,1996(3):46.

[7] 王胜华. 戏剧人类学 [M]. 昆明:云南大学出版社,2009:159.

[8] 王胜华. 戏剧人类学 [M]. 昆明:云南大学出版社,2009:184.

[9] 王胜华. 戏剧人类学 [M]. 昆明:云南大学出版社,2009:231.

[10] 利普斯. 事物的起源·序言 [M]. 兰州:敦煌文艺出版社,2000:2.

Research on "Story" of Shehuo from the Perspective of Drama Anthropology — Taking Henan Folk Drama "Xiaosan" as an Example

Abstract: Xiaosan, a song and dance drama popular in Xingyang area of Henan province, which integrates music, dance and drama together. As a part of the pluralistic composition of Chinese culture, Xiaosan has a high literary value, historical value and aesthetic function, while its lyrics are rich in content, with documentary and literary characteristics, and are especially worth studying. The study of dramatic anthropology is in the ascendant in recent years, and its emphasis on observation, comparison and field work not only provides a new academic perspective for the study of Xiaosan, but also helps to rescue endangered literature and art and obtain first-hand data. Xiaosan is performed by five people in roles of Cheng Yaojin, swordsman and female warrior, etc. Dancing, singing and allegro are performed alternately. Through on-the-spot investigation, the Xiaosan has been on the edge of extinction and needs urgent research by experts and scholars and necessary protection and rescue by cultural departments, whose protection should be effectively carried out from aspects of optimizing its literary and artistic ecological environment, strengthening inheritance and training, improving the quality of performance programs, information processing and industrial operation.

Key words: dramatic anthropology; Xingyang City of Henan Province;Song and dance drama; Xiaosan

Drama is an overall art with literary, documentary and artistic characteristics. Influenced by differences in time, region and culture, drama takes on various forms. A folk song and dance drama called "Xiaosan" was bred and popular in Xingyang area of Henan province, which is a combination of music, dance and opera, with lively rhythm, jokingly singing and funny actions. It is regarded as one of the representatives of Xingyang regional culture. According to local artists, Xiaosan was very popular in the local area as early as before the "Cultural Revolution". Almost all villages and towns in Xingyang had their own Xiaosan story teams. During the "Cultural Revolution", as a remnant of feudal culture, the play boxes and props used for Xiaosan were burned up one after another and the performance team almost disappeared in Xingyang. After the end of the "Cultural Revolution", Xiaosan was restored and prospered briefly. With the coming of reform and opening up, people's aesthetic and entertainment choices have been greatly enriched, and the folk arts such as Xiaosan have gradually declined. Up to now, there are very few performing teams that can perform the whole story of Xiaosan, while only a few artists can organize small-scale performances to amuse others and themselves. The study of drama is ultimately the study of "people" and theatrical anthropology has brought us a brand-new academic vision, which has landed the focus of attention and research on "people", artists, audiences and so on. The creation, inheritance and aesthetics of folk literature and art cannot be separated from the practical activities of "people", especially aesthetics is necessarily a two-way interaction between "actors" and "audience". From 2016 to 2018, the author and his party carried out on-the-spot investigation and visiting activities in villages and towns around Xingyang on the folk song and dance drama Xiaosan. He went to Guandimiao Village in Yulong Town and Longquansi Village in Chengguan Town to interview artists and villagers, such as Li Tongzhong, etc. Through many contacts with local dancers and on-the-spot investigations, we feel that Xiaosan, as a local song and dance drama, has been integrated with the life of the local people. Just as Wang Ningsheng mentioned in his book *Cultural Anthropology Survey*, "art is the product of human using imagination to express thoughts and feelings symbolically, and it is the most infectious part of human culture." [1]. The relevant investigation and reflection reports are as follows.

1. The Origin and Development of "Xiaosan"

As an important Shehuo story in Xingyang area, Xiaosan has a long history. According to the words from local artists, the "Xiaosan" originated from the historical incident of the war against Xingyang City by the Wagang Army at the end of the Sui Dynasty. At the end of the Sui Dynasty, Emperor Yang showed little concern for the people, plundered the people and enslaved them, which caused widespread resentment and local rebellions. In the 12th year of Daye of Sui Dynasty (616 AD), the Wagang Army wanted to attack Xingyang City, which was the place that all previous generations of soldiers in the central plains had to contend for and it was firmly established and surrounded by the moat. In addition, faced with the desperate resistance of the defending Sui Army, Wagang soldiers struggled in the battle, and the city could not be taken for a long time. Wagang Army Commander Zhai Rang adopted the plan of counselor Li Mi. On the 15th of the first month, when the Lantern Festival was going on, he took advantage of the slack defense of the soldiers in the city and sent Cheng Yaojin to lead his soldiers. He disguised himself as a funny old man dancing with a flower umbrella and infiltrated into Xingyang City with the sound of gongs and drums. Finally, he took the

Xingyang City at one stroke with the ambushed soldiers outside the city. Later, local folk artists took the story and form as their creation prototype and created a unique folk art category, namely the Xiaosan.

Since the Xiaosan was performed in Xingyang, it has been deeply loved and sought after by the local people, and on this basis, it has been continuously spread to the nearby villages and towns and has been spread to this day. Since the Qing Dynasty, the performance of Xiaosan has entered a heyday, especially in the Emperor Kangxi's ruling years of the Qing Dynasty, when Xiaosan blossomed everywhere in villages and towns near Xingyang City. During the period of the Republic of China, many local folk art performance teams in Xingyang took to the streets to perform Xiaosan. "In primitive times, if any kind of artistic and cultural phenomenon is not based on any religion, it is doubtful whether it can be produced and maintained." [2] It is understood that sacrificial activities to God of Fire were popular in Xingyang area in the past. Almost every village has a temple of Fire God, and every village has a meeting of Fire Gods. Some remains of the Temple of Fire God are still preserved in Guandimiao Village in Yulong Town and Longquansi Village in Chengguan Town, which we visited and investigated on the spot. In the past, in order to meet the basic needs of offering sacrifices to Fire God, Guandimiao Village has set up a total of 9 artistic performance teams, including Lion Drum, Xiaosan, Dragon Lantern, Stilts, Handcart, Land Boat, Single-pole Sedan, Real Monkey (jumping monkey) and Overlord Whip. Every lunar new year, every "story" from the first day of the first month to the seventh day of the first month will be performed in the village and nearby villages and towns. Before going out to perform each time, one must perform in front of the Fire God Temple in the village to appreciate the gods and protect the story team. Longquan Temple, located in Chengguan Town, is a Buddhist Temple in Xingyang where the incense is very popular. The partial temple in Longquan Temple worships the image of Fire God. The Fire God sacrifice tradition in

Longquan Temple is the largest and most influential Shehuo activity in the area. The Shehuo story teams from several nearby villages will all attend the sacrificial ceremony and devote the performance of worshiping gods. The ancient temple fair of Longquan Temple is centered on the former site of the present Longquan Temple. The performance teams of several villages to the west are collectively called "West Fair" and those to the east are called "East Fair". The performance of the "East Fair" is exciting and fascinating, which occupies the highest position in the ancient temple fair of Longquan Temple. In every year's activities, there will be the "Major Fair", that is, the first performance to enter the temple to participate in worship and sacrifice activities. After all the "stories" of the "East Fair" have been performed, the other leaders can lead the "stories" of their villages and towns into the temple to perform. The "stories" of the "East Fair" where Guandimiao Village is located are played in every village along the way, which is usually at the noon time when arriving at Longquan Temple. Even if the "stories" of other villages arrive at Longquan Temple before the "East Fair", they must wait outside the temple until all the "stories" of the "East Fair" enter the temple to perform in turn. At the same time, during the conversation with Chen Wei, a local cultural scholar, we learned that the Xiaosan used to be the center of the whole Longquan Temple Shehuo show, and other "stories" were all performed around the Xiaosan, which can be seen that the status of Xiaosan in the local fire show is indeed higher than other "stories".

In the early days of the founding of People's Republic of China, that is, a period of time before the "Cultural Revolution", Xiaosan, as an important form of literature and art loved by the local people, was once active in the streets and lanes and fields. However, with the change of social ideology and public aesthetics, primitive beliefs or feudal beliefs have been subverted and destroyed, which has led to a sharp decline in the original ecological environment of Xiaosan. "during the 'Cultural Revolution', it basically disappeared." [3] After the end of the "Cultural Revolution", some of the

Xiaosan story teams were able to recover and develop briefly. However, due to the influence of various factors, many classical lyrics and aria are missing, and some of the story teams that resumed their activities have experienced a period of reform and opening-up in which the public's choice of aesthetic entertainment is extremely rich, and eventually they have fallen silent.

The survival situation of the Xiaosan art is really worrying, and its development is even more impossible. The Xiaosan that used to be scattered all over Xingyang area is few and far between now as the years change and the artists age and lack the replacement of new generation power. At present, only the old man Li Tongzhong from Guandimiao Village is left on the Xiaosan story team that can take part in all kinds of theatrical performances and folk Shehuo activities in Xingyang City. After many twists and turns, we finally found Li Tongzhong, an old entertainer performing with Xiaosan, through the staff of the local cultural management department in Guandimiao Village, Yulong Town. He said that now it is only during the Chinese New Year's Day that they will still play Xiaosan in the village, which is already unsustainable for the performing members of the traditional art to rely solely on the spontaneous participation of the villagers in the village. Mr. Li had to either request or mobilize his children and his little grandson (in his teens) to perform. The performance standard and content presented to the aesthetic audience cannot naturally be compared with the past it was. In a word, the current Xiaosan art is facing a serious crisis on the issue of survival and development, and it is on the verge of extinction.

It is now known that the "existing" Xiaosan story team, with registration information in the local cultural administration department, is the Guandimiao Village Xiaosan story team, and the main actor Li Tongzhong has passed 80 years old. Zhang Haishan, Li Huiyou, Li Shitou and others who were able to perform with him in the past have either died or are no longer able to perform due to illness. In order to prevent this folk song and dance drama from being lost, Li Tongzhong did all he could and even started several young daughters-in-law in the village to learn and play Xiaosan. However, they were still constrained by the consideration of economic benefits and they expressed their reluctance to take part in such meaningful activities without any economic benefits. In desperation, Li Tongzhong mobilized his wife, Wang Xiuzhi, to study and take part in the performance of Xiaosan. After that, he successively mobilized his children and grandchildren to take part in it. In the past, the performance of Xiaosan was based on god, who provided spiritual power and material support to the prestigious elders in the village. In the course of the investigation, we learned that the past performance of Xiaosan was mainly held in various temple fairs with sacrifices for gods. In the past, all kinds of sacrificial activities in Xingyang area (especially the large and small sacrificial activities during the Spring Festival) were the most concentrated time for Xiaosan performances. Folk beliefs and related sacrificial ceremonies (activities) provide an excellent display platform and development opportunity for folk literature and art, including Xiaosan. Today, after experiencing the impact of the "Cultural Revolution" and the great enrichment of modern art forms, the survival foundation on which Xiaosan relied collapsed, making it difficult to sustain its spiritual power and material support. At present, there is by no means only one who is struggling to maintain the traditional art, just like the Xiaosan artist Li Tongzhong, depending on his personal interests or his sense of responsibility and belief in protecting cultural heritage. When talking about the development of Xiaosan, Li Tongzhong said with great anxiety: "I want to inherit the Xiaosan. However, a skillful woman cannot cook without rice and a lot of things can't be done without the foundation we need!" [4]

2. The Basic Form of "Xiaosan"

Gertz once said that it is feasible to take behavior (practice) as the starting point for studying literature and art. "We must pay attention to behavior and have some accuracy, because cultural forms are expressed in the flow of behavior." [5] The Xiaosan performance is jointly performed by five people playing different roles. The main character is dressed as "Cheng Yaojin", wearing a red and white flowered felt hat, a black and white clown makeup, a red beard, an ancient yellow robe with wide sleeves, loose white trousers, black cloth shoes that look like the nose of an ox, a wide and thick white ribbon around the waist, a broken cattail leaf fan in the left hand and a flowered umbrella more than one meter high in the right hand. The remaining four people, two as swordsman, two as female warrior. The five performed with the accompaniment of small gongs, tambourines and other musical instruments. Props used include cattail leaf fan, flower umbrella, silk ribbon, etc. When performing Xiaosan, one usually chooses an open plot of land, five people form a circle one by one, turn two or three times, then sing, turn and sing. Usually sing twice, turn twice, and finally say an allegro, that is, perform according to the procedure of "turn—sing—turn—sing—say".

"Drama is an artistic form that reflects social life and expresses subjective feelings through dance, music, language and other forms." [6] The dance footwork of Xiaosan is basically to dance in circles, with slow rhythm and overlapping with swaying, squatting and umbrella dancing movements. The content of the lyrics is varied and rich, and the lyrics are easy to understand. The content is both documentary and literary. The content is mostly the stories of common people's farming, family life and their expectation of plain and beautiful life in the future. Singing tune is a variety of folk opera minor and dialect fusion. For example, "The Ballads of Four Seasons":

In the first day of the first month of lunar year,
Zhao Zilong was in front of of Changbanpo.
In order to save the crown prince,
he defeated the troops of Cao Cao by himself.
In the second day of the second month of lunar year,
rich family's daughter throws the hydrangea for a spouse.

Lv Mengzheng got the hydrangea by accident,

he became a duke finally from being an impecunious man.

In the third day of the third month of lunar year,

Wang Zhaojun married to the Xiong-Nu chieftain out of national peace.

She missed her parents with tears streaming down her eyes,

while looking at the south direction of home with great bitterness.

In the fourth day of the fourth month of lunar year,

incense was inserted by Grandma in the temple.

In order to pray to the gods for falling raining,

all the crowds knelt down in front of the temple.

In the fifth day of the fifth month of lunar year,

people were harvesting wheat and barley during the Dragon Boat
Festival.

Every harvest equipment was gathered around,

people would do farming while playing as singing loudly.

In the sixth day of the sixth month of lunar year,

younger sister sat in ivory bed alone to avoid high temperature.

She still felt hot with holding a fan,

Suddenly realized her husband was farming under the sun.

In the seventh day of the seventh month of lunar year,

Niu Lang was dating with Zhi Nv in the sky.

Zhinv will meet her husband eventually,

They meet each other with tears in their eyes.

...

From January to December, this aria has been sung in one go, continuously linking up and discussing the past and the present, with long implications. Among them, there are not only praise and admiration for the heroic figures and deeds that have emerged in history, but also praise and pray for the hard work and simple life of the plowmen in the real agricultural life. Moreover, there are also myths and stories that run wild and unconstrained, reflecting the intelligent wisdom and artistic creativity of our simple working people. This fully reflects Plekhanov's view that "labor precedes art", that is, such lyrics are accumulated, polished and continuously recreated in the accumulated agricultural life of the working people, which is far earlier than the form of performance with "Xiaosan" as the carrier.

Working people are not only the creative subject of folk literature and art, but also the aesthetic subject. As a unique form of folk art, Xiaosan must have the embryonic form of two-way construction and interaction between creative subject and aesthetic audience. That is, the main body of the performance is the peasant masses, and the audience is also the peasant masses, which contains the plain artistic pursuit of our working people. Among many Xiaosan lyrics that have been handed down so far, there are also some lyrics that are quite humorous. Working people use their intelligence and wisdom to create and reprocess their simple and unadorned life. While the art reproduces the scenes of working people's daily life, it focuses more on realizing the practical demands of working people, such as "Coax Children Minor":

> One went to Beipo at his spare time,
> the old graves were more than the new ones.
> New graves had white paper at their tops,
> old graves had a sea of briars at their peaks.
> Half-naked children caught crickets,
> but the briars pricked his feet.
> He touched and pulled them again and again,
> the pain he suffered was in the limited spots of his feet.
> Looking to the west and the sun was setting,
> the toad croaked and ghost screamed.
> A group of wolves ran from the mountain,
> like hungry tigers looking for food.
> Some lyrics focus on the reproduction and artistic restoration of the

working people's working life scenes, as well as showing the workers'
yearning and longing for a happy and happy life, such as "The Hoe Song":

Early in the morning I carry a hoe,

then I went to Nanhu to hoe corn.

After hoe after hoe,

my stomach was growling with hunger.

Looking up towards north,

I saw my wife shouldering a pole.

One side of the pole was black steamed corn bread.

The other was bran polenta.

Darling, I asked you to bake oil buns and eggs for me.

Who told you to cook bran polenta?

My wife said: It is not easy until May, let's just wait.

At that time, you can eat baked bun oil and eggs in the morning.

And eat garlic noodles at noon.

At night we sleep together, your arm resting on me...

"The artistic form of drama depends on the difference of cultural soil." [7] The Xiaosan lyrics collected during the investigation are very rich in content and full of emotional appeal of life, which also reflect the life portrayal of the working people in the Central Plains who have worked hard for thousands of years, digging in the soil for food, and the simple life ideal of longing for bumper harvest of crops and harmony of family. Xiaosan is not only a ceremony in folk temple fairs, but also an activity closely related to life and the needs of the body (human) in the eyes of actors and inheritors, which enables the actor to obtain sufficient material basis for life, and the performance also provides people with sufficient spiritual food for praying gods and entertaining people. All these fully fit the cultural creativity and artistic ecological environment of the working people in Xingyang City. In addition to the above excerpts for analysis, there are also more than 30 pieces of Xiaosan texts circulating in the local area, such as "the Burning Warship", "the Kingmaker Entering Beijing" and "the Fourth Generation Going to Work". Since most folk artists did not receive good cultural education in the old days, most of these lyrics were handed down from generation to generation by artists, and some of them still need to be corrected. At the same time, there are also many lyrics improvised by Xiaosan artists of past dynasties, which mostly reflect the working people's real living conditions and plain life expectations.

3. The Reflection on the Theatrical Anthropology of "Xiaosan"

Xiaosan has a long history and its performance program is unique compared with other types of operas, which is a wonderful flower among numerous folk songs and dances in Henan Province. From the perspective of dramatic anthropology, it is one of the colorful folk art forms derived from dramatic live transmission under the influence of many factors such as time changes, cultural differences and regional differences. The unique performance form of Xiaosan and the content of lyrics that can give consideration to both freehand brushwork and realism greatly enrich the connotation of Chinese excellent traditional culture and national identity, whose special form of dramatic performance not only enriches the categories of Central Plains operas, but also contributes to the diversity of Chinese excellent traditional culture. It is not only an important symbol and artistic carrier of the Chinese nation's long civilization, but also an indispensable part of local people's education, culture, entertainment and even their own development. In the long process of human development and evolution, Xiaosan has brought spiritual pleasure and satisfaction to the local people. At the same time, it also plays a positive role in the symbiosis and competition of local literature and art, which absorbs the nutrition of other arts to seek its own new development in different periods, while it also contributes to the development of the diversity of dramatic art forms; especially in Xingyang's folk Shehuo activities, Xiaosan, as the core program of the local social fire, plays a positive role in harmonizing the harmonious coexistence of many folk art performance forms in the whole rural cultural activities. In today's life, although the influence of folk beliefs is weakening, thus restricting the survival and development of Xiaosan, it still has its unique literary value, historical value and aesthetic function. Under the background of flourishing socialist cultural undertakings, it is playing and contributing its own value.

（1）The Value of Xiaosan

Xiaosan not only meets the basic aesthetic needs of local people, but also exerts profound and lasting influence on local economy, social concepts and artistic theories. In the local Shehuo performance over the years, the Xiaosan has been closely linked with the spiritual sustenance and entertainment of the local people, and it has become an important part of the spiritual sustenance of the people in festivals, temple fairs, Shehuo sacrifices and other activities. At present, Xiaosan and other intangible cultural heritage projects have been listed at different levels. They are gradually getting rid of the mire of "remnants of feudal culture" and the state is increasing its efforts to justify, support and promote Chinese excellent traditional culture. As one of the representatives of Xingyang's regional culture, Xiaosan seeks its own development and meets its times, whose value can be roughly understood from the following aspects.

First, Xiaosan is the spontaneous demand of local people. According to the viewpoint of dramatic anthropology, what kind of aesthetic audience, there will be what kind of dramatic form; what kind of cultural ecology, there will be what kind of artistic connotation; what kind of material and non-material conditions, there will be what kind of dramatic style. As a unique song and dance drama in Xingyang area, Xiaosan has been enduring since its formation, which is bound to be inseparable from regional culture and people's needs. The content of Xiaosan lyrics is mainly divided into two aspects. One is historical stories, myths and legends, and the other is the reappearance of people's life content. The lyrics of Xiaosan are not only the true portrayal and artistic reflection of people's life, but also the concise expression of regional culture and people's needs.

Second, Xiaosan is an important part of enriching people's spiritual and cultural needs. "Drama art has basically gone through a process of development from entertaining gods to entertaining people since it took place." [8] Xiaosan originated in the era of small-scale peasant economy in feudal society, whose main activities are religious temple fairs, Shehuo sacrifices and other activities, and it plays its role as a reward for the original dramatic form. In the long-term historical development process, the aesthetic needs of the people have gradually become active, making folk song and dance operas such as Xiaosan no longer limited to entertaining gods, but also having the effect of entertaining people. In today's society, people's material needs have been greatly met, and the pursuit of spiritual culture has become urgent. With the upsurge of carrying forward the excellent traditional Chinese culture, the Xiaosan, as an important part of enriching the people's spiritual and cultural needs, plays an important role in people's life.

Third, Xiaosan is an important resource for the prosperity of Chinese culture. The development of human civilization is endless, and the culture produced during this period is endless. "Drama in the Perspective of Drama Anthropology is an Important Component of Culture"[9], while Xiaosan is a category with cultural connotation and artistic characteristics. The present excellent traditional Chinese culture must have been formed over the years on the basis of the culture of the previous generation. Completely abandon the previous generation of culture and avoid talking about it, only saying that the excellent traditional Chinese culture we advocate at present must be castles in the air and beautiful scenery. The breadth and depth of Chinese culture lies in the historical achievement rattan frame jointly constructed by various cultural resources with distinct regional characteristics, such as Xiaosan. In today's unprecedented prosperity of art categories, Xiaosan, as an important component of Chinese cultural resources, should not only arouse people's attention and awareness of protection, but also make full use of this important resource to construct the framework of Chinese excellent traditional culture.

（2）The Inheritance and Protection of "Xiaosan"

Through investigation and research, it is found that Xiaosan, as a song and dance drama with regional characteristics in Xingyang City, Henan Province, is on the verge of extinction and needs to be excavated, sorted out, protected and inherited urgently. "The commonness of all nationalities revealed by anthropological materials will eventually contribute to the realization of the world's great harmony." [10] As an important component of rich cultural diversity, Xiaosan should be protected and inherited as soon as possible, while the local protection work is not satisfactory. Under the trend of market economy and cultural diversity, the survival situation of Xiaosan is not optimistic, especially when it comes to development. Artists tend to be older and have obvious distribution faults, the performance team is difficult to sustain, and the performance market is shrinking, which makes it extremely urgent to take necessary measures to protect Xiaosan. In view of the crisis that the Xiaosan art is on the verge of extinction, we should do the following work well.

First, adapt to the laws of literary and artistic development and improve the ecological environment of literature and art. The good development of the Xiaosan for a long time has benefited from the effective ecological mechanism established in compliance with the scientific laws of literary and artistic development. At the same time, Xiaosan thrives in the original literary ecological environment in Xingyang. The cultural connotation and dramatic form of Xiaosan have changed with the regularity and periodicity of the social form. With the rise and fall of social forms, great changes have taken place in folk beliefs and thoughts, resulting in an imbalance in the ecological environment of the original literature and art of Xiaosan and difficulty in self-development. The development of Xiaosan should still follow the scientific law of literary and artistic development and reconstruct the ecological field suitable for the development of Xiaosan with the support and efforts of various parties, which requires the relevant government departments to spare no effort to support and encourage the activities of non-governmental organizations and folk customs, to continuously strengthen the protection of local literature and art, to establish cultural and ecological protection zones, and to continuously improve the ecological environment of local literature and art such as Xiaosan.

Second, strengthen the inheritance and improve the performance quality. The main body of folk literature and art is human, which refers to both actors and performers. On the issue of the inheritance of Xiaosan, how to make the inheritance strong must be based on a clear understanding of the main body of artist, who is the focus and foothold of its inheritance and protection. Therefore, talking of the inheritance and protection of Xiaosan, the excavation and cultivation of artists and audience are in the first place. People are the core and foundation for the survival and development of all folk arts. In recent years, the relevant departments of all levels of government have continuously increased their funding and policy support to the inheritors from different levels, and have continuously created a good opera ecology through such forms as the government sending plays to the grassroots, in order to enable folk arts such as Xiaosan to re-activate on the stage of cultural diversity. In fact, it has little effect. The reason is that there is no reference to successful cases when policies are translated into practice, and all localities are flinched in order to avoid mistakes in actual work. Xiaosan artists and audience tend to be aging and lack young people's strength to continue, which is by no means a case in folk literature and art. Imagine how a group of artists who have passed the age of 60 can well adapt to the current aesthetic trend and needs of the public and create new works that conform to the current era. Even for classic plays, it is difficult to guarantee the integrity and quality of their performances with the current strength of the team. In order to change the present situation that the arts are not inherited and the performances are not of high quality, we must do both. One is to "enter the campus", while students are the development vane and potential audience group of China's aesthetic needs. Only by grasping the folk literature and art publicity and communication platform such as campus and creating and edifying a good traditional and excellent cultural aesthetic environment can the difficult problems of development be fundamentally improved. The other is ideological changes and economic means should be handled with both hands firmly. Not only should the masses change their ideological attitude towards learning folk arts such as Xiaosan, but also some economic encouragement and compensation should be given to meet the basic survival problems of the inheritors.

Third, information processing and industrial management must be implemented. Xiaosan is a folk song and dance drama on the verge of extinction. As an important component of literary and artistic projects, its dramatic texts should be recorded and preserved by means of digital audio and video recording. At the same time, the collapse of the belief in folk gods and the opening of the market economy make Xiaosan try to meet the needs of market development and industrialization. Relying on the cultural industrialization of colleges and universities, let Xiaosan operate comprehensively in the fields of theatrical performances, cultural product sales, Internet publicity, etc. To build a good operation mechanism, it is necessary to gradually make profits from performances and cultural products to achieve the balance of artists' survival and development, or even to turn from balance of income and expenditure to profit.

The Xiaosan is a fascinating but vulnerable cultural heritage in the fine traditional culture of China. We firmly believe that through our unremitting efforts, Xiaosan can usher in a better tomorrow with its own development, government support and prosperity of the literary and art market. Xiaosan is unique in form and value and used to be the sustenance and catharsis of the simple life of the local working people. Today, the survival and development of Xiaosan are hindered to some extent, but this is definitely not the reason for the restriction and stagnation. Through the ages, the development of any kind of folk literature and art will definitely not be smooth sailing, which will be a difficult course with ups and downs. This requires all sectors of society to make joint efforts to deal with and grasp the relationship between the survival, development, protection and inheritance of Xiaosan.

Reference:

[1] Wang Ningsheng. Cultural Anthropology Survey [M]. Beijing: Heritage Publishing House, 1996: 188.

[2] Ding Yaping. Art and Culture [M]. Beijing: Culture and Art Publishing House, 2005: 232.

[3] Du Zhiqing. Xingyang City Records [M]. Beijing: Xinhua Publishing House, 1996: 731.

[4] Interview with Li Tongzhong in Guandimiao Village, Yulong Town, Xingyang City on October 2, 2016.

[5] Gertz. Cultural Interpretation [M]. Shanghai: Shanghai People's Publishing House, 1999: 20.

[6] Chen Yan. Dynamic Analysis of Artistic Essence [J]. Research on Literary Theory, 1996 (3): 46.

[7] Wang Shenghua. Drama Anthropology [M]. Kunming: Yunnan University Press, 2009: 159.

[8] Wang Shenghua. Drama Anthropology [M]. Kunming: Yunnan University Press, 2009: 184.

[9] Wang Shenghua. Drama Anthropology [M]. Kunming: Yunnan University Press, 2009: 231.

[10] Lips. Origin of Things. Preface [M].Lanzhou: Dunhuang Literature and Art Publishing House, 2000:2.

艺术人类学视阈中的河洛"狮子鼓"
文化生态研究

摘要：狮子鼓是流行在河洛地区的民间乐舞。它的发展深受河洛自然和社会环境的影响。二十世纪中期以前，当地狮子鼓队曾达几百家，之后迅速减少，目前只剩少数鼓队还在活动。狮子鼓的表演由鼓乐、武术、狮舞三部分构成。鼓乐由大鼓、大镲等乐器演奏，在整个表演中起着指挥的作用；武术主要是人与狮斗，分平地斗、高台斗和高空斗，使用的器械有大刀、三股叉等；狮舞是狮子鼓表演的核心，分地摊、中摊、高摊三个环节。狮子鼓融武术、杂技、舞蹈等多种艺术于一体，内容丰富，技艺精湛，极受群众喜爱。狮子鼓在文化多样性、民众精神生活丰富、文化及其产业创造等方面有着重要价值。其保护应该从生态环境的优化入手，不断提高表演水平，积极探索现代发展的新路子。

关键词：艺术人类学；河洛文化；狮子鼓；非物质文化遗产保护

艺术是人类高级精神存在的重要表征。不同民族、不同地区的人民在各自的实践中得以创造了不同的艺术。中华民族艺术的宝库就是在各地区民众的共同创造中得以不断丰富的。在河南省郑州、洛阳一带的河洛地区流行着一种独特的民间艺术——狮子鼓。它融音乐和舞蹈为一体，争斗激烈、动作惊险、节奏鲜明，被看作是河洛文化的代表之一，并于2008年被列入了国家级非物质文化遗产保护名录。狮子鼓是河洛文化孕育的独特文化物种。它的成长方式、运作规律及其与环境的互动在非物质文化遗产中有着很强的代表性。从狮子鼓的产生、成熟以及曲折的发展过程中,我们能体悟到民众与民间艺术的关系,也能感受到民间艺术发展的一些生态规律。2016年,作者带领学生多次到河洛地区调查狮子鼓,并将狮子鼓表演队请到本校的"文化遗产活动月"中进行表演。通过调查以及与狮鼓队的多次接触,我们感到,狮子鼓已与当地的民众生活融为一体。正如艺术人类学家所说,它是仪式在生活中的具体体现。现将有关调查及思考报告如下。

一、河洛狮子鼓成长的生态环境

河洛地区位于河南省中西部,其核心地区是黄河和伊洛河交汇处的荥阳市、巩义市一带。但在文化研究上,河洛文化区涉及的范围要广泛些,并有广义和狭义之分。广义的河洛文化区是指北起中条山、南达伏牛山、西至潼关、东到开封的广大区域。狭义的河洛文化区是指黄河中游潼关至郑州段的南岸,洛水、伊水及嵩山周围地区,大致包括北纬34°至35°、东经110°至114°之间的地区,即今天河南省的西部地区。狮子鼓流行的荥阳、巩县一带正处于河洛文化的核心区域。应该说,狮子鼓是河洛地区特定生态环境孕育的文化成果。

河洛地区的自然环境是河洛文化发展的基础。文化生态学认为,文化"是由一个社会与其环境互动的特殊适应过程造成的"。[1]河洛地区特定的气候、水土、交通等条件决定了河洛文化的形态、特征与风貌。河洛地区地处黄河中下游平原西端。这里日照充分,气候温暖,降雨适中,水利条件优越。良好的自然条件使这里的农业自古就比较发达。河洛地区古代还是中国的交通中心。"秦汉实现了国家的统一,秦始皇修筑'驰道'和'直道'。从咸阳到东方的主干道,出潼关经函谷关到达洛阳,再向东出虎牢关到达荥阳,可以向北到燕赵,向东到齐鲁,东南到江淮。东汉时期洛阳成为通往西域和欧洲的丝绸之路的东方起点。洛阳往南经南阳可达江汉地区,向北经河内可达太原、雁门,东北可达幽、冀。隋代修通了以洛阳为中心,北起涿郡、南达余杭的大运河,极大地方便了河洛地区的水上交通……总之,河洛地区不仅交通便利,而且长期是全国的交通中心。"[2]河洛地区不仅陆路交通便利,其水上交通也曾相当发达。这里曾是大运河的必经之地,是古代的水上交通枢纽。"按照新旧《唐书地理志》的记载,隶属江南道的有苏州、润州和越州,隶属淮南道的有楚州和滁州,隶属河北道的有邢州、冀州、德州和魏州。这些地方的租粮均能够通过大运河,由江南运河、邗沟、通济渠,或者由永济渠,来到含嘉仓。在这样的经济地理形势下,加之河山控带的形胜,东都洛阳成为经济区与政治中心之间的最佳平衡点,'有河朔之饶,食江淮之利,九年之储已积,四方之赋攸均'。也因此,洛阳成为大运河的中心,盛况空前。"[3] 水运对河洛地区的政治、经济和文化的发展产生了至关重要的影响。直至近代,伊洛河与黄河的航运仍然对当地的社会发展发挥着重要作用。明清之际兴盛了几百年的康百万家族就是靠伊洛河和黄河的航运做生意起家并持续繁荣的。至二十世纪中期,当地仍然有很多人在以航运谋生。我们在调查时,巩义市神南、神北村的村民说,过去这里大部分人都是玩船的(即以航运谋生)。直至抗日战争爆发,大量的船只被日本飞机炸毁,航运才逐渐萧条。[1] 自然条件的优越、交通中心的位置,这些都为当地经济和文化的发展创造了良好的条件。

河洛地区的社会环境对文化的发展产生了更重要的影响。我们知道,河洛地区曾长期是中国的政治、经济和文化中心。这里丰富多彩的政治、经济、宗教、文化活动对当地民间文艺的发展产生了深刻影响。对狮子鼓影响最大、最直接的是当地的宗教活动。众所周知,中原地区是佛教在中国发展最早的地区。洛阳白马寺是中国第一个佛教寺庙。佛教在中原地区的迅速发展对当地的社会生活和文化发展都产生了深刻影响。河洛地区曾拥有大量的佛教寺庙。如白马寺、少林寺、唐僧寺(玄奘寺,原名灵岩寺)、香山寺、福仙寺、龙马负图寺、广化寺、观音寺、黄觉寺、风穴寺、古唐寺、藏梅寺、灵山寺、石窟寺、皇觉寺、看经寺、花山庙、奉先寺、潜溪寺、大福先寺、大海寺、龙泉寺、周固寺、等慈寺、兴国寺、洞林寺、蔡村寺、高村寺、蟠龙寺、南大寺、北大寺、佛姑寺等。此外,还有大量的道教庙观。如关林庙、白云观、中岳庙、吕祖庵、高龙中岳庙、神灵寨、上清宫、下清宫、长春观、飞龙顶、逍遥观、玉皇庙、老君庙、三官庙、二郎庙、吕祖庙、龙王庙、火神庙、大王庙、关帝庙、岵山庙等。这里先后拥有的寺庙道观加起来有几百座之多。大量寺庙道观的存在意味着这里有着大量的庙会等宗教仪式活动。"河南各县庙会每年少者百余次,多者千余次。林州每年有庙会 231 次,温县 243 次,荥阳市 247 次……"庙会作为民间文艺发展的重要平台和载体为民间文艺的发展提供了很好的机会。如洛阳关林庙会,"明清时期的洛阳关林庙会,可以说是盛大的文艺汇演,千姿百态的戏曲和美不胜收的民间文艺表演,具有浓郁的时代特色和地方特色,对于长期生活在乡间,过清苦生活的农民和手工业者来说,具有强烈的吸引力。"在关林庙会上不仅有大量的戏曲表演,还有跑阵、高跷曲子、舞狮子、旱船、竹马、秧歌等多样化的民间文艺表演。舞狮子是关林庙会极富特色的项目,常有上老杆、上天梯、走软索等惊险节目。调查中河洛地区的艺人们多次谈到,狮子鼓是一项大型的表演节目,需要的人多,动静很大,仪式威严,过去主要是在庙会上表演。大量的庙会等仪式活动为狮子鼓表演提供了舞台,由此极大地推动了狮子鼓的发展。

综上所述,河洛地区优越的自然条件、良好的社会环境为狮子鼓的发展创造了良好的条件。狮子鼓正是在这样独特的环境中逐步成熟和发展起来的。

二、河洛狮子鼓的历史发展及艺术构成

中国舞狮的历史相当悠久。据考,其源头可追溯到汉代。"舞狮始于汉代长安(公元前20—公元25年),盛于南北朝(公元420—589年),至今已有两千多年的历史。"[3] 至唐代,舞狮已成为上至宫廷下到民间都非常喜欢的一种舞蹈活动。唐代诗人白居易曾有"假面胡人假面狮,刻木为头丝作尾。金镀眼睛银帖齿,奋迅毛衣摆双耳"的诗句,对当时的舞狮进行了很形象的描写。狮舞经长期发展,并在各地演变,形成了不同的风格。大致说来,中国舞狮分南狮、北狮两大类型。北狮动作灵活,舞动以扑、跌、翻、滚、跳跃、擦痒等为主。南狮威猛,色彩艳丽,制作考究、机巧,眼帘、嘴巴可以活动,舞动时注重马步。具体到各地又有不同的类型,如山西天塔狮舞、广东席狮舞、上海手狮舞等。河南各地也有不同的舞狮类型,如豫北舞狮、豫西狮舞、沈丘回族文狮舞、双狮舞(漯河)、五花营狮子舞、砖井狮虎舞等,相互之间差别也很大。河洛狮子鼓是中国众多舞狮中极为独特的一种形式。

(一)河洛狮子鼓的产生与发展

河洛狮子鼓产生的具体时间没有明确的记载。据民间传说,狮子鼓是李世民于虎牢关以少胜多大破夏王窦建德后,唐军兵士为庆贺大捷而作《秦王破阵乐》,后来该乐在当地流传并与舞狮子结合逐步形成了狮子鼓。

国家级非物质文化遗产项目"小相狮舞"所在地巩义市小相村的艺人则说,狮子鼓"起于清初,其时村中'霍乱'肆虐,死伤无数,求医无门,久病无方。当时民间尚迷信,认为'霍乱'由妖魅作祟引起,而狮子又称为'神兽''辟邪''天禄',是守护人间的瑞兽,于是大家自发组织狮舞活动以驱病、逐恶。'霍乱'过后,狮舞活动就保留下来。"[1]"起于清初"这种说法值得进一步考证。如前所述,中国舞狮的历史相当悠久。河洛地区作为当时中国的政治和文化中心,狮舞出现得也相当早。北魏杨炫之的《洛阳伽蓝记》中就有"辟邪狮子,引导其前"的描写。我们在荥阳市蒋头村调查时,当地艺人说狮子鼓产生于明代。到底是产生于清代,还是产生于明代,抑或更早?这都还有待于进一步考证。但可以肯定的是,狮子鼓的历史已经相当悠久了。

明清时期是河洛狮子鼓迅速发展的时期。这一时期狮子鼓已遍布各地并成了社火的重要组成部分。我们在调查时很多老艺人都谈到,过去河洛地区的狮鼓社非常多。一般在春节祭祀时与其他民间艺术一同"出社"(演出)。其形式往往非常隆重,表演也极为讲究。狮子鼓出社的阵容通常是:放铳人在前面打场开道,掌班人(狮社首领)手持令旗居首,写有社火名称的门旗紧随其后。之后依次是:竖幅大旌旗,小家什社,龙、凤、虎、雀大花旗,帅字旗,黄罗伞,八面大鼓,镲、铙、圪垯锣,狮舞"回回"(斗狮人),几架狮子,以及呐喊助威人员等。据说,过去巩义、荥阳、偃师一带的大鼓社多达400余家,可见当时狮子鼓是相当繁盛的。

新中国成立后,社会安定,人民当家作主,各项事业欣欣向荣,狮子鼓也有了进一步的发展。狮社数量增多,演员也大量增加。"文革"开始后,在一片反对迷信声中,多数狮鼓社停止了活动。二十世纪七八十年代以后,狮子鼓的活动又逐渐恢复。近年来,随着社会对非物质文化遗产保护的重视,狮子鼓的发展出现了新的转机,不少鼓社又趋活跃。如巩义市小相村、荥阳市王村镇王村和蒋头村等的狮鼓队都相当活跃。但近年也有一些新情况出现。由于受经济等因素的影响,一些曾恢复的鼓队在活动了一段时间后又趋于了沉寂。如荥阳市高村乡高村的狮子鼓,原曾极有特色,在当地很有影响。"文革"后鼓队恢复活动,一度曾相当活跃。但近年来由于演员外出打工等,组织工作变得越来越困难,现已基本停止活动了。当前传承比较好的是巩义市小相村的狮鼓队。小相狮子鼓（小相狮舞）2007 年入选河南省第一批非物质文化遗产名录，2008 年入选国家级非物质文化遗产名录。小相狮舞技艺高超、动作惊险、观赏性强，曾获得"中原第一狮""中华第一狮"等称号。在原村委会主任李金土的带领下，小相村已成立"巩义市金王狮鼓文化传播公司"。他们承接商业演出，举办狮子鼓培训班，目前正在积极探索市场经济条件下狮子鼓发展的新路子。[1] 荥阳市也曾是狮子鼓比较发达的地区。荥阳市文化学者陈玮说："荥阳过去是水乡。旱船、推小车、跑驴、高跷、狮子鼓、笑伞等文艺形式非常盛行。……狮子鼓的鼓谱与陕西'秦王破阵乐'相似。本是打虎，因讳李世民，后来改为打狮子。"荥阳市王村镇王村的狮子鼓在当地非常有名。该村的狮子鼓技艺高超、表演精彩，曾参加多种活动夺得大奖。1992 年起该村狮子鼓先后六次受邀到郑州表演，曾荣获"河南省第一届艺术节优秀节目奖""郑州国际少林武术节特别贡献奖""'威震中州'盘鼓狮舞比赛一等奖""河洛一绝""郑州市 2002 年狮舞大赛一等奖"等多种荣誉称号。荥阳市王村镇蒋头村的狮子鼓是当前比较活跃的表演队。领队茈毛孩说，本村的狮子鼓明朝初期就有。清朝末期本村的狮子鼓表演达到了很高的水平，出现了多位技艺高超的艺人，如赵锡纯（高台）、金臭（耍大刀）、茈坡（上老杆儿）、李贺喜（地摊，春秋刀）等。本村狮鼓队表演的四排鼓、大炸鞭、双交（凤展翅）、上老杆儿、霸桥、拿顶、踩绳等都很叫好。蒋头村的狮子鼓队曾多次参加中国少林武术节、河南省首届艺术节、洛阳牡丹节、黄河大观开园仪式、中国中西部会议开幕式等活动，并多次获奖。2016 年 11 月，蒋头村狮子鼓还应邀到河南师范大学开展进校园表演，受到了师生们的好评。

（二）河洛狮子鼓的艺术构成

在河洛地区，狮子鼓通常是社火的重要组成部分。狮鼓社少则五六十人，多则百人以上。过去表演时演员常穿古代兵丁、将士服装，在帅字旗、都督旗、令旗等的指挥下进行表演。狮子鼓表演综合了武术、杂技、舞蹈等多种技艺，特别是融合了当地著名拳种茈家拳的武术动作，刚柔并济、攻守兼备、自成特色。狮子鼓出会表演常常会有各种名堂，如龙凤鼓舞、群狮闹喜、刀山火海、神仙下凡、嫦娥奔月、蹿火奔月等。狮子鼓艺术通常由三部分构成：鼓乐、武术、舞狮。其中，鼓乐在表演中起着指挥的作用。武术、狮舞是表演的核心。狮子鼓表演时,轰鸣多变的鼓乐、激烈热闹的打斗、惊险绝妙的狮舞常令观众拍手叫好。

鼓乐。鼓乐是狮子鼓表演的基础,它起着指挥和控制节奏的作用。鼓乐演奏常用的乐器有:大鼓8面、大镲12副、大铙8副、大京10面、圪垯锣2面。改革开放后,经济条件好转,有些地方鼓的数量增至20面,甚至还有更多的。其他乐器数量也会随着鼓的增加而增加。鼓乐的核心是大鼓,其轰鸣的声音、多变的节奏指引狮子不停地舞动。其他乐器都配合着大鼓进行演奏。鼓乐演奏按鼓谱进行,内容相当丰富,并且各地差别很大。以荥阳市高村乡高村的狮子鼓为例,其鼓的打法有:老长套(鼓的基础点)、反棰、行路交(青龙探爪、猴上杆)、交棰(单叉花、双叉花、金蝉脱骨、五虎下西川、青龙上桥)等。狮子鼓的曲牌则更多。《河洛鼓谱》的作者李戊辰说:"(狮子鼓)所演奏的曲牌,流传下来的就有近千首,按一首一首的鼓歌计,一个鼓社至少也有十四五首,河洛地区估计就有近万首。在调查中发现,各鼓社所演奏的鼓歌,除个别特殊情况外,基本上没有一首是完全相同的。不同地区即使曲牌名称相同,它的曲谱、韵律、结构形式都不一样。"[1]可见,狮子鼓的鼓乐内容是相当丰富的。不同地区的狮子鼓在发展中融入了当地民众的创造,形成了自己的特色,这恰是民间艺术发展的典型特征。鼓歌是珍贵的文化遗产,在狮子鼓的保护中应予以高度重视。除了鼓、镲等演奏,狮子鼓表演时还有好多人配合演出放炮、吹螺号、吹尖子号等,周边还有人挥动器械呐喊、吹口哨助威,这都可看作是狮子鼓表演的组成部分。可以说,狮子鼓表演首先是一场声乐的艺术盛宴。

武术。狮子鼓融合了当地苌家拳的武术内容,全程贯穿着人狮相斗(当地称"斗狮")。斗狮分三种情况:平地斗、高台斗和高空斗。平地斗多用器械,如大刀、单刀、双刀、枪、大镰、三股叉、梢子棍、绣球等。斗狮人使用各种器械与狮子相斗。斗狮者功夫高超、动作激烈,狮子则腾挪闪跃、威猛异常。高台斗主要是在桌子上进行打斗。狮子在桌子上做出各种高难动作,斗狮人桌上桌下闪跃腾窜,也相当激烈。高空斗主要是引狮上"山"。所谓"山"是用长条凳叠起,高达十几米。斗狮人在平地、高台斗完后,再引狮上"山"。斗狮者身手灵巧,狮子窜上窜下追逐,在"高山"之上人狮相斗,显示了表演者极为高超的武术和艺术功力。

舞狮。舞狮是整个狮子鼓表演的核心。据说,舞狮最初只是"文狮"表演,后经过荥阳地区武术大家苌大炮、苌小旦等人的精心设计、加工,融武术动作于狮舞,最后形成了"武狮"。现在河洛地区流行的多为"武狮"。其表演着重于高难度的技巧展示,动作多粗犷、激烈,常展示的动作有跳跃、跌扑、登高、翻滚、直立、抖毛、钻火圈、走钢丝、穿口、蹦桌子、蹬球以及上"高台"、爬"老杆儿"等。舞狮表演也分三个部分:地摊(平地表演)、中摊(桌上表演)、高摊(高空表演)。地摊表演主要是人狮平地相斗,狮子与持各种器械者相斗。地摊表演在展现狮子威猛的同时,也展现狮鼓队高超的武术功夫。中摊表演主要是狮子在桌子上表演,狮子通过腾跃、叠立等,展现高超的技艺。高摊表演主要是在长条凳叠起的"高山"上进行。狮子在斗狮人的引逗下,逐级上爬,至顶常常做出站立、衔凳等各种高难度动作。高潮时狮子嘴里吊出"祝×××人民新年愉快!"等条幅,引起观众热烈鼓掌。高空表演结束后,狮子逐级"下山",并将长条凳用嘴衔扔而下,至底表演结束。有时狮子还要表演上老杆儿项目。上老杆儿是狮子鼓表演中最惊险的项目。老杆儿通常为十几米高的长杆,四面由粗绳固定,表演时狮子沿绳而上,最终到达长杆之巅做出各种惊险动作。老杆儿表演是展示狮子鼓队表演水平的标志性活动。只有高水平的舞狮队才敢进行这项表演。

狮子鼓就是这样,它融音乐、武术、舞狮为一体,与生活紧密结合,内容丰富、套路复杂、技艺高超,展现了河洛民间艺术的卓越风采。狮子鼓表演常常会吸引大量观众,并不时引起阵阵喝彩。

三、关于河洛狮子鼓的艺术人类学思考

狮子鼓是河洛文化孕育的艺术奇葩。经长期发展,它已与民众生活紧密地联系在一起,并成了民众精神生活的重要依托。今天,随着非物质文化遗产保护工作的深入,狮子鼓的生存环境有了明显改善,但其生存危机还远远没有解除。那么,狮子鼓的价值究竟应该怎么认识,今后的保护工作又该怎么做呢?

(一)狮子鼓的价值

对民间艺术价值的认识涉及政治、社会观念、艺术理论等方方面面。中国近代以来对民间艺术价值的认识经历了一个十分曲折的过程。以"文

革"为代表的否定传统运动曾使我们迷失方向、疏离民间文艺,从而导致了大量民间艺术的衰败和消亡。近些年来,随着政治的拨乱反正以及学术研究的进步,特别是进入 21 世纪以来联合国教科文组织倡导的非物质文化遗产保护运动的兴起,使我们对民间文化有了全新的认识。今天,狮子鼓已从"迷信""糟粕"的污名中脱身而出,成了非物质文化遗产,这确实是狮子鼓发展中的一大幸事。狮子鼓的价值大致可以从如下这几个方面理解。

第一,狮子鼓是人类文化多样性的重要组成部分。人类文化是在多样化的民族和地区生活中不断丰富和发展的。文化人类学家认为,任何一种文化都有它独特的价值,任何一个民族的文化都应该受到尊重,在民族文化上没有高低贵贱、先进与落后之分。正如人类学家博厄斯所强调的,"根本就不存在人类文化发展的普遍法则,每一种文化都有其存在的价值,每一个民族都有其值得尊重的价值观,都在人类进化的历程中作出了不可磨灭的贡献,不同的文化背景有着不同的价值和功能。"[1] 文化的多样发展正是在不同民族、不同地区人民的共同努力下实现的。不同的生产方式和生活方式产生了不同的文化。每一种文化都是在特定的自然和社会环境中造就出来的,都有着独特的价值。狮子鼓也一样,它是河洛地区人民的独特创造,是对人类文化多样性的重要贡献。近代以来,我国社会所形成的重西方文化、轻民族文化的现象对民间文化的发展造成了极为不利的影响。很多人不能正视自己的民族文化。特别是年轻一代,一切以西方文化马首是瞻,崇美、哈韩、逐日,唯独对自己民族的文化不感兴趣。这种情况是不利于民间文化发展的。所幸近年来兴起的非物质文化遗产保护热潮逐步改变了人们对民间文化的认识。民间文化发展的环境在日趋好转。但思想认识的提高不是一日能完成的。我们还应该加强宣传,将艺术人类学等有关理论应用到实践中,提高保护的科学性,从而真正使非物质文化遗产得到有效的保护。

第二,狮子鼓是河洛人民丰富精神生活的重要工具。艺术人类学告诉我们,艺术是人类生活不可缺少的重要组成部分。广泛的人类实践表明,广大民众的精神充实离不开根植于生活的民间艺术。即使是在生活困苦的旧社会,人们依然可以通过自己所喜爱的民间艺术实现"诗意栖居"。狮子鼓就是河洛地区人民实现诗意栖居的重要工具。在漫长甚至困苦的生活中,人们正是通过狮子鼓等民间艺术愉悦了精神、凝聚了力量、充实了生活。狮子鼓之所以能持续到今天,就在于它所拥有的这种精神审美价值。

第三,狮子鼓是文化发展和文化产业创造的重要资源。人类文化的发展是个永不停息的过程。后代文化的发展和创造离不开前代文化的积累。抛开前代文化基础进行所谓的创造,往往是空中楼阁,是不可行的。中国文化发展中最值得珍惜的就是我们在漫长的历史发展中所积累的大量艺术成果和艺术经验。狮子鼓作为文化发展的历史成果,也是当代文化创造的重要资源。更值得注意的是,随着当代文化产业的迅猛发展,狮子鼓还将是文化产业发展的重要资源。

(二)关于河洛狮子鼓保护的思考

通过研究我们知道,狮子鼓是河洛人民在长期生产和生活实践中创造的伟大成果,是河洛文化的优秀代表。然而,随着时代的变迁,狮子鼓几经沉浮,今天又面临着重重危机。在市场经济、文化多元化等因素冲击之下,狮子鼓的生存变得越来越困难,演出市场不断萎缩、表演队越来越少、演员青黄不接。如不采取有效措施进行保护,狮子鼓将来可能就会失传。鉴于此,当前我们应该做好以下工作。

第一,重视艺术规律,加强生态保护。从文化生态学的视角来看,狮子鼓是河洛地区特有生态环境孕育出的一朵美丽鲜花。历史上狮子鼓的良好发展乃得益于其良好的生态环境。"文革"时期它的寥落和衰败也是由于生态环境恶化所致。可见,生态环境在很大程度上决定着狮子鼓的兴衰。因此,要保护狮子鼓,就必须优化狮子鼓的生态环境。具体地说,就是要从恢复和保护河洛地区的自然和社会环境做起。如尽力维护自然的多样性、减少环境污染、美化自然;恢复一些有益的习俗与信仰、增进人际关系的和谐、推动狮子鼓与生活的结合等。将来如果在更多的人生仪式、节日活动、重要庆典中有更多的机会来表演狮子鼓,也许狮子鼓的生存状况就会有所好转。

第二,加强技艺传承,提高演出水平。狮子鼓是历史的产物,是千百年来劳动人民智慧的结晶。在长期的历史发展中,狮子鼓表演形成了丰富的艺术技巧。这些艺术技巧不是一个人在短时间内能学到的,也不是单靠灵感就能悟出的。狮子鼓演员应该虚心地向老艺人学习,传承其独特的技艺,提高表演的水平。有关部门应有意识地引导、支持狮子鼓的传承。可以通过开设狮子鼓培训班、组织狮子鼓传承人到各村镇教授等形式,推动狮子鼓的传承。各表演队也要积极行动,主动向有经验的老艺人学习,邀请老艺人到本队传教。相关高校、研究部门也应该加强社会服务意识,积极与狮子鼓队结合,通过申报各级艺术基金、研究项目等,研究狮子鼓的艺术规律、记录狮子鼓的资料、培养狮子鼓的传承人,全面地帮助狮子鼓发展。更需要注意的是,在新的时代条件下,观众的审美水平越来越高、眼光越来越挑剔。狮子鼓队应当拿出更多、更高质量的作品来服务社会。特别是在新媒体条件下,艺术打破了地区的界限和传播的旧模式,不同地区甚至不同国家的艺术要在同一竞技场中竞争。今后,狮子鼓要面临的很可能是与一些国际大公司精心打造、倾力投入的大制作、高水平的艺术作品进行竞争。这显然是极为艰难的。这就要求,狮子鼓一定要与时俱进,不断提高表演水平,以更加精彩的表演来吸引新时代的观众。

第三,适应时代需要,探索发展新路。传统的狮子鼓多依附于敬神祭祀等活动,是社火活动的主要组成部分。其发展主要靠信仰和仪式的力量。新中国成立后,随着反对迷信运动的开展以及"文革"的来临,信仰活动遭到了严重的冲击,仪式的力量迅速衰弱,狮子鼓赖以生存的环境和动力消失,发展随之陷入困顿。今天狮子鼓发展的环境虽有一定改善,但其传统的发展机制和动力已难再恢复。在这样的条件下,我们就必须去寻找新的动力源泉、建立新的发展机制。在当前的市场经济条件下,狮子鼓的发展也应该充分考虑市场的规则和经济的手段,尝试运用现代公司管理模式进行管理。如实行公司化运营和股份制,尽快建立科学的人事管理制度、财务制度、企业管理制度等。在经营上,积极创造文化精品,以高质量的艺术产品去占领市场,积极开发新媒体产品,如影视、网络、手机传媒产品等。同时,加强宣传,扩大狮子鼓的影响,树立狮子鼓品牌形象,引导观众消费等。

我们相信,通过不断的努力与发展,狮子鼓会迎来一个更美好的未来。当然,这是一个艰难的过程,也许它并不会那么一帆风顺。这需要社会各界共同努力与配合,也需要处理好保护、创新、发展等各方面的关系。

参考文献：

[1] 程金成．文艺人类学的理论与实践 [M]．北京：民族出版社，2007：243．

[2] 朱利安·H·斯图尔德．潘艳,陈洪波译．文化生态学 [J]．南方文物，2007（2）．

[3] 程有为．河洛文化概论 [M]．郑州：河南人民出版社，2007：14-15.

[4] 王伟．洛阳与隋唐大运河 [J]．中原文物，2014（5）．

[5] 相关情况来自 2015 年 7 月 16 日作者在巩义市神北村对张瑞敏等人的调查。

[6] 河南省地方史志编纂委员会．河南省志·文化志 [M]．郑州：河南人民出版社，1994：391.

[7] 韩维鹏．明清时期洛阳关林庙会研究 [D]．硕士论文,广西师范大学，2012.

[8] 高谊、姚贵树．中国舞狮 [M]．天津：南开大学出版社，2007：1.

[9] 白晓玉．浅析小相狮舞之美 [J]．语文知识，2012.

[10] 李戊辰．河洛鼓谱 [M]．郑州：大象出版社，2013：2.

[11] 相关情况来自作者 2016 年 7 月 20 日在巩义市鲁庄镇小相村对小相狮舞国家级传承人李金土的采访。

[12]2016 年 10 月 2 日作者在荥阳市对文化学者陈玮的采访。

[13]2016 年 10 月 2 日作者在荥阳市蒋头村对苌毛孩的采访。

[14] 李戊辰．河洛鼓谱 [M]．郑州：大象出版社，2013：3.

[15] 张今杰,林艳．弗朗兹·博厄斯的整体论思想研究 [J]．武汉理工大学学报（社会科学版），2012（5）．

Study on the Cultural Ecology of Heluo "Lion Drum" from the Perspective of Artistic Anthropology

Abstract: The Lion drum is a popular folk music and dance in Heluo area. Its development is deeply influenced by Heluo natural and social environment. There were several hundred local lion drum troupes before the middle of the 20th century, but they declined rapidly and only a few drum troupes are still active. Lion drum performance consists of three parts which are drum music, martial arts and lion dance. The drum music is played by the big drum and the big cymbals that play the role of the conductor in the entire performance. Martial arts refers to the fight between people and lions which includes flat fighting, high platform fighting and high-altitude fighting with the use of equipment such as broadsword and three branch hayfork. Lion dance is the core of lion drum performance with three rounds which are ground move, middle move and high move. Lion drum, a combination of martial arts, acrobatics, dance and other arts, attracts people by its rich contents. Lion drum is of great value in cultural diversity, spiritual life of the people and cultural and industrial creation. Its protection should start from the optimization of the ecological environment so as to improve the performance level constantly and explore new ways of modern development actively.

Key words: artistic anthropology; Heluo culture; the lion drum; protection of intangible cultural heritage

Art is an important representation of the existence of the advanced human spirit.People of different nationalities and regions have created different arts through their own practices.The treasure house of Chinese national art is constantly enriched in the joint creation of people in various regions.A unique folk art—lion drum was popular in Heluo area of Zhengzhou and Luoyang in Henan Province.It integrates music and dance into a whole with fierce fighting, thrilling action and distinct rhythm. It is regarded as one of the representatives of Heluo culture and was listed in the National Intangible Cultural Heritage Protection list in 2008.Lion drum is a unique cultural species bred by Heluo culture.

Its growth mode, operation rules and interaction with the environment are very representative in the intangible cultural heritage. From the emergence, maturity and tortuous development process of lion drum, we can understand the relationship between the people and folk art and also feel some ecological rules of the development of folk art.In 2016, the author led students to investigate the lion drum in Heluo district for many times and invited the lion drum performance team to perform in the cultural heritage activity month of our school.

We feel that the lion drum has been integrated into the local people's life through investigation and many contacts with the lion drum team.

It's said by the art anthropologist that the lion drum is the concrete embodiment of ritual in daily life. [1] The relevant investigation and reflection report is as follows.

1.The Ecological Environment of HeluoLion Drum Growing

Heluo area is located in the central and western part of Henan Province which the core areas are Xingyang City and Gongyi City around the intersection of the Yellow River and Yiluo River. However, we mentioned the cultural research about Heluo area which has the broad sense and the narrow sense. The narrow sense of the Heluo cultural area refers to the vast area from Zhongtiao Mountain in the north to Funiu Mountain in the south to Tongguan in the west and Kaifeng in the east.The narrow sense of the Heluo cultural area refers to the Tongguan in middle of the Yellow River to south bank of Zhengzhou City and the surrounding area of Luoshui, Yishui and Songshan which generally include 34° to 35° north latitude and 110° to 114° east longitude between regions, namely the current western region of Henan Province. Xingyang and Gong County area is at the core of the Heluo culture where the Lion drum has its popularity. It should be said that the lion drum is a cultural achievement created by the special ecological environment in Heluo area.

The natural environment in Heluo area is the basis of the development of Heluo culture. Cultural ecology holds that culture is caused by a special adaptive process in which a society interacts with its environment. The specific climate, water and soil, transportation and other conditions in Heluo region determine the form, characteristics and style of Heluo culture.Heluo area is located in the western end of the middle and lower Yellow River plain.

The good natural conditions here like full sunshine, warm climate, moderate rainfall and superior water conservancy conditions to make agriculture here more developed since ancient times.Heluo area was also the traffic center of ancient China.

The Qin and Han dynasties achieved the unification of the country. Meanwhile, first emperor of Qin Dynasty ordered to construct the high-speed way and stright way. From Xianyang to the main road of the east, out of Tongguan, through Hanguguan, pass to Luoyang, then east out of Hulaoguan pass to Xingyang, one can go north to Yanzhao, east to Qilu, southeast to Jianghuai. During the Eastern Han Dynasty, Luoyang became the eastern starting point of the silk road to the western regions and Europe.

Luoyang can reach Jianghan area through Nanyang in the south, Taiyuan and Yanmen in the north, and You and Ji in the northeast.In Sui Dynasty, the grand canal was built which took Luoyang as the center, north rose Zhuojun, south to Yuhang. The canal greatly facilitated the aquatic traffic of Heluo area....In a word, Heluo area is not only convenient in transportation, but also the transportation center of the whole country for a long time. [3] Heluo area not only has a good land transport, but also has an advanced water transportation. It was once the only passage of the grand canal and the ancient water transportation hub. According to the old and new edition of *Geography Records of the Book of Tang History*, Suzhou, Runzhou and Yuezhou belonged to Jiangnan Dao, Chuzhou and Chuzhou belonged to Huainan Dao, and Xingzhou, Jizhou, Dezhou and Weizhou belonged to Hebei Dao. Grain rents in these places were routed through the grand canal, by the Jiangnan Canal, Han Channel, the Tongji Channel or the Yongji Channel and got to the Hanjia Granary. Under such economic and geographical situation, together with the advantage of being surrounded by the river and mountain and difficult to attack, the eastern capital of Luoyang has become the best balance between the economic zone and the political center. There was a poem said that Luoyang enjoyed the benifits and advantages of Heshuo area and Jianghuai area, which made it a great amount of goods and materials, and at the same time, it had got fair taxes from places nearby. Therefore, Luoyang became the center of the grand canal with unprecedented prosperity . [4]

Water transport has a vital influence on the political, economic and cultural development of Heluo area. The shipping between the Yiluo river and the Yellow River still played an important role in local social development until modern times.The Kangbaiwan family which flourished for hundreds of years during the Ming and Qing dynasties, started their business by shipping along the Yiluo and Yellow rivers and continued to prosper.Many local people were still making a living by shipping in the middle of the twentiethcentury, .

Villagers from Shennan and Shenbei villages in Gongyi City said that most people here used to play with boats (it means making a living by shipping) during our survey. The shipping was gradually depressed when the outbreak of the War of Resistance against Japanese Aggression and a large number of ships were bombed by Japanese aircraft.[5] The superior natural conditions and the location of the transportation center create favorable conditions for the development of local economy and culture.

The social environment in Heluo area has more important influence on the development of culture. As we all know, Heluo region has long been the political, economic and cultural center of China. The colorful political, economic, religious and cultural activities here have had a profound impact on the development of local folk literature and art. The local religious activities have the most direct influence on lion drum. It is widely known that the central plain is the earliest region where Buddhism developed in China.The White Horse Temple in Luoyang is the first buddhist temple in China.The rapid development of Buddhism in the central plains has had a profound impact on the local social life and cultural development. The Heluo region once had a large number of buddhist Temples.Such as the White Horse Temple, the Shaolin Temple, Tangseng Temple (Xuan Zang Temple, formerly known as Lingyan Temple), Xiangshan Temple, Fuxian Temple, Longmafutu Temple, Guanghua Temple, Guanyin Temple, Huangjue Temple, Fengxue Temple, Gutang Temple, Cangmei Temple, Lingshan Temple, Shiku Temple, Huangjue Temple, Kanjing Temple, Huashan Temple, Fengxian Temple, Qianxi Temple, Dafuxian Temple, Dahai Temple, Longquan Temple, Zhougu Temple, Dengci Temple, Xingguo Temple, Donglin Temple, Caicun Temple, Gaocun Temple, Panlong Temple, Nanda Temple, Beida Temple, Fogu Temple and so on. In addition, there are many Taoist Temples. Such as Guanlin Temple, Baiyun Temple, Zhongyue Temple, Lvzu Temple, Gaolong zhongyue Temple, Shenling Village, Shangqing Palace, Xiaqing Palace,

Changchun Temple, Feilong Peak, Xiaoyao Temple, Yuhuang Temple, Laojun Temple, Sanguan Temple, Erlang Temple, Lvzu Temple, Longwang Temple, Huoshen Temple, Dawang Temple, Guandi Temple and Gushan Temple, etc. It once had hundreds of Temples and Taoist Temples in this place.

The presence of a large number of temples and Taoist temples means that there are a large number of temple fairs and other religious rituals here. There are hundreds of temple fairs in every county in Henan every year. There are 231 times temple fairs in Linzhou County, 243 times in Wenxian County and 247 in Xingyang City.[6] As an important platform and carrier of the development of folk literature and art, temple fair provides a good opportunity for the development of folk literature and art.Such as Luoyang Guanlin temple fair. In Ming and Qing dynasties, Luoyang Guanlin Temple fair can be said to be the grand literary performance; various opera and beautiful folk art performances with strong characteristics of the times and local characteristics have strong attraction for farmers and craftsmen who are living in the country for a long time. [7]

In Guanlin temple fair, there are not only a large number of opera performances, but also running time, stilt music, lion dance, land boat, bamboo horse, Yangko and other diversified folk art performances.Lion dance is a very characteristic item of Guanlin temple fair with some risky performances like climbing the old pole and sky pole and walking on a soft rope.According to the survey, many artists in Heluo region said that the lion drum is a large performance program which requires a large number of people, a big movement and a dignified ceremony. In the past, the lion drum was mainly performed at the temple fair.A large number of temple fairs and other ceremonial activities provided a stage for the lion drum performance which greatly promoted the development of the lion drum.

To sum up, the superior natural conditions and favorable social environment in Heluo region create favorable conditions for the development of lion drum. Lion drum is gradually becoming matured and developed in such a unique environment.

2. The Historical Development and Artistic Composition of Heluo Lion Drum

Chinese lion dance has a long history.According to research, its origin can be traced back to the Han Dynasty.Lion dancing started in Chang'an (206 BC—25AD) in the Han Dynasty and flourished in the Southern and Northern Dynasties (420—589). It has a history of more than 2,000 years. [8]

Until the Tang Dynasty, lion dance has become a popular dance from the court to the folk. Tang Dynasty poet Bai Juyi once had a poem says that "Masked Huren, masked lion, carved wood for the head and silk for the tail. Gold plated eyes silver for teeth, be swift and powerful with sweater, put double ears sway" which had the very vivid description about the lion dance at that time. After a long period of development, the lion dance has evolved into different styles. Generally speaking, Chinese lion dance is divided into two types: southern lion and northern lion. The movements of the north lion are flexible, mainly including flapping, falling, turning, rolling, jumping and scratching. Southern lion is fierce, colorful and its material is with niceness and smartness. Its eyes and mouth can move and pay attention to the firm stance when it is dancing.There are various types in different places, such as Shanxi tower lion dance, Guangdong lion dance and Shanghai hand lion dance. There are also different types of lion dance in Henan, such as the lion dance in northern Henan, the lion dance in western Henan, the lion dance in Shenqiu Hui culture, the double lion dance (Luohe), the lion dance in Wu huaiying, and the lion and tiger dance in Zhuanjing, which are also very different from each other. Heluo lion drum is a unique form of lion dance in China.

（1）the birth and development of Heluo lion drum

The exact time of Heluo lion drum was not clearly recorded.According to folklore, arfter the victory when Li Shimin won Dou Jiande, Tang army soldiers celebrated the success of victory and made a song *King of Qin*

Broken Music; later the music in the local spread and with the lion dance gradually formed the lion drum. An artist from Xiaoxiang Village in Gongyi City where the National Intangible Cultural Heritage Project Xiaoxiang Lion Dance is located said that the lion drum "was started in the early Qing Dynasty when the village was plagued by 'cholera' and suffered numerous casualties.At that time, people were still superstitious and believed that 'cholera' was caused by the worship of evil spirits. At the same time, the lion, also known as 'god beast', 'warding off evil spirits' and 'sky fortune', was the auspicious animal guarding the world. Therefore, people spontaneously organized lion dance activities to drive away diseases and pursue evil.The lion dance was kept ever since." [9]

The saying that the lion drum started in the early Qing Dynasty needs a further research.As mentioned above, Chinese lion dance has a long history. Heluo area was the political and cultural center of China, and the lion dance appeared quite early in Heluo area. *Luoyang Qielan Ji*, written by Yang Xuanzhi of the Northern Wei Dynasty. has a description of "guarding off evil lions and guiding them before".

In our survey of Xingyang Jiangtou Village, a local artist said that the lion drum was created in Ming Dynasty.Was it born in Qing Dynasty, Ming Dynasty or earlier?All this remains to be further verified.But one thing can be sure of is that the lion drum has a long history.

The Ming and Qing dynasties were a period of rapid development of Heluo lion drum. During this period, the lion drum has spread all over the country and become an important part of the celebration of Spring Festival. Many old artists mentioned that there were many lion drum clubs in Heluo area in the past. Usually in the Spring Festival fete, the clubs with other folk arts together "out of the club" (performance). Its form is often very ceremonious and the performance is also extremely fastidious.

Lion drum's performance squad usually can be: put a spear in a rough way, the manager of a theatrical troupe (lions club leader) in front carries the flag first, the flag written with Shehuo name follow by. What after are vertical banners, small items club, dragon, phoenix, tiger, finches flag, general flag, yellow umbrella, eight-directions drums, small cymbals, big cymbals, Ge Da gong, lion dances "Hui Hui" (people fighting with lions), several lions and cheerer, etc. [10] It is said that the past Gongyi, Xingyang, Yanshi area got more than 400 big drum clubs, so it is obviously that lion drum is quite prosperous at that time.

The society has been stable, and the people are the masters of the country; various undertakings are thriving and the lion drum has made further progress since the founding of New China. The lion club and the cast grew in number. After the beginning of the "Cultural Revolution", most of the lion drum clubs stopped their activities in a voice against superstition. After the 1970s and 1980s, the lion drum activities have gradually resumed. With the society's attention to the protection of intangible cultural heritage in recent years, the development of lion drum has taken a new turn and many drum clubs have become active. For example, the lion drum team from Xiaoxiang Village of Gongyi City, Wangcun Town Wangcun and Jiangtou Village from Xingyang City are quite active. But something new has emerged in recent years.

Some of the restored drum corps tend to be silent after a period of activity due to the influence of economy. For example, lion drum from Gao Cun of Xingyang City was very distinctive and has its influential in the local. The drum troupe resumed its activities and was once quite active after the "Cultural Revolution". However, owing to the actors out of work in recent years, the organizing work has become more and more difficult and has now basically stopped activities. The lion drum team in Xiaoxiang Village of Gongyi City has a good inheritance. Xiaoxiang lion drum (Xiaoxiang lion dance) was included in the first batch of Intangible Cultural Heritage List of Henan Province in 2007 and the National Intangible Cultural Heritage List in 2008. Xiaoxiang lion dance is superb in skill, breathtaking in action and highly ornamental. It has won the title of "the First Lion in Central China" and "the First Lion in China".

Under the leadership of Li Jintu, the former director of the village committee, Xiaoxiang Village has established "Gongyi Golden King Lion Drum Culture Communication Company".They undertake commercial performances and hold lion drum training classes. At present, they are actively exploring new ways for the development of lion drum under the conditions of market economy. [11] Xingyang City also used to be a relatively developed area of lion drum.

"Xingyang used to be a water town that some literature and art stuffs, like land boating, pushing carts, running donkeys, stilts, lion drums and Xiaosan are very popular. Lion drum's drum manual is similar to that of 'King of Qin' in Shaanxi Province. It was supposed to beat the tiger, but for some reason of Li Shimin,they had to change it to beat the lion," said Chen Wei, a cultural scholar in Xingyang. [12] Wangcun lion drum from Xingyang City in the local is very famous.The lion drum in the village is superb in skill and performance and won a lot of highest prize.

The lion drum in the village has been invited to perform in Zhengzhou for six times since 1992. It has won many honorary titles such as "Excellent Program Award of the First Henan Arts Festival", "Special Contribution Award of Zhengzhou International Shaolin Martial Arts Festival", "First Prize of Pandrum Lion Dance Competition of Weizhen Zhongzhou", "First Prize of Heluo Lion Dance Competition" and "First Prize of Zhengzhou Lion Dance Competition in 2002". Lion drum from Jiangtou Village of Wangcun Town in Xingyang City is the current relatively active performance team.

The leader Changmaohai said that the village lion drum came into being during the early Ming Dynasty.

Many excellent entertainers appeared at the end of the Qing Dynasty and the lion drum performance in this village reached a high level,such as Zhao xichun (Gaotai), Jin chou (Shuadadao), Chang po (Shanglaogan), Li hexi (Ditan,Chunqiudao), etc.

The village lion drum team performed four rows of drums, big fried whip, double cross (phoenix wings), Shanglaogan, Baqiao top, trampling rope are very well.[13] The lion drum team of Jiangtou Village has participated in the Shaolin Martial Arts Festival of China, the First Henan Arts Festival, Luoyang Peony Festival, the Opening Ceremony of the Yellow River Grand View, the Opening Ceremony of the Central and Western China Conference and other activities for many times and won many awards .

In November 2016, lion drum from Jiangtou Village was invited to perform on the campus of Henan Normal University which was well received by teachers and students.

（2）the artistic composition of Heluo lion drum

In Heluo area, lion drum is usually an important part of Spring Festival celebrations. The club member of lion drum club is 50 or 60 people to 100 people.In the past, performers often wore ancient military uniforms and performed under the command of flag with the Chinese character shuai, flag with the Chinese character du and command flag.

Lion drum show combines martial arts, acrobatics, dance and other skills, especially the integration of the local famous boxing Chang-style martial arts movements with flexibility, offensive and defensive and its own characteristics.Lion drum will often have a variety of performances, such as dragon and phoenix drum dance, lion trouble, mountain of sword and sea of fire, immortals descend to the earth,Chang'e to the moon, flam to the moon and so on.Lion drum art usually consists of three parts which are drum music, martial arts and lion dance. Among them, drum music plays a commanding role in the performance. Martial arts and lion dance are the core of performance. The roar of changeable drum music, fierce lively fighting, breathtaking wonderful lion dance in Lion drum performance often make the audience clap.

Drum music. Drum music is the basis of lion drum performance which plays the role of command and rhythm control.The instruments commonly used in drum music are 8 drums, 12 small cymbals, 8 big cymbals,10 DaJing and 2 Ge Da gong. After the reform and opening up with economic conditions improved, the number of drums in some places increased to 20 and even more resulting in the number of other instruments also increasing. The core of drum music is the big drum whose roaring sound and changeable rhythm guide the lion to keep dancing.All the other instruments are played coordinating with the drum.Drum music is performed according to the drum manual which is quite rich in content and varies greatly in different places.

Take lion drum from Gao Village of Gaocun Village in Xingyang City as an example, the drumming methods are including old Changtao (drum base point), fanchui, xinglujiao (Tsing Lung displaying claws, monkey on the pole), jiaochui (single forked flower, double forked flower, golden cicada off bone, five tigers going down Xichuan, Tsing Lung on the bridge), etc.The lion drum has more music tune.

As the author of *Heluo Drum Spectrum*, Li Wuchen said that (the lion drum) by playing the music tune, there are nearly a thousand songs spread down. A drum club has at least 14 or 15 by drum song, so that the Heluo area is estimated to have nearly ten thousand.In the survey, we found that except for some special cases, none of the drum songs played by the drum clubs were exactly the same.

Even if the name is same in different regions, the music, rhythm and structure are different.[14] Thus, the content of lion drum is quite rich. The lion drum in different areas integrates the creation of local people in the development and forms its own characteristics, which is a typical characteristic of the development of folk art. Drum song is a precious cultural heritage and should be highly valued in the protection of lion drum.

Except the drums and cymbals, there are a lot of people with the performance of the gun, blowing the nut, blowing the horn, and there are people around waving equipment shouting or whistling to cheer for it when lion drum's performance is on going. This can be seen as a lion drum part of the performance. It can be said that the lion drum performance is a vocal art feast.

The martial arts. The lion drum incorporates the martial arts style of Chang-style boxing which allows the men and lions to compete (known locally as "fighting lions").

The three types of lion fighting are flat fighting, high platform fighting and high-altitude fighting. Flat fighting is usually performed with equipment, such as broadsword, single broadword, double broadsword, spear, big sickle, three-tined fork shaozi cudgel, hydrangea and so on. The lion fighters use all kinds of equipment against the lions. They do so skilfully and are in intense action; the lion is moving and jumping extremely bravely and fiercely. The higt platform fighting is mainly performed on the table.The lion will make a variety of difficult movements on the table, the lion-fighting man jumps up and down on the table which is also quite intense.High-altitude fighting is mainly to lead the lion on the "mountain".The so-called "mountain" is a long bench stacked with the height of over ten meters.

After the flat fighting and high platform fighting finished, the fighter will lead the lion on the "mountain" again. The lion-fighting man is dexterous; the lion jumps up and down to chase; on the "high mountain" there is a fighting between people and lions, which shows the performer's extremely superb skills of martial arts and art.

Lion dance. Lion dance is the core of the whole lion drum performance. It is said that the lion dance was originally a "silent lion" show; after martial arts masters of Xingyang area Chang Dapao, Chang Xiaodan and others, elaborate design, processing, incorporating martial arts movements in the lion dance, finally a "martial lion" was formid. Now Heluo area the "martial lion" is popular.

Its performance focuses on the display of difficult skills; the movements are more rough, fierce. The movements often showing are jumping, diving, climbing, tumbling, vertical, shaking hair, drilling fire ring, walking wire, weaving, weaving table, pedal ball and on the "high table", climb "old pole" and so on. Lion dance performance is also divided into three parts which are the ground (flat performance), middle booth (table performance), and high booth (high-altitude performance). The flat performance mainly shows the fighting between people and lions, and the fighting between the lion and the people holding a variety of equipments. The performance not only shows the lion's mighty strength, but also shows the superb martial arts of the lion drum team. The table performance is mainly performed by the lions on the table. The lions show their superb skills by prancing and stacking up. The high booth performance is mainly done on the "mountain" which is fomed by the stacking of the long benches stack. The lions are enticed by the lion-fighter to climb up the ladder, and on the top often make standing, holding stools in the mouth and other difficult movements. The banner of "Happy New Year to the People" would come out of the lion's mouth to cause the audience to applaud warmly. After the high-altitude performance, the lions "descend the mountain" step by step and throw down the bench with their mouths until the end of the performance. Sometimes the lions even perform on the old pole. The old pole is the most dangerous event in the lion drum show. The old pole is usually a long pole more than ten meters high, fixed all around by the thick rope; in the performance the lion goes up along the rope, and finally reaches the top of the pole to make a variety of breathtaking action. The old pole performance is a symbolic activity to show the performance level of the lion drum team. Only a high level lion dance team dares to perform this performance.

This is the Lion drum that integrates music, martial arts and lion dance as one, closely combined with life and rich in content, with complex routines and superb skills; it shows the outstanding style of Heluo folk art.Lion drum performances often attract large audience and always cause applause.

3. Artistic Anthropology Thinking about Heluo Lion drum

Lion drum is an outstanding artistic work of Heluo culture. It has been closely linked with people's life and has become an important support for people's spiritual life after long-term development. Today, the living environment of lion drum has been significantly improved with the deepening of the protection of intangible cultural heritage. But its existential crisis is far from over. So, how should we recognize the value of the lion drum and how should we do about the protection work in the future?

（i）The value of the lion drum

The understanding of the value of folk art involves politics, social concept, art theory and other aspects.China's understanding of the value of folk art has undergone a tortuous process since modern times.The movement of negating tradition represented by the "Cultural Revolution" once made us lose our orientation and alienate folk literature and art which led to the decline and extinction of a large number of folk arts. In recent years, with the improvement of politics and academic research, we have gained a new understanding of folk culture especially after the rise of the intangible cultural heritage protection movement initiated by UNESCO in the new century. Today, lion drum has got rid of the stigma of "superstition" and "dregs" and becomes an intangible cultural heritage. This is indeed a great blessing for the development of lion drum.The value of lion drum can be understood from the following aspects.

Firstly, the lion drum is an important part of human cultural diversity. Human culture is constantly enriched and developed in the life of diverse ethnic groups and regions.Cultural anthropologists believe that any culture has its unique value, that the culture of any nation should be respected and that there is no distinction of being high or low, advanced or backward in national culture.As anthropologist Boas stressed that there isn't any universal law of development of human culture; every culture has its existence value, and every nation has its respectable values.In the course of human evolution it has made indelible contributions. Different cultural background has different value and function.[15] The diverse development of culture has been achieved through the joint efforts of people of different ethnic groups and regions. Different modes of production and lifestyles produce different cultures.

Each culture is created in a specific natural and social environment and has its own unique value. The lion drum is also a unique creation of the people of Heluo and is an important contribution to the cultural diversity of mankind. Since the modern times, the phenomenon that Chinese society emphasizes the western culture and neglects the national culture has exerted a negative influence on the development of folk culture. Many people cannot face up to their national culture.Especially for the younger generation, they follow the western culture and worship the USA, Korea and Japan, but they are not interested in their own culture.This situation is not conducive to the development of folk culture.Fortunately, the boom of intangible cultural heritage protection in recent years has gradually changed people's understanding of folk culture.The environment for the development of folk culture is improving day by day.However, the improvement of ideological awareness can not be completed in a day.We should also strengthen publicity, apply relevant theories such as artistic anthropology to practice, and improve the scientific nature of protection, so as to truly ensure the effective protection of intangible cultural heritage.

Secondly, the lion drum is an important tool for Heluo people to enrich their spiritual life.Artistic anthropology tells us that art is an indispensable and important part of human life.Extensive human practice shows that the spiritual enrichment of the general public is inseparable from the folk art rooted in life.Even in the poor old society, people can still realize "poetic dwelling" through their favorite folk art.Lion drum is an important tool for people to realize poetic inhabitation in Heluo area.In the long and even difficult life, just through the lion drum and other folk art people please spirit, concentrate strength, and enrich life. The reason why lion drum can continue to this day is that it has this spiritual aesthetic value.

Thirdly, lion drum is an important resource for cultural development and cultural industry creation.The development of human culture is a never-ending process. The development and creation of the culture of the next generation cannot be separated from the accumulation of the culture of the previous generation. The so-called creation without the cultural foundation of the previous generation is often a castle in the air, which is not feasible. The most cherished thing in the development of Chinese culture is the large amount of artistic achievements and experience we have accumulated in the long history of development. As a historical achievement of cultural development, lion drum is also an important resource of contemporary cultural creation. More notably, with the rapid development of contemporary cultural industry, lion drum will also be an important resource for the development of cultural industry.

（ii）thoughts on the protection of Heluo lion drum

We know that the lion drum is a great achievement created by Heluo people in long-term production and living practice and is an excellent representative of Heluo culture. However, with the change of times the lion drum is facing a heavy crisis after its ups and downs.Under the impact of marketing economy, cultural diversity and other factors, the survival of lion drum is becoming more and more difficult. The performance market is shrinking, the performance team is fewer and fewer and the performers are in short supply.If no effective protection measures are taken, the lion drum may be lost in the future.In view of this, we should do the following work at present.

Firstly, pay attention to the law of art and strengthen ecological protection. From the perspective of cultural ecology, lion drum is a beautiful flower bred by the unique ecological environment in Heluo region. Historically, the lion drum's good development is due to its good ecological environment.During the "Cultural Revolution", its decline was also caused by the deterioration of the ecological environment.It can be seen that the ecological environment to a large extent determines the rise and fall of the lion drum.Therefore, in order to protect the lion drum, we must optimize the ecological environment of the lion drum.To be specific, it is necessary to restore and protect the natural and social environment in Heluo area.Such as trying to preserve the diversity of nature, reduce environmental pollution, and beautify nature. Restore some beneficial customs and beliefs, promote harmony in relationships and promote the integration of the lion drum and life.If there are more opportunities to play the lion drum in more life ceremonies, festivals and important celebrations in the future, perhaps the survival situation of the lion drum will be better.

Secondly, strengthen the inheritance of skills and improve the performance level. Lion drum is the product of history and the crystallization of the wisdom which working people have been collecting for thousands of years.Lion drum performance has developed rich artistic skills in its long history.These artistic skills are not something one can learn in a short time, nor can they be learned by inspiration alone.Lion drum performers should learn from old artists with an open mind and inherit their unique skills and improve their performance.Relevant departments should guide and support lion drum inheritance consciously. The inheritance of the lion drum can be promoted by setting up lion drum training classes and organizing lion drum inheritors to teach in villages and towns.The performing teams should also take active actions to learn from experienced artists and invite them to teach their teams.Relevant universities and research departments should also strengthen the sense of social service, actively combine with the lion drum team, study the artistic rules of the lion drum, record the materials of the lion drum, train the successors of the lion drum and comprehensively help the development of the lion drum team by applying for art funds and research projects at all levels. It should be noted that in the new era, the audience's aesthetic level is getting higher and more discerning.The lion drum team should serve the society with more and higher-quality works.Especially under the condition of new media, art has broken the boundaries of regions and the old mode of communication. Art from different regions or even different countries must compete in the same arena. In the future, lion drum is likely to face competition with big-budget and high-quality art works, which are crafted and invested by some of the world's largest companies, which is obviously extremely difficult. This requires that the lion drum must keep pace with the era, constantly improve the performance level to attract the audience of the new era with a more exciting performance.

Thirdly, to adapt to the needs of the era and explore new ways of development.The traditional lion drum is mainly attached to the activities of worship and sacrifice which is the main part of the Spring Festival celebration activities.Its development depends mainly on the power of faith and ritual.After the founding of the People's Republic of China, the anti-superstition movement was carried out and the "Cultural Revolution" came. The belief activities suffered a serious impact. The power of ritual weakened rapidly, and the environment and power that lion drum depended on disappeared.Although the environment for lion drum's development has improved to some extent, its traditional development mechanism and driving force have been difficult to recover.Under such circumstances, we must seek new sources of driving force and establish new development mechanisms. The development of lion drum should also fully consider the rules of the market and economic means in the current market economy and try its best to use the modern company management mode for managing. Such as implementing of corporate operations and joint-stock system and establishing a scientific personnel management system, financial system, enterprise management system as soon as possible.In terms of operation, we should actively create high-quality cultural products, occupy the market with high-quality art products and actively develop new media products, such as film and television, Internet and mobile media products. At the same time, we should strengthen publicity, expand the influence of the lion drum, set up the brand image of lion drum and guide the audience consumption.

We believe that lion drum will have a better future through continuous efforts and development. Of course, this is a difficult process and may not be so smooth.This requires the joint efforts and cooperation of all sectors of society, as well as a good balance between protection, innovation and development.

References:

[1] Cheng Jincheng. Theory and practice of literary anthropology [M]. Beijing: Minorities Press, 2007:243.

[2] Julian H. Stewart. Translated by Pan Yan, Chen Hongbo. Cultural Ecology [J]. Southern Heritage, 2007(2).

[3] Cheng Youwei. Introduction to Heluo Culture [M]. Zhengzhou: Henan People's Publishing House, 2007: 14-15.

[4] Wang Wei. Luoyang and the Grand Canal of Sui and Tang Dynasties [M]. Zhongyuan Cultural Relics, 2014(5).

[5] Relevant information comes from the author's investigation of Zhang ruimin et al in Shenbei Village, Gongyi city, on July 16, 2015.

[6] Local historiography compilation committee of Henan Province. Records of Henan Province · Cultural Records [M]. Zhengzhou: Henan people's Publishing House, 1994:391.

[7] Han Weipeng. A Study on Guanlin Temple Fair in Luoyang during the Ming and Qing Dynasties [D]. master's thesis, Guangxi Normal University, 2012.

[8] Gao Yi, Yao Guishu. Chinese Lion Dance [M]. Tianjin: Nankai University Press, 2007:1.

[9] Baixiaoyu. A Brief Analysis of the Beauty of the Lion Dance, Chinese Knowledge, 2012(3).

[10] Li Wuchen. Heluo Drum Spectrum [M]. Zhengzhou: Elephant Publishing House, 2013:2.

[11] Relevant information comes from the author's interview with Li jintu, national inheritor of Xiaoxiang lion dance, Xiaoxiang Village, Luzhuang Town, Gongyi City, on July 20, 2016.

[12] An interview with cultural scholar Chen Wei by the author in Xingyang City on October 2, 2016.

[13] An Interview with Chang maohai by the author in Jiangtou Village, Xingyang City on October 2, 2016.

[14] Li Wuchen. Heluo Drum Spectrum [M]. Zhengzhou: Elephant Publishing House, 2013:3.

[15] Zhang Jinjie, Lin Yan. A Study of Franz Boas's Holistic Thought [J]. Journal of Wuhan University of Technology (social science edition), 2012(5).

在困难中坚守

——河南新乡王官营怀梆剧团调查

摘要：河南新乡王官营地理位置闭塞，文化环境相对独立闭锁。怀梆作为流行于河南焦作一带的地方戏曲，传入王官营由来已久且保存和发展状况良好，是一个值得研究的文化现象。怀梆作为中华文化多样性的重要构成部分，具有较高的现实价值、文化价值和审美价值，是当地民众的重要精神食粮。王官营怀梆剧团至今仍保留大量艺人的口述唱本，尤其值得研究。王官营怀梆在清代和民国时期最为兴盛，"文革"后短暂恢复又迅速衰败，生存发展现状堪忧。王官营怀梆的保护和抢救已迫在眉睫。应尽快优化其文化生态环境、加强传承人的培养、运用现代科学技术手段和传播方式等对其进行有效的保护。

关键词：怀梆；王官营；河南新乡；价值

怀梆，是以旧时怀庆府（今河南焦作一带）为主要流行地域，由怀庆府语系发展演变而来的地方戏曲。王官营地处新乡西南，旧时属卫辉府获嘉县管辖。在过去陆路交通尚不发达、水系建设亦不完备之时，其地理位置实属闭塞。加之"十年九旱"、年降水量十分稀少的自然地理条件制约，王官营全境基本都是沙质壤土，旧时村人称这样的地块为"气死龙王地"（不怕水淹光怕旱）。[1]46-47 村人只能靠外出经商、做学徒挣些银两养家糊口。依靠着与怀庆府比邻而居的地缘关系，王官营村人多在怀庆府经商、做学徒，这也就为怀梆这一地域特色戏曲传播到王官营埋下了伏笔。考察怀梆在这样一个自然地理位置极为恶劣的村落的生存发展现状,有助于我们更深刻地认识、了解怀梆的原始模样、艺术魅力,也有助于我们探究怀梆艺术的传播规律和有效保护方法。

长期以来的闭塞和落后使得在王官营传播的怀梆保留了最质朴的模样。新中国成立后,随着社会主义建设事业的蓬勃发展,旧时闭塞的环境得到改善,这颗遗失在王官营的戏曲明珠才得以再现在我们的视野之中,为我们研究怀梆戏曲的艺术本体及其流变提供了绝佳的机遇和个案分析,可谓是千载难逢。王官营怀梆艺人大多年事已高且村中青壮年多外出务工而少有传承,对王官营怀梆戏曲的调查研究也就迫在眉睫。正是带着寻访最"质朴"的怀梆艺术,理清怀梆戏曲发展、流变的脉络等目的,笔者一行人对王官营怀梆戏曲艺术的生存发展现状展开了一些调查研究。

一、王官营怀梆剧团的产生及其发展

怀梆传入王官营历史悠久。依据马紫晨先生主编的中原戏曲文化丛书《怀梆·怀调》一书中"过筛子"式的梳拢、探讨,所得出的比较确切的推论就是,怀梆形成大致不早于清乾隆末年(即公元 1780 年),至今已有二百余年历史。在对王官营怀梆戏曲艺人的口述史采集过程中,我们理清、梳理得出,王官营怀梆大致是在清光绪十六年(即公元 1890 年)前后传入王官营的,迄今为止已有近 130 年的历史。怀梆艺人师义天,自幼在怀庆府一带随班学唱怀梆,后学有所成而带班演出,人称"师老板"。王官营乡绅倪景岳生于同治元年(即公元 1862 年),喜爱戏曲,师义天每逢回乡探亲途径王官营都要指导倪景岳练习怀梆戏。经年累月得此机缘,师义天倾囊相授给倪景岳,也使之成了王官营怀梆的第一代传人。第二代传人倪鸿年(倪景岳之子),打小受到了家庭戏曲氛围的熏陶而学唱怀梆,后又得到"师老板"口传身授。及至王官营怀梆的第三代传人倪修全、倪修才(均为倪氏子嗣)等学习怀梆之时,师义天因卧病在床只能是对其口传指点。王官营三代怀梆戏曲艺人的刻苦努力与师义天先生的悉心栽培,使得王官营怀梆传人个个都练就了"手、眼、身、法、步"俱佳的真本领,也对"生、旦、净、丑"各色行当的把握和演绎臻于精妙。其中,倪清领先生演绎的白脸、花脸,倪修全先生饰演的老旦、花旦和青衣在怀梆戏演出中可谓是声震

"十里八乡"。怀梆戏曲艺术就此在卫辉府王官营扎下了艺术的根苗。

王官营怀梆剧团始终保持农闲时清唱的形式,深受地方村人的喜爱。据现年62岁的樊旺真先生讲,"(唱怀梆)全庄人民都拥护"。在实地调研过程中,发现王官营现今的村民几乎"人人听怀梆,人人唱怀梆",足可佐证怀梆戏曲艺术在王官营颇受喜爱,"是情感的传达","是情感的对象化形式"。[2]7"文化大革命"的十年浩劫对王官营怀梆的发展可以说是毁灭性的,怀梆艺人纷纷被要求改唱京剧《红灯记》《智取威虎山》《奇袭白虎团》等样板戏,而怀梆的《反西京》《困南唐》《五凤岭》等传统经典剧目则被当作"毒草"毁坏和打压,剧团服装、道具等多数被烧毁。但是,怀梆戏曲艺术就是风雨中的浮萍,任凭风吹雨打,但其艺术生命力仍然凭借着王官营村民的广泛喜爱而再度辉煌起来。"文化大革命"结束后,全国各地方剧种纷纷开始恢复演出,王官营怀梆也在其中。在辉县的戏曲大汇演中,王官营怀梆剧团演出几乎是年年获奖。现年66岁的王修龙老艺人当年的扮唱"四县八区没人比",足可见怀梆戏曲艺术虽长久偏安于新乡西南一隅,却在王官营的田间地头焕发出了诗意的盎然光辉。

二、王官营怀梆剧团发展现状

缺人才、缺钱财、缺政府扶持,王官营怀梆剧团发展现状实在堪忧。王官营全村目前有600余户居民,不足3 000人口,爱好怀梆戏曲艺术的村民普遍年龄都在50岁以上, 50岁以下的村民尽管多数喜爱怀梆戏,却也是迫于生计,多外出务工,很难组织其学习、传承和演唱怀梆戏曲。就是这样50岁到80岁的村民群体,出于对诗意生活的向往,凭对怀梆戏曲的一腔热爱坚守着,实在令人钦佩至极。作为一个完全由村民自发经营、组织、演出的民间剧团,王官营怀梆剧团至今仍保存着比较完整的戏箱和"四蟒四靠"等戏曲服装和道具,其中绝大多数是村民因为热爱而自筹资金购置的戏曲服装和道具。在经济建设高速发展的当今社会,这样一个全凭发自内心对怀梆戏曲艺术的热爱而支撑下来的团体,依靠着自筹经费的发展路子究竟能走多远,尚是未知之数。当下的王官营,怀梆仍然是村民农闲娱乐、迎神赛会的重要表演节目。村人迎亲添丁、升学乔迁、亲人亡故等,依旧会邀请王官营本村的怀梆剧团搭台唱戏。在谈及演出收费问题时候,

82岁的怀梆艺人史建新老先生（王官营怀梆第四代传人）说："不图挣钱，管个吃喝就行。有时候一人分上10块钱、一盒烟的，也能演。正月十三、十四、十五，给村子里的人免费演。"王官营怀梆至今仍保留着质朴的演出风格，外出商演收费一场大概千元左右，远低于当下市场同等级别剧团的商演收费标准，这主要是由于剧团的成员不计个人得失而单凭着喜爱坚持着。近些年来，王官营怀梆剧团营利性质演出每年平均在村内是十多场，赴外演出更少，笼统计算，一年下来总共20多场的样子。外出演戏场次不多的原因并非剧团演出水平不高，而是在于王官营地处偏僻，知名度不高，缺乏商业化运作等，这才是造成王官营怀梆剧团面临生存窘境的最根本原因。但也正是基于如此的"先天不足"，才使得王官营怀梆这块被遗失的璞玉保持着最原汁原味的怀梆风骨。

"传承事业难以为继，保留剧目自然风光不再。"[3]32 王官营怀梆的生存发展问题已然是摆在我们面前的一项亟待解决的难题，其保留剧目的传承也必然是被包括其中的。保留剧目经过了历史文化的积淀和洗礼，仍然充满着勃勃生机。它是除了戏曲演绎者以外的另一项亟待重视和传承的宝贵财富。王官营怀梆的精湛演绎莫不是得益于对保留剧目文本的完好保存和使用。王官营怀梆应属东路怀梆，多是征战杀伐的戏曲演出，整体风格较之西路怀梆更多的是高亢、挺拔、奔放的激荡之情。王官营怀梆剧团至今仍保留着怀梆演唱老唱本、口述唱本多本，基本都是征战杀伐类。经过整理，目前保存完好的怀梆老唱本有：1.《二龙山》；2.《两狼山》（提寇选段）；3.《麒麟山》；4.《黄三耀闯山》；5.《反长安》；6.《反徐州》；7.《反西京》；8.《反洪山》；9.《铡西宫》；10.《铡太师》；11.《赶秦三》；12.《五凤岭》；13.《丁郎认父》；14.《黄巢别家》；15.《火烧岳王庙》；16.《骂殿》；17.《雷振海征北》；18.《白玉杯》；19.《包公辞朝》；20.《刘墉平五虎》；21.《穆杨会》；22.《收杜府》；23.《收马岱》；24.《困南唐》；25.《薛仁贵征东》；26.《哑女告状》；27.《辕门斩子》等。其中，征战杀伐类居多，且多是薛家戏、杨家戏等。与河南境内多数怀梆剧团的"大多数情况下是以演出豫剧为主，整本的怀梆已几乎无法演出"[4]124 的现状相比较，王官营怀梆剧团能够整出戏演唱的还有十六七部，实属鲜有。这在以往调研走访的现有怀梆演出的地市一级剧团中也十分罕见，可以说是凤毛麟角，这为我们更好地研究怀梆戏曲艺术提供了绝佳的机会。

王官营怀梆剧团角色行当完整,琴师乐师功底深厚,足可与专业怀梆剧团相媲美。在近些年来豫剧发展势头正盛的情况下,多数的河南地方小剧种基本上不见当年风采,纷纷改学、改唱、改演豫剧。仍在演唱怀梆戏的剧团也多是艰难维持,"除了少数能整场演出外,多数剧团已是行当不足、角色不全。有些只能和别的村庄联合组团才能演出。"[4]124 偏安于一隅的王官营怀梆剧团则是个像模像样的"草台班",绝不像一般村民自娱的"耍笑班",可谓是麻雀虽小、五脏俱全。从服装的"四蟒四靠",到各色戏曲道具一应俱全,这就为整本怀梆戏的演出和各色行当粉墨登场提供了坚实的物质基础。一个好的戏曲班子了看"角儿",其次就是看乐队。戏曲音乐很重要,乐队人才更重要。王官营怀梆剧团的板胡、二胡、三弦、点鼓、电子琴等乐器相当齐备,演奏者受整个村子怀梆氛围的熏陶而自幼有一定的怀梆基础外,例如倪清和老先生当过乡村学校教师和校长,懂得一些乐理常识,具备识谱能力;樊振安、朱好文(土高村人,现年68岁)等乐队成员对怀梆的板式、演奏都有着独到的见解和丰富的演奏经验。这些都为王官营怀梆整体演出的效果增香添色,就演出的整体效果来讲,足可以媲美专业怀梆剧团。与王官营相近的西河、大块等村子的怀梆演出,有时也要来王官营怀梆剧团请人去帮忙奏乐,足可见王官营怀梆剧团这样一个完整的班底是难得而重要的。

三、王官营怀梆的价值及保护设想

王官营怀梆良好的保存现状,在已知的怀梆戏曲艺术相关研究调查成果中实为罕见,对于我们认识和探究怀梆戏曲艺术具有十分重要的研究价值和艺术价值。从非物质文化遗产保护视野审视王官营怀梆,它是中华文化多元化、多样性的重要构成部分。其质朴的音韵唱腔和演出形式,丰富了学界对怀梆戏曲艺术的认识。其保存完整的怀梆唱本,为抢救和复原怀梆戏曲艺术,学界开展老唱本文本分析具有极强的现实价值和学术价值。它是中华民族悠久文化历史的表征,更是当地村民迎神赛会、农闲娱乐的精神食粮和朴素信仰。正如丁永祥教授在《当代美学视野中的非物质文化遗产》一文中所谈到的:"传统的民间艺术仍然有着独特的魅力,它的独特功能和地位是其他艺术不能替代的。"[5]238 在漫长的历史发展演变过程中，怀梆戏曲为王官营村民带来了祥和、欢乐和精神寄托。特别是旧社会的迎神赛会，怀梆一直是王官营的主要演出形式，环绕村庄一圈进行演出，为民间社火表演发挥了积极的、不可替代的作用。在今天的生活中，怀梆仍然有着它独特的价值和作用。它在丰富王官营村民精神生活的同时，还能够为怀梆艺术的现代发展和王官营文化产业化发展提供资源和动力。因此，我们应当珍视、保护王官营怀梆这样一种乡野艺术，加紧对王官营怀梆戏曲的传承、保护和创新发展。

王官营怀梆戏曲的良好基础与发展陷入窘境的现状形成了强烈的反差。改善王官营怀梆的发展窘境以更好地保护怀梆戏曲艺术，成为促其发展的当务之急，提出可行性保护和发展设想是必要的。在调查过程中，通过对大量王官营怀梆艺人进行口述史记录，笔者得知，他们都在为王官营怀梆下一步的发展担忧。王官营大量的怀梆艺人都已经上了岁数，少部分四五十岁的演唱者都被称作"年轻人"。老艺人们还在凭借着对怀梆的满腔热爱而坚守，许多高难度技巧性动作都因后继无人，只能是凑合着演。演唱的水准和内容自然也很难与过去同日而语。传承人员青黄不接，难以为继；日常演出因乡野闭塞，难以走出去；政府政策性支持力度虽大，最后一公里却往往很难施展。针对滞阻王官营怀梆戏曲发展的诸多因素，笔者认为，政府和民间的携手共进乃当务之急。基于此项调研提出以下设想仅供参考：

一是重新建构适宜的文化生态机制。营造良好的文化生态，有助于怀梆艺术的自我良性发展，王官营怀梆商业运营机制的可行性论证尤为重要。"在更高的人文审美上回归传统，让悠悠历史更加精炼地浮现和融合于当代社会。"[3]37 需要政府拿出足够的魄力支持和鼓励民间艺术研究，加强民间文艺的保护，建立文化生态保护区。通过像王官营怀梆剧团一样的民间演艺团体商业化的运作和文化生态保护区的良性循环发展，不断改善文艺的生态环境，使"作品更加关注人性、人心，关注民生，关注底层话语，以人为本，'文学是人学'，戏剧舞台也是人生舞台"，[3]7 给予文艺事业发展以更加广阔的空间和市场，而绝非单纯地、强硬地将民间文艺团体推向市场，任其自生自灭而不管不顾。

二是依托国家政策导向，创新培养传承人机制。2017 年来，国家层面多部委先后联合印发《关于实施中华优秀传统文化传承发展工程的意见》（中共中央办公厅、国务院办公厅印发）、《关于戏曲进农村的实施方案》（中共中央宣传部、文化和旅游部、财政部印发）、《关于新形势下加强戏曲教育工作的意见》（中共中央宣传部、文化和旅游部、教育部、财政部印发）等的意见、方案，足可见得国家在繁荣社会主义文艺事业方面拿出了攻坚破难的勇气、毅力和空前的支持力度。从印发的文件来看，国家注意到了戏曲文化汲取营养的土壤在广大农村，这是以往戏曲发展滞阻的症结所在。实施中华优秀传统文化传承发展工程和加强新形势下的戏曲教育工作有助于营造良好的文艺生态，加强传承与教育工作是医治文艺事业发展落后病灶的精准药方。依托国家政策导向的指挥棒，创新培养传承人机制，建立戏曲教育、戏曲演出进校园进农村两者并举的基本模式，通过校园文化环境的营造和受众文艺熏陶，培养戏曲发展的新生力量，通过戏曲在校园和农村的演出来引导受众逐步重新悦纳戏曲艺术，摆正内心对中华传统文化的位置。

三是运用先进的技术和理论手段对王官营怀梆现有资料进行记录和传播。即充分运用现有科技资源，对王官营怀梆戏曲艺术通过录音、录像等技术手段进行有效的资料记录和保护。同时，借助"互联网＋"的大趋势和互联网平台，利用微信、微博、H5等新网络文化载体对王官营怀梆戏曲进行传播和宣传，扩大王官营怀梆戏曲艺术的影响力。利用市场营销学理论对王官营怀梆戏曲的有效市场进行分析、划定，为王官营怀梆的商业化运营机制进行沙盘模拟和可行性论证。不仅要吸引更多的世人来关注和助力怀梆的发展，更应该自我突破，增强怀梆艺术本体的生命力。

总而言之，王官营怀梆是怀文化圈诗意的表征，更是中华多元文化的瑰宝。它以其质朴的唱腔和表演形式，百年来，在当地村民的诗意生活中发挥着难以估量的积极作用。如今王官营怀梆戏曲生存前景堪忧，急需拯救，相信在政府和社会各界的共同努力之下，王官营怀梆这颗隐匿在乡野的明珠定能够再一次散发出诗意的光辉！

参考文献：

[1] 定曼. 引黄灌溉区中的一农村——王官营 [J]. 新黄河.1952（4）：46-47.

[2] 王胜华. 戏剧人类学 [M]. 昆明：云南大学出版社，2009.

[3] 吴新斌. 新语境下的话语重构——当代戏剧丛论 [M]. 北京：中国文联出版社，2015.

[4] 卢跟上. 怀庆府民间怀梆剧团调查 [J]. 戏曲艺术.2006（2）：124.

[5] 丁永祥. 当代美学视野中的非物质文化遗产 [J]. 中州学刊.2011（3）：238.

Holding Fast in Difficulties
—The Investigation of Huaibang Opera Troupe in Wangguanying, Xinxiang, Henan Province

Abstract: The geographical location of Wangguanying in Xinxiang, Henan Province is blocked, which is in a relatively independent and closed cultural environment. As a local opera popular in Jiaozuo, Henan Province, Huaibang Opera has been introduced to Wangguanying for a long time and is well preserved and developed. It is a cultural phenomenon that deserves studying. As an important component of Chinese cultural diversity, Huaibang Opera has high practical, cultural and aesthetic values, and is an important spiritual food for the local people. Huaibang Opera troupe in Wangguanying still retains a large number of artists' narrative albums, which are especially worth studying. It was in the Qing Dynasty and the Republic of China that Huaibang Opera in Wangguanying flourished most. After the Cultural Revolution, it had a short period of resumption and then declined rapidly. The current situation of its survival and development is worrying. The protection and rescue of Huaibang Opera in Wangguanying is imminent. We should optimize its cultural ecological environment as soon as possible, strengthen the cultivation of inheritors, and apply modern scientific and technological means and communication methods to effectively protect it.

Key words: Huaibang Opera, Wangguanying, Xinxiang City, Henan Province, value

Huaibang Opera is a local opera that originated from the language family of Huaiqing Prefecture, with the former Huaiqing Prefecture (now in Jiaozuo, Henan Province) as its main popular region. Wangguanying is located in the southwest of Xinxiang, formerly under the jurisdiction of Huojia County, Weihui Prefecture. In the past, owing to its undeveloped land transportation and incomplete water system construction, it is hard to get to Wangguanying. In addition, due to the natural and geographical constraints, especially the droughts, the annual precipitation of Wangguanying is very scarce, therefore the whole area of Wangguanying is basically sandy loam. [1]46-47 The villagers can only earn some money to support their families by going out to do business or being apprentices. Neighbouring to the Huaiqing Prefecture, most of the villagers of Wangguanying do business or become apprentices in the Huaiqing Prefecture, which laid the groundwork for the spread of Huaibang Opera, a regional characteristic opera, to Wangguanying. The studying of the present situation of Huaibang Opera's survival and development in such a village with extremely bad natural and geographical location is helpful for us to have a deeper understanding of the original appearance and artistic charm of Huaibang Opera, as well as to explore the dissemination rules and effective protection methods of the art of Huaibang Opera.

The long-term occlusion and backwardness have made Huaibang Opera spread in Wangguanying contain its simplest form. After the founding of the People's Republic of China, with the vigorous development of socialist construction and the improvement of the former isolated environment, this opera pearl lost in Wangguanying has been able to reappear in our vision. It provides us with an excellent opportunity and case analysis to study the artistic ontology of Huaibang Opera and its evolution. This may be the chance of a life-time. Most of the artists of Huaibang Opera in Wangguanying are advanced in years, and the young adults in the village are more willing to go out to work, so there is few people to inherit the Huaibang Opera. Therefore, the study of Huaibang Opera in Wangguanying is extremely urgent. The author and his partners have launched some investigations and studies on the present survival and development situation of Huaibang Opera's art in Wangguanying to search for the simplest art of Huaibang Opera, and sort out the development and evolution of Huaibang Opera.

1.The Formation and Development of Huaibang Opera Troupe in Wangguanying

The introduction of Huaibang Opera into Wangguanying has a long history. According to Central Plains Opera Culture Series *Huaibang · Huaidiao* edited by Mr. Ma Zichen, who has carefully combed and discussed Huaibang Opera, we can get a more accurate conclusion that the formation of Huaibang Opera was not earlier than the late period of the reign of Emperor Qianlong of the Qing Dynasty (i.e.1780 A.D.) and it has a history of more than 200 years. In the process of collecting the oral history of Huaibang Opera artists in Wangguanying, we sort out that Huaibang Opera was introduced to Wangguanying roughly in the 16th year of the reign of Emperor Guangxu of the Qing Dynasty (i.e. 1890 A.D.) and has a history of nearly 130 years so far. Shi Yitian, an artist of Huaibang Opera, learned to sing Huaibang Opera along with the Huaibang Opera troupe in the area of Huaiqing Prefecture when he was a child. Then, after he has acquired achievements from study, he performed the Huaibang Opera with leading an opera troupe, and became known as "Boss Shi". Ni Jingyue, a landed gentry of Wangguanying, was born in the first year of the reign of Emperor Tongzhi of the Qing Dynasty (i.e.1862 A.D.) and loved opera. Every time Shi Yitian returned home to visit his relatives, he always instructed Ni Jingyue to practice Huaibang Opera in Wangguanying. Over the years, Shi Yitian instructed Ni Jingyue without reservation, which made Ni Jingyue become the first generation of Huaibang in Wangguangying. The second generation, Ni Hongnian (the son of Ni Jingyue), learned to sing Huaibang Opera under the influence of the family drama atmosphere, and received oral instruction from the "Boss Shi". When Ni Xiuquan and Ni Xiucai (the descendants of Ni family), the third generation of Huaibang Opera in Wangguanying, studied Huaibang Opera, Shi Yitian was confined to bed by sickness, so he could only give them oral instruction. Thanks to the hard work of the three generations of Huaibang Opera artists in Wangguanying and the careful cultivation of Mr. Shi Yitian, all the descendants of Huaibang Opera in Wangguanying have mastered five techniques of opera performing art: gesture, eye expression, figure, performing techniques and gait, as well as the performance of various roles, such as male role, female role, painted face role and clown role. Among them, Ni Qingling's performance of the white face and the painted face, and Ni Xiuquan's performance of the pantaloon and young female role were famous in the performance of Huaibang Opera. In this regard, the art of Huaibang Opera has rooted in Wangguanying, Weihui Prefecture.

The Huaibang Opera troupe has always maintained the form of singing unaccompanied during the slack season, and it is deeply loved by local villagers. According to Mr. Fan Wangzhen, who is 62 years old now, "all the villagers support singing Huaibang Opera". In the process of field research, it is founded that nearly all the villagers of Wangguanying today listen to and sing Huaibang Opera, which can fully prove that Huaibang Opera art is very popular in Wangguanying. It is not only the transmission of feelings of the Wangguanying's people but also the objectified form of emotion. [2]7 The ten-year catastrophe of "the Cultural Revolution" can be said to be devastating to the development of Huaibang Opera in Wangguanying. Huaibang artists were forced to sing Beijing Opera, such as *The Red Lantern, The Taking of Tiger Mountain, Legendary Voluntary Army* and other model operas, while the traditional classic plays of Huaibang Opera were destroyed and suppressed as "poisonous weeds", such as *Xijing Rebellion, Trapped in Southern Tang Dynasty* and *Wufeng Mountain*, and most of the costumes and props of the troupe were burned down. However, Huaibang Opera art is like the floating duckweed in the storm. Despite the hardships and difficulties, its artistic vitality thrives again thanks to the widespread love of the villagers of Wangguanying. After "the Cultural Revolution", local operas across the country began to resume their performances, including Huaibang Opera in Wangguanying. In the opera joint performance of Hui County, Huaibang Opera troupe in Wangguanying won awards almost every year. And the performance of 66-year-old Wang Xiulong, who is an experienced artist, has no parallel in the surrounding regions, which shows that though the development of Huaibang Opera art has long been hindered by the partial control of the southwest of Xinxiang City, it advances with poetic brilliance in the fields of Wangguanying.

2. The Current Development Situation of Huaibang Opera Troupe in Wangguanying

The shortage of talents, money and government support has impeded the development of Huaibang Opera troupe in Wangguanying, whose current development situation is really worrying. At present, there are more than 600 households in Wangguanying village, with a population of less than 3,000. The villagers who love Huaibang Opera art are generally aged 50 or above. Although most of the villagers under 50 like Huaibang Opera, they have to go out to work for earning a living, which makes it difficult to organize learning, inheriting and singing Huaibang Opera. It is the group of villagers aged 50 to 80 that yearn for the poetic life and stick to it with their love for Huaibang Opera, which is really admirable. As a folk troupe that is operated, organized and performed by villagers, Huaibang Opera troupe in Wangguanying still keeps relatively complete opera trunks, costumes and props, and most of which are purchased by the villagers through self-raised funds because of their love to Huaibang Opera. In today's society, where economic construction is developing at a high speed, it is still unknown that how far such a group, which has deep love for Huaibang Opera art, can go by relying on self-raised funds to develop itself. In the present Wangguanying, Huaibang Opera is still an important performance program for villagers to organize entertainment activities and celebrate religious festivals. The villagers will still invite the Huaibang Opera troupe in Wangguanying to perform when there are joyous occasions (e.g. wedding, enter a higher school, move to a better place) or funeral arrangements. When talking about the issue of performance fees, the 82-year-old Huaibang artist Shi Jianxin (the fourth generation of Huaibang Opera in Wangguanying) said, "our main purpose is not to earn money, but have enough to eat and drink. We can also perform although sometimes each of us is paid only 10 *yuan* or a pack of cigarettes. On the 13th, 14th and 15th day of the Lunar New Year, we will perform to the villagers without payments." Huaibang Opera in Wangguanying still retains its simple performance style, and the charge for a commercial performance is about 1,000 *yuan*, which is far lower than the current charging standard of commercial performance compared with the same level troupes in the market. The main reason is that the members of the troupe hold fast to Huaibang Opera is just for love not considering of the personal gain or loss. In recent years, the average annual profit-making performance of Huaibang Opera troupe in Wangguanying is more than 10 performances in the village, let alone go out to performance. Generally speaking, the total number of performances in a year is roughly over 20. The reason why there are fewer chances to go out to perform is not the lack of performance level of the troupe, but because the remote geographical location, low popularity and the lack of commercial operation of Wangguanying. This is the most fundamental reason why Huaibang Opera troupe in Wangguanying is facing a dilemma of survival, but it is also based on such "congenital deficiencies" that Huaibang Opera in Wangguanying, a lost unrefined jade, maintains its original Huaibang style.

The inheritance cause of the Huaibang Opera in Wangguanying is difficult to further develop, and the repertory operas are not popular as before. [3]32 The survival and development of Huaibang Opera in Wangguanying is already a difficult problem that needs to be solved urgently. The inheritance of the repertory operas must also be included. The repertory operas are still full of vitality after the accumulation and baptism of history and culture. It is another precious treasure that needs to be paid more attention to and to be inherited urgently besides opera and performers. The masterly performance of Huaibang in Wangguanying is benefited from the intact preservation and use of the repertory operas. The Huaibang in Wangguanying belongs to the Donglu Huaibang, whose performance is mainly about war or massacre. Compared with Xilu Huaibang, its overall style is more sonorous, powerful and unrestrained. The Huaibang Opera toupe in Wangguanying still retains many old and oral versions, which basically are about war or massacre. After being organized, the well-preserved old Huaibang versions are as follows: Erlong Mountain, Lianglang Mountain (the selections of Tikou), Qilin Mountain, Huang Sanyao Rushes through the Feihu Mountain, Chang'an Rebellion, Xuzhou Rebellion, Xijing Rebellion, Hongshan Rebellion, The Killing of Imperial Concubine, The Killing of Grand Tutor, The Expelling of Qinsan, Wufeng Mountain, Dinglang Recognizes His Father, Huangchao Leaving Home, Burning Yuewang Temple, Madian, Lei Zhenhai's Expedition to the North, White Jade Cup, Baozheng Resigns from the Official Position, Liuyong Suppresses the Rebellion of Wuhu, The Meeting of Yang Zongbao and Mu Guiying, The Recovering of Du Mansion, The Recovering of Madai, Trapped in the Southern Tang Dynasty, Xue Rengui's Expedition to the East, Dumb Woman's Complaint, Yang Yanzhao Kills His Son in the Barracks Gate etc. The majority of them are about war or massacre, and most of the operas tell the story about Xue family and Yang family. Compared with the current situation of Huaibang Opera troupes in Henan Province, which mainly perform Henan Operas, and are almost impossible to perform complete Huaibang Opera. [4]124 While there are 16 or 17 operas that Huaibang Opera troupe in Wangguanying can completely perform, which is hard to see. This is also very rare among the existing municipal first-class Huaibang Opera troupes that have been visited and investigated in the past. It provides us with an excellent opportunity to study Huaibang Opera art better.

The role of Huaibang Opera troupe in Wangguanying is complete and its musicians have a solid foundation of basic techniques, which is comparable to that of the professional Huaibang Opera troupe. With the rapid development of Henan Opera in recent years, the development of most of the small local Operas in Henan is not as prosperous as before, and they have changed to study, sing and perform Henan Opera one after another. Most of the troupes that are still perform Huaibang Opera are hard to survive; only a few troupes can completely perform the opera, and the roles of the majority of the troupes are already incomplete. Some can only perform in groups with other villages' troupes. [4]124 The Huaibang Opera troupe in Wangguanying, which is situated at a remote area, is like a professional, small, poorly-equipped travelling theatrical troupe, but, not the amateur troupe for villagers to entertain themselves. Just as a Chinese saying goes, "A sparrow may be small but it has all the vital organs; small but complete". All varieties of costumes and opera props are available, which provide a solid material basis for the complete performance of Huaibang Opera and the various roles. A good opera troupe not only depends on the outstanding actors but also on the orchestra. Opera and music are very important, and orchestra and talents are even more important. The Huaibang Opera troupe in Wangguannying is equipped with different kinds of musical instruments, such as, Banhu, Erhu, Sanxian, Diangu, electronic piano and so on. Influenced by the environment of the whole village, the players have laid a certain foundation of Huaibang Opera since childhood. For example, Mr. Ni Qinghe, who used to be a teacher and principal of a rural school, grasps some common music theory and has the ability to read music. Besides, Fan Zhenan, Zhu Haowen (they come from Tugao Village, and are 68 years old now) and other members of the orchestra have unique insights and rich experience in Huaibang Opera's various types of beats and performance. These all make the overall performance of Huaibang Opera in Wangguanying more excellent, which is comparable to the professional Huaibang Opera troupe in terms of overall performance. Sometimes, the Huaibang Opera troupes from Xihe and Dakuai villages, which are close to Wangguanying, need to invite the Huaibang Opera troupe of Wangguanying to help play music. This shows that a complete troupe like Huaibang Opera troupe of Wangguanying is uncommon and important.

3. The Value of Huaibang Opera in Wangguanying and the Ideas for Its Preservation

The Huaibang Opera in Wangguanying has been well-preserved so far, which is rare in the known research results of Huaibang Opera art. Besides, it has very important research value and artistic value for us to understand and study Huaibang Opera art. As an intangible cultural heritage, Huaibang Opera in Wangguanying is an important component of the diversity of Chinese culture. Its simple rhythm, singing style and performance form have enriched the academic circle's understanding of Huaibang Opera art. In addition, the well-preserved Huaibang Opera scripts are of great practical and academic value not only for the rescue and restoration of Huaibang Opera art, but also for the academic circles to carry out the analysis of the old Huaibang Opera scripts. It is not only a symbol of the long cultural history of the Chinese nation, but also the spiritual food and simple belief of the local villagers in celebrating regional festivals and organizing entertainment activities. As Professor Ding Yongxiang said in his article *Intangible Cultural Heritage in Contemporary Aesthetics Perspective*, "Traditional folk art still has its unique charm. Its unique function and position cannot be replaced by other arts." [5]238 In the long process of historical development and evolution, Huaibang Opera has become a spiritual habitat for the villagers of Wangguanying, bringing them peace and happiness. Especially in the old society, Huaibang Opera has always been the main performance form of Wangguanying when celebrating regional festivals, which played an active and irreplaceable role in traditional festivities performances. In today's life, Huaibang Opera still has its unique value and function. It not only enriches the spiritual life of the villagers of Wangguanying, but also provides resources and motivation for the modern development of Huaibang Opera art and the industrialization development of Wangguanying's culture. Therefore, we should cherish and preserve the rural art like Huaibang Opera in Wangguanying, and step up the inheritance, preservation and innovative development of Huaibang Opera in Wangguanying.

The good foundation for the preservation of Huaibang Opera in Wangguanying is in sharp contrast to the present situation where the development is in a dilemma. It is necessary to improve the development dilemma of Huaibang Opera in Wangguanying for better preserving Huaibang Opera art, promoting its development, and putting forward feasible preservation and development ideas. In the process of investigation, based on the oral history records of a large number of Huaibang Opera artists in Wangguanying, the author knows that they are all worried about the future development of Huaibang Opera in Wangg was ying. A large number of Huaibang Opera artists in Wangguanying are already old, and a small number of performers aged 40 and 50 are called "young people". The old artists are still sticking to it with their ardent love for Huaibang Opera, and many difficult and skillful movements can not be performed completely because there are no successors. The standard and content of performance are naturally hard to keep pace with that of the past. It is difficult for Huaibang Opera in Wangguanying to further develop because the shortage of talents.

Hampered by the geographical isolation, the troupes are difficult to get out to perform. Besides, although the government's policy support is strong. In view of the many factors that hinder the development of Huaibang Opera in Wangguanying, the author believes that it is imperative for the government and the people to work together. Based on this research, the following ideas are proposed for reference only:

First, we should reconstruct the appropriate cultural ecological mechanism. Creating a sound cultural ecology is conducive to the self-healthy development of Huaibang Opera art. The feasibility demonstration of Huaibang Opera's business operation mechanism in Wangguanying is particularly important. In order to return to tradition in a higher humanistic aesthetics, and make the history integrate into contemporary society, [3]37 the government should show enough courage to support and encourage the research of folk arts, strengthen the preservation of folk arts and establish cultural ecological protection zones. Through the commercial operation of folk performing groups like Huaibang Opera troupe in Wangguanying and the virtuous circle development of cultural and ecological protection areas, the ecological environment of literature and art can be continuously improved. The works should be people-oriented, paying more attention to human nature, human feelings, people's livelihood, and the will of the grass-roots people. The literature is hominology, and the opera stage is also the stage of life. [3]7 So we should provide a broader space and market for the development of literature undertakings, instead of pushing the folk art groups to the market in a simple and tough way and leaving them to operate on their own.

Second, we should rely on national policy guidance and innovate the mechanism of training inheritors. Since 2017, many ministries and commissions at the national level have jointly issued Opinions on Implementing the Project of Inheritance and Development of Chinese Excellent Traditional Culture (issued by the general office of the CPC Central Committee and the State Council), On the Implementation Scheme of Opera

Entering Rural Areas (issued by the Propaganda Department of the CPC Central Committee, the Ministry of Culture and the Ministry of Finance), and Opinions on Strengthening the Education of Traditional Opera under the New Situation (issued by the Propaganda Department of the CPC Central Committee, the Ministry of Culture, the Ministry of Education and the Ministry of Finance), all of which fully demonstrate the country's courage, perseverance and unprecedented support in flourishing socialist literature undertakings. Judging from the documents issued, the state has noticed that the vast rural areas are where opera culture draws nourishment, which is the crux of the stagnation of opera development in the past. The implementation of the inheritance and development project of Chinese excellent traditional culture and the strengthening of opera education work under the new situation show that creating a good literary ecology and strengthening the inheritance and education work are necessary to resolve the backward development of literature undertakings. Relying on the national policy, we should innovate the mechanism of training inheritors, and establish the basic mode of promoting opera, opera performance and opera education entering into the campus and rural areas simultaneously. Through the construction of campus cultural environment and the nourishment of literature, we can cultivate new forces for the development of opera, and through the opera performances on campus and in rural areas, we can guide the audience to gradually re-accept opera art and straighten out their inner position towards traditional Chinese culture.

Third, we should apply advanced technology and theoretical means to record and propagate the existing materials of Huaibang Opera in Wangguanying. That is, we should make full use of the existing scientific and technological resources to effectively record and protect the materials of Huaibang Opera art in Wangguanying through sound recording, video recording and other technical means. At the same time, with the help of the general trend of "Internet plus" and the Internet platform, we can apply

WeChat, microblog, H5 and other new network cultural carriers to spread and publicize Huaibang Opera in Wangguanying, and expand its influence. We can apply the marketing theory to analyze and delimit the effective market of Huaibang Opera in Wangguanying, thus conducting sand table simulation and feasibility demonstration for the commercial operation mechanism of Huaibang Opera in Wangguanying. We should not only attract more people to pay attention to and promote the development of Huaibang Opera, but also break through ourselves and enhance the vitality of Huaibang Opera art.

In a word, Huaibang Opera in Wangguanying is a poetic representation of Huai Culture circle and a treasure of Chinese multi-culture. With its simple singing style and performance form, it has played an immeasurable positive role in the poetic life of local villagers for a hundred years. At present, the survival prospect of Huaibang Opera in Wangguanying is worrying and needs to be rescued urgently. The author believes that with the joint efforts of the government and all sectors of society, Huaibang Opera in Wangguanying, a pearl hidden in the countryside, will once again brim with poetic brilliance!

References:

[1] Dingman. Wangguanying, a countryside in the irrigation area of the Yellow River Diversion Project [J]. New Yellow River. 1952 (4): 46-47.

[2] Wang Shenghua. Theatre Anthropology [M].Kunming: Yunnan University Press, 2009.

[3] Wu Xinbin. Discourse Reconstruction in the New Context — Contemporary Theatre Series [M].Beijing: Chinese Federation Press, 2015.

[4] Lu Gensheng. The Investigation of Folk Huaibang Opera Troupe in Huaiqing Prefecture [J]. Opera Art. 2006 (2): 124.

[5] Ding Yongxiang. Intangible Cultural Heritage in Contemporary Aesthetic Perspective [J]. Zhongzhou Academic Journal. 2011 (3): 238.

论小说的影视改编

——文本选择和剧情剪辑模式探讨

摘要：影视剧本在对小说进行筛选的同时，需进行非线性剪辑，通过非线性剧情表述让观众一次性接受更多的剧情信息。制片人与导演对筛选小说作品各有见解，很难形成统一的模式。在选择小说进行影视改编的过程中，制片人和导演最关注的是小说作品的影视改编可行度是否高，较高的影视改编可行度能缩短改编周期，降低改编成本，成为改编的大前提。本文从选择合适的小说作品入手，阐述如何建立清晰的故事线与情节结构，并对剧情进行筛选与对比，重点强化曲折的剧情，最后统一对剧情进行剪辑；探寻现代影视的创新模式，介绍并总结剧本筛选与剪辑的方法，为影视工作者提供参考，同时希望能拓展影视剧的开发模式，以提高影视作品的文化水准与市场效益。

关键词：小说剧情；文本转换；故事线；非线性剪辑

　　小说被改编为影视剧本，进而被拍摄为影视作品已成为当代影视创作的主流趋势之一。近些年来，广大制片人与导演均在大力挖掘各种优秀小说，希望能将其进行筛选、改编，搬上屏幕，借此来获取良好的市场效益与社会效益。

　　从20世纪90年代冷战结束后，全球经济、文化发展进入了一个新的历史时期。随着影视作品将小说故事素材引入到影视叙事当中，其对情节的编辑与设置的要求越来越高，同时小说被改编为影视剧本的趋势日益增强。为了契合时代与观众的审美需要,影视作品的质量在不断提高。影视剧本创作在对小说进行筛选的同时,需进行错位性质的情节安排和设置,以让观众获得更为丰富的感受和信息。近 30 年来,影视剧本创作模式虽然在不断变化,但遗憾的是,真正具有独创性的只是少数,多数乃是跟风仿效的平庸之作。正所谓,好的小说常见,但好的影视作品却不常见。故而在小说选择、整体架构、情节改编等方面急需摸索出一套成熟的审读评判模式。

一、选择小说的因素

大多数小说改编的影视作品,其原创文本都是由制片人或导演来筛选。作为影视作品产出的决策者,他们关注的是小说的预期经济效益,及潜在的社会效应。例如,该小说看的人是否多,反应是否强烈,原创作者是否有名气等。如果小说具有较高的社会认知度,那么这个片子上座率不会低于平均水准,将来的票房和广告费将会达到一个令制片人和导演都满意的结果。成熟的影视制片人与导演不会在某一部影视作品成功后停滞,而是会持续地做下去。如果该影视作品不能达到预期的效益,他们会挖掘其他小说,以期再战。

选择一部小说进行改编,除了以上提及的考量因素外,最关键的还在于小说文本自身,不是所有小说都能被完美地打造成影视剧本并搬上屏幕。在剧本的选择问题上,它必须遵循着自己的规则,专业规则、市场规则、团队要求等。小说给读者带来的是思考和遐想,而影视作品给观众带来的则更多的是娱乐和休闲。简单地说,"喜欢读书和喜欢看电影是两类不同的人群"。[1] 因此,在小说的选择与改编问题上,编剧、导演和制片人都有着自己的评判标准。总的来讲,就是他们清楚地知道哪些适合改编成电影,哪些不能改编成电影。

选择一部能够给人以思考和启迪的小说并将其改编为给人感官冲击的影片,筛选条件就是这部小说应当具备改编成为影视作品的基本特质。其依据就是:情节丰富、形象多变、角色量大、主题导向正、感官冲击力强。"要让观众享受到在日常生活、工作中所无法体验的视觉盛宴,达到娱乐和休闲的目的。"[2] 这样一来,引发人深刻思考与启迪的小说就不能作为最佳的影视改编文学备选素材。这是一个理念,并不是所有的小说都适宜改编为影视剧作。小说的种类有很多，中篇小说、长篇小说、小小说、网络小说，依据不同的分类标准划分。面对种类各异的小说，一任简单粗暴地改编、拍摄，会直接导致现在影视市场烂片频出。编剧、导演和制片要做一个分辨、一个判断、一个选择，这既是个人经验的积累所致，也是影视改编行业内模式化操作不成体系的症结。最终，由于泛滥的、缺乏模式化的小说改编成为影视剧作，导致影视业走向平庸化、机械化，无法带给审美受众不同以往的视听体验。

因此，各路制片人、导演、编剧均在寻求一套妥善的处理方法，既能筛选出适宜改编成为影视作品的优秀小说，又能保证影视作品的剧情深度与层次，还能满足观众日新月异的审美需求。所以，需探寻一种甚至多种模式来延续影视作品在观众审美定位中的影响力和认可程度。

二、解析故事线与情节结构

当下在对原著小说的筛选过程中，制片人和导演最关注的是小说的影视化程度是否高。较高的影视化程度能有效地降低改编难度，缩短改编周期，控制改编成本，是选取小说进行影视改编的大前提所在。对小说本身而言，故事线和情节要求结构尤其清晰。至于情节是简单还是复杂都不重要，简单的情节可以改编为爱情片、战争片、动作片，复杂的情节可以改编为推理片、惊悚片、剧情片。

美国作家大卫·米切尔的畅销小说《云图》（2011 年）经由华纳兄弟影片公司改编制作成为同名剧情片，并于 2013 年在中国内地上映。这部由畅销小说改编并由老牌影视制作公司制作的电影却并未有受众所预想和期待的完美。因它的故事结构分为 6 部分，在阅读小说时给读者以前后关联的联想，具有很强的对比与想象空间，让每个故事的情节都复杂有趣。但最终在影像化时，由于牵连的时空跨度太大，编导将精力都集中到塑造不同时空的人物个性上，很多有关联的寓意就无法顺利地通过影像可视化处理。穿越时空的遐想是文学创作留给读者的最开阔的空间。现被编导搬上屏幕，打破了读者的想象思维，认为与自己的理解截然不同，于是众说纷纭产生负面的效果，影响了该电影的社会接受度。

影视作品一般会在开场 10 分钟内，交代清楚影片的基本情况。一部影片是否能够抓住观众的审美趣味，其关键在于其开篇概述的影视内容。如果不能在这 10 分钟的叙事过程中在观众的头脑里建构出一条清晰的故事线，必然会令观众在后续的观影体验中信马由缰地进行剧情揣测。观众猜测正确，会显得编导水平低；观众猜测错误，会损害到观众继续观看的兴趣。因此，影视作品对原著小说进行改编，改编的不应是故事线，相反应当是保留这条故事线，让它更清晰。虽然通过改编情节结构，让情节多样化、曲折化更能够借助影视语言的叙事得以可视化，但始终不能离开整条故事线。

可见，剧情丰富化与多样化是影视作品的主要特征。在原创小说中纵向贯穿的情节，可在影片中横向展现，通过蒙太奇的处理手法强化剧情结构。其中，必然有一条情绪明了的故事线贯穿于整部影片的始终，提升小说对影视作品的文本转化效果。

三、剧情选择与对比

剧情的结构与虚实关系，也是小说和剧本改编的差异所在。小说需要读者通过阅读与遐想来自行脑补，或者说需通过许多个人的想象力来建构具体故事空间，那么这部小说进行影视改编的难度和强度会更大。关于这一点，特别显著的例子便是古龙小说和金庸小说。

在古龙的小说中，两个角色决斗时一般会附有高深的对话。他们互相凝视并沉默后，其中一个说："你输了。"然后掉头离开，另一个也心安理得地认输。当然，古龙会描述一些解释，如手中无剑、心中有剑等。如果读者仅仅是阅读小说，看到这样的文字，是可以自主填补、想象出各种场景。但改编成影视作品，就会过于单调、静态，观众看着屏幕上两个演员互相瞪眼，最后用语言来决出胜负，观众的反应肯定是无法认同，因为观众要看的是过程和武打动作。因此，这种剧情会加大改编难度。

相比较而言，金庸的武侠小说是比较容易进行影视化改编的。金庸的小说故事线和脉络架构相当完整和清晰，对于人物故事情节发生的场面表述颇具画面感，这为小说与影视的文本转化奠定了良好基础。同样是描述男女相爱，却不能终成眷属，古龙在描述李寻欢与林诗音之间的情节时，写李寻欢站在林诗音家外的巷子，对着房子饮酒，没有其他言语。但是金庸笔下的周芷若在大庭广众下一剑刺穿张无忌,改编成影视作品后加入了动作与语言,让观众更易接受。

因此,在小说到影视作品的转换过程中,对情节人物的处理需要做到四个"告诉",即:告诉观众这个角色是谁;告诉观众这是个怎样的角色;告诉观众角色要做什么;告诉观众角色在完成这些事情之后会发生哪些变化。后来被改编成为影视剧《小李飞刀》(1999年)的古龙小说《多情剑客无情剑》中,李寻欢是谁?李寻欢是小李飞刀吗?小说并没交代。因为小说在一开始,李寻欢就已经是名满天下的绝顶高手了。改编为电视剧时,对小说做了相当大的补充和改动,使其得以成为一部较成功的影视剧作。而在金庸的小说《射雕英雄传》(1983年同名电视剧)中,所有角色都有来龙去脉,尤其是对郭靖、杨康的人物背景表述得更是详尽,这样复杂的背景又深刻影响了两个角色的性格;不仅对武戏有深度包装,创作出"九阴真经""降龙十八掌""一阳指"等如雷贯耳的名词,而且对文戏部分的爱情、事业纠葛也有着深刻的现实映照。整部小说不再是小说,而是一部相对成品的影视剧本。

适宜进行影视改编的小说文本应当具象化、细腻化。对小说的情节应当进行筛选,预估影视作品商业娱乐、休闲的一面,以形象的方式,蕴含思想深刻、寓意深刻的部分,做到既保留小说的神韵和精神主旨,又能以生机盎然的方式展现视听过程。

四、强化曲折的剧情

将剧情曲折化是影视片对小说创新改编的主要形式,遇到不适合改编却又很优秀的小说时,编剧们都会发挥自己独特的想象力来丰富剧情,但若不能在同一规格上妥善处理,就会被观众识破。[3]当剧情发展到中间时,很多观众通过习惯模式就能猜到结果,这对影视片是一种最致命的打击,其口碑往往会因此跌落到低谷。所以,如何创新性强化曲折剧情成为关键所在。

热播电视剧《甄嬛传》(2011年)对于原创小说的影视化改编可谓是革命性的颠覆,是强化曲折剧情的成功案例。剧情首先提出疑问:甄嬛是谁?答:甄嬛在入宫前是小官僚的女儿。甄嬛入宫后为什么会被皇帝选中?答:

因为她长得和故去的纯元皇后相像,得到了皇帝青睐。剧情中人物历程开始发生转变,由最初不谙世事,无意争宠,到后来花园邂逅皇帝,陷入爱河,人物心理也悄悄转变。她发现皇帝并非自己的真心人,所谓的"四郎"也不过就是自己内心对爱情的画地为牢,从真情转折到假意。对于当下观众的娱乐审美趋向而言,这样的故事是吸引观众感慨猜测的正确方式。

将小说成功改编并搬上屏幕的影片例证是可供参考和借鉴的。而失败的影视改编更多地源自小说文本的影视转换性不强,基本相当于重构故事结构、编织故事情节。为此,编剧做了大量改编工作,添加了很多原著小说中没有的情节,让故事情节符合影片拍摄要求。但是往往偏离了小说内涵主旨,无法获得社会的认同,也就无法获得成功的社会和经济效应,流行了近20年的抗战神剧就是我们身边最为典型的反面例子。

曲折的情节能让观众品味日常生活中所无法品味到的思考乐趣。不断强化且曲折的剧情更适合悬疑片、推理片、侦探片,这类商业影片若能兼顾文艺影片的高雅,甚至哲理意蕴,便能提升商业影片的思想层次感、审美水准,满足观众猎奇与提升素养的多重心理需求,成为经典之作。在实际编写剧本的过程中,利用非线性编辑的模式创作,将合理的剧情打断,穿插遭遇反复失败、困难等矛盾冲突的剧情,配合多线索同步表述能将剧情不断强化,最终达到理想效果。

五、剧情剪辑的突破模式

选定改编的小说后,需对小说内容进行整体提升。让小说文字的遐想转变为影视的形象可感,这种转变来自编剧和导演的二度创造。剧本的改编过程是对小说中空间想象的建构过程,建构得成功便叫座叫好双丰收。

当然,想象是一种感性行为,成功的概率是未知数。要获得成功,应给影视剧本注入理性思维。对剧情进行剪辑是对小说作品改编的理性思维。剪辑的过程也是进一步塑造想象空间的过程。[4]虽然广大编剧、导演和制片人都寄希望于剪辑给影片注入全新的活力,但可供参考和借鉴的模式甚少,以下列举出三种具有创造性的剪辑模式。

（一）选择正确的剧情表述方式

剧情的视听语言叙述是最关键的改编方式。用什么样的方式和时空结构去讲好一个故事,对于影视片十分重要。影片的剧情表述最忌讳拖沓冗长和平铺直叙。开场 10 分钟内必须吸引观众眼球。好莱坞的大片之所以受欢迎,其叙事的灵活多变、情节的峰回路转、情感的一波三折是重要的参考。从剧情剪辑的角度上来看,相对于线性剧情表述的单调,大多数片子需善于利用非线性剪辑思维调度和统筹视听语言,制造情节的颠覆性,把控时空结构的心理自由度,从而完成影视片的剧情表述。[5]

电影《肖申克的救赎》(1994 年)改编自美国作家斯蒂芬·金的中篇小说。讲述银行家安迪被当作杀害妻子的凶手送上法庭。安迪面对着人生的种种困境,走进人间地狱。在狱中发生的一系列事件终让他忍无可忍越狱而出。当典狱长发现安迪越狱后,极其不安而畏罪自杀。安迪本来是一个无辜的好人,几任典狱长却都不清白。在这样一个错乱、颠倒的世界,斯蒂芬·金笔下塑造的安迪像一只浴火后重生的凤凰飞出了牢狱。结局设计寄托着作者"振奋"起善良的人性的创作主旨。影片通过对情节的叠化和重复,对主角的狱中生活进行浓缩,将原著中 20 多年的牢狱生活剪辑浓缩在一部电影的时长中,删繁就简地将主线的关键情节进行影视叙述。虽是线性表述,但是大胆剪辑让情节变得紧凑、生动,成为美国监狱题材商业影片的典范,同时为美国 89 集五季电视剧《越狱》(2005 年)打下坚实的技术基础。

(二)塑造剪辑节奏的生命力

节奏在影片剪辑中能控制时空关系和心理情绪。节奏决定着镜头在场景上停留的时长,直接影响一部电影的叙事方式和影像风格。因此剪辑师对于节奏的把控是评判其影片改编成功与否的关键要素之一。节奏的把控并非量化,不能以多少个镜头数来划分一部电影的节奏快慢,但每个镜头该用多长确能影响观众达到观影的情绪和效果。

电影《盗梦空间》(2010 年)是一部获得超高票房的影视佳作。影片中造梦师柯布带领着他的团队进入他人梦境,并从他人的意识中盗取秘密,同时能重塑他人梦境。柯布这一绝技使他成为一名国际逃犯。如今柯布只要完成最后一项任务就可以恢复原来的生活。但无法预料的是对手早已熟悉他们的行动。该片在剧情剪辑上运用频繁,节奏操控得着实恰到好处。前几次行动虽然是快节奏剪辑和拼凑贯连,但每次都有细腻缓慢的表述穿插其中,本应当放慢节奏表述的最后一次行动却没有被观众猜到结局,多次反复剧情反而加快了剧情的节奏。这种出乎观众意料之外的节奏剪辑,成为影视片抓住观众思想情绪的关键。[6]

（三）多重线索形成立体剧情

现代影视创作不再是单一的线索串联和线性叙事的方式,常使用大量的省略和抽离,其作用就在于扩增影片传达的信息量,所以多条线索并进的立体叙事成为现代电影的主要方式。多线索并进,再加上快的节奏和炫目的视听技巧,如果线与线之间的转换稍不加注意,就会引起观众对故事的理解错乱,让叙事变得混乱。剪辑师在遇到多线索叙事的影片时会保持审慎与清醒展开工作,要在万千头绪中找准自己的着眼点在何处。也就是说,用什么来串起整个故事,做好转场是一个使情节和线索清晰化的重要技巧。

电影《速度与激情7》（2015年）是美国环球影业出品的赛车动作片续集。故事开始于多米尼克和布莱恩带着赦免令回到美国。他的本过着平淡的日子,但是危险来了,英国特勤杀手肖不断追杀着在上一部影片中杀掉了欧文的团队成员,因为欧文是他的弟弟。多米尼克寻求政府帮助。多米尼克和布莱恩唯一的生机就是继续开着赛车保护一个追踪设备的样品。该影片的剧情线索特别多,每个人都有自己的故事线索。影片将多条故事线环绕在主线周遭,构成一套立体剧情,让观众的神经时刻保持绷紧的状态。多重剧情线索融合在一起就需要剪辑,这种剪辑的最大魅力在于能满足不同层次的观众。大家希望得到的是对影片的回忆和畅想,剧情线索多,回忆和畅想就多,看后耐人寻味,这从另一方面凸显了该片的价值。

除了上述三种影视剪辑方式外,尚有很多未被大力挖掘和推广的剪辑方法,需要进一步在影视剧本改编创作中实践尝试。商业影片作为电影产业的支柱,其重要性已经被好莱坞票房神话反复论证过。对小说改编后进行视听剪辑,就成为提高商业与艺术水准的关键性突破口。

结　语

小说、剧本、影视作品为文化艺术传播的重要形式,文化艺术传播的是思想,理念应当是积极向上的,而相互转化的形式也将日新月异。在一个开放的世界当中,艺术同样参与着国际市场的竞争,没有竞争就没有生命力。^[7]因为近些年的努力,在电影领域,国外影片并没有冲击到我们的国产影片,反而刺激了国产影片在不断提高质量,形成了更强的竞争力。

提升影视作品竞争力关键在于创新,我国影视产业在近 30 年的高速发展过程中一直在学习、借鉴外国的创新点。从选择合适的小说开始,建立清晰的故事线与情节结构,接着对剧情筛选与对比,重点强化曲折的剧情,最后统一对剧情进行剪辑。这种探寻过程本身就是一部规律性与创造性兼顾的大片,其中筛选与剪辑时时刻刻都在绽放新意。编剧、导演将能在探寻过程中找到理想的创新模式,并运用这种模式来给影片增添无穷的创意。

参考文献:

[1]理查德·沃尔特.剧本:影视写作的艺术、技巧和商业运作 [M].天津:天津人民出版社,2017:45.

[2]悉德·菲尔德.电影剧本写作基础 [M].北京:北京联合出版公司,2016:85.

[3]克劳迪娅·亨特·约翰逊.短片剧本写作 [M].北京:世界图书出版公司,2017:103.

[4]周倩雯,吴丽娜,吕永华.剧本写作元素练习方法 [M].北京:中国戏剧出版社,2012:67.

[5]徐燕.剧本写作教程 [M].北京:中国传媒大学出版社,2017:222.

[6]埃里克·埃德森.故事策略——电影剧本必备的 23 个故事段落 [M].北京:人民邮电出版社,2013:96.

[7]中共中央宣传部.习近平总书记在文艺工作座谈会上的重要讲话学习读本 [M].北京:学习出版社,2015:23.

On the Film Adaptation of the Novel
—The Discussion on Text Selection and Plot Editing Mode

Abstract: While screening novels, movie scripts need to be edited in a non-linear way through which the audience can accept more plot information at one time. However, in this aspect producers and directors have their own opinions and it is difficult to form a unified model. In the process of selecting novels for adaptation into a film or a TV series, what the producers and directors most concern is whether it is feasible. For them, high feasibility means shorter adaptation cycle and lower cost, thus becoming the major premise. Starting with the selection of appropriate novels, this paper elaborates how to establish a clear story line and plot structure and then screen and contrast the plot, focusing on strengthening the tortuous plots and and finally editing the plots in a unified way. Besides, it also explores the innovative mode of modern films and TV series, introduces and summarizes the methods of scripts screening and editing, and provides reference for films workers, hoping that the development mode of films and televisions can be expanded to improve the cultural levels and market benefits of film and television works.

Key words: novel plots, text conversion, story line, non-linear editing

It has become one of the mainstream trends in contemporary movie and television creation that novels are adapted and then filmed as movies and TV series. In recent years, many producers and directors are vigorously hunting for kinds of brilliant novels, hoping to adapt and put them onto the screen in order to obtain good market and social benefits.

Since the end of the Cold War in the 1990s, the development of global economy and culture has entered a new historical stage. Under such an environment, with novel materials being introduced into film and television works, the requirements for plot editing and setting are getting higher and higher. At the same time, more and more novels are being adapted into film and television. In order to meet the aesthetic needs of the times and the audience, the quality of film and television works needs to be improved. That is to say, while screening the novels for adaptation, it is necessary to carry out the dislocated plot arrangements and settings so that the audience can get more information. In the past 30 years, although the creative mode of film and television scripts has been constantly changing, it is regrettable that only a few are truly original and most are mediocre works that follow the trend. As we all know, good novels are common, while few are good movies and television works. Therefore, there is an urgent need to find a set of mature mode for review and evaluation in the aspects of novel selection, overall structure and plot adaptation.

1. The Factors of Choosing a Novel

Most original texts of novels adapted into film and television works are screened by producers or directors who most focus on the expected economic benefits and potential social effects of the novels. They care about the number of readers, whether the reaction is strong and the original author is famous or not, etc. If the novel has a high social awareness, then it will attract much more viewers, making the attendance rate of the film higher than the average level. And in the future the box office and advertising expenses will satisfy both producers and directors. Instead of stopping after a successful film or TV series, they will continue to do it. If the work fails to achieve the expected benefits, they will hunt for another novel.

Apart from the considerations mentioned above, the most important factor in screening a novel for adaptation lies in the novel text itself. That is to say, not all novels can be perfectly created into movie scripts and put on the screen. On the issue of script selection, it must follow its own rules, like rules of profession, market and team requirements, etc. What the novels bring the readers are thinking and imagination, while the film and television works bring more entertainment and leisure to the viewers. In brief, "people who like reading books and watching movies are two different groups." [1] Therefore, the screenwriters, directors and producers all have their own criteria in the selection and adaptation of novels. In general, they know clearly which can be adapted into a movie or a TV series and which cannot.

If a novel can enlighten and give the audience sensory impact when it is adapted, there is a condition that the novel should have the basic characteristics of adaptation, which include rich plots, changeable images, large amount of characters, positive theme, and strong sense of impact. "To make the audience enjoy a visual feast that they cannot experience in their daily life and work, making them entertain and relax themselves." [2] In this way, novels that make people think deeply cannot be used as the best materials for adaptation. Also not all novels are suitable for adaptation into films or televisions. According to different classification standards, novels can be divided into novellas, novels, short novels and online novels. Faced with various novels, casual adaptation and shooting will directly lead to current movies with low quality in the film and television market. Screenwriters, directors, and producers must distinguish and make a correct choice. Otherwise due to the massive film adaptation of those novels which are non-model novels, film industry will become mediocre and mechanized, and it is impossible to bring unique audio-visual experiences to the audience.

Therefore, all film producers, directors, and screenwriters are hunting for a proper method, which can not only select excellent novels suitable for adaptation, but also ensure the level of the film works, meeting the audience's ever-changing aesthetic needs. That is to say, it is necessary to explore one or more modes to last longer the influence and recognition of film and television works.

2. Analysis of the Story Lines and Plot Structures

In the process of screening the original novels, what the filmmakers and directors concern most is whether the film is highly filmed. Adaptation with a higher degree of film or TV series can effectively reduce the difficulty of adaptation, shorten the adaptation cycle and control the cost, which is the major premise of selecting novels for adaptation. For the novel itself, there must be a particularly clear structure in the story line and plot. It doesn't matter whether the plot is simple or not. Because simple plots can be adapted into love movies, war movies and action movies, while complex plots can be adapted into mystery movies, thrillers and feature films.

One of David Mitchell's best-selling novels "Cloud Map" (2011) was adapted into a feature film by Warner Bros and was released in mainland China in 2013. (David Mitchell: an American writer) The film, adapted from best-selling novels and produced by established film and television production companies, has not met the audience's expectations. Because its story structure of novel is divided into 6 parts with strong space of contrast and imagination, making every plot complex and interesting. When reading it, the readers can associate its past with the future plot. However, in the final visualization, because the space-time span involved is too large and the director concentrates on the personality of the characters in different time and space. As a result, many related meanings cannot be smoothly processed through the image visualization. Literary creation can give people enough space for imagining through time and space. However, now the imagination is moved onto the screen, which breaks the readers' imagination. As a result, the audience imagines differently from before. Therefore, the various opinions have left a negative influence and affected the social acceptance of the film.

For a film or television, it will generally explain what the work mainly tells within the first 10 minutes. That is to say, whether a film can attract the audience successfully, the film and television content outlined in the opening is very important.

However, the opening cannot construct a clear story line, which will inevitably lead the audience to speculate in the follow-up movie watching. If the audience guesses correctly, it will show that director is unprofessional; while if the audience produces wrong guesses, it will damage their interest to continue watching. Therefore, if a novel is adapted, the adaptation should not just be the story line. On the contrary, the story line should be kept and made clearly. Although by adapting the structure, the plot is diversified and the twists and turns can be visualized by the narrative of the film and television language, but the whole story line cannot be adapted.

It can be seen that the rich and diversified plots are the main features of film and television works. The plots that run through in an original novel can be displayed horizontally in the film, and the structure of the plot can be strengthened through montage. Among them, there must be a story line with clear emotions through the whole film to enhance the text conversion of the novel on film and television works.

3. Selection and Comparison of the Plots

Another difference between the original novel and the adaptation is that the structure of the plot and the relationship between truth and falsehood. If a novel requires the readers to imagine for constructing a specific story space, then it will be much more difficult to adapt it. Particular examples are Gu

Long's novels and Jin Yong's novels.

In Gu Long's novels, two parts usually talk with each other profoundly when fighting. After staring at each other silently, one said to the other one: you lost. Then he will turn around and leave, with the other one admitting the defeat. Gu Long will also give some explanations, such as no swords in the hand, a sword in the heart, and so on. If a reader is reading such words, he can imagine various scenes by himself. However, if the novel is adapted into a film or television, the plot will be too monotonous and static. On the screen, what the audience watches is two actors winking each other and using words to determine the result. In fact, the audience cannot recognize it because they want to see the motion and process. Such plots will increase the difficulty of adaptation.

In comparison, Jin Yong's martial arts novels are easier to be adapted. The story line and vein structure of Jin Yong's novels are quite complete and clear, and the scene expression of the characters' story line is quite vivid, which lays a good foundation for the text transformation of novels and movies. Similarly, describing the love between men and women, in Gu Long's novel they cannot get married. When describing the plot between Li Xunhuan and Lin Shiyin, Gu Long wrote that Li Xunhuan stood in the alley outside Lin Shiyin's house and drank alcohol at the house without any other words. However, in Jin Yong's novel, Zhou Zhiruo pierces Zhang Wuji in public, which was added actions and language in adapted TV series, making them more acceptable to the audience.

Therefore, in the process of the conversion of novels to film or television works, four "telling" s need to be achieved about the handling of the characters, namely: telling the audience who the character is; what kind of role he/she is; what the role will do; what changes will happen to the character after finishing these behaviors. Later, in the television *"Throwing Knife of Li Xunhuan"* (1999) adapted by Gu Long's novel *"Affectionate Swordsman and Ruthless Sword "*, there is a character, Li Xunhuan. But who is Li Xunhuan? Is Li Xunhuan equivalent to Xiao Li Fei Dao? The novel didn't tell us. At the beginning of the novel, Li Xunhuan was already a world-renowned master. There are considerable additions and changes in the adaptation of TV series, making it a more successful TV play. In Jin Yong's novel "*The Legend of the Condor Heroes*" (the eponymous TV series in 1983), all the characters have their ins and outs, especially the characters' background of Guo Jing and Yang Kang is more detailed, and this complicated background has profoundly affected the two characters. Not only does it have deep packaging for martial arts, but also creates some famous terms such as "Jiu Yin Zhen Jing" (a scripture of Kungfu), "the 18 palm attacks to defeat dragons" and "One-finger death touch", and it has a profound realistic reflection on the love and career entanglement of the literary drama. The whole novel is no longer a novel, but a relatively complete film and television script.

The novels suitable for adaptation should be figurative and exquisite. The plot of the novel should be screened to estimate the commercial entertainment and leisure side of the film and television works. In the image mode, it contains profound meanings, so as to not only preserve the charm and spiritual theme of the novel but also present the audio-visual process to live in a vibrant way.

4. Strengthening in the Twists and Turns of the Plot

Turning twists and turns of the plots is the main form of innovative adaptation of novels in movies or TV programs. When confronted with a novel that is not suitable for adaptation but is very excellent, the screenwriters will use their unique imagination to enrich the plots. But if they cannot properly handle it in the same specification, the flaw will be seen through by the audience. [3] When the story develops to the middle stage, much audience can guess the result through the habit pattern, which is the most fatal blow to the film, and its reputation will often fall to the bottom. Therefore, how to creatively strengthen the tortuous plot becomes the key.

The popular TV series *"Biography of Zhen Huan"* (2011) is a revolutionary subversion of the film and television adaptation of original novels, which is a successful case of strengthening the twists and turns. The play first raises a question. Who was Zhen Huan? Then it tells that she was the daughter of a small bureaucrat before entering the palace. Why was she chosen by the emperor after entering the palace? Because looking like the deceased Queen Chun Yuan, so she was favored by the emperor. In the play, the character began to change from being ignorant of the world at first and having no intention of competing for favor, to meeting the emperor in the garden and falling in love with him. The character's psychology also changed quietly. She found that the emperor was not her sincere person. The so-called "Four Lang" was just her inner plot of love, turning from true feelings to hypocrisy. For the current entertainment aesthetic trend of the audience, such a story attracts the audience to draw a sigh on the speculate in a correct way.

The film examples that successfully adapted the novel and put it on the screen can be used for reference. However, the failure of adaptation stems more due to the weak film and television conversion of the novel text, which is basically equivalent to reconstructing the story structure and weaving the story plot. For this reason, the screenwriter has done a lot of adaptation work, adding many plots not found in the original novel, so that the plots of the story can meet the requirements of film shooting. But it often deviates from the main connotation of the novel, making the adaptation cannot obtain the social identity and achieve the social and economic effects. The anti-Japanese play that has been popular for nearly 20 years is the most typical negative example around us.

The tortuous plots can make audience enjoy imaging that they cannot feel in daily life. The constantly intensified and tortuous plots are more suitable for suspense films, reasoning films, and detective films. If such commercial films can take both the elegance and even philosophical implication of literary films into account, they can enhance the ideological layering of commercial films, aesthetic standards, and satisfy the multiple psychological needs of audiences for novelty-seeking and quality improvement, becoming classic works. In the process of writing the script, using the mode of nonlinear editing and breaking reasonable plots with interspersing repeated failure, and difficulties and so on plots plus the multi-cue synchronous expression can continuously strengthen the plot and finally achieve the desired effect.

5. The Breakthrough Mode of Plot Editing

After selecting the adapted novel, the content of the novel needs to be improved as a whole. The illusion of the novel's words is transformed into the image of the film. This transformation comes from the second creation of the screenwriters and the directors, which is a process of constructing the spatial imagination in the novel. If the construction is successful, it is like a good harvest.

Of course, imagination is sentimental and the probability of success is unknown. To get success, rational thinking should be injected into the film and television script. Editing the plot is rational thinking for the adaptation of novels and the process of editing is also the process of further shaping the imagination space. [4] Although the majority of screenwriters, directors and producers all hope that the editing will inject new vitality into the film, there are few models for reference. Here are three creative editing modes.

(a) Choosing a right way to present the plot

The audio-visual language narration of the plot is the most crucial way in adaptation. It is very important for a film or television to be told in which way or space-time structure. If a film or TV series is too long and straightforward, it will make the viewers feel bored. So it must be eye-catching within the first 10 minutes. Why are the Hollywood blockbusters so popular? Flexible narratives, twisted plots and emotions are the keys. From the point of view of plot editing, compared with the monotony of linear plot expression, most films need to be good at using nonlinear editing thinking to schedule and coordinate audio-visual language, to make plot subversive, and to control the freedom of mind in time and space structure, so as to complete plot expression of television films. [5]

The film "*Shaw Shank Redemption*" (1994) is adapted from the novella of American writer Stephen King. It tells the story of a banker, Andy, who was sent to court as the murderer because of killing his wife. Facing the dilemma of life, Andy walked into death. A series of events in prison finally made him unable to escape. When the warden found that Andy had escaped from prison, he was extremely upset and committed suicide. Andy was originally an innocent man, but several wardens were not innocent. In such a chaotic, upside-down world, Andy, who was created by Stephen King, flew out of jail like a phoenix rising from the ashes. The ending reposes the author's creative theme of "inspiration" of kindness. Through the episode and repetition of the plot, the film condenses the protagonist's prison life by condensing the prison life of more than 20 years in the original book into a film's duration, and then simply tells the main plot of the main line. Although it is a linear expression, bold editing makes the plot compact and vivid, and it has become a model for American prison-themed commercial films. At the same time, it has laid a solid technical foundation for the 89-episode five-season TV series "*Prison Break*" (2005).

(b) Shaping vitality of the editing rhythm

Rhythm can control space-time relations and psychological emotions in film editing. It also determines how long the scene will stay, which directly affects the narrative style and image style of a movie. Therefore, the editor's control of the rhythm is one of the key elements to judge the success of the film adaptation. Rhythm control is not quantitative, and the tempo of a movie cannot be divided by the number of shots. However, the length of each shot can definitely affect the audience's mood and effect of watching the movie.

The movie *"Pirates of the Dream"* (2010) is a masterpiece that has won a high box office. In the movie, dream maker Cobb leads his team to enter other people's dreams and steal secrets to reshape other people's dreams. Cobb's unique skill made him an international fugitive. Now Cobb can restore his life as long as he finishes his last task. But what is unpredictable is that the opponents are already familiar with their actions. Plot editing is used frequently in this movie, and the rhythm is really well controlled. Although the previous few actions were fast-paced editing and patchwork, each time there was a delicate and slow expression interspersed among them. The last action that should have slowed down the rhythm expression was not guessed by the audience. Instead, repeated plots accelerated the rhythm of the plot. This kind of rhythm editing that is unexpected to the audience has become the key to capturing the audience's thoughts and emotions. [6]

(c) Forming a three-dimensional plot with multiple clues

Modern film or television creation is no longer a single way of clue concatenation and linear narration. It often uses a lot of omission and abstraction to amplify the amount of information conveyed by the film. So the three-dimensional narrative with multiple clues becomes the main way of modern film. If the transition between lines and lines is slightly unnoticed, it will cause the audience to misunderstand the story and make the narrative messy with multiple clues, fast rhythms and dazzling audiovisual techniques. When encountering a multi-cue narrative film, editors must be cautious and awake, and find out what their focus is through a myriad of clues. In other words, what is used to string up the whole story and make the transition is an important skill to make the plot and clues clear.

The film *"Speed and Passion 7"* (2015) is a sequel to the racing action film produced by Universal Pictures of the United States. The story begins when Dominic and Brian return to the United States with a pardon. They live a common life, but the danger is coming. The British Secret Service killer Shaw keeps chasing after Owen's team members who killed Owen in the last film because Owen is his younger brother. Dominica begins to turn to the government. Dominic and Brian's only hope is to continue driving the car to protect a sample of tracking equipment. There are many plot clues in the film where everyone has his own story clues. The film encircles many story lines around the main line to form a set of three-dimensional plots, attracting the audience at all times. What's more, multiple plot clues need to be edited when combined together of which the biggest charm is that it can satisfy audience of different levels. What everyone hopes to get is memories and imagination of the film. The more plot clues, the more memories and imagination, which is interesting after watching. On the other hand, it also highlights the value of the film.

In addition to the above three kinds of film editing methods, there are still many editing methods that have not been vigorously explored and promoted, and further practice is needed in the adaptation of film and television scripts. As the pillar of the film industry, commercial films have been repeatedly demonstrated by Hollywood box office myth. The audio-visual editing of the adaptation of the novel has become a key breakthrough in improving business and artistic standards.

The Ending

Novels, plays and movies are important forms of cultural and artistic communication. Cultural and artistic communication is about ideas, which should be positive. Besides, the forms of mutual transformation will change with each passing day. In an open world, art also participates in the competition in the international market. Without competition, there would be no vitality. [7] As a result of the efforts in recent years, foreign films have not impacted our domestic films, instead they have stimulated domestic films to continuously improve their quality and make them more competitive.

The key to enhancing the competitiveness of film and television works lies in innovation. China's film and television industry has been learning from foreign innovations in the past 30 years of rapid development. The stage is that starting with the selection of appropriate novels, establishing a clear story line and plot structure, then screening and contrasting the plot, focusing on strengthening the tortuous plots and and finally editing the plots in a unified way. This process of exploration itself is a blockbuster of both regularity and creativity, in which screening and editing are always in full of new ideas. Besides, the screenwriters and directors will be able to find an ideal innovative mode in the process of exploration, and then use this mode to make the film or TV series creative and attractive.

References:

[1] Richard Walter. Script: The art, skills and business operations of film and television writing [M]. Tianjin: Tianjin People's Publishing House, 2017: 45.

[2] Sid Field. The basis of film script writing [M]. Beijing: Beijing United Publishing Company, 2016: 85.

[3] Claudia Hunter Johansson. Short script writing [M]. Beijing: World Book Publishing Company, 2017: 103.

[4] Zhou Qianwen, Wu Lina, Lv Yonghua. Practice Methods of Script Writing Elements [M]. Beijing: China Drama Publishing House, 2012: 67.

[5] Xu Yan. Script Writing Course [M]. Beijing: Communication University of China Press, 2017: 222.

[6] Eric Edersen. Story Strategy—23 Story Paragraphs Required for Movie Scripts [M]. Beijing: People's Posts and Telecommunications Press, 2013: 96.

[7] The Propaganda Department of the Central Committee of the Communist Party of China. General Secretary Xi Jinping's important speech at the Symposium on Literature and Art Learning Reader [M]. Beijing: Learning Press, 2015:23.

且读且悟　亦史亦灯

——评郭晓霞、刘道全主编的《西方戏剧史》

　　摘要：《西方戏剧史》思路开阔、气魄宏伟，是一部富有新意的探索性学术著作。其要旨虽在还原西方戏剧史的真实全貌，但在针对每个时代重点介绍一个或两个国家的作家所取得的戏剧成就时，将其放在全球化大语境、整个西方国家文化大视野，以及中国和西方文化交流的宏大平台上考察、比较，为我所用。它力图抑恶扬善，从正反方面证明人类文明文化的最高价值：真的、善的、美的理念必须坚守；力图以更科学、更正确的立场，以更知性的方式，传递当代文学影视戏剧新理念。

　　关键词：西方戏剧史；文化视野；梳理

　　这是一部表现出史家之汇通赅博又具有论者之专精明睿的关于西方戏剧研究的扛鼎之作。进入 21 世纪以来，中国高等教育悄然进入一种世界性的文化格局。在这种全球化语境中，怎样看待西方历史，卓有成效地进行中外文学文化戏剧之间的影响研究？面对这个关涉全球化学术视界和文化襟怀的时代考题，作家兼学者的郭晓霞、刘道全两位先生主编的《西方戏剧史》（河南人民出版社，2013 年版）为此提供了崭新的学习范本，提交了一份优秀的答卷。

　　习近平总书记说："世界的今天是从世界的昨天发展而来的。今天世界遇到的很多事情可以在历史上找到影子，历史上发生的很多事情也可以作为今天的镜鉴"。他强调领导干部多读外国历史，不仅是个人素质提升的

且读且悟　亦史亦灯

一个途径,更是经济社会发展的必然要求。换言之,高校莘莘学子(戏剧专业)学习历史(尤其是西方历史),其不再是一个纯粹被动的接受体,而是悠久历史文化的创造者。中国文学只有与外国戏剧(尤其是西方戏剧)在同等的研究平台之上相互学习借鉴,才能站在时代的制高点上,融会贯通,取长补短,为我所用,为他们筑就中华民族伟大复兴时代文艺高峰搭建好的平台、提供强有力的保障。这部系统梳理、阐释西方戏剧历史发展状况的学术著作,凝结着编者所在院校及诸多致力于学术研究的教授、学者、教师同仁、朋友的智慧结晶。

据悉,郭晓霞、刘道全之所以编著《西方戏剧史》教材,源自教学的实践和困惑,源自对党的教育事业那一份可贵的责任担当。之前,虽有武汉大学郑传寅、黄蓓合著的《欧洲戏剧史》,但内容主要是从古希腊戏剧到19世纪中期戏剧,存在时间跨度不足之弊端(作者在后记中声称19世纪以后的西方戏剧要另书出版)。廖可兑先生的《西欧戏剧史》(研究者和戏剧专业学生使用)比较系统全面地介绍了自古希腊以来直到20世纪80年代整个西方戏剧的发展历程,尤其侧重于戏剧艺术和剧场艺术的发展。它虽然是国内该领域代表性的专业研究书籍,但在地域上有局限性,不能涵盖西方戏剧的全部内容。尤其是它的"阳春白雪"味道并不适合新升入本科院校戏剧影视文学专业学生的实际知识状况。此刻,为培养创新型、开发型人才,编写好的教材是刻不容缓的重要任务。因为,熟知他山之"石","攻玉"的事业也会事半功倍,产生积极正向的效果。从这个角度说,郭晓霞、刘道全呼应时代、敢着先鞭、集众人之力,主编完成的《西方戏剧史》一书可谓非常宝贵,值得点赞!

且读且悟,亦史亦灯。《西方戏剧史》按照时间顺序,对西方三千年戏剧史上出现的戏剧思潮、剧场艺术的演变以及代表性的作家和作品进行逐一论述,每一章第一节先概述本时期戏剧发展的基本情况,之后介绍一般性的作家和作品,接着选择有代表性的重点作家和作品进行细致全面分析。它要言不烦地阐述自己的理论主张,让远去的历史渐渐清晰、渐渐鲜活;让创造这历史的一代戏剧大师生动、亲切起来,甚至栩栩如生,毫发毕现。恩格斯说:"中世纪是从粗野的原始状态发展而来的。它把古代文明、古代哲学、政治和法律一扫而光,以便一切从头做起。它从没落了的古代世界承受下来的唯一事物就是基督教和一些残破不全而且失掉文明的城市。"[1]《西方戏剧史》在"中世纪戏剧"一章的小序里指出,欧洲中世纪的戏剧与骄矜倨傲的古希腊罗马戏剧迥然不同,其主要类型是发源于基督教堂式的宗教剧,以及发源于异教仪式和民间艺术的世俗戏剧,并强调指出中世纪戏剧和古希腊罗马戏剧两者一起成为"西方现代戏剧的发展源头"[2] 的重要性。在第二节里以宗教剧《第二个牧羊人的戏》和世俗戏剧《巴特兰律师》为例证,详细分析了其产生背景、主要类型以及它所产生的巨大社会意义和艺术贡献。作品写道,《第二个牧羊人的戏》)全剧两部分的结构安排表面看似乎有偏离主题之嫌,实际上,这恰是该剧的突出成就,一定程度上,"这出戏的结构之美就在于威克菲尔德大师从中为我们勾画了一个对偶式的世界"[3]。这样的教材编写体例,论点明确,论据翔实而有说服力,做到了"既见森林,又见树木"。在朴实亲切而形象生动的基础之上,意在笔先,气韵贯通,为后来者留下了西方戏剧历史原生态的样貌,更便于学生理解和学习。(此类例子举不胜举,限于篇幅,不再赘述)"冰冻三尺,非一日之寒。"能达到如此境界,显然是与编写者郭晓霞、刘道全潜心搜找、灯窗埋首、严谨治学的态度密不可分的。

　　真诚追溯往事,总结成败得失,洞察未来趋势。《西方戏剧史》论述用语严谨周密、实事求是,不夸大其词,也不模棱两可;既论述每个时期的辉煌成就,又和过去曾流行的戏剧相互比较优劣,给予合适定论。第四章论述17 世纪戏剧史,表明了欧洲戏剧的主要潮流体现为古典主义戏剧,它于法国形成并达到全盛,进而传播到欧洲其他国家。同时也指出之前的中世纪宗教剧和文艺复兴时期的戏剧仍然在一定时期内存在,但影响及成就远不及古典主义戏剧。还有对古典主义的创作艺术规范和标准"三一律"(即用一地、一天完成一个故事)也用一分为二的观点审视,既褒扬其使剧本情节更紧凑突出,促进了戏剧文本规范的完善和发展,又指出其"束缚和压抑"剧作家的创作思维的弊端。显然,这种来自文学、源于作家笔下的责任和担当,体现出的是中国知识分子那种特立独行的个性与人格,敢说实话、说真话的一种高尚品质。它使当下读者至少避免了在文化和历史戏剧方面走进误区。它以文学的回眸、审视方式,为西方戏剧颠踬蹉跎的坎坷历程,做了认真的剖解与探询,也给这段遥远的戏剧史事,做了拾漏补遗和校准完善。从这个角度说,学者兼作家郭晓霞、刘道全,在培养人才、融通学科方面,表现得目光敏锐、动作迅速,其将史识、史笔融入文本,以言简意赅的文字还原西方戏剧历史现场,保存西方戏剧历史真相。随意翻开其中一页,读者(学生)便能看到时代潮汐的涨落,看到戏剧风云的激荡。掩卷遐想,犹如林涛喧响,山风呼啸,不惟在耳,亦入于心。《西方戏剧史》的出版,无疑给学术领域和高校的教育事业吹来一股清新的春风,具有非常强烈的时代意义和现实意义。

《西方戏剧史》力图以更科学、更正确的立场,以更知性的方式,传递其文学影视戏剧新理念。它的要旨虽在还原西方戏剧史,却并不孤立地写一个或两个国家,而是将其放在整个西方国家文化大视野之中,放在中国和西方文化交流的宏大语境里考察、比较,思路开阔、气魄宏伟,为读者形象生动地传递了耳目一新的文学影视理念。譬如对英国、法国、意大利、葡萄牙、美国等戏剧史进行叙述时,尽量选择中国读者所熟悉的剧作家,挖掘其深刻的思想内涵,以引起受众的共鸣。英国文艺复兴时期人文主义戏剧作家莎士比亚,被称为"欧洲戏剧史乃至世界戏剧史上当之无愧的泰斗"[4]。在介绍他创作的四大喜剧《威尼斯商人》《无事生非》《皆大欢喜》《第十二夜》时,《西方戏剧史》就选择了争议较多的喜剧《威尼斯商人》进行评述。争议的焦点是该剧在欢快的基础上注入了深刻的思绪,触及了一些社会问题,而主题的复杂性使剧中人物不再是单一的形象。法庭上,夏洛克慷慨激情地道出了犹太人的心声:

他曾经羞辱过我,夺去我几十万块的生意,讥笑着我的亏蚀,挖苦着我的盈余,侮辱着我的民族,破坏我的买卖,离间我的朋友,煽动我的仇敌;他的理由是什么?只因为我是一个犹太人。难道犹太人没有眼睛吗?难道犹太人没有五官四肢、没有知觉、没有感情、没有血气吗?……你们要是用毒药谋害我们,我们不是也会死吗?那么要是你们欺侮了我们,我们难道不会复仇吗?(《威尼斯商人》第三幕第一场)[5]

《诗大序》有云:"情动于中而形于言,言之不足,故嗟叹之,嗟叹之不足,故咏歌之,咏歌之不足,不知手之舞之,足之蹈之也。"[6]显然,在喜剧《威尼斯商人》里,夏洛克这番声泪俱下的演讲和控诉(说白),几乎使他成为一个悲剧英雄——为自己遭受蹂躏欺凌的犹太民族鸣不平。同时,它通过韵律之美和语言表现力,展现鲜明的抑扬跌宕和顿挫变化的艺术美感,"使诵念本身体现出一种'乐化'之美"[7]。在这里,形象的多面性使得夏洛克这一人物形象获得了不朽艺术生命,并与福斯诺夫、哈姆雷特一起,在中国读者中家喻户晓,被评论家认为是莎士比亚戏剧人物中最为复杂的三大典型。在这里,编写者正是希望借喜剧的艺术魅力使人们(学生)从世界文学、世界文化的背景中,去考察、发现莎士比亚戏剧自身的独特价值。而对作品的叙述由点到面,由浅入深,既有共性,又有个性,贴近生活,走进受众的心灵。

秉笔直书,直面问题,不为尊讳。因为,真实的历史是无法遮蔽的;而还原历史过程中的个性生命力量,更具有珍贵的文化价值。历史回望,不是简单的历史考据和追溯,而是着眼于现实社会生活。"戏剧应该是史学的原则和抒情性的原则经过调解(互相转化)的统一。"[8]众所周知,西方戏剧作品广受读者和作家青睐。这类作品大多有揭示历史真相或隐情的意味,是一种旧闻新知,同时,又指向当下社会的现实生活。《西方戏剧史》注入了作者的精神与责任担当,写出了历经磨难后人性的温暖与坚韧。它充分发挥文字的力量和韵致,尽量原汁原味地去还原遥远年代的气息和氛围,在人物、事件的推进中,细致地刻画人物的内心情感,给人以新异的阅读感受。19世纪下半叶,欧洲"新戏剧"抛弃了陈旧的情节结构模式,大大拓展了人们对于戏剧性的认识,尤其是契诃夫剧作中对于"内在戏剧性"的成熟表现,更让人们认识到戏剧性不仅存在于那些罕见的、突转的、宿命的历史故事中,不仅存在于那些充满巧合、带有神秘色彩的传奇故事中,而且也存在于被人们司空见惯的平淡无奇的日常生活之中。契诃夫强调他的剧作《樱桃园》是"四幕抒情喜剧",斯坦尼斯拉夫斯基(世界著名演员、导演)从自身体验,把《樱桃园》排演成了一出悲剧,演出时观众席几成泪海。契诃夫对此极端不满,称之为"愚蠢的感伤主义"。之后,斯坦尼斯拉夫斯基为了迎合契诃夫,在人物舞台动作上增加了许多滑稽逗乐动作,结果人物乐了,观众没乐,这让契诃夫更加不满。为什么呢?《西方戏剧史》的编著者站在时代的高度,从深处找出了症结之所在:"……有许多喜剧给人的印象往往是悲剧,如果人物不符合悲剧的要求,那么这部剧也不会符合于喜剧。使人发笑和催人泪下的东西是微妙地交织在一起的。

（因为）《樱桃园》从情感的角度去体验是悲剧,从理性的角度思索是喜剧。"[9]故笔者认为,《西方戏剧史》以《樱桃园》为例,对两位戏剧大师之间的内心世界给予了从未有过的充分的尊重,对悲、喜剧这两种艺术价值存在的认识分歧的理解思考,既兼文学性与思辨性,又含历史性与可读性,从而使作品呈现出了一种内在丰盈的特质。无疑,这对今天的读者(学生)探寻西方戏剧史真相、勾勒文本生成中的人物谱系、人物背后的历史以及历史背后的精神内涵,有着十分重要的启迪作用。

以史为鉴,扬长避短;继往开来,再跃新程。在20世纪中外文学关系中,西方戏剧史已被置于世界文学背景下考察、比较,其方法是跨越语言、国别和民族的比较研究,也正是在这一点上,它对传统的学术(历史)的研究方法和观念具有颠覆性的挑战味道。毋庸讳言,当下学术界的历史戏剧研究,越来越注意科学性,其文体也多以纯粹的逻辑说理为主流。然而,那些在撰写历史专著的论述时依然能时时保持一种对"文学"本身的敏感与自觉的学者,委实不多见。文化事业的本质实际上是寻觅失去的精神家园。笔者从郭晓霞、刘道全两位学者兼作家的《西方戏剧史》著述里,不仅对其结构之宏大印象深刻,更品尝到它在细节上的种种人生况味;不但时时会被文本流淌出的哲理感喟所震撼,还会时时被其睿智、生动出彩的剖析所折服。"庄子以旷世文章放飞了他的思想、我们是否也能从他那里学到一点灵性,把庄子鲜活的生命放飞起来?"这句话是谁说的,已经记不清了,但郭晓霞、刘道全的《西方戏剧史》充分满足了广大读者(学生)的这一阅读期待,其展现出来的开拓和创新的勇气,应该是高校学术研究领域人们的学习楷模。

参考文献：

[1]恩格斯.德国农民战争[M]//中共中央马克思恩格斯列宁斯大林著作编译局.马克思恩格斯全集(第7卷).北京:人民出版社,1959:400.

[2]郭晓霞,刘道全.西方戏剧史[M].郑州:河南人民出版社,2013:50.

[3] 孙柏. 丑角的复活：对西方戏剧文化的价值重估 [M]. 上海：学林出版社，2002:268.

[4] 郭晓霞，刘道全. 西方戏剧史 [M]. 郑州：河南人民出版社，2013：79.

[5] 莎士比亚. 莎士比亚全集 [M]. 朱生豪译. 北京：人民文学出版社，1994.

[6] 路应昆. 戏剧艺术论 [M]. 北京：北京广播学院出版社，2002：4.

[7] 阮元. 十三经注疏（上册）[M]. 上海：上海古籍出版社，1962：149.

[8] 黑格尔. 美学（第三卷）[M]. 朱光潜译. 北京：商务印书馆，1981：242.

[9] 郭晓霞，刘道全. 西方戏剧史 [M]. 郑州：河南人民出版社，2013：172.

History as a Guiding Light while Reading —A Review of *The History of Western Drama* Compiled by Guo Xiaoxia and Liu Daoquan

Abstract: Possessing broad threads and bold vision, *The History of Western Drama* is an innovative and explorative academic composition. It aims to restore the true features of the western drama history. However, when describing the writers' drama accomplishments in one or two countries in each period, Guo and Liu don't limit them in their own country. Instead, the writers of this book put these achievements in a global stage, in the whole vision of western countries' culture and the platform of Chinse and western culture communication. Therefore, Chinese people can absorb its essence by comparison. In addition, this book tries its best to press the evil and support the good, and prove the highest value of human cultural and civilization from both the positive and negative aspects, which is to hold fast to the theory of truth, goodness and beauty. It strives to transmit the new theory of modern literature, television, film and drama in a more scientific, more proper and more intellectual way.

Key Words: the history of western drama; culture vision; analyses

This is a leading composition on western drama studying that shows the writers' erudite knowledge and professional skills as historians. Since the beginning of the 21st century, Chinese higher education has quietly entered a worldwide cultural pattern. In such a globalized situation, how should we view the western history and effectively study the influence between Chinese and foreign literature and culture plays? Confronted with the global epochal issue of academic horizon and cultural sense, Guo Xiaoxia and Liu Daoquan, who are both writers and scholars, compiling *The History of Western Drama* (Henan People's Publishing House, 2013), provided a new learning model and submitted an excellent solution.

General Secretary Xi Jinping said that Today's world is derived from yesterday's world. Many of what happens nowadays can be found in the past, and many of what happened in history can serve as a mirror for today. He emphasized that leaders and cadres should read foreign histories, which is not only a way to improve their personal qualities, but also can satisfy the essential needs of economic and social development. In other words, students in university (students majored in theater) should learn history and especially western history. Moreover, they can no longer be containers that just receive knowledge passively. They should be creators of our long history and culture. Chinese literature can stand on a "high ground" and make good for deficiency only by absorbing and learning from foreign drama (especially western drama) on an equally important research platform. Thus, it offers an opportunity and a powerful guarantee for rejuvenation of the Chinese nation. Having explained and figured out the development of western drama history systematically, this academic composition comprises the wisdom of many people who devoted their lives into academic researches, including these two writers' institution, many professors, teachers and other friends who work with them.

It is learned that the reason why Guo Xiaoxia and Liu Daoquan wrote this book is the puzzles generated by teaching and practicing process and the invaluable responsibility for our party's educational task. Earlier before this book, Zheng Chuanyin and Huang Bei in Wuhan University compiled *The History of European Drama* together. However, it has some weaknesses such as its insufficient time span, only ranging from ancient Greece to the middle of 19 century (the writer said in the postscript that the western drama after 19th century would be published in another book later). *The History of Western Europe Drama* compiled by Liao Kedui (used by researchers and students who major in drama) systematically and comprehensively introduces the development process of western drama from ancient Greece to the 1980s, with particular emphasis on the development of drama and theater art. Although it is a representative professional research book in this field in China, it is limited geographically and cannot cover all contents of western drama. In particular, its "highbrow" flavor is not suitable for the newly promoted undergraduates who major in drama, film and television literature. They do not have enough knowledge background to support themselves. Thus, at this moment, it allows of no delay to develop innovative talents and compile proper textbooks. If we study western drama thoroughly, we can make big progress in our own history research and have a positive effect. From this point of view, *The History of Western Drama* written by Guo Xiaoxia and Liu Daoquan who echoed the society, took their initials and work with other people, is invaluable and deserves a big thumbs-up.

When reading the history repeatedly, we will know the history is not just things happened in the past, but a guiding light for our future. According to the chronological sequence, *The History of Western Drama* discusses the dramatic trend of thought, the evolution of theater art, and the representative writers and works in three thousand years of western drama history one by one. The first section of each chapter first summarizes the basic situation of drama development in this period, and then it introduces general writers and works, and finally it selects some representative key writers and works for detailed and comprehensive analyses. It briefly elaborates its theory and makes the distant history much clear and vivid gradually. It also makes the theater masters who create the history kind and dynamic, even more lifelike. Engels once said, "The middle ages are derived from an uncivil primitive state. It swept away ancient civilization, ancient philosophy, politics and laws to start from scratch. The only things it has inherited from the ruined ancient world are Christianity and a few ruined and uncivilized cities". [1] It is said in the preface of the chapter of the Medieval Drama that the drama in middle ages of Europe is totally different from the drama in ancient Greece and Rome. The former is developed from Christianity church plays, ceremonies of other religions and folk arts plays. This book also states the importance of these two dramas combing with each other and becoming "the source of western modern drama development". In the second section, the religious drama *The Play of the Second Shepherd* and the secular drama *The Lawyer of Bartlett* are taken as examples to analyze in detail their background, main type as well as their great social significances and artistic contributions. It seems like digression because of its divided text structures in *The Play of the Second Shepherd*. However, it is exactly the most successful part in that Wakefield sketches the contours of a dual world. [2] The compilation of this textbook has clear theses and convincing arguments so that readers can have a comprehensive understanding. It is plain and vivid, but it also remains the writer's unique personal characteristic. The true features of western drama history are still left for descendants in order to make it easier and more convenient for students to study. (Because of limited words, we will not pick other similar examples) As the saying goes, Rome is not built in a day. It is Guo Xiaoxia and Liu Daoquan's hard work and serious attitude that leads to such accomplishments.

We can only see the future trend through clearly by dating back to history and reviewing the failures and success. *The History of Western Drama* uses accurate and true words, neither exaggerated nor ambiguous. It describes the achievements in each period and compares the drama with the past popular plays to get a proper argument. The fourth chapter discusses the history of drama in the 17th century, affirming that the main trend of European drama is classical drama, which came into being in France and reached full bloom, and finally spread to other countries in Europe. At the same time, it also points out that the medieval religious plays and Renaissance plays still exist in a certain period, but their influence and achievements are far less than that of classical plays. When it comes to "the Three Units" (finishing a story in a place within one day), the artistic criterion of classic literature creation, the writers adopted a dialectical method. They appreciated this method for making the plot more compact and improving the development of dramatic texts. However, it also has the weakness, which is limiting and restricting the writer's creativity and inspiration. Obviously, this sort of responsibility manifests the eccentric personality and character of Chinese intellectuals: daring to tell the truth. This brave trait is a noble quality. It avoids the embarrassment of being misguided in culture and history drama. These two writers review, explore, summarize and finally supplement and rectify the rough and rich western drama history. From this perspective, writers and scholars Guo Xiaoxia and Liu Daoquan both have sharp eyes and quick actions in terms of cultivating talents and digesting different subjects. They restore the western drama history and maintain its true features with its brief words. If you open the book and go through it, you can see the changing of time and charm of drama. If you close the book, you can also imagine the picture and hear the voice, and you can even feel it in your heart. Therefore, the publication of *The History of Western Drama* undoubtedly brought a fresh spring breeze to the academic field and the educational cause of colleges and universities, which has a very strong historical and practical significance.

The History of Western Drama tries to convey its new ideas of literature, film and drama in a more scientific, correct and intellectual way. Although its main purpose is to restore the history of western drama, it does not describe one or two countries in isolation. However, the writers put them in the broad cultural vision of the whole western countries, and in the grand context of the cultural exchange between China and the West to observe and compare. Thus, it has broad threads and is full of spirits. It delivers a brand-new literature, television and film theory to the students with a more scientific, more proper and more intellectual way. When describing the history of Britain, France, Italy, Portugal and America, the writer chooses some famous foreign playwriters to explore its ideological implication and strike the readers' resonance. Shakespeare, the British humanist dramatic writer during the Renaissance, was called "the worthy leader in the history of European drama and even in the world drama". [3] When introducing the four comedies of Shakespeare, *The Merchant of Venice, Much ado about nothing, As you like it, Twelfth night*, the writers chose the most controversial *The Merchant of Venice*. The main dispute is that there are many deep thoughts in this bright comedy. It triggered out some social problems and the characters in this book are more complicated than before because of the complexity of the theme. In court, Shylock spoke generously and passionately for the Jews:

He hath disgraced me and hindered me half a million, laughed at my losses, mocked at my gains, scorned my nation, thwarted my bargains, cooled my friends, heated mine enemies; and what is his reason? I am a Jew. Hath not a Jew eyes? Hath not a Jew hands, organs, dimensions, senses, affections, passions?... If you poison us, do we not die? And if you wrong us, shall we not revenge? (The Merchant of Venice, Act 3 Scene 1) [4]

The Great Preface to the Book of Odes once said that if people feel something happy from the bottom of their heart, they would say it out loudly. However, sometimes words are not enough to express their feelings, thus they extol. And it fails again, they sing for it. Nevertheless, singing is a little monotonous. Finally, they sing, dance and sign it with their body language. [5] Obviously, the tearful talks and complaints of Shylock in comedy *The Merchant of Venice* almost made him a tragic hero—to express the unfairness for the bullied Jews. At the same time, it shows the aesthetic feeling of the changing tones and rhymes by its rhythm and words of power, which makes only reading the book is like singing it[6]. Therefore, the character of Shylock obtains an immortal life by his multi-dimensional personality. Shylock, Falstaff and Hamlet are regarded by reviewers as the most complicated characters in Shakespeare drama characters and are familiar by Chinese readers. And the writers want to arouse students' desire to explore and observe the unique value of Shakespeare drama by its comedy charm from the perspective of world literature and world culture. Moreover, the narration of this book is from one point to the whole work, from surface to the depth. It has something in common with other works. But it has its own personality, and it is close to real daily life and can touch readers' heart easily.

When we are writing historical books, we should face the problems directly without hiding the truth and dare to challenge the authority. Because the true history cannot be hidden. Besides, restoring the powerful and vivid characters in the history process has more precious culture value. Reviewing the failures and success in history is not simply focusing on the past life. It also pays attention to the real social life. "Drama should be a unification of historiography principle and lyricism principle after mutual transformation and combination." [7] As is well known, western drama works are popular and highly praised by readers and writers. These works reveal the true history and hidden truth, which tell the things happened before but rare to know. Meantime, they point to the real social life nowadays. Infused with the writers' spirits and responsibilities, *The History of Western Drama* describes humans' kindness, toughness and tenacity after suffering from ordeals. It gives full play to the words power and rhymes to restore the atmosphere of those distant ages originally. With the development of the plot, the characters' inner feelings are described in detail, which makes people feel novel and interested. In the late 19th century, the "new drama" in Europe abandoned the old model of plot structure and greatly expanded people's understanding of drama. In particular, the mature performance of inherent drama in Chekhov's drama made people realize that theatricality exists not only in those rare, unexpected, destined, mysterious and quite coincidental historical stories and legendaries, but also can exist in common and unromantic daily life which is always being ignored by people. Chekhov once emphasized that his drama *The Cherry Orchard* is a "lyrical comedy in four acts", but Stanislavski (a worldwide famous actor and director) stared it as a tragedy from his personal experience. The audience were full of tears. However, Chekhov was extremely unsatisfied with his performance and called it as "stupid schmaltz". Later, in order to cater to Chekhov, Stanislavski added many funny actions and humorous body languages for this character. Nevertheless, the problem is this character was amusing but audience were not amused, which made Chekhov much more disgruntled than before. Why is that? The writers of *The History of Western Drama* stood in a higher level and finally found the root of this problem : "Many comedies left a tragic impression on people, and if characters in the play are not qualified for tragedy, then this drama belongs to a comedy neither. Actually, things that make people laugh and those make people cry are subtly intertwined with each other instead of being independent. And *The Cherry Orchard* is a tragedy if you immerse yourself in that situation. But it is also a comedy from the perspective of rationality". [8] Thus, the author of this essay thinks *The History of Western Drama*, taking *the Cherry Orchard* as an example, gives full respect to those two theater masters' inner world that they never obtained before. The understanding and reflection of the divergence of tragedies and comedies is full of literariness and dialectics and makes this work present a rich and dynamic trait. It is of great historic significance and worth of reading. There is no doubt that it plays an enlightening role to readers (students) today. It can help them explore character pedigree described by western drama history, the history behind the characters and the spiritual connotation.

Take history as a mirror, make the best of it, avoid the worst of it, and we will keep going and make a new leap. In the relations between Chinese literature and foreign literature in the 20th century, the history of western drama has been examined and compared in the context of world literature. Its main method is comparative research across languages, countries and nationalities. In addition, it is exactly in this respect that it challenges traditional academic (historical) research methods and concepts in a subversive way. Needless to say, the current academic research on historical drama is paying more and more attention to scientific nature, and its style is mainly based on pure logic. It is rare, however, for scholars to write historical treatises with a constant sensitivity and self-consciousness to "literature" itself. The essence of cultural business is actually seeking lost spiritual homeland. From *The History of Western Drama* written by writers and scholars Guo and Liu, the author of this essay feels not only its impressive and magnificent text structures, but also the human moods and sentiments in some details. The author of this essay is constantly shocked by the philosophy in this book and conquered by their smart and wonderful analyses. "Chuang Tzu liberated his mind by his unique articles, but can we learn a little bit from him and liberate Chuang Tzu's life thereby?" There is no need to care who said it. However, *The History of Western Drama* written by Guo Xiaoxia and Liu Daoquan fully satisfied the reading expectations of the majority of readers (students), and their courage of pioneering and innovation should be the learning models for people in academic research fields in universities.

Bibliographies:

[1] Engels. German Peasants' War [M]// Central Compilation and Translation Bureau. Karl Marx and Frederick Engels (Volume 7). Beijing: People's Press, 1959:400.

[2] Guo Xiaoxia, Liu Daoquan. The History of Western Drama [M].

Zhengzhou: Henan People's Publishing House, 2013:50.

[3] Sun Bai. The Resurrection of the Harlequin: A Reassessment of the Value of Western Drama Culture [M]. Shanghai:Xuelin Publishing House, 2002:268.

[4] Guo Xiaoxia, Liu Daoquan. The History of Western Drama [M]. Zhengzhou: Henan People's Publishing House, 2013:79.

[5] Shakespeare. The Complete Works of William Shakespeare [M]. Translated by Zhu Shenghao. Beijing: People's Literature Publishing House, 1994.

[6] Lu Yingkun. The Theory of Drama Art [M]. Beijing: Beijing Broadcasting Institute Press, 2002: 4.

[7] Ruan Yuan. Notes of the Thirteen Confucian Classics (Volume 1) [M]. Shanghai: Shanghai Ancient Books Publishing House, 1962: 149.

[8] G. W. F. Hegel. Lectures on Fine Art (Volume 3) [M]. Translated by Zhu Guangqian. Beijing: The Commercial Press, 1981: 242.

[9] Guo Xiaoxia, Liu Daoquan. The History of Western Drama [M]. Zhengzhou: Henan People's Publishing House, 2013: 172.

燃亮中国笔记小说研究的航行灯塔

——评孙顺霖、陈协琹《中国笔记小说纵览》

摘要：笔记小说是文言文小说中的一大门类，在历史的长河中留下了众多异彩纷呈的作品。然而，当前笔记小说的研究中存在着不容忽视和乐观的情况：现存作品版本复杂，载录的卷帙、年代、书名等信息多有不同，综合研究和全面分析的学术论文和著作较少，等等。孙顺霖、陈协琹共同撰写的《中国笔记小说纵览》一书，立意高远，纲目细密，理论架构合理而全面，并且思路新颖，开拓面广，成为笔记小说研究领域中涌现的又一丰硕成果。它不仅弥补了笔记小说研究的不足，而且对笔记小说这一优秀文化遗产的传承也具有重大意义，堪称当代笔记小说研究的开拓之作。

关键词：笔记小说；纵览；现实

孙顺霖、陈协琹共同撰写的《中国笔记小说纵览》（2013 年华东师范大学出版社出版）装潢精美、厚重大气、资料翔实、论证全面深入细致，可谓是我国学术研究领域涌现的又一丰硕成果，堪称当代笔记小说研究的开拓之作。在此，笔者向两位资深的学者（作家）表示热烈的祝贺和深深的敬意！

中国的笔记小说是文言文小说中的一大门类。在各种体类的古典小说中，笔记小说以其最悠久的历史，贯穿于中国古典小说的全过程，而传奇小说、白话小说中的章回小说和拟话本小说，都直接或间接地受其影响，有的样式甚至可以说是从笔记小说中脱胎而成。因此，对笔记小说开展深入细致的研究,对于继承中国传统文化、汲取前人优秀的哲学精粹和艺术精华以古为今用、促进学术研究和实现当代的"中国梦"有着不可估量的现实意义。

"相对于诗文、小说、戏曲而言,笔记的研究显然比较冷清"[1],在笔记小说研究领域中存在着不容忽视和乐观的现实情况:中国笔记小说浩如烟海、汗牛充栋,在历史的长河中那些现存的作品版本复杂多样,所载录的卷帙、年代、书名等信息多有不同。研究一人一书者多,综合研究者少;论述一朝一代者多,全面分析研究者少。因为纵使是笔记小说研究领域的学者大家也未必能够全面地、一个不漏地去认识它。管中窥豹,难免挂一漏万;而光阴如箭一般飞快、短促、易逝,我们常常在沧桑变动中丢失历史,丢失类似笔记小说这样的优秀文化;倘不及时对这些文化遗产整理和研究并传承下去,将愧对历史,遗憾终生。如何让研究笔记小说的人少走弯路,收到事半功倍的效果,成为摆在学术领域里一个迫切需要解决的重大课题。值得欣慰的是,孙顺霖、陈协琹两位学者(作家)为了实现这个梦想,兀兀穷年,废寝忘食,甘于寂寞,甘于清贫,坚持为文学耕耘,力求严谨的治学态度,在长达15年的时间里查看和阅读了历朝历代的大量文献,单是阅读各个朝代的笔记小说就有700余种,或积累,或钩沉,或校正,或圈点,耗费无数的心血和体能,才著成了《中国笔记小说纵览》这本工具书,给有志对笔记小说进行研究的人们提供了一条便捷的途径,燃亮了一盏灿烂的航行灯塔。

立意高远,纲目细密,理论架构合理而全面,是《中国笔记小说纵览》的最鲜明特点。此书将中国笔记小说总论细分为四个章节对笔记小说的概念、价值、发展脉络、类别和形式的结构顺序进行介绍;章节之间环环相扣、丝丝相连,衔接极为严密。同时,对历史发展脉络过程的阐述做到详略得当、要言不烦、条理清晰,其中不乏真知灼见。开篇总论一开始就指出:"笔记小说"一词从出现到而后被社会承认,经历过一番实践和论争。唐代以后,不少文史学家或分别论述,或综合考究,最终对此达成共识。明代胡应麟在《少室山房笔丛·九流绪论》中说:"小说家一类,又自分数种:一曰志怪;《搜神》、《述异》、《宣室》、《酉阳》之类是也。"[2]这个观点对后世影响很大。其又指出,笔记小说是中国古典小说的最初形式。它讲究布局谋篇，推敲斟酌文字，描写细腻，情节曲折，语言简约，是中国小说史上最早产生并贯穿于其发展过程的、对其他文学体裁产生过大量影响的小说文体。这里所谓的"小说"，一是基于耳闻目睹的现实性，二是内容的庞杂与丰富性，三是"小说"、"小语"与形式的灵活性等。与史记类、纪程类、考据类、诗话类之笔记不同，它是一种有人物活动、有言语交流、有情节、有感情互动之物，是对历史文化发展有较大影响的作品。此书对笔记小说一词的起源及影响的阐述高屋建瓴、思维缜密、论证严密、重点突出而又顾及全局，让读者在极短的时间里对笔记小说的概念产生、发展及嬗变获得清晰明了的认知。

征引繁博，引著翔实，剖析深刻，是本书的另一大学术特点。其以词条形式呈现，着实令观者有眼前一亮的感觉。如此匠心独运，便于读者按需检索和查阅，体现了其作为工具书的最基本性质。书中开篇有"总论"，各章前有"概述"，分别对笔记小说的源流、发展、嬗变、传承、影响，以及各朝代的名家名篇等，作了提要钩玄的评析，将其精要摘出纵览，不啻一篇比较完整的"笔记小说简史"。正文中的作家介绍词条，主要介绍其活动年代、籍贯、生平事迹、代表作品等；作品词条，则介绍书名、卷次、名篇（条）、主要特色和影响、版本和流传情况等。全书从宏观到微观层面，比较完整清晰地呈现了中国笔记小说的发展概貌。

作为文献学研究者，孙顺霖、陈协琹两位对中国笔记小说作品的版本考证、钩沉着力颇深。书中所辑录的每部作品，均详列其版本种类、成书年代，并指出其传世的最佳版本。如东晋葛洪的《西京杂记》条，说明"以清卢文昭《抱经堂丛书》二卷本为最佳版本；罗根泽校注的该书与《燕丹子》合刊本（北京，中华书局 1985 年版）为较精当的校本。"此外，该书中还针对一些作品版本在历史流传问题上出现的篇牍讹误问题进行考证，如在介绍南宋刘昌诗《芦浦笔记》时，认为其中"草鞋大王"条是存在讹误的，该条称"绍兴癸丑余客淮南"云云，癸丑乃绍兴三年（即公元1133 年），距作者捐俸刻书之时的"嘉定二年"（即公元 1210 年），其间足有七十七年。如是计，作者年且百余岁，记其尚居县令之位断无可能，亦不合乎情理。据作者推断，此处疑为"绍熙癸丑（1193）"之误。经此考订，于情于理均合。

再如"行卷",起于唐代科举之时,作为引荐投状的文字出现。行卷一般指举子的诗文写卷,里面一般都写诗文,只有宋人赵彦卫提及行卷内容为小说。他在《云麓漫钞》卷八中说:"唐世举人,先藉当世显人,以姓名达之主司,然后以所业投献。踰数日又投,谓之温卷。如《幽怪录》《传奇》等皆是也。盖此等文备众体,可以见史才、诗笔、议论。"[3] 但是在唐代史料中仅见《南部新书》甲卷中记李复言曾记以《纂异》一部十卷献省卷,被主司李景让斥责退回。这只是孤证。赵彦卫的说法有待继续发现佐证,以小说作行卷的说法似显牵强。在总论中对笔记小说中的词条"行卷"所做的解释和界定范围的分寸把握恰当,不粉饰,不隐恶,客观、公正、全面而又博采众长。书中的资料引证博繁,资料丰富,落笔有据,较为完整地勾勒了笔记小说的发展概貌,有一种返璞归真、大象无形的艺术美感。

思路新颖,开拓面广,是本书的另一个显著特点。显然,作为一本全面系统论述中国笔记小说流派、分支及个性特征(包括各个朝代作家所处的时代背景和作品的社会影响)的工具书,其中所要涉及的历史和文学的理论问题包罗万象、极为繁复,而各种资料又浩如烟海,要给予分条缕析和校对如同大海捞针,其难度是相当大的,然而孙顺霖、陈协琹两位却能分析得非常透彻到位。譬如书中对元代笔记小说之所以发展曲折缓慢因素的探究即如此。因为蒙古游牧民族并不注重文治,因而废止科举制度,中断了读书人的仕途之路,文人在权力阶层中的下移使得戏曲、通俗小说等逐步在元代文学中占据主导,进而影响了包括笔记小说在内的文学形式在元代文学中的发展,致使文人有"嗟乎卑哉,介乎娼之下,丐之上者,今之儒也!"[4]之叹,导致笔记小说式微,两宋时的高峰期已然是"风光不再"。即使如此,仍然涌现出了陶宗仪的《说郛》如此令人眼亮的作品,对小说的普及做出了不小的贡献。自然,无论从哪个角度看,这里所研究的对象和种类都是"偏僻"和罕见的,但由于著者能够广征博引,探本清源,落笔有据,故其使读者在查阅中既能开阔视野,又能俯首心折。而要做到这一点,不付出艰苦卓绝的体力与智力劳动是达不到的。

清代是中国历史上的最后一个封建朝代,笔记小说创作在《聊斋志异》《阅微草堂笔记》的问世下,进入到一个新的创作高潮;而随着文言文的式微,笔记小说也画上了句号。作者在《中国笔记小说纵览》一书中,披沙拣金、芟芜举要，论证了先秦、魏晋南北朝、清代等笔记小说的"新的特色"：第一，通俗化倾向；第二，主观色彩加强；第三，形式更加多样。与传统笔记小说相关的几乎全部类型，至清代都有作品出现。但同时，也有一些博物小说意蕴不浓，甚至有一些诗话考证充斥其中。"笔记小说极有历史价值，可补正史之不足，以供在消遣中而达消遣之目的，著作既非牟利求名，更不料能流传至今，故所记见闻大都可信……"[5]足可见其史料价值远高于文学价值。同时，插入了"卖饼者记"之类的短故事或者传说，"友人言市有卖饼者甚佳，见者辄云，买与儿女吃，鲜言与父母吃者。"仅以26个字"短小的篇幅记叙人物的故事"[6]，一幅父母爱儿女但少有儿女记住父母的悲凉画图呼之欲出。此实例既有典型性，也有一定的独特性和趣味性，不仅充分论证了清代笔记小说主观色彩加强的特点，也力避了工具书枯燥乏味的弊端；同时，此书对笔记小说的部分常用词语单独列出章节给予解释阐述，把笔记小说的标题按音序编成作品索引，在方便受众查阅的同时，也烛照出作者严谨治学和心中有读者的负责态度。

脉络清晰，普及力强，知识面广，是本书的又一大特色。在历史发展的过程中，由于各时期的经济、政治和文化发展的状况不一，人们的知识水准和文体演绎情况也不尽相同，加之历朝历代对笔记小说的名称不断有所更新、演绎和变化，为了便于读者了解笔记小说的历史与现状，书中专门列出了109种词目，并作了解释，以期使读者对笔记小说的历史演变作概略了解。

综观全书，孙顺霖、陈协琹两位虽用功颇勤，但仍稍有不尽善尽美之处。突出表现在作者对近年来的笔记小说的研究成果吸收工作似有不足。如介绍宋代文莹《湘山野录》的版本时，只提及1984年由中华书局出版的郑世刚先生校点本。事实上，朱易安、傅璇琮等主编的《全宋笔记》丛书，共分十集，2003年由大象出版社陆续出版，其中有不少笔记小说的点校成就是承袭先贤之绝学，具有继往开来之功。郑世刚先生的《湘山野录》点校本在《全宋笔记》本中亦有收录，并更正了原版本的一些讹误，更为谨严、缜密。这些"白璧微瑕"，虽不能于此苛求著者，但就学术研究的严谨性和科学性而论，如果能博采众书、缜密论证，当是可以避免的。

植物需要阳光的照耀，并不是希望自己成为阳光。《中国历史小说纵览》这本学术工具书的问世,对源远流长的笔记小说所做的全面而深入透彻的探索和研究,填补了文言历史研究的空白,可谓功德无量;通读全书,能够对笔记小说这类文学体裁的艺术特色、思想内涵和学术价值,有更深刻的了解和感受,其对继承博大精深的古代文化遗产发挥的不可估量的影响及作用,早已超越了此工具书客观存在意义的本身。古语有云:"涉浅水者见虾,其颇深者察鱼鳖,其尤甚者观蛟龙。"——对于孙顺霖、陈协琹这两位学者来说,在自己的劳动成果受到读者认可和悦纳之时,既快乐于为文学做出的点点滴滴,也享受着笔耕不辍的快乐!

参考文献:

[1] 陶敏,刘再华."笔记小说"与笔记研究 [J]. 文学遗产,1988(3):107.

[2] 胡应麟. 少室山房笔丛·九流绪论 [M]. 北京:中华书局,1988:374.

[3] 赵彦卫. 云麓漫钞·卷八 [M]. 北京:中华书局,1996:135.

[4] 谢枋得. 叠山集·卷二·送方伯载归三山序 [M]. 北京:中华书局,1985:21.

[5] 袁文春. 百年来笔记小说概念研究综述 [J]. 学术界,2012(12):216.

[6] 苗壮. 笔记小说史 [M]. 杭州:浙江古籍出版社,1998:6.

The Navigation Lighthouse for Lighting up the Study of Chinese Literary Sketches —Comments on *A Comprehensive Survey of Chinese Literary Sketches* of Sun Shunlin and Chen Xieqin

Abstract: Literary sketches are a large category of classical Chinese novels, which have left many colorful works in the long history. However, there are some problems that are not optimistic and cannot be ignored in the current study of literary sketches: the editions of the existing works are complicated, the recorded information such as volume, age and title are different, the lack of comprehensively studied and analyzed academic papers and works, etc. The book *A Comprehensive Survey of Chinese Literary Sketches* wrote by Sun Shunlin and Chen Xieqin, which has wise conception, detailed outline, reasonable and comprehensive theoretical framework, novel ideas and broad scope. It has become another fruitful achievement in the field of literary sketches research. The book not only makes up for the shortage of literary sketches research, but also has great significance for the inheritance of literary sketches which are an outstanding cultural heritage. And it can be regarded as a pioneering work in contemporary literary sketches research.

Key words: literary sketches, comprehensive survey, reality

With exquisite decoration, lofty writing style, complete and accurate data and thorough argumentation, the book *A Comprehensive Survey of Chinese Literary Sketches* (published by East China Normal University Press in 2013) written by Sun Shunlin and Chen Xieqin is a fruitful achievement in the field of academic research, and it can be regarded as a pioneering work in the study of contemporary literary sketches. On this occasion, I would like to express my warm congratulations and deep respect to the two senior scholars (writers).

Chinese literary sketches are a large category of classical Chinese novels. Among all kinds of classical novels, literary sketches, with their longest history, have run through the whole process of Chinese classical novels. While legendary novels, chapter novels and simulated stories in vernacular novels are all directly or indirectly influenced by them, and some styles can even be said to be derived from literary sketches. Therefore, the deep and meticulous research on literary sketches has immeasurable practical significance in inheriting the traditional Chinese cultures, drawing on the outstanding philosophical and artistic essence of our predecessors, promoting academic research and realizing the contemporary "Chinese dream".

"Compared with poems, novels and operas, there are few studies on sketches" [1]. In the field of study of literary sketches, there are some realistic situations that are not optimistic and can not be ignored: the Chinese literary sketches are numerous, the editions of those existing works in the long history are complicated and various, and the recorded information such as volume, age and title are different. There are many researchers studying one person or one book, but fewer researchers can make comprehensive studies; in the same way, there are more researches on one generation, but fewer researches on comprehensive analysis. Because even scholars in the field of study of literary sketches may not be able to fully understand all of them. Just like a Chinese saying goes, "we all have a limited view of something." How time flies! We often lose our history and excellent culture such as

The Navigation Lighthouse for Lighting up the
Study of Chinese Literary Sketches

literary sketches in the vicissitudes of life. If these cultural heritages can not be sorted out, studied and inherited in time, we would shame on history and always regret it. It is an urgent and important issue in the academic field to let the researchers of literary sketches yield twice the result with half the effort. It is gratifying that in order to realize this dream, the scholars (writers) Sun Shunlin and Chen Xieqin, who lived in poverty, devoted themselves to literature with rigorous scholarship. During the 15-year period, they have looked over and read a large number of documents of all dynasties, and among these documents, there are more than 700 kinds of literary sketches. The two scholars have spent all their efforts and energies in writing the reference book *A Comprehensive Survey of Chinese Literary Sketches*, which provides a convenient way for people who are interested in studying literary sketches and lights up a brilliant navigation lighthouse.

The most distinctive feature of *A Comprehensive Survey of Chinese Literary Sketches* is its wise conception, detailed outline, reasonable and comprehensive theoretical framework. According to this book's introduction, which is divided into four chapters to introduce the concept, value, development context, category and structural order of the form, and the four chapters are closely linked and connected with each other. Besides, the exposition of the historical development process in this book is clear, detailed and concise, with many insightful comments. At the beginning of the introduction, it is pointed out that the word "literary sketches" experienced some practice and controversy from its appearance to its recognition by the society. Since the Tang Dynasty, many literary historians have discussed the issue separately or comprehensively, and finally reached a consensus on it. According to *The Series of Shaoshi Shanfang·Jiuliu Introduction* written by Hu Yinglin in Ming Dynasty, "The novels can be divided into different categories. One is mythical stories, such as *Soushen, Shuyi, Xuanshi and Youyang*" [2] This view has great influence on later generations. It also points out that literary sketches are the original form of Chinese classical novels. The literary sketches pay attention to the composition and words, with delicate description, attractive plots, simple language and brief outline. And it is the earliest novel in the history of Chinese novels and runs through its development process, and has had a great influence on other literary genres. The so-called "novels" here refers to the reality based on what we hear and see, the complexity and richness of the content, and the flexibility of "novels", "notes" and forms. Being different from the notes of historical records, chronicle notes, textual research and poetry, the book *A Comprehensive Survey of Chinese Literary Sketches* has character activities, verbal communication, attractive plots and emotional interaction. And it is a work that has great influence on the development of history and culture. This book elaborates the origin and influence of the word "literary sketches" from a strategic perspective, with meticulous thinking, rigorous argumentation, prominent focus and overall perspective, so that readers can gain a clear understanding of the generation, development and evolution of the concept of literary sketches in a very short period of time.

Another major academic feature of this book is its quotes extensive, detailed and accurate citation and profound analysis. It appears in the form of entries, which leaves a deep impression on the readers. It is so ingenious and convenient for readers to search and consult on demand, which reflects the most basic nature of reference books. The book begins with an "introduction" and each chapter is preceded by a "summary", which makes a critical analysis of the origin, development, evolution, inheritance and influence of the literary sketches, as well as famous articles of various dynasties, etc. And the book summarizes the main contents to do a survey, which is no less than a relatively complete "A Brief History of Literary Sketches". The writers' introduction entries in the main text mainly introduce the writers' age, native place, life story, representative works, etc. The entries of the works introduce the title, volume, famous article, main features and influence, edition and circulation, etc. From the macro level to the micro level, the book presents a relatively complete and clear overview of the development of Chinese literary sketches.

As philological researchers, Sun Shunlin and Chen Xieqin have a deep understanding of the textual research on the versions of Chinese literary sketches. There are detailed information about the type of version, the completion date and the classical edition of each work compiled in the book. Such as *Notes Xijing* written by Ge Hong in Eastern Jin Dynasty; its classical edition is the second volume of *Baojingtang Series* written by Lu Wenzhao in Qing Dynasty; and the more accurate collated edition is the joint edition (Beijing, Zhonghua Book Company, 1985 edition) of Luo Genze's collated edition and *Yandanzi*. In addition, the book also makes a textual research on the errors in some versions of the works in the process of historical circulation. For example, when introducing *Lupu Notes* written by Liu Changshi in the Southern Song Dynasty, it is believed that there is an error in the entry of "The King of Straw Sandals", which says "I lived in Huainan in the period of Shaoxing Gui Chou". Gui Chou was the third year in the period of Shaoxing (i.e.1133 A.D.), and the author donated his salary and inscribed the book in the second year of Jiading (i.e. 1210 A.D.). The two events are separated in time by seventy-seven years. If so, the author was over 100 years old, and it is impossible that he still assumed the office of county magistrate. According to the author's inference, the mistake here is suspected to be in the period of Shaoxi Gui Chou (1193)".Through this textual research, all is reasonable.

Another example is "Xingjuan", which originated from the imperial examination in the Tang Dynasty and appeared as an introduction letter. "Xingjuan" generally refers to the poetic proses written by the candidates for the imperial examinations, and the content of it is mainly poems, only Zhao Yanwei in Song Dynasty mentioned the content of "Xingjuan" is novels. He said in Volume 8 of *Yunlu Manchao*, "The imperial officials of the Tang Dynasty firstly deliver their works to the present-day distinguished person, and after a few days they deliver their works again, which is called 'Xingjuan'. Such as *The Tales of Ghosts, The Legend* and so on. Such literary forms as this can be seen in the works of historical talents, poetry and comments". [3] But only in one of the Tang Dynasty's historical materials, the first volume of *Southern New Book*, it was recorded that Li Fuyan delivered *Zuanyi* with ten volumes to the provincial government, which was reprimanded and returned by Li Jingrang, the chief secretary. This is just an isolated case. Zhao Yanwei's statement needs to be further proved, and it seems far-fetched to use the novel as a "Xingjuan". In the introduction, the explanation and definition of the entry "Xingjuan" in the literary sketches are appropriate, objective, fair and comprehensive, without over decorating and concealing. The cited materials in the book are abundant, wide-ranging, and well-documented, which outline the development of the literary sketches in a relatively complete way, and leave the readers an artistic aesthetic feeling of returning to nature.

The novel thinking and broad scope are another remarkable feature of this book. Obviously, as a reference book that comprehensively and systematically discusses the genres, branches and personality characteristics of Chinese literary sketches, including the era background of writers of various dynasties and the social influence of their works, since the theoretical issues involved in history and literature are numerous and extremely complicated, and various kinds of materials are voluminous, it is quite difficult to analyze and proofread them in detail like looking for a needle in a haystack. However, Sun Shunlin and Chen Xieqin can analyze them thoroughly. For example, the book's exploration of the slow development of Yuan Dynasty's literary sketches are very thorough. Because Mongolian nomads did not pay attention to literature and politics, the imperial examination system was abolished and the official career of scholars was interrupted. The downward movement of literati in the power class led to the gradual dominance of operas and popular novels in Yuan Dynasty literature, which further affected the development of literature in Yuan Dynasty, including literary sketches. As a result, the literati sighed "it is sorrowful that we literati are just inferior to prostitutes but superior to beggars!" [4] All of that led to the decline of literary sketches, and the peak period of Southern Song Dynasty and Northern Song Dynasty was already the past tense. Even so, it still emerged a brilliant work *Shuofu* written by Tao Zongyi, which contributed a lot to the popularization of novels. Naturally, no matter from which point of view, the objects and types studied here are seldom seen. However, due to the author's ability to cite numerous and wide-ranging materials which are well-documented, it makes readers not only broaden their horizons, but also admire the authors greatly in the process of reading. And it is not possible to do this without painstaking physical and intellectual work.

Qing Dynasty was the last feudal dynasty in Chinese history. The creation of literary sketches reached a new climax with the publication of *Strange Tales from a Lonely Studio* and *Sketches of Yuewei Humble Cottage*. However, with the decline of classical Chinese, the development of literary sketches has come to an end. In the book *An Comprehensive Survey of Chinese Literary Sketches*, the author demonstrates the "new features" of the literary sketches in the pre-Qin days, Wei-Jin and Southern and Northern Dynasties and Qing Dynasty. First, the tendency of popularization. Second, the subjectivity is strengthened. Third, the forms are colorful. Almost all the types of novels related to traditional literary sketches appeared until Qing Dynasty. However, at the same time, there are also some geographical and botanical stories that have little implication, and even some textual research of notes on classical poetry is included. "Literary sketches are of great historical value and can supplement the shortcomings of official history. The works are neither seeking fame nor profit, and it is unforeseen that they can be spread to this day, so most of the stories recorded are credible ..." [5] It can be seen that the historical value of literary sketches is far higher than that of literature. At the same time, short stories or legends are inserted too, such as "The Records of Cake Sellers," "there are friends say that the cakes sold in the market are delicious, and those who have tasted the cakes also say that, but most of them buy the cakes for their children while few of them buy the cakes for their parents." Only with a few of words, (to narrate the stories of characters with short space) [6], a sad picture of all parents loving their children, but few children remembering their parents emerges. This example is not only typical, but also unique and interesting. It not only fully demonstrates the characteristics of strengthening subjectivity in Qing Dynasty's literary sketches, but also makes up for the disadvantages of boring of reference books. Meanwhile, this book gives explanations to some commonly used words in literary sketches by listing chapters separately, and compiles the titles of the literary sketches into a work index according to the phonetic ordering, which not only makes it convenient for the readers to consult, but also reflects the author's responsible attitude of rigorous scholarship and being eaders-oriented.

Clear skeleton, strong popularity and wide-ranging knowledge are another major feature of this book. In the process of historical development, due to the different economic, political and cultural development in different periods, people's knowledge level and stylistic deduction are also different. In addition, the names of the literary sketches have been updated, deduced and changed continuously in the past dynasties. In order to facilitate readers to understand the history and current situation and historical evolution of the literary sketches, this book has listed 109 lexical entries with detailed explanation.

The overview of this book shows that Sun Shunlin and Chen Xieqin have devoted to it, but there are still some imperfections, which mainly reflected in that the authors have done little to absorb the research results of recent years' literary sketches. For example, when introducing the edition of *Non-official Historical Works of Xiang Mountain* written by Wen Ying of the

Song Dynasty, this book only mentions the proofreading edition of Mr. Zheng Shigang published by Zhonghua Book Company in 1984. In fact, the series of *Notes of the Song Dynasty* edited by Zhu Yian, Fu Xuancong and other editors has ten volumes, and was successively published by Elephant Press in 2003. Among them, many of the proofreading editions of literary sketches draw lessons from the scholars of the past and carry forward the cause into the future. The proofreading edition of *Non-official Historical Works of Xiang Mountain* written by Mr. Zheng Shigang is also included in the *Notes of the Song Dynasty*, with correcting some errors of the original version and being more cautious and meticulous. Although these are trivial problems, and we cannot make excessive demands of the authors, the imperfections could be avoided if the authors have learned widely from others' books and made careful demonstration in terms of the strictness and scientificity of academic research.

Plants need sunshine, but not to be sunshine. The publication of *A Comprehensive Overview of Chinese Literary Sketches*, an academic reference book, has made a comprehensive and thorough exploration and study of long-standing literary sketches, filling in the gaps in the study of classical Chinese history, which makes great contributions to the development of literary sketches. Throughout the book, one can have a deeper understanding and feeling of the artistic features, ideological connotation and academic value of literary genres such as literary sketches. This book plays an immeasurable influence and role in inheriting the extensive and profound ancient cultural heritages, and it has already gone beyond the objective meaning of the reference book itself. As the old Chinese saying goes, "Those who wade in shallow water only can see shrimps, those who are in deeper water can see fishes and turtles, while those who are in the deepest water can see dragons." For the two scholars Sun Shunlin and Chen Xieqin, when their work achievements are recognized and accepted by the readers, they are not only happy with the little things they have done for literature, but also enjoying the happiness of writing without giving up.

References:

[1] Tao Min, Liu Zaihua. Literary Sketches and Notes Research [J]. Literary Heritage, 1988 (3): 107.

[2] Hu Yinglin. The Series of Shaoshi Shanfang·Jiuliu introduction [M]. Beijing: Zhonghua Book Company, 1988: 374.

[3] Zhao Yanwei. Yunlu Manchao · Volume 8 [M]. Beijing: Zhonghua Book Company, 1996: 135.

[4] Xie Fangde. Die Mountain Collection · Volume 2 · The Preface of Sending Uncle Fang to Sanshan [M]. Beijing: Zhonghua Book Company, 1985: 21.

[5] Yuan Wenchun. A Review of Conceptual Studies on Literary Sketches in the Past 100 Years [J]. Academia, 2012 (12): 216.

[6] Miao Zhuang. History of Literary Sketches [M]. Hangzhou: Zhejiang Ancient Books Publishing House, 1998: 6.

青春志愿行　亮丽的风景

楚　惬

点击时代的星空

刷新晨曦的黎明

啊　我们听到的第一组乐章

便是青春志愿者之歌

我们看到的第一幕风景

便是青春志愿者匆匆的身影

在盛世中华的大地上

在复兴筑梦的潮汐中

青春志愿者

这支勇立潮头的风华一代

让我们感到无比的艳羡啊

让我们温润的心境

荡起了和合的春风

看啊　青春志愿者

这支新思想哺育出的青春团队

这支拥抱未来的时代先锋

从他们登上筑梦的舞台之后

便演绎出一个个感人的故事

便爆屏出一幕幕精彩的纷呈
打开历史叠加的画面吧
我们不会忘记
在临危抢险的第一线
是他们冒着生命的未卜
用青春写下无私奉献之歌
用大爱植下友爱互助之情

我们不会忘记
在扶贫攻坚的日子里
是他们用双手
改变了穷山野岭的面貌
是他们用智慧
点亮了百姓心中的希望之灯
我们不会忘记
在防治污染的攻坚战里
是他们用汗珠
洁净了山水廊道
是他们用心灵
擦亮了一碧如洗的长空
我们不会忘记
在学习雷锋的春风里
他们用真善美的性灵
濡染了多少人们的身心
方便了多少过往的群众

他们的故事啊
伴随着每一天翻开的日历
从交通路口到车站码头
从大街小巷到万千家庭

甜美的问候是第一个开心的导语

热情的帮助

是故事启动的第一段场景

捡垃圾　清污水

擦护栏　美市容

这点点滴滴的文字符号

这红红火火的画意诗情

是青春志愿者

那闪光的帽徽

那红色的衣领

那擎起的手旗

那殷殷的笑容

共同写就的感人的故事

共频流动的筑梦的风景

啊　不妨让我们

打开中华文明的宝典吧

东方智慧如玉之润泽

让修身行善、激浊扬清

定格成中华儿女守仁的情怀

舍生取义、乐善好施

是中华民族生生不息的火种

尚德明礼、推己惠人

是人格品质之澡雪

奉献爱心、和合为公

是赓续文明的大道之风

这就是炎黄子孙的基因啊

这就是中华儿女的心灯

这就是民族魂魄的正气啊

这就是五千年华夏文明

凝聚成的精神之灵
这信仰　这担当
这情怀　这认同
在一代代青春志愿者的传承中
已化成九州时空绚丽的彩虹

是的　青年是人类的春天
青年是时代的先锋
青年是祖国的未来
青年是筑梦的英雄
看　泱泱神州大地
民族复兴之伟业
正如潮涌之洪波
浩浩乎　惊涛骇浪
中华崛起之巍然
正如巨龙之飞腾
断断乎　凌越太空
国势之强在乎人
人才之用在青春
青春的理想　青春的活力
青春的奋斗　青春的锦程
在因势勃兴的志愿者行动中
已成为中国精神之光照
已成为青春力量之奔腾
已成为复兴筑梦之呐喊
已成为核心价值观之践行

让我们以青春之我
谱写新时代的壮美之歌
以青春之美

青春志愿行　亮丽的风景

彩绘九州大地之胜景
以青春之行
传递青春志愿者之活力
以青春之光
锃亮伟大民族复兴的中国之梦
啊　青春志愿行
中华大地一道亮丽的风景

写于戊戌年夏

小戏剧

寻恩人

楚 惬

时间　2018 年春末

地点　河南某地山区

人物　时旺财　男　50 岁　农民　被帮扶对象　简称：财。

　　　二　花　女　40 岁　农民　小化工厂老板娘　简称：花。

　　　艾　民　女　30 岁　市某单位干部　扶贫第一书记　简称：民。

（幕启　山区春末景象，舞台右后有灌木丛，远山上矗立着一座古塔。）

（财上。）

财　（唱）小步快走把山岗上，

　　　　　寻亲人了却那心事一桩。

　　　　　踮起脚尖四下望，

　　　　　咋不见艾民在何方？

（财急转身，与风风火火从下场门上的花，撞了个满怀，财倒地。）

花　（气恨状）你没长眼！

财　哎哟！（自语）是个人呐，我当撞树上了啦。大婶！

花　我有那么老？

财　（揉眼，仔细看）大妹子！

花　这还差不多？

财　你，没事吧？

花　我这身板（显示强壮）能有啥事？

财　那就好，那就好。哎……

花　啥事？

财　向你打听个人。

花　打听谁呀？说吧！这村里的人都知道。

财　她不是这村的。

花　邻村的？

财　也不是。

花　那我哪儿会知道。（欲走）

财　别急着走嘛。恁这儿的第一书记。

花　你说的是艾　民。

财　对，对。以前在俺村当过第一书记，现在来恁这儿当第一书记了。

花　国家女干部？

财　是，是。

花　认识，认识！哪儿会不认识。你是哪儿嘞？

财　我是那儿嘞，（指）万山南坡。

花　哟！也是老山窝儿。恁村啥样？

财　你说以前还是现在？

花　变化大吗？

财　大了去咯！以前，一个字——穷。俺村儿有个顺口溜。

花　顺口溜？说说。

财　吃水水囤担，吃饭靠老天，道路窄又陡，一群光棍汉。

花　哈哈哈！还怪押韵咧。现在嘞？

财　三个字——脱贫了。

花　你们既然都脱贫了还找她干啥？

财　报恩哪。

花　你们村脱贫是党的政策好，要报恩，只能报共产党的恩，不能报某个人的恩吧？

财　共产党的恩情比山高、似海深，世世代代都不会忘记。艾民书记对我帮助太大了，对我有恩哪！人要知恩、感恩、报恩，知恩不报那还算是人吗？！

花　　你打算咋报恩？

财　　我打算成立个"万山波尔山羊养殖公司"，让她……（猛然觉着不妥）

花　　让她咋着？

财　　不说了。走了半天口渴了先喝点水。（去一旁从包里拿出水瓶喝水）

花　　艾民来俺村先关停了俺家的小化工厂，说俺那厂，属于"小、散、乱、污"的四小企业。谁要不关停就触犯了法律。我去找她想通融通融，谁知道，她是粉面无私、铁面无情。这个女人呐，我早就对她有意见了。她还说俺村属于那个啥——生态扶贫，可以建成旅游区，让大家投资入股。看来那人（指财）的养殖公司，给她有好处。将来俺这旅游区建成了，她得的好处才多呐。嗨！表面上装得廉洁，实际上是假公济私。我得想法让他说出来，弄个证据举报她。咋弄证据呢？对！录个视频。只要……哼哼。（走向财，用手机录像）

花　　大哥！你是哪个乡镇，哪个村的，叫啥名字？

财　　你是给我照相嘞还是录像嘞？

花　　你是脱贫的好典型，录个视频发到朋友圈，让大家给你点赞。我问你啥，你就回答啥。

财　　中。电视台录像也是这么说的。

花　　你是哪个乡镇、哪个村的，啥名字？

财　　哦！我是张河镇时坡村嘞。

花　　石头的石？

财　　不是。是时间的时，山坡的坡。我叫时旺财。

花　　时旺财？

财　　旺是左边一个日，右边一个王，财是发财的财。

花　　你的名字起得多好，啥时候财都旺。

财　　呷！哪像你说嘞。以前穷帽子就有摘过。地是山坡地，人畜吃水都是水囤里嘞水。唉！缺水呀。

花　　那是望天收哇。

财　　可不是嘞！

花　　你不会外出打工？

财　　前些年也出去打过,这几年出不去了。

花　　咋了？

财　　父母七八十岁了,身体不太好。

花　　恁老婆嘞？

财　　唉！别提了。

花　　咋了？年轻漂亮,丢在家不放心？

财　　俺老婆是老实巴交的乡下娘们,脸晒得黑儿吧唧,手粗糙得跟砂纸一样。除了我,没人看上她。哪像你细皮嫩肉,穿着打扮跟城里人一样,看上去你也就小三十？

花　　哎,哎！打住,打住。扯远了。那你咋不出去打工？

财　　老婆前几年在山上摔了一下,腰摔坏了,重活干不了。

花　　你吃低保了冇？

财　　吃了好几年啦,穷根刨不了哇。

花　　后来呢？

财　　艾民来俺村当第一书记的第三天,就找我商量脱贫的事。俺村就在万山坡,春、夏、秋三季儿有青草,冬天有秸秆,既可以养羊又避免了焚烧秸秆污染环境。

花　　以前你就没想到过养羊？

财　　想是想到了,一只半大的山羊,就得千把块,再少不得两只羊,这就得两千多块钱哪！咱不是锅,腰上树——缺钱嘛。

花　　艾民咋帮你嘞？

财　　艾民书记用自己的钱,买了两只山羊,还是好品种波尔山羊。这波尔山羊长得快,肉质好,免疫力强,不咋生病。

花　　哦！你现在有多少只？

财　　三年的时间,就有二三十只啦！

花　　那你现在生活好多了。

　　　　（民在上场门内喊：旺财叔！旺财叔！）

财　　哎！（从上场门下）

花　　艾民来了，我不能在这录像啊。可是，关键的证据还有嘞。这……（四处看）这儿是他们去村委的必经之路，我……（眼四处看，看到灌木丛）就这么办。

　　　　（财、民同上）

民　　旺财叔，您昨天打电话说今天上午来，都快 11 点了没见到您，打您的手机关机，我去那边处理点事，走到这儿看着像您。

财　　手机没电了。遇到个女的打听你嘞，在这喷了一会儿。（看）哎！人哪？走了？

民　　别找了。时坡村现在咋样？

财　　你听我说。

　　　　（唱）自从你进村当书记，

　　　　　　　　福民事做的都是大工程。

　　　　　　　　全村人吃上了自来水，

　　　　　　　　哗啦啦水声赛过钢琴声。

　　　　　　　　村民古来都是梦，

　　　　　　　　美梦成真感恩情。

　　　　　　　　水泥路修到家门口，

　　　　　　　　大小车辆都通行。

　　　　　　　　桃杏鲜果城里卖，

　　　　　　　　钞票装兜你说那是啥心情？

民　　这是党的政策好，加上群众的干劲大，扶贫攻坚才能开花结果。您自己咋样，温饱了吗？

财　　不光是温饱，还小康了哪！

　　　　（唱）穷帽子摘掉扔得远，

　　　　　　　　新房建了五六间。

　　　　　　　　腰杆挺起人前站，

　　　　　　　　办事不用再借钱。

　　　　　　　　出门开的小皮卡，

　　　　　　　　（嘀，嘀——汽车喇叭声）

　　　　　　　　喇叭一响跑得欢。

民　　旺财叔,您真能干,我为您点赞! 大老远来找我有啥事?

财　　有,有! 我打算成立个"万山波尔山羊养殖公司",挂牌儿咯请你给挂。

民　　好哇! 旺财叔您不但能吃苦、有干劲,还有远大的梦想。到时候您和我说一声,我一定去。

财　　还有一件事。

民　　您说。

财　　这个公司,你得入股,当股东。

民　　您说啥?

财　　让你入股当股东。

民　　让我入股,当股东?

财　　是啊! 当初不是你送我两只羊,哪有现在的一大群羊。你是当然的股东,还该是大股东。(灌木丛晃动)

民　　谁! (二花学猫叫)

财　　不是人,是野猫。现在是春天,猫叫春嘞。我说的那个事,你就答应了吧,要不然我这心里过意不去呀!

民　　旺财叔啊!

　　　(唱)习主席心系咱百姓,

　　　　　　人民的福祉在他心中。

　　　　　　扶贫攻坚大战略,

　　　　　　全民富国家才能兴。

　　　　　　做实事要让百姓笑,

　　　　　　做不好百姓哭了可不行。

　　　　　　我做好工作是本分,

　　　　　　做不好还请大家多批评。

　　　　　　入股的事儿啊别再讲,

　　　　　　那是万万行不通。

　　　　　　不能假公把私济

　　　　　　事儿大了可要上法绳。

财　　我听懂了,你恁好嘞书记,我可不能把你坑了。

民　　旺财叔，您想建股份公司，可以找愿意合伙干的村民哪！哎！对了，您让需要脱贫的人和您一块儿干。

财　　你是说穷帽子冇摘嘞，俺邻村有哇。

民　　他们跟您一块儿干，既可以让他们到您那儿打工，您也可以送给他种羊，传授给他技术和经营方法，他只要达到了脱贫线，一个人就可以补助你一万元的资金。

财　　咱脱贫了，不能忘了穷帽子还戴着的乡亲们，政府补不补咱都得帮。槐树坡的孙二拐子在我那儿半年了，管吃、管住，还发工资。

民　　公司成立了，赶快报项目，经过审查验收，补助就会到位。不过股份公司的管理也是一门学问，还得学会才行。

财　　我弄不懂的，你教我。

民　　这没问题。哎！有个事还得求您呀。

财　　呷！看你外气了不是，啥求不求嘞！你说！

民　　想让您把脱贫致富的经验，给周山村的村民们讲讲。

财　　我没上过几年学，怕讲不好给你丢人。

民　　实话实说就行。走，去村委会再好好商量商量。（民、财下）（花现身）

花　　恁看看，本来想录个证据，抓住她腐败的把柄，倒录了个先进的典型。这不能送到纪检会了，得送到电视台了。（下）

剧　终

中原　出彩的天空

回眸泱泱华夏的历史
刷新九州大地的彩屏
一方秀甲天下的山河
一部历史厚重的文明
那便是古老的中原大地啊
她用母亲的乳汁　她用炎黄的血精
哺育了勤劳勇敢的中华儿女
开创了秦皇汉武　唐宗宋祖
那曾经瞩目世界的鼎盛

啊中原　这里有大河不息的奔流
这里有炎黄二帝创业的身影
这里有仓颉造字契刻的符号
这里有裴里岗　仰韶
见证下的数千年历史文明
不妨让我们点读一下
那精彩凝重的历史章节吧
"得中原者得天下"的战略之道
已成为中原独特的历史回声
七朝古都让汴梁开封
书写下多少英雄豪杰的故事

九京阊阖的洛水之阳
粉墨了多少牡丹的天香芳容
轩辕黄帝的故里
已成为炎黄子孙寻根拜祖的圣地
嫘祖缫丝的玉泉山洞
见证了人类文明初始的进程
广武山头的嘶鸣战马
刻录下楚汉子弟多少铁血的呐喊
少林功夫的远扬名声
让世界感受中华武术的魅力无穷
还有那千古名画"清明上河图"
既是大宋开封鼎盛繁华的写真
更是中国文化自信最早的见证

俱往矣　中原大地让我们如此憧憬
看今朝　改革开放的强劲东风
让中原大地一时间便成为九州的明星
看啊　被誉为中国粮仓的河南
连连丰收的喜讯　刷新着
世界期货交易的屏幕
实现全面小康目标的步伐
是那么坚实有力而铿锵有声
中原经济区发展的科学定位
催生出现代化城市群崭新的风貌
引领全国的立体交通网络
向全国及世界传递着中原的追梦
应时而勃兴的高科技产业
为河南插上腾飞的翅膀
兴国大计的文化教育
几年间便凸起一个个高峰

更有那一片片青山绿水
更有那一方方蓝天白云
和谐文明的中州大地啊
让中原的天空更加出彩
让我们的筑梦指日可成

啊　中原的热土正喷薄着激情与活力
啊　中州的儿女正释放着智慧与精诚
为实现河南更加恢宏的蓝图
我们将乘着改革开放之势
我们将怀着迎接十九大召开的满腔激情
高歌猛进　砥砺前行

写于丁酉年夏